DOUGLAS COUPLAND was born
Baden-Söllingen, Germany, in 1
Generation X, Shampoo Planet, Life After God, Microserfs, Polaroids from the Dead,
and *Girlfriend in a Coma.* He works as a designer and sculptor in
Vancouver, British Columbia, and is currently writing his next
novel.

From the reviews for *Miss Wyoming:*

'An astonishing novel… To imagine characters such as these finding
redemption through mutual love should be impossible. Except, of
course, that it is what many of us spend our time imagining
every day, whenever we pick up a copy of *Hello* magazine or read a
celebrity love story in a tabloid. This is Coupland's genius. He creates concepts that allow us to get to grips with our unimaginable,
real-life, end of the world news.'   NICHOLAS BLINCOE, *Literary Review*

'An extraordinary 21st century love story… Coupland isn't just
funny, he is smart. What is striking is the way he organizes his
sociological titbits, how he makes patterns out of the fuzz. *Miss
Wyoming* can be read and greatly enjoyed as a jaunt, a merry frip-
pery. At the same time though, there is something darker going on,
beneath the stardust.'   EMRAN MIAN, *Glasgow Herald*

'If *Girlfriend in a Coma* was Coupland's dark, difficult Tricky album of
a novel, then *Miss Wyoming* is his perky, polished Britney Spears radio
edit. Its terrain is the trash-strewn byways of failed celebrity, its
principal characters a washed-up action-movie producer and a
fallen beauty queen. Both seek to escape their punchline fate through
doomed bids for anonymity, finally finding some meaning among
the wreckage of their lives… That might sound worryingly insub-
stantial, but with such acute social commentary and sparkling
prose, who's complaining?'   *The Face*

'Another fantastically affecting tour through latter-day
Americana… its seemingly effortless understanding of the modern
world is a joy.'   *Select*

'Coupland manipulates the two narratives with devilish mastery: Susan and John's stories mirror each other, almost touch, then move away… As John notes, you reach a moment in life when thereafter "it's reruns". For Coupland, soothsayer of the anxious generation, the only way to break the loop is with love, and that's exactly what his characters are holding out for. There is more than enough fret and fizz here to keep you simmering.'

JAMES HOPKIN, *Guardian*

'Along the way, as ever, Coupland sets out wonderful observations… Much more entertaining than reading any of those worthy tomes about changing your life.'

PETER CARTY, *Time Out*

'Coupland's smartly written, satirical novel, animated throughout by his trademark exaggerated similes, takes a scalpel to various kinds of plastic American celebrity. He is remarkably good at entertainingly sending up the grotesque milieux from which his protagonists flee, and atmospherically depicting the altered perspectives they gain in flight.'

Sunday Times

'As his characters yearn for purity, the prose and the story itself sparkle with the cleanliness of the polished phrase. There are marvellous asides of oddness righting itself, and Coupland knows enough about the worlds he satirizes for the ring of truth to come through… For better or worse you feel at home in Coupland's world, not so much because of the snap, crackle, pop references – the electric current of the insistent *now* – but because threading beneath it is the familiar tale of the love story as redemption. And in the world as Coupland writes it, an old-fashioned love story is all you need.'

WILLIAM GEORGIADES, *Spectator*

'*Miss Wyoming*, like all his novels, is weird, wonderful, highly original, on occasion laugh-out-loud funny, yet always underpinned by an air of desperation.'

NICK JOHNSTONE, *Uncut*

'Coupland at his best can make a single phrase say more than many another writer's whole novel.' JENNY TURNER, *London Review of Books*

DOUGLAS COUPLAND

Miss Wyoming

Flamingo
An Imprint of HarperCollins*Publishers*

Flamingo
An imprint of HarperCollins*Publishers*
77–85 Fulham Palace Road,
Hammersmith, London W6 8JB

www.**fire**and**water**.com

Published by Flamingo 2000
9 8 7 6 5 4 3 2 1

First published in Great Britain by Flamingo 2000

First published in the USA by Pantheon Books 2000

ISBN 0-00-655206-4

Set in Joanna

Printed and bound in Great Britain by Clays Ltd, St Ives plc

Miss Wyoming

Chapter One

Susan Colgate sat with her agent, Adam Norwitz, on the rocky outdoor patio of the Ivy restaurant at the edge of Beverly Hills. Susan was slightly chilly and kept a fawn-colored cashmere sweater wrapped around her shoulders as she snuck bread crumbs to the birds darting about the ground. Her face was flawlessly made up and her hair was cut in the style of the era. She was a woman on a magazine cover, gazing out at the checkout-stand shopper, smiling, but locked in time and space, away from the real world of squalling babies, bank cards and casual shoplifting.

Susan and Adam were looking at two men across the busy restaurant. Adam was saying to Susan, "You see that guy on the left? That's 'Jerr-Bear' Rogers, snack dealer to the stars and the human equivalent of an unflushed toilet."

"Adam!"

"Well, it's true." Adam broke open a focaccia slice. "Oh *God*, Sooz, they're looking at us."

"Thoughts have wings, Adam."

"Whatever. They're both still staring at us."

A waiter came and filled their water glasses. Adam said, "And that other guy—John Johnson. Semisleazebag movie producer. He vanished for a while earlier this year. Did you hear about that?"

"It sounds faintly familiar. But I stopped reading the dailies a while ago. You know that, Adam."

"He totally vanished. Turns out he OD'd and had some kind of vision, and then afterward he gave away everything he had—his house and cars and copyrights and everything else, and turned himself into a bum. Walked across the Southwest eating hamburgers out of McDonald's dumpsters."

"Really?"

"Oh yeah. Hey . . ." Adam lowered his voice and spoke out the side of his mouth. "Oh Lordy, it looks like John Johnson's fixated on you, Sooz, gawping at you like you were Fergie or something. Smile back like a trouper, will you? He may be gaga, but he's still got the power."

"Adam, don't tell me what to do or not to do."

"Oh God. He's standing up. He's coming over here," said Adam. "Lana Turner, be a good girl and tuck in your sweater. Wow. John Johnson. Whatta sleazebag."

Susan turned to Adam. "Don't be such a hypocrite, Adam, like you're so pure yourself? Know what I think? I think there's a touch 'o the 'bag in all of us."

John was by then standing a close but respectful distance from Susan. He looked at her with the unsure smile of a high school junior bracing himself to ask a girl one social notch above him to dance at the prom, his hands behind his back like a penitent child.

"Hello," he said. "I'm John Johnson." He stuck out his right arm too quickly, surprising her, but she took his hand in hers and slid her chair back onto the flagstones so that she could survey him more fully—a sadly handsome man, dressed in clothes that looked like hand-me-downs: jeans and a frayed blue gingham shirt, shoes a pair of disintegrating desert boots with a different-colored lace on each foot.

"I'm Susan Colgate."

"Hi."

"Hi to *you*."

"I'm Adam Norwitz." Adam lobbed his hand into the mix. John shook it, but not for a moment did he break his gaze on Susan.

"Yes,'" said John. "Adam Norwitz. I've heard your name before."

Adam blushed at this ambiguous praise. "Congratulations on *Mega Force*," he said. Owing to John's radical decision of the previous winter, he was not making a single penny from his current blockbuster, *Mega Force*. In his pocket were ninety $20 bills, and this was all the money he had in the world.

"Thank you," said John.

"Adam told me that you're a sleazebag," said Susan. John, caught completely off guard, laughed. Adam froze in horror, and Susan smiled and said, "Well, you *did* say it, Adam."

"Susan! How could you—"

"He's *right*," said John. "Look at my track record and he'd be bang on. I saw you feeding birds under the table. That's nice."

"You were doing it, too."

"I like birds." John's teeth were big and white, like pearls of baby corn. His eyes were the pale blue color of sun-bleached parking tickets, his skin like brown leather.

"Why?" Susan asked.

"They mind their own business. No bird has never tried to sneak me a screenplay or slagged me behind my back. And they still hang out with you even if your movies tank."

"I certainly know *that* feeling."

"Susan!" Adam interjected. "Your projects do well."

"My movies are crap, Adam."

Across the terrazzo, Jerr-Bear made the *ah-oooo-gah, ah-oooo-gah* noise of a drowning submarine in order to attract John's attention, but John and Susan, alone among the annoyed lunchtime crowd, ignored him.

Adam was trying to figure a way out of what he perceived as a dreadful collision of *faux pas*, mixed signals and badly tossed banana cream pies, and said, "Would you and your, er, colleague, like to join us for lunch, Mr. Johnson?"

John suddenly seemed to realize that he was in public, in a restaurant, surrounded by people bent on eating food and gossiping, and that this was the opposite of the place he wanted to be. He stammered, "I—"

"Yes?" Susan looked at him kindly.

"I really need to get out of here. You wouldn't want to come with me on a—I dunno—a *walk*, would you?"

Susan stood up, catching Adam's bewildered eyes. "I'll call you later, Adam."

Staff scurried about, and in the space of what seemed like a badly edited film snippet, John and Susan were out on North Robertson Boulevard, amid sleeping Saabs and Audis, in dazzling sunlight that made the insides of their eyeballs bubble as though filled with ginger ale.

"Are you okay for walking in those shoes?" John asked.

"These? I could climb Alps in these puppies." She smiled. "No man's ever asked me that before."

"They look Italian."

"I bought them in Rome in 1988, and they've never let me down once."

"Rome, huh? What was going on in Rome?"

"I was doing a set of TV commercials for bottled spaghetti sauce. Maybe you saw them. They were on the air for years. They spent a fortune getting everybody over there and then they shot it inside a studio anyway, and then they propped it with cheesy Italian stuff, so it looked like it was filmed in New Jersey."

"Welcome to film economics."

"That wasn't my first lesson, but it was one of the strangest. You never did commercials, did you?"

"I went right into film."

"Commercials are weird. You can go be in a reasonably successful TV weekly series for years and nobody mentions it to you, but appear at three A.M. in some god-awful sauce plug, and people phone to wake you up and scream, 'I just saw you on TV!' "

A mailman walked by, and once he'd passed John and Susan, in cahoots they copied his exaggerated stride, then made devilish faces at each other.

"You gotta hand it to him," Susan said about the mailman, now out of earshot, "for a guy his age, he sure works it."

"How old do you think I am?" asked John.

Susan appraised him. "I'll guess forty. Why do you ask?"

"I look forty?"

"But that's good. If you're not forty, then it means you've accrued wisdom beyond your, say, thirty-five years. It looks good on a man."

"I'm thirty-seven."

"You still haven't told me why you asked."

"Because I think about how old I am," John replied, "and I wonder, *Hey, John Johnson, you've pretty much felt all the emotions you're ever likely to feel, and from here on it's reruns.* And that totally scares me. Do you ever think that?"

"Well, John, life's thrown me a curveball or two, so I don't worry about the rerun factor quite so much. But yeah, I do think about it. Every day, really." She looked over at him. "For what it's worth, today is my twenty-eighth birthday."

John beamed. "Happy birthday, Susan!" He then shook her hand in a parody of heartiness, but secretly savored how cool her palms were, like a salve on a burn he didn't even know he had.

The novelty of strolling in their city rather than barreling through it inside air-conditioned metal nodules added an unearthly sensation to their steps. They heard the changing gears of cars headed toward the Beverly Center. They listened to birdcalls and rustling branches. John felt young, like he was back in grade school.

"You know what this feels like—our leaving the restaurant like that?" Susan asked.

"What?" John replied.

"Like we're running away from home together."

They walked across a sunbaked intersection where a Hispanic boy with a gold incisor was selling maps to the stars' homes. John asked Susan, "You ever been on one of those things?"

"A star map? Once, for about two years. I was deleted in a reprinted version. Cars would drive past my place and then slow down to almost a stop and then speed up again—every day and every night. It was the creepiest thing ever. The house had good security, but even then, a few times I was spooked so badly I went and stayed at a friend's place. You?"

"I'm not a star." Just then the Oscar Mayer wiener truck drove by and cars all around them honked as if it were a wedding cortège. Screwing up his courage, John asked, "Susan—Sue— speaking of curveballs, here's one for you. A simple question: do you think you've ever met me before?"

Susan looked thoughtful, as though ready to spell out her reply in a spelling bee. "I've read about you in magazines. And I saw a bit of stuff about you on TV. I'm sorry things didn't work out for you—when you took off and tried to change yourself or whatever it was you were trying to do. I really am." The wiener hubbub had died down, and Susan stepped in front of John to survey him. His eyes looked like those of somebody who's lost big and is ready to leave the casino. "I mean, I've been pretty tired of being 'me' as well. I sympathize."

John moved as if to kiss her, but two cars behind them squealed their tires in a pulse of road rage. They turned around and the walk resumed.

"You were a beauty queen, weren't you?" John asked. "Miss Wyoming."

"Oh Lord, yeah. I was on the beauty circuit since about the age of JonBenet-and-a-half, which is, like, four. I've also been a child TV star, a has-been, a rock-and-roll bride, an air crash survivor and public enigma."

"You like having been so many different things?"

Susan took a second to answer. "I never thought of it that way. Yes. No. You mean there's some other way to live?"

"I don't know," said John.

They crossed San Vicente Boulevard, passing buildings and roads that once held stories for each of them, but which now seemed transient and disconnected from their lives, like window displays. Each recalled a bad meeting here, a check cashed there, a meal. . . .

John asked, "Where are you from?"

"My family? We're hillbillies. Literally. From the mountains of Oregon. We're nothing. If my mother hadn't escaped, I'd probably be pregnant with my brother's seventh brat by now—and somebody in the family'd probably steal the kid and trade it for a stack of unscratched lottery cards. You?"

In a deep, TV-announcer voice he declared, "The Lodge Family of Delaware. 'The Pesticide Lodges.' " His voice returned to normal. "My maternal great-grandfather discovered a chemical to interrupt the breeding cycle of mites that infect corn crops."

A light turned green and the boulevard was shot with traffic and the pair walked on. Susan was wrapped in a pale light fabric, cool and comfortable, like a pageant winner's sash. John was sweating like a lemonade pitcher, his jeans, gingham shirt and black hair soaking up heat like desert stones. But instead of seeking both air-conditioning and a mirror, John merely untucked his shirt and kept pace with Susan.

"You'd think our family had invented the atom bomb from the way they all lorded about the eastern seaboard. But then they did this really weird thing."

"What was that?" Susan asked.

"We went through our own family tree with a chain saw. Ruthless, totally ruthless. Anybody who was found to be socially lacking was erased. It was like they'd never even lived. I have dozens of great-uncles and aunts and cousins who I've never met, and their only crime was to have had humble lives. One great-uncle was a prison warden. *Gone.* Another married a woman who pronounced 'theater' *thee-ay-ter. Gone.* And heaven help anybody who slighted another family member. People weren't challenged or punished in our family. They were merely *erased.*"

They were quiet. They'd walked maybe a mile by now. John felt as close to Susan as paint is to a wall. John said, "Tell me something else, Susan. Anything. I like your voice."

"My voice? Anybody can hear my voice almost any time of day anywhere on earth. All you need is a dish that picks up signals from satellite stations that play nonstop cheesy early eighties TV shows." They were outside a record store. Two mohawked punk fossils from 1977 walked past them.

John looked at her and said, "Susan, have you ever seen a face, say—in a magazine or on TV—and obsessed on it, and maybe secretly hoped every day, at least once, that you'd run into the person behind the face?"

Susan laughed.

"I take it that's a yes?"

"How come you're asking?"

John told Susan about a vision he'd had at Cedars-Sinai Medical Center the year before that led him to make a drastic life decision. He told Susan that it was *her* face and voice that had come to him during his vision. "But what happened was that months later, after I'd gone and completely chucked out all of my old life, I realized I didn't have this great big mystical Dolby THX vision. I realized that there'd merely been some old episode of that TV show you used to star in playing on the hospital's TV set beside my bed. And it must have melted into my dream life."

It made a form of sense to Susan that this man with sad, pale eyes like snowy TV sets should have seen her as a refuge and then found her. Years before she'd stopped believing in fate. Fate was corny. Yet with John that long-lost tingle of destiny was once again with her.

A leaf blower cut the moment in two, and just as John was about to raise his voice, Cedars-Sinai came into view far in the distance, between a colonnade of cypress trees and a billboard advertising gay ocean-liner cruises. John's shirt was now soaked through with sweat, so they stopped at a convenience store and bought an XXL I-LOVE-LA white cotton shirt and two bottles of water. He changed out in the parking lot to the amused ogling of teenage boys who yelled out, "Boy supermodel steals the catwalk!"

John said, "Fuck 'em," and they crossed Sunset. It was getting to be late in the afternoon, and the traffic was crabby and sclerotic. They entered a residential neighborhood. Susan was feeling dizzy and sleepy and said, "I need to sit down," so they did, on the curb before a Wedgwood-blue French country-style house under the suspicious gaze of an Asian woman on the second floor.

"It's the sun," said Susan. "It's not like it used to be. Or, I can't take as much as I used to." She lay back on the Bermuda grass.

Suddenly worried he'd been the only one spilling the beans, John said, "Tell me about the crash. The Seneca crash. I'll bet you never talk about it, do you?"

"Not the full story, no."

"So tell me." Susan sat up and John put his arm around her. Staring at the pavement, like Prince William behind his mother's coffin, she told the story. And she might have talked to him all night, but two things happened: the lawn sprinklers spritzed into frantic life, and a Beverly Hills police patrol car soundlessly materialized. Two grim-faced officers got out, hands on weapons on hips. Soaked, Susan started to stand up, but her tired knees buckled. John helped pull her up, saying, "Jesus, we try and take a quick rest and in comes the SWAT team. Who pays your salaries, you goons? I pay your salaries. . . ."

"There's no SWAT team, Mr. Johnson. Stay calm," said one of the officers. "Ma'am"—he looked more closely at her—"Mrs. Thraice? Can we help you? Give you a lift? You were great in *Dynamite Bay*." *Dynamite Bay* was a low-budget action picture now in wide video release and not doing too badly. Adam had been proclaiming it as the revival of Susan's acting career.

She took a professional tone. "Hello, boys. Yes, I'd love a ride." She turned toward John and smiled regretfully. "I'm great for long walks but otherwise I'm not really Outward Bound material. Another day, another pilgrimage." She entered the rear passenger seat, and the officer shut the door. She rolled down the window. "To Beechwood Canyon, boys." She looked out at John. "You know—I don't even know my own phone number.

Call Adam Norwitz." Just as the cruiser pulled away, she rolled up a silk scarf, wet from the sprinkler, and handed it to John. "What actually happened *after* the crash is a much better story. I should have told you *that* instead. Phone me." And then she was gone and John stood, clutching the silk to his heart while the sprinkler drenched his feet, as though they were seeds.

Chapter Two

Two days before she turned twenty-five, Susan took a plane from New York, where she'd gone to audition for the part of a wacky neighbor on a sitcom pilot. Not the lead—the wacky neighbor. Next stop: mother roles. The audition hadn't gone well. The producer's Prince Charles spaniel had the runs, which had the hotel management badgering him with phone calls and door knocks while Susan was bravely making the most of stale coffee-tea-or-me jokes written by USC grads weaned on a lifetime of *Charles in Charge*, plus four years of Gauloises and Fellini ephemera.

In beaten retreat she boarded Flight 802 from New York to Los Angeles, sitting in Coach Class, as Where-Are-They-Now? waves of pity washed over her from the other passengers eagerly attuned to the scent of celebrity failure. Thank heaven for the distracting tarmac rituals—the safety demonstration, the small tingle of anticipation just before acceleration and lift-off. Banks of TV screens dislodged from the ceiling hawking Disney World, the Chevy Lumina and sugary perfumes. A *Cheers* rerun began.

The seat-belt light went off, and the flight attendants glumly hurled packets of smoked almonds at the passengers. Airlines were so disinterested in food these days, thought Susan, who had once been reigning queen of the old MGM Grand airline flights between coasts, playing poker with Nick Nolte, polishing toenails with Eartha Kitt and trading gossip with Roddy McDowell. Her fellow Flight 802 passengers ripped into their nuts all at once, a planewide locustlike chewing frenzy followed by the salty solvent odor of mashed nuts. *Ah, the fall from grace.*

Susan sat in her window seat, 58-A, and idly watched the landscape below. To her left was an older couple—he an engineer of some sort, and she a mousy 1950s wife. Mr. Engineer was convinced they were currently flying directly over Jamestown, New York, "the birthplace of Lucille Ball," and craned over Susan, jabbing at what looked like just another American town that bought Tide, ate Campbell's soup and generated at least one weird, senseless killing per decade. Later, Susan would look at a map of the eastern United States and realize how truly wrong Mr. Engineer had been, but at the time she gawked downward in some misplaced mythical hope of seeing a tiny little dot of flaming red hair.

It was at this point the engine blew—the left engine, clearly visible to Susan from her seat. Like a popcorn kernel—*poomp!*— the blast was muffled by the fuselage. The recoil shot flight attendants and their drink trolleys into the center bank of seats, while oxygen masks dropped like lizard tongues from the ceiling. The jet began tumbling and the unseat-belted passengers, such as Susan, floated like hummingbirds. She thought to herself, *I can float.* She thought, *I'm an astronaut.* Everything was moving too quickly for fear. There was some moaning during the drop, some cursing, but no hysteria and little other noise.

Then the pilot regained control of the plane, and the harnessing of its reins made it feel as if its bulk had walloped onto concrete. The oxygen hoses swooned like cartoon water lilies, and the TV screens resumed playing *Cheers.*

For the next two minutes normal flight resumed. Susan felt some relief as Mr. Engineer described to Mrs. Engineer exactly why the plane would remain flyable.

Then the descent began again, a descent as long as a song on the radio, a downward free float—smooth and bumpless. Susan felt as though the other passengers must be angry at her for jinxing their flight—for being the low-grade onboard celebrity who brought tabloid bad luck onto an otherwise routine flight. She avoided looking at them. She put on her seat belt. She felt clenched and brittle. She thought, *So this is how it ends, in a crash over Lucy's hometown, amid syndicated TV reruns, spilled drinks, and moaning engines. Once the plane hits the ground, I'll no longer be me. I'll go on to being whatever comes next.*

She felt a surprising relief that the plastic strand of failed identities she'd been beading together across her life was coming to an end. *Maybe I'll blink and open my eyes and I'll find myself hatching from a bird's egg, reincarnated as a cardinal. Maybe I'll meet Jesus. But whatever happens, I'm off the hook! Whatever happens, I'll no longer have to be a failure or a puppet or a has-been celebrity who people can hate or love or blame.*

Then, like the yank of a cyclone roller coaster, the plane sheared and bounced and slid into soil. The noise was so loud that it overpowered all other sensations. The visions she saw came at her fast as snapshots—bodies and dirt and luggage strewn toward her as though from a wood chipper—the screams of tortured metal and compressed air. And then silence.

Her seat had come to a stop along with a section of fuselage. The engineer, his wife and their two seats were . . . *gone.* Her chair rested alone, bolted to its piece of fuselage, perfectly vertical. She was still for about a minute, a small plume of smoke rising far off to the right. She smelled fuel. Gently she unclasped the seat belt of 58-A and rose to look across a fallow sorghum field. A brief survey of her body showed she was unscratched, yet it appeared to her that all the other passengers were crushed and broiled and broken along a debris path that stretched half a mile across the sorghum field hemmed with tract housing. There was a brief gap between when her plane crashed and when people began streaming from the suburb toward the wreckage. During that moment Susan had the entire plane wreck and the crumpled passengers to herself, like a museum late on a rainy Tuesday afternoon. The bodies around her seemed as though they'd been flocked onto the plane's hull and onto the gashed sorghum field from a spray can. A clump of unheated foil-wrapped dinners covered a stewardess's legs. Luggage had burst like firecrackers and was mixed with dirt and roots and dandelions, while cans of pop and bottles of Courvoisier were sprinkled like dropped marbles. Susan tried to find somebody else alive. There were limb fragments and heads. The soot-covered fuselage contained a cordwood pile of dead passengers.

She felt like a ghost. She tried to find her bodily remains there in the wreckage and was unable to do so. She grew frightened that the relationship between her mind and body had been severed.

Teenage boys on bicycles were the first to arrive, dropping their bikes as they began sleepwalking around the perimeter. They looked so young and vital. Susan approached them and one of them shouted out, "Hey, lady, did you see that?! Did you see it come down?" to which Susan nodded, realizing the boys had no idea she was a passenger and didn't recognize her.

Then she was lost in a crowd of local onlookers and trucks, parping sirens and ambulances. She picked her way out of the melee and found a newly paved suburban road that she followed away from the wreck into the folds of a housing development. She had survived, and now she needed sanctuary and silence.

She looked at the street names: Bryn Mawr Way, Appaloosa Street, Cornflower Road. After a short walk down Cornflower, past its recently dug soils and juvenile trees, she saw a newly built home with a small pile of newspapers accumulated on the front stoop. She went to the door, rang the bell and felt her shoulders relax when no one answered. Peeking in, she saw a cool, silent middle-class chamber, as quiet and inviting as the treasure vaults of King Tut must have seemed to their discoverers. She felt a calm that reminded her of riding in the back of the family's Corvair at night as a child, looking up to see stars through the sun roof, the most glamorous concept in the world.

She tried opening the front door, but it was locked. At the side of the house, the garage door was locked, and at the back she tried the kitchen's sliding door. No luck. With a rock the size of a peach, she smashed a hole in the glass, released the latch, and entered the kitchen. She made a quick scan for alarm systems—life in Hollywood had made her an expert—but there were none. Relief! And so quiet.

She smelled the air, poured a glass of tap water and scanned the various items magneted onto the fridge door: family photos, two attractive children, a boy and a girl, and a photo of the mother, who looked to Susan like one of those soccer moms she saw profiled in women's magazines, the sort of woman who endures childbirth with a brave smile, incapable of preparing nutritionally unbalanced picnic lunches. There was a photo of the father, athletic, in a blue nylon marathon outfit with the daughter papoosed onto his back. Also on the fridge was a calendar whose markings quickly let Susan know that "The Galvins" were going to be in Orlando for seven more days. She looked in the fridge and found some forgotten carrot sticks and nibbled on them as she walked into the living room and lay on the couch. The faint barks and wails of sirens reached her and she turned on the TV. A local news affiliate's traffic helicopter was covering the crash. The events on TV seemed more real to her than did her actual experience. Rescue workers, she was told, had yet to locate a survivor. The death toll was placed at 194. Susan took it all in. She was frightened by her inability to react to the crash. She was old enough to know about shock, and she knew that when it came, its manifestation would be harsh and bizarre.

Late afternoon sun filtered in through the living room sheers. Susan turned on the air-conditioning and walked through the silent house, and paused to press her cheek against the cool plaster of the upstairs hallway. She saw a warren of three bedrooms and two bathrooms, whose normalcy was so extreme she felt she had magically leapt five hundred years into the future and was inside a diorama recreating middle-class North American life in the late twentieth century.

The bathroom was large and clean. Susan drew a bath, disrobed and entered the tub, submerging her head in the chlorinated gem-blue water, and when she came up for air, she began to cry. She had emerged flawless—unpunctured and unbruised, like a Spartan apple fresh from the crisper at Von's. Her skin clammy, her knees pulled up to her chin, Susan thought of her mother, Marilyn, and of Marilyn's addiction to lottery tickets: Quick Picks, Shamrock Scratches, 6/49s. From an early age Susan had a deep suspicion of lotteries. Sure, they gave a person the opportunity to win $3.7 million, but in opening the doors to that possibility, they also opened *other* doors— doors a person probably didn't want opened, and doors that would remain uncloseable. A person opened herself up to the possibility of both catastrophic good and bad. Was deliverance Susan's repayment for years of refusing to scratch Marilyn's Pokerinos?

She splashed water on her face, rinsing away her tears. Her teeth felt gluey, and she spritzed water into her mouth and rubbed her tongue around them. She no longer felt she might be dead or a ghost.

Her chest stopped heaving. The sky was darkening, and she toweled herself dry, put on Karen Galvin's terry robe and returned to the kitchen, where she heated a can of cream-of-mushroom soup. Once the soup was ready, she took it and a box of Goldfish crackers into the living room to watch TV. Would the neighbors see the lights and suspect an intruder? She pushed the thought away. The neighborhood seemed to have been air-freighted in from the Fox lot, specifically designed for people who didn't want community, and she suspected she could probably crank up a heavy metal album to full volume and nobody would bat an eye.

The local news teams were out in force, and Susan wasn't surprised when an old news service head shot of herself appeared on screen behind the anchor's head. She remembered the day she'd posed for that particular shot. Her husband Chris, the rock star, had stood behind the photographer making quacking noises. She was happy to be away from Chris and auditions and mean tabloid articles. Wait—where *was* she? Ohio? Kentucky? She got up and went to check mail on a small credenza by the front door. Seneca, Ohio. Good.

She returned to the couch to hear more about her supposed death, wondering how long it would take the authorities to reassemble the bodies and dental fragments and realize she wasn't there. She wondered if her unbuckled seat belt in 58-A would be a giveaway.

She fell asleep on the couch, and woke up the next morning hungry and curious. The TV was still on, and as she surfed its channels, she learned the truth of the axiom that the last thing we ever learn in life is the effect we have on others. She was also able to calculate with disheartening precision the exact caliber of her rung in entertainment hell:

- "Forfeited a middling acting career for the trash of rock and roll."
- "Small-town girl makes it big and then small again."
- "Smart enough, but made some bad decisions."
- "Long-suffering wife of philandering rocker hubby."
- "A recent small brainless part in a small brainless movie."

She saw her mother and stepfather being interviewed on CNN on their lawn in Cheyenne. Marilyn held a framed photo of Susan up against her stomach as though hiding a pregnancy. It was an early teenage photo taken about three minutes before she became famous, just before her world expanded like an exploding spacecraft in a movie. Her stepfather, Don, was cross-armed and stern. Both were speaking about Susan's death, both uttering "No comment" to the prospect of suing the airline. Following them was a ten-second clip of Susan in her most remembered role as Katie, the "good" daughter in the long-running network series *Meet the Blooms*. Following the clip, the newscaster added gravely, "Susan Colgate—beauty queen, child star, rock-and-roll wife and devoted daughter. Her star now shines in heaven," at which Susan took a deep breath and said, "Ugh."

She made orange juice from frozen concentrate, and then a plate of cooked frozen peas served in a puddle of melted margarine, with two well-done hamburger patties garnished with Thousand Island dressing, served with dinner rolls, each stuffed with a once-folded-over processed cheese slice. The meal reminded her of a childhood hospital stay for an appendectomy, and she was conscious of this regression.

On CNN there was no real news footage to add to yesterday's. By tomorrow she figured there would be no mention of her, and by the day after, the nation's memory scar would be healed over completely. The world would forget her and she would forget the world. Whatever trace she'd left on the world would vanish as quickly as a paper cut. All that work and time and spirit she'd spent trying to become a plausible Susan Colgate— for nothing.

She zapped off the TV and upstairs tried on some of Karen Galvin's clothes, her own size, but a bit on the athletic side. A few pieces of okay jewelry—her husband's taste?

Later that week, Susan caught a snippet of her memorial service on *Entertainment Tonight*, with Chris Thraice, flown in from Germany to lead well-wishers at the Westwood Memorial Chapel in a painful, rockified version of "Amazing Grace" that sounded like a Live Aid hugging anthem. She was ashamed of the shallow, pathetic tribute arranged by God only knows whose people—Chris's probably—but then realized that it would have been the PR people for her action-adventure movie, masterminding some contorted variation of a pity fuck to get people into the theaters and pump up the third weekend's gross.

Her mother and stepfather, interviewed again after the service, had become key figures in the class-action suit being launched against the airline. "We'd sacrifice anything we might gain from this suit just to have our precious Suzie back in our fold." Suzie? Marilyn had called Susan many things before, but Suzie had never been one of them.

In more local crash news, the airline had paid the sorghum farmer for three years' worth of crops and, using sifting devices borrowed from a local mine, had already sanitized the site of all fragments. The county coroner admitted that many passengers had been too badly charred to be identified, and any fears Susan might have had that authorities had noticed her absence were scotched by an interview with a teary-eyed gate attendant who recounted how thrilled she'd been showing Susan into the jet ramp ("So real! And in coach class, too"). The gate attendant's testimony was the one moment of sincere warmth during the whole memorial charade.

At any rate, Susan was taking a risk that the Galvins, as a thrifty, bulk-purchasing family, would remain in Orlando for the fully-paid-for extent of their holiday, regardless of having one of North America's largest civil aviation disasters a short walk from their back door. The fridge calendar indicated an arrival in Columbus the next day at 6:10 P.M., in Seneca by 8:00.

On the morning of the Galvins' scheduled return, she went around the house with rags and Windex to wipe clean any surface that might conceivably bear her fingerprints. She washed sheets and towels and restored them to their original positions. She rearranged the remaining foods in the cupboards and deep freeze so that they appeared undepleted.

She then selected items stuffed in the back of Karen Galvin's wardrobe, and from boxes where evidence indicated garments that looked rarely if ever used. Also at the back, buried behind shoes and a stack of energy-rich athletic candy bars, she found ash blond wigs in a style she associated with women connected in some way to second- and third-generation entertainment money. She placed some of the wigs and a selection of clothes into a disused athletic bag from a shelf beside the washer and dryer, along with a box of energy bars, some older cosmetics, and a pair of Karen's almost touchingly practical shoes. She improvised a look for the day to come, and then nodded to the mirror.

Done.

Now she had one more job to do. She went into Mr. Galvin's liquor cabinet and selected what she thought would appeal most to teenagers—Jack Daniels—and poured three-quarters of the bottle down the sink. She took the partially filled bottle as well as some emptied beer cans and arranged them in a semicircle around the TV set. Then, with a thick-pointed Sharpie in what she hoped was teenage boy-looking handwriting, she scribbled on the TV screen, "Metallica rocks on." She also put out six drinking glasses tinged with Jack Daniels, two of them with lipstick traces. She mussed up the couch and a few pieces of bric-a-brac. The returning family would find evidence only of a low-threat minor occupation by teens.

Bewigged and sporting Karen's clothes, Susan was feeling good as she walked out the unlocked patio door, onto a back lane, where she heaved a plastic bag of her week's garbage into a stranger's trash can. She tried to think of a place to go. She chose Indiana.

Chapter Three

In the hospital John woke up long enough to hear the doctor tell a nurse that his lungs were plugged up with "about five cans of cream-of-mushroom soup," followed by, "Christ, he looks awful. I've eaten steaks healthier than this guy. He's down to what, sixteen T cells? He looks familiar. Movie guy?"

"Johnson. He did *Bel Air PI*."

"No way. What else?"

"*Bel Air PI 2*."

"Oh yeah—that was one of the few sequels better than the original."

"Yeah, sure, but did you see *The Wild Land*?"

"Nope. Never heard of it."

"Join the club. Didn't even go to video. I think it went, like, straight to Malaysia."

"Wait—didn't this guy do *The Other Side of Hate*?"

"Guilty. It went straight to in-flight. They might as well have shipped the dailies directly up to the Boeing factory."

"He deserves *Holy Retribution* for that one. I flew across the country about eight times one year and that movie was like a curse on my life. It haunted me no matter what flight or which direction I was flying in."

"At least it paid for Fun Boy's toy box. Check the rope burns on the wrists and ankles."

The doctor and nurse inspected his body like it was a skimpy Christmas tree. "Well, like I say, whatever floats your boat. Time to Hoover out the lungs again. And monitor his CNS for the wobblies. This guy's pill soup. Christ, whatta mess. He's like the undead Sno-Kone that is Walt Disney."

The nurse turned on a suction tube, but turned it off when John made a noise. "Didnaw go vee-oh."

"He's saying something. What's he saying?"

"Didnaw go vee-oh."

"It sounds like mush. Listen harder . . ."

"I think he's saying, 'It didn't go straight to video.' "

"What didn't?"

"*Wile Lann.*"

"*The Wild Land.*"

"Yoo azzhoe."

"Well, Doctor, I think he just called *you* a prince."

That it was something bacterial, and not, say, an overdose of five different prescription drugs mixed with cognac and two Slimfast strawberry shakes that nearly killed him was a fact not lost on him, regardless of what his medical team thought.

The night he died was to have been a typical Thursday evening: out of the house around 11 P.M., party with a friend of Ivan's who was coming in from New York, some guy with a hot play for sale—maybe take him up to Melody's for a quick hug or two. But John woke up around midafternoon feeling achy and nauseous, his thinking foggy, and he mistook this to be a bad reaction to the previous evening's methamphetamine, Serax and bondage. After all, a leather hood had chafed his Adam's apple. He seemed to recall a rope he pulled too hard. There was a sore at the base of his penis—*ouch*—was the skin surface broken? And the Vasarely ashtray as-expensive-as-a-new-small-car had been cleaved into three valueless chunks.

Kay finished cleaning the kitchen and Saran-wrapped his lunch around sunset. He heard her car exit the driveway. A pulse of seasickness surged, and his breathing grew limp. He dragged his torso to the shower stall to vomit, afterward grabbing and chewing a stray Serax tablet lying beneath the sink's kick. He stripped while leaning crumpled against the slate tiles, then ignited the hot water faucet and felt what little food he'd had that day—seaweed, basmati rice, grapefruit, algae drink and six Kit Kats. Rinsing off his skin, he blacked out.

When he came to, the water dowsing him was nearly cold and the sky outside had gone fully dark. He turned off the faucet. He was shivering and realized he was merely sick—sick! He hadn't been sick in decades, but his heart leapt with the knowledge that it wasn't drugs or excessive living that had his jaws chattering like a tree full of birds. He reached for the wall phone beside the toilet to slap the speakerphone button with his palm, triggering a dial tone that sliced the silence like a razor.

Who to call? He had to think quickly because he felt numbers leaving him. Kay would be back home in Inglewood now, well into her second bottle of Chablis. Melody was over in Rancho Mirage organizing a fantasy weekend for bankers. Ivan was in Davos, Switzerland, nookying with investors. His mother? No way was he going to let *her* see him like this. His assistant, Jennifer, had quit yesterday when she found the nannycam that Lopez, his security man, had installed in the bathroom's plug-in deodorizer. ("John, I can't believe you'd sink to accusing me of stealing your coke." "But Jennifer, you *were* stealing my coke." "Even still, how could you harbor such ugly thoughts about me in your head?") Bridge burned.

And then John couldn't remember numbers, period, so he pushed the "Old Lady Button," the one marked with the little red cross, and he croaked to the teenager manning the dispatch to "send me a goddamn ambulance," which finally showed up what seemed like two REM cycles later, after he'd squirreled himself into a pair of track pants and scooped a Halloween sack of pills into their baggy pockets, which rattled out, one by one, as he inchwormed his way down the staircase to the front door just as the paramedics arrived, at which point he passed out again.

Hours later, after the medical help had analyzed his career arc and removed the soup from his lungs, he lay in a cool, quiet room at Cedars-Sinai. Beside the bed there was a TV the size of a pack of Marlboros. He heard the sound of a laugh track, a few commercials, and then he used the sum of his strength to turn his head to watch. It was some piece-of-crap show from the early eighties. A bunch of has-beens.

He was dizzy sick, feverish. He remembered being young in Kentucky with his mother when a freak tornado had hit. He had walked through a street across the town that had been flattened. A cow was lying beside a pickup truck with its hide sucked right off. A horse was stuck up inside the one standing tree, its leaves plucked off in the middle of summer. Thousands of perch flopped inside a swath of Russian thistle as though the earth had sprouted erupting, percolating sores.

He suddenly felt sixteen years old again; his body was clean. He felt springy and he wanted to do somersaults off the high school's trampette. He wanted to ski a glacier. He wanted to climb the glass windows of the First Interstate Bank Tower with suction cups. He felt like flying. And so he flew, up above the Cedars-Sinai Medical Center and Los Angeles, toward the sun, into the upper atmosphere where he rapped his knuckles on the Mir Space Station, and then he heard a woman's voice and saw her face. It said to him, "No, John. Time to go back."

"Oh, you have *got* to be kidding." John kept propelling himself toward the sun.

"I don't kid, John Johnson. It's not a part of my job description."

John turned and saw Susan's face and voice, so recently stolen from the TV. It was a lovely, TV-proportioned all-American face—the face of a child raised with tetracycline, baton twirling and kung fu lessons. "Like *you* run the studio or something?"

"John, we're not here to cut a deal for Canadian and Mexican distribution rights. We're here to make you better."

"Better? I've never *been* better. Shit, I just rang the doorbell on the Mir Space Station." He could feel himself falling back down to earth again, through the ionosphere and the troposphere and the creamy blue atmosphere. "Stop that!" he shouted. "And who are you—do I know you or something? Send me back up!"

"Look at me, John."

"I'm looking. I'm *looking*."

"No you're not. You're looking for a way to get rid of me and fly back into space again."

"Okay, okay, you're *good*. But do you blame me? I don't want to go back down there to my crappy little life."

"Your life is crappy?"

His body stopped where it was, his feet inside the atmosphere, his head out in space, as though he were wading in the planet. "It's not what I would have wanted, no."

"What *would* you have wanted, then?"

"Like I keep that information at the top of my 'To Do' list, or something?"

"What would be wrong with keeping that at the top of your 'To Do' list?"

This gave John pause. "Nothing, I guess." He looked east, toward the seaboard. "Hey, look at New York! You can see the lights! It's night there now." The view was indeed splendid.

"Sure, John, the world is beautiful. But you were telling me what you would have wanted to do differently in your life."

"I dunno. Be one of those guys who buy short-sleeve golf shirts with olive checks at the pro shop—the ones who drive their kids to judo lessons and then to the pancake house afterward."

"*You?*"

"Well, it'd be a start. I see these guys on the San Diego Freeway on Saturday afternoons. They're married to soccer moms and they don't have affairs."

"John, let's be serious. Stop wasting my time."

"Okay, okay. Take a sip of water, fer Chrissake. Let me think."

"Oh *Johnnnn*," the vision cooed, "I'm not a table full of suits from Disney."

"You know what?" John said. "I'd like to simply stop being *me*. I'd like to be somebody anonymous, without any luggage. I want a clean slate."

"So then go clean your slate. Enter your own private witness relocation program."

"It's too complex. You can't do it anymore. Too many computers and stuff."

"It's not complex. It's the opposite of complex. What could be simpler?"

"Who *are* you?"

"I'm not the issue here."

"I *know* you from somewhere. Sundance? Tristar?"

"You're wasting your time."

"So what happens now?"

"Back to the hospital."

"Oh."

"You sound disappointed."

John went quiet as an empty room. And then he said, "I want to see you again."

"I don't know, John."

"Please?" John's body began zooming down to California at telescopic speed.

"I have a call on another line, John."

Whamp!

He felt as though he'd fallen onto concrete.

Two days later, he was lying on his hospital bed, wide awake, and his confidant-madam, Melody, was sitting across his dark private room watching *Dr. Quinn, Medicine Woman* on the TV screen.

"You're awake! Hello!" Melody shouted. She pushed the MUTE button and scampered toward him, kissing him on the forehead.

"Melody—shit—what day is it?"

"It's Saturday, you brute. You had the flu. And pneumonia. The doctors said they thought you had AIDS because you have almost no immune system left." The sun had nearly set outside. A supply trolley rolled past the door.

"You've been here all this time?"

Melody looked guilty. "Well, only about ten minutes, really."

John flopped his head sideways, caught a glimpse of his face in the mirror. He closed his eyes. "Jesus."

Melody was rustling about in her purse and found some mints. "Want a mint?"

John's stomach turned. "No."

"Spoilsport."

Melody popped a mint and then stared at John, who closed his eyes and tried to recapture the face and voice he'd just seen. Instead he heard Melody tell him what had happened and how sick he'd been, then bridge into snatches of gossip. The captive nature of the sickbed reminded him of his childhood illnesses. He didn't want to remember that, and he brusquely let Melody know it.

"*Excusez-moi*. I'm just trying to be friendly. I didn't *have* to come down here, you know. Ivan called from Switzerland and put me on sentry duty. Me and all none of your friends."

"Mel—"

"Oh shit." Melody felt she'd gone too far. "I'm sorry, John. For what it's worth, your mother's been camping out here for forty-eight hours. I sent her home to sleep."

"Forget it."

"No. I feel terrible for being so mean when you're so sick." Her eyes became frantic. "I know—I've got some wonderful welcome-back pussy for you—twins!"

"I don't want twins, Mel. Shit, I don't want anybody. Or anything."

"How about a bit of toot, John?" Melody removed a pink plastic Hello Kitty heart-shaped box from her fetal calf leather handbag. "Straight from Miss Bolivia's falsies. Yummie, yummie." She held out the box to John, and he slapped it with a wave that was just forceful enough to read as purposeful. The box fell onto the floor and exploded.

"John! That was really stupid."

"Mel, please. I don't feel so good. I want to be alone."

"Oh cute—like a Simon and Garfunkel song. You remember who your friends are. And remember—twins! From Florida no less."

John stared at her.

"I'm going to leave now, John, before you go and say something else stupid. I'll tell Nurse Ratchet outside that you're awake. *Au revoir*, Johnniepoo."

Chapter Four

Susan's earliest memory was powerful and clear. She was four and a half, and she was in the elevator of the Benson Hotel, Portland, Oregon, wearing a beaded strapless evening gown paid for with the proceeds of rabbits her mother Marilyn sold from hutches adjoining the double-wide trailer back in McMinnville.

Marilyn had toiled for umpteen hours on each of the gown's beaded filaments, in between furtive glances at walls papered with gown photos ripped from ladies' magazines and special- ized pageantry publications. Marilyn had also recently purchased a glue gun and she had had great plans for fastening sparkly ob- jects to belts and accessories.

Susan's face was heavily pancaked in a manner calculated to add fifteen years to her age. She was wearing a diagonal rayon sash across her chest reading PETITE MISS MULTNOMAH COUNTY— FIRST RUNNER-UP, and her face was so moist from tears it felt like an unsqueezed dish sponge. She remembered pushing a button for each of the floors. The doors opened sixteen times from penthouse to basement, each time revealing the absence of Marilyn.

Earlier, just before Susan had gone onstage, Marilyn had clasped her shoulders, looked her dead in the eyes and said,

"Only the prettiest and the best-behaved girl gets to win, and if you don't win, I'm not going to be here waiting for you afterward. Do you understand this? Is this clear?" Susan had nodded and gone onstage with the fluid military precision drummed into her on a mock catwalk Marilyn had chalked onto the concrete at the cul-de-sac's end back in McMinnville. And yet she hadn't won, and had no idea what mistake had caused her to lose.

Once the elevator reached the lowest level, Susan pushed all the buttons on the pad again, and rose upward. When the doors on the main floor opened, she saw dozens of the mother-daughter molecules specific to pageantry, milling their way out the front door. Marilyn was speaking to the concierge. She looked at Susan exiting the elevator and, cool-as-you-will, said, "Oh my, a runner-up." As Susan came closer she added, "I have a daughter, yes, but she's a winner, and you couldn't possibly be her because your sash says FIRST RUNNER-UP, which means the same thing as losing."

Susan burst into tears.

"Oh, shut up," said Marilyn, and she gave her daughter a handkerchief. "You'll stain the dress. Come on. Let's walk to the car."

Susan followed, brimming with the shameful gratitude of a puppy in training. The night was cool, on the brink of discomfort.

"Oh Susan," began Marilyn, "You know how long we worked on this one. It's been weeks since I've touched a bingo card with Elaine or even watched TV. I think of the time I spend trying to make you the winningest little girl in Oregon and I start to feeling like those inmates in orange jumpsuits picking up litter on the sides of the Interstate."

Bums heckled them as they walked through the town center.

Marilyn looked their way and said: "They can't pave this city fast enough. Put a ten-lane freeway right through these old heaps, call it a mall, and gas those wretched winos."

Susan sniffled and her heels clicked on the sidewalk like a sous-chef's cutting knife on a board.

"Don't you have *anything* to say?" asked Marilyn. "You're so quiet, like a Barbie doll, except Barbie wouldn't have muffed her lighting cue on the 'Spirit of Recycling' dance routine." Marilyn breathed a sigh like a deflating parade balloon. She lit a cigarette. "You could at least show a bit more spunk with me— fight back—a little bit of give-and-take."

But Susan remained silent. Susan was going to *be* Barbie. She was going to be more Barbie than Barbie, and in having made this decision, she unwittingly followed Marilyn's dancing lead.

They reached the car, the sunroofed Corvair Susan considered the one truly glamorous aspect of her family's life. It appeared that Marilyn was not going to assist her, so as she got in, she carefully lifted and folded her dress so as not to damage it when shutting the door.

Marilyn started the car, and they pulled out of the downtown core. "Okay then, Susan. Your ramp walking was pretty good. A good stride. And the makeup worked well under that lighting. A bit too tarty, maybe, but good."

"Mom?"

"Yes?"

"What's 'tarty'?"

Marilyn deemed it inappropriate to discuss tartiness with her four-and-a-half-year-old. She ignored the question. "Next time you're going to have to approach the fore-catwalk more naturally, and I truly think those bangs of yours are going to have to grow out some." She looked over at her daughter. "Susan, your eyes look like two cherry pits spit onto the floor," but Susan was drifting off to sleep. A gentle rain was falling and the wipers were slapping. "I was never able to enter pageants myself, Susan. I could only dream of them. The excitement. The dresses. The winning. I was stuck out in the boondocks with my wretched family." She pulled onto the highway back to McMinnville. "I never had what you have now—a mother who cares for you and who wants you to win. And certainly not what you're going to have—a big success in life—and trust me, you're going to have it. Me, I'll never be the prettiest or the purest or the best, but you—you will."

Susan, sleepy, hoped Marilyn's good mood would stretch all the way home.

"I shouldn't bitch. I did end up getting your father—your stepfather—but he's as good as a real father." Her voice relaxed. "Don the Swan." She looked kindly over at Susan. "Baby, you'll win next time, won't you, sweetie?"

Susan looked up at her mother, rain splashing on the windshield and her small mouth emitted a calm, clear, and hopefully Barbie-like "Yes."

Chapter Five

"Suzie, do be a love and whack this evil little Kinder Egg into the Grand Canyon for me." Chris handed Susan a 5-iron. It was near dawn and she, Chris, two band members and an arty black-and-white photographer named Rudy were sitting atop the tour bus in lawn chairs, sipping Benedictine and taking turns trying on silvery-orange nipple tassels that Chris, back in Las Vegas and crashingly drunk, had purchased from an off-duty lap dancer for $500.

"Okay, guv," said Susan, "but we'll never know what the little toy was inside the egg."

"That's the point, you evil, evil girl," replied Chris. "Is the eggy-weggy properly teed up?"

"Chris, your London vocabulary is really driving me crazy."

"Be that as it may, I repeat, is the eggy-weggy properly teed up?"

Susan checked the foil wrapped chocolate egg perched on a Marlboro box. "Ready for action."

"Okay then, Sooz, it's time for whackies!"

Rudy, sensing a trophy, slunk into a shooting angle behind Susan, then in tassels, while Chris called out, "Wait! Your tassels are a mess." With the fingertips of one hand he held her nipples in place while using his other hand to rake the tinsel. "There."

"Thank you, *husband*."

"We Brits are so dominant, so forceful."

"Sun's almost up," called Nash, the drummer.

Susan moved into position. Far across the vast geographical sore, the first chinks of sunlight were breaking through the horizon's rock. Susan shouted, "Foreplay!" and walloped the Kinder Egg with such force that it vaporized and fell into the canyon as a mist. Rudy's flash coincided with the sunrise entering into her eye, and she wasn't sure which was which. The photo was a winner: faded child star now in second bloom as rock-and-roll mama.

"*Ravishing*," said Chris.

"You liar. You just like me because I got you a green card."

"You just like *me* because I let you sing backup vocals on tour."

"That's not true. I *love* you for the 10K a month you put into my savings account."

"You just love *me* for the manliness of my member." Chris dropped his trousers and wagged his hips back and forth, establishing a lewd pendulum as the crowd on the roof shrieked in unison.

And so went life on tour. Susan was alpha road-rat on the North American tour of Chris's band, Steel Mountain, the highly caste-conscious temporary family fueled by drinking, smoking, copious drugs and arcade games inside buses that stank of the ghosts of a hundred previous bands.

Susan married Chris two years after the network canceled *Meet the Blooms*, and her TV career vanished in a puff of dust. Her then agent-manager-lover, Larry Mortimer, phoned her with news of the cancellation while she was in Guam shooting a Japanese commercial for a lemony sports beverage called Pocari Sweat ("Hey team—*let's Pocari!*"). Larry was getting bored with

TV and had just entered the world of rock management and had connected Susan to Chris.

The match had its pluses and minuses. Chris had money and Susan did not. Her earnings from her years in TV had been squandered and lost by her mother and stepfather, a fact that she had laboriously kept out of the media. Also, Chris was gay, information that would surely have given surprise to his head-banging musical constituency. Above all, Susan was still in love with the Catholic, divorce-phobic Larry Mortimer. While once it had been easy to find reasons to be around Larry, now Susan needed a better pretext—marrying Chris to land him a green card restored her to Larry's inner-circle. The green-card deal with Chris seemed like just the ticket, and for a while it worked. But when Chris wasn't touring, he lived in London. Susan stayed in California, the partnerless weeks and months adding up across the years. She lived by herself most of the time, in Chris's Space Needle–like orb atop a pole that had the distinct aura of having been handed down from a long succession of emotionally adolescent, newly monied entertainment people. It had filthy shag carpets in long-discontinued colors, appliances that probably hadn't worked since the dawn of TV dinners, and the impending sensation that the Monkees would pop in through a window at any moment and burst into song. In the Space Needle, Susan realized that the phone really didn't ring too often, and when it did, it was for Chris. Any scripts Larry sent her were for titty flicks. Their phone calls were many: "Oh, come on, Larry. We can do better than this. How hard can it be to land a TV movie?"

"You're rock and roll now, Sue. You need to be a Young Mom for TV movies. You know—two kids—those new minivans people are driving. Fridge magnets. People read about you and

Chris and the rest of those gorillas trashing a Ramada on a tour and it scares them off."

"I'm unbankable, Larry. Say it."

"You're crazy. I send you a dozen scripts a week."

"Slashers and titties."

"That's not true. They're entry points."

"Entry to nowhere. I'm stereotyped as either the sucky little Bloom daughter or the slutty rock bitch."

"I'm not going to have this conversation, Susan, because it goes nowhere."

"Don't hang up, Larry."

"Take acting lessons. Karate. Put on that blue lace number you wore for me down in Laguna Niguel and give Chris a peek. It's so hot, he'll switch."

"You *liked* that negligée?"

"Liked? Ooh—*Susan.*"

"I looked hot in it? You didn't act like it."

"I've got worries."

Larry went quiet. After a while, Susan said, "Can you come over tonight?"

No answer.

"Good-*bye,* Larry." She slammed down the receiver and it rang almost simultaneously; she picked up the phone and barked, "Hello."

"*Suzie,* if you're going to be such a shit about a simple little ringy-dingy, then I needn't waste my time here."

"Hey, Chris. Larry's being a jerk. Where are you?"

"At a chic little Kensington soirée, and it's so lofty I feel faint. I'm hiding in the library right now."

"Whose party is it, Chris?"

"Guess."

"I'm not in the mood to—"

41

"Think 'palace.' "

"No!"

"Yes."

"Oh God. Oh God. I can't believe I'm going to ask you the question I'm about to ask: what's *She* wearing?" Susan's preoccupation with Larry's dwindling role in her life, for the moment, was deflected. "Steal me a pair of Her shoes and I'll never de-alphabetize your tapes ever again."

Chapter Six

Two weeks after John had left Cedars-Sinai, he was physically restored, but his old life and its trappings felt archaic, slightly silly, and woefully inadequate to meet the changes he felt inside—as if he were now expected to play CDs on a wobbly old turntable with a blunt needle. He kept trying to see his life as Susan saw it, or rather, how his life might seem to the woman in his vision, whose identity remained unknown. He was thumping out tuneless rhythms as he walked through the fuck-hut's slate and aluminum walls. Yes, he was experiencing a type of freedom associated with no longer caring about keeping up the appearance of wealth, but with this freedom came a rudderless sensation, one that made him giddy, the way he'd felt as a child as he waited for week upon agonizing week for the postman to deliver a cardboard submarine he'd sent away for—a device that had promised to take him far away into a fascinating new realm, but which upon arrival was revealed to be as substantial and as well constructed as a bakery's cardboard cake box. But *ahhh*, the waiting had been so wonderfully sweet.

The sun had set. Another day was over. He'd spent the morning speaking with a lawyer inquiring about his will. He'd spent the afternoon at City Hall doing some paperwork. He was still thumping when the doorbell ran (two bars of Phillip Glass). It was the twins Melody had promised. He sighed and buzzed them into his polished-steel atrium. "I'm Cindy," said the sister in the pink angora sweater with bare midriff. "And I'm Krista," said the other in green. They looked at each other, smiled, and overstated the obvious: "We're twins!"

"Yeah, yeah."

He showed them the living room with its suede walls and panoramic windows exposing a constellational view of the city lights below. "Can I fetch you drinks?" he asked, inwardly noting how many times he'd asked this same antique question.

The girls exchanged looks. "Just one," said Krista.

"That's all we're allowed," added Cindy. "Jack Daniels if you have it. With maraschino cherries. I just *adore* them."

"Why just one drink?" John asked.

More looks were exchanged: "We've heard you can be demanding," said Cindy, to which Krista added, "We're going to need our wits here."

"Wits?" said John. "Oh God, *relax.* Sit down. Look at the view. I don't want anything. Wait. Yes I do. I just want to talk."

"That's okay. We get that all the time," said Krista.

"What—guys who only want to talk?"

"No. More like guys who don't want to feel like they're consorting with hell-bound floozies, who believe that a cozy chat beforehand will absolve them of moral contagion."

John looked at Krista: *"Absolve them of moral contagion?"*

"I'm an educated woman," said Krista.

Cindy said, "Krista, *don't.*"

"Don't *what?*" asked John.

There was a pause: "Don't be smart."

"Why not?" John asked.

"It's a turnoff to customers."

John howled. "You can't be serious!"

Krista said, "Mention politics or use a big word and a guy deflates like a party balloon."

"Now you've done it," said Cindy.

"You've done *nothing*," said John.

"I've got a degree in organic chemistry," said Krista. "That's the study of molecules containing carbon."

"Thank you, Madame Curie," said John. "What about you, Cindy, what do you have a degree in?"

"Hot nourishing lunches," Krista inserted quickly.

"I have a degree in nutrition. Florida State University, class of '97."

"Phone the Nobel Committee," said Krista.

"Krista, just can it, okay?"

"So what are you two baccalaureates doing in a fuckhouse like Melody's? There must be test kitchens all over America begging for a team like you two."

"Very amusing, Mr. Johnson," said Krista. "We both want to act. In high school I did *Joseph and the Amazing Technicolor Dreamcoat*—in drag, no less." John's heart was sinking. "I'm good. So's Cindy. And this kind of thing just pays the bills."

"Look," said John, "you've gotta know that if you hump one of us producer guys, you've humped all of us—which means there's probably all kinds of other junk you've done that the *Enquirer*'s going to zoom in on like a smart bomb the moment you get a walk-on part in a cable-access slasher. You won't even get a job as a body double in a Cycle dog food commercial."

"We'll take that risk."

"Okay," said John. "You guys want to do some acting tonight?"

Cindy winked at Krista: "Sure. And by the way, *Bel Air PI* was great. I saw it three times in a row in Pensacola this spring after my wisdom teeth got yanked."

"How do you want us to act, Mr. Johnson?"

"Oh Jesus. How about normal."

This remark drew a blank.

"Normal?" Cindy asked. "Like housewives? Like people who live in Ohio or something?"

"No. Be yourselves. Talk to me like I'm a person, not a customer."

"We can do that," said Krista, communicating with Cindy in what appeared to be their personal Morse of winks. "Yes—let's."

And so the three of them sipped drinks and watched the city lights for a moment or two.

"My panties feel too tight," said Cindy.

"And my sweater's too hot," added Krista. "I'm so hot. I'm going to have to remove my sweater."

"Cut!" John was upset. "I don't mean normal dirty talk. I mean normal. Like we're talking in a restaurant and there's no possibility of sex."

The twins had heard rumors at Melody's about some of John's kinkier scenes. Maybe this was how they started out.

"I'm going to freshen your drinks," John said, "and then you're going to tell me about yourselves. How you got to where you are now. Your life if it was a movie."

"More like a beauty pageant," called Cindy as John jiggled with bottles and crystal glasses.

"I was Miss Dade County," said Krista.

"And I was Miss United Fruit Growers," added Cindy.

"And we were both Junior Miss Florida Panhandle," continued Krista. "One year apiece, one right after the other, but because we're twins people weren't sure if we were technically the same person. *USA Today* did a thing on us. It's real scary how evil the pageant circle is."

"Tell me," John said, returning with the drinks.

"Oh! Where to begin?" said Cindy. "At birth, I guess. The important thing is to have a hungry unfulfilled mother who needs a piece of herself up there on the winner's dais being bathed in adulation. There's no such thing as a child star by herself. Child stars exist only in conjunction with a stage mother. Earth and sun."

"We really lucked out in that department," said Krista. "In her sophomore year at U. of F., Mom got the heave-ho from *Godspell*, and she vowed to wreak vengeance on the state of Florida. We're her weapons."

Said Cindy: "You have to have a mother pushing you the whole way from, like, two onward. For most of us show dogs, we're not even aware of how distorted and grimly fucked up we are until it's too late. They have to get you when you're young."

"And your mom has to buy and make you, like, a thousand little outfits a year," said Krista, "and your mother has to make you dress like a stripper at the age of, like, five."

"Some parents will do anything. There's this actress out there—Susan—oh—what's her name, Kris? She's in the Where-Are-They-Now? file—the one who disappeared for a year."

"Colgate. Susan Colgate," Krista answered.

"Yeah. In junior high her parents moved to Cheyenne, Wyoming, just to improve their chances of being able to represent an entire state in the national competitions. Yeah—Miss Wyoming. Ha!"

"Missed her," said John. "I don't pay attention to TV. It turned to trash in the eighties. I stopped watching it, period."

Music then swirled through the room's air—horns and jazz, and the lights dimmed to candle strength. "The lights are on a timer," John said, but it didn't matter, because the room became smaller, the air charged like summer's eve, and the three of them clinked the ice that remained in their glasses. The sisters began to remove their angoras. "No, don't," John said. "No. Let's keep it perfect." And the girls said, "Fine."

"Come work for me," he said.

"What?" came the reply in stereo.

"Be my assistants. I need help right now."

There was a pause. Krista said, "I don't know, Mr. Johnson."

"No. No. It's not a sex thing. I swear, no sex. You guys are smart and ambitious," John said.

"Is that what you look for in assistants?" Krista asked.

"Fuck, yes. Smartness, hipness, alertness, greed and speed."

Krista continued: "Is this how you normally hire assistants?"

"Nahhh. What I normally do is put ads in the paper advertising Eames furniture at ridiculously low prices."

"That's that 1950s stuff, isn't it?" asked Cindy.

"Bingo. It's this furniture designed for poor people, but poor people never liked it, and the only people who know about it or care about it are rich or smart. So anybody who answers that ad really quickly is de facto smart, alert, greedy and hip."

"What's Melody going to say?" asked Cindy.

"Mel has two ugly little brats I helped put through Dartmouth and Neufchâtel. She owes me."

"But then what about, say, the salary?"

"See—I was right. You're a little bit greedy," at which point the girls quickly huffed up and their spines straightened. "Relax. In the film business it's a compliment."

"So what do you want?" Cindy asked.

"Truth be told," John said, "the one thing in this world I want more than anything else is a great big crowbar, to jimmy myself open and take whatever creature that's sitting inside and shake it clean like a rug and then rinse it in a cold, clear lake like up in Oregon, and then I want to put it under the sun to let it heal and dry and grow and sit and come to consciousness again with a clear and quiet mind."

The CD player clicked and purred as it changed albums, and

Cindy and Krista kept their bodies still. Cindy said, "Okay. I'll work for you."

Krista said, "Me, too. I'm in."

John said, "Good," and music came on, Edvard Grieg, a flute solo. "What's going to be your next move then—John?" asked Krista.

"I'm going to liquidate myself."

"Like going offshore or something? Taxes?" asked Cindy.

"No. I'm going to erase myself. I'm going to stop being me." John saw the look on the twins' faces, and it wasn't fear, but neither was it comprehension. "No. Not suicide. But suicide's cousin. I want to disappear."

"You've lost me," said Cindy.

"I'm going to start my own witness relocation program."

"Help us out here, John."

"It's easy. I don't want to be me anymore. I think I've gone as far as I can go in this body."

"In this body?"

"Yeah."

"Who gets your money?" Cindy asked.

"Probably the IRS."

"Who gets your residuals and your copyrights?"

"I don't know. Crack babies. Jerry's Kids. Something like that. That's a detail. Think of the bigger picture here."

He would be *gone*. Completely. He would no longer be John Lodge Johnson. He would be—*nobody*—he would have nothing: no money, no name, no history, no future, no hungers—he would merely be this sensate creature walking the country's burning freeways, its yawning malls, its gashes of wilderness, its lightning storms, its factories and its dead spaces. "Ladies, my atom's stopped spinning. The twitching barnyard animal lies silent in a heap. The machine has *stopped*."

Cindy and Krista made ooh . . . noises.

Two drinks later, John, Cindy and Krista were going through John's house, with Cindy pushing a SmarteCarte and Krista holding a clipboard on which she recorded each item John tossed into a box on the cart, the contents bound for the local Goodwill drop box.

"DKNY blazer. Unworn. Charcoal."

"Check."

"Prada slacks, cocoa. Unworn."

"Check."

"Where'd you get a SmarteCarte?" Cindy asked.

"Stole it from SeaTac Airport up in Seattle. I've spent so much on those goddamn things over the years—I put the Smarte-Carte children through beauty school. They owed me one after all this time."

Cindy said, "You seem to put a lot of people through a lot of things, John."

The doorbell rang—it was his business partner, Ivan McClintock, with his wife, Nylla. John buzzed them in and called from upstairs, Ivan and Nylla climbed a series of chilly aluminum slabs that led up to the bedrooms. "John-O?"

"We're in here, Ive."

The couple rounded a corner. "Guys, this is Krista and Cindy. Gals, this is Ivan and Nylla. Ivan and I have been making movies ever since we both had acne."

The group exchanged hellos, and the work of emptying John's wardrobes of conspicuously expensive clothing continued.

"See anything you want, Ivan?" John asked, holding out a nest of ties.

Ivan was doing his best to keep his cool.

"Our styles are opposite, John-O. That's why we make a good team."

Nylla, pregnant and wrapped in one of her trademark silk shawls, asked, "John, Melody called Ivan at work and then me at home. She said you were making plans to—." She paused. "*Erase* yourself or something. Something radical."

John was silent.

Nylla persevered. "So what's the score?"

A TV-sized Tiffany box full of enema tools clattered down from an upper shelf, bouncing on the sisal flooring and rattling onto the white limestone hallway. "Why don't we go downstairs?" John said to Ivan and Nylla.

From the landing, he shouted back, "Remember gals— *everything* goes."

They went into the living room. It was night outside. Ivan and Nylla drank in the view. "I never get tired of looking at the city, John-O. It's like we're flying over it, about to land at LAX."

"It's like upside-down stars," said Nylla.

John handed Ivan a scotch with branch water. Nylla took cranberry juice.

Ivan said, "Melody phoned. She told me about your name change application."

"She narced?"

Nylla said, "Oh, don't be so corny. Of *course* she did. She's worried sick about you. We all are."

Ivan burst in. "Fortunately between me and Mel we have enough contacts at City Hall to retrieve your forms, no harm done."

"John," said Nylla, "You were going to change your name to 'dot'?"

"Not 'dot'—just a simple period. When I filed my Change of Name affidavit at City Hall, they told me I had to use at least one keyboard stroke. A period is the smallest amount of ink and space a name can be."

Ivan put his drink on a glass-block table and made I-told-you-so eyes at Nylla.

"There's more, Ivan. I'm going to renounce my citizenship."

"Oh, John-O, that is a lousy idea—it's—it's—un-*American*."

"What country *do* you want to be a citizen of, then?" asked Nylla. The three sat themselves down on Ultrasuede couches in John's high-tech conversation pit. John clapped his hands and the fire started.

"I don't want to be a citizen of anywhere, Ny."

"Can you *do* that?" she asked. "I mean, be a citizen of nowhere?"

"I don't know. I'm seeing an immigration lawyer tomorrow. I'm wondering if I can get citizenship in Antarctica."

"Antarctica?" said Ivan.

"Yeah. It's not like it has a king or queen or president or anything. I want to give it a try."

"I think Antarctica's presliced into pieces from the South Pole outward," said Nylla, "and a different country regulates each slice. So maybe not there. Maybe you can get citizenship in a country that's so useless it's almost the same thing as being stateless. Some country that only exists when the tide's out."

"Nylla," Ivan interrupted, "you're only feeding his bullshit idea."

"It's not bullshit, Ivan," John said.

"How about Pitcairn Island?" Nylla suggested. "One square mile in the middle of the South Pacific Ocean, the most remote inhabited place on earth."

"My wife the *Jeopardy* champion."

"England owns it," said John. "I checked."

Ivan asked listlessly, "How about one of those African countries held together with Scotch tape and Popsicle sticks?"

"I'm considering them, too."

"John-O—if you renounce your U.S. citizenship, you'll have no protection. With citizenship, the U.S. government can step in and help you wherever you go. And besides, you'll always have your Social Security number no matter what else happens."

"Not if I renounce my citizenship. I *do* know that."

Ivan was sulky: "Just try renting a car with no credit card and a passport from Upper Volta."

"It's called Benin now," said Nylla.

Ivan glowered her way: "Please phrase your answer in the form of a question."

"Ivan, you're getting distracted. You're missing the spirit of the thing. I won't be *wanting* to rent cars anymore. I'll be completely *gone.*"

"You're really pushing me with this new hobo kick, John-O. Sleeping in rain culverts and stealing fresh clothes from laundry lines is going to wear thin awful quickly."

"Ivan, let me pitch it to you: This is the *road* we're talking about—the romance of the *road.* Strange new friends. Adventures every ten minutes. Waking up each morning feeling like a wild animal. No crappy rules or smothering obligations."

Ivan was appalled. "The road is *over,* John-O. It never even *was.* You're thinking like a kid behind a Starbucks counter sneaking peeks at his Kerouac paperback and writing '*That's so true!*' in the margins. And if nothing else, Doris is freaked out by this totally."

"You told my *mother?*"

"Of course."

John paused. "Another drink, Ivan?"

As he looked for ice cubes in the kitchen's two deep freezes, John considered Ivan and Nylla. He heard them talking back in the living room. They were now discussing carpeting: prices per square yard, *World Book Encyclopedia*–style. "I want the good type," said Ivan, "the kind that looks like pearl barley packed together. Really smooth."

"But if the wool's too smooth, it looks like Orlon. It needs character. A bit of sheep dung mixed into it maybe."

"We're going to have Beverly Hills's first Hanta virus carpet?"

"Sheep don't get Hanta virus. Just rodents, I think. And raccoons."

John listened in and ached to have somebody to discuss rugs and raccoons with. He felt intact but worthless, like a chocolate rabbit selling for 75 percent off the month after Easter. But it went beyond that, too. He felt contaminated, that his blood stream carried microscopic loneliness viruses, like miniscule fish hooks, just waiting to inflect somebody dumb enough to attempt intimacy with him.

His mind wandered. There had to be hope—and there was. He remembered the woman in his hospital vision had made him feel that somewhere on the alien Death Star of his heart lay a small, vulnerable entry point into which he could deploy a rocket, blow himself up and rebuild from the shards that remained.

In the second freezer John found the ice cubes clumped frozen together inside a sky blue plastic bag. He opened up the bag and tried to pry a few cubes away from the lump. Daydreaming, he wondered if he could ever be unselfconsciously chatty and loose with someone. If Ivan=Nylla, then John=blank. Maybe his mother Doris's years of prayers had begun to inch their way onto God's "To Do" list: *Dear Lord, please take care of the late Piers Wyatt Johnson, a king among men. Also bless the pesticide industry, our boys in Vietnam, (still, even at the century's end) and please find a nice young wife for John, preferably one who doesn't mind the smell of cigarette smoke, which is so hard to find in California. . . .*

He heard Krista and Cindy come downstairs and begin

chatting with Ivan, then returned his attention to the ice. He lifted up the bag of fused ice cubes and dropped it, shattering its contents into individual cubes. The noise was fearsome, and Ivan called from the living room asking if John was okay, and John called back, "Fine—couldn't be better," and it was easy to take as many cubes as he liked.

Chapter Seven

Standing alone on the sidewalk, John watched the police car drive Susan away. He was as still as a statue as the sun went down behind the hill. Had he left a car at the restaurant? No, Nylla had dropped him off there. So he decided to walk the rest of the way home. Home was temporary digs in Ivan's guesthouse, the house he grew up in and in which his mother still lived. John had been staying there since his return two months earlier from his disastrous experiment in hobodom.

He headed along Sunset Boulevard and was oblivious to the stares of passing drivers, many of whom punctuated their cell phone calls with such comments as:

- "Good Lord—it's John Johnson—walking—yes, that's right, with his *feet*—on Sunset!"
- "*Yow*, he looks like crap—what were the numbers on *Mega Force* in the end?—*yeee*—that much?"
- "Maybe he's doing his walking thing again—I mean, he looks like a Mexican gonna sell you a bag of oranges at a streetlight for a dollar."
- "Yes, I'm absolutely sure it's him—he looks really thin, or should I say, not sort of bloated like he was before detox number 239."

- "Wasn't he in the hospital?—pneumonia? AIDS?—no, if it was, we'd all know."
- "Maybe he's gone and found God again. Whatta case."

Ivan spotted John from his Audi and pulled over just past the corner at Gretna Green. "John-O, what the fuck are you doing? Hop in."

"Ivan, what do you know about Susan Colgate?"

"Susan Colgate? TV—rock and roll. Get in the car and I'll tell you. Jesus, you smell like the carpet in a Gold's Gym changing room."

"I walked here from the Ivy."

"The Ivy? That's, like, a jeezly number of miles away."

"Ivan, what do you know about Susan Colgate?"

Ivan cut the car back into traffic. "Later. Later. Did you see the weekend numbers from France and Germany? Whoosh!"

"Ivan—" John was firm: "Susan Colgate."

"Everybody in town is going to think you've gone crazy again. Walking. On Sunset, no less. Shit."

"I don't care, Ivan. *Susan*."

"What—you want to, uh, cast her in a *movie*?"

"Maybe."

"You're gonna make her a *star*?" They both laughed. Ivan pulled the Audi into his driveway, entered a code into his dash panel, releasing the gate. They drove through, depositing the car by the front steps instead of the garage. They got out. Ivan stopped and grabbed John's arm before he walked down the hill to the guesthouse. "God, whatta gorgeous day, John-O. Look at the light coming through that mimosa tree. It looks backlit, like it's on Demerol."

Both men sat down on the front entryway's limestone pavers and watched the late afternoon's solar aureoles around the plants and birds and insects of Ivan's garden.

"Where were you coming from just now?" John asked.

"Temple, temple, temple."

"Three times a week still?"

"*Sí.*" The sprinklers kicked in by a dahlia patch. Ivan said, "So you're in love, then, John-O? With Susan Colgate—ha!"

"I'm in . . . *need*. Desperate need."

"Where'd you meet?"

"The Ivy. Today."

"Lunch? Today?" He whistled. "*That's* a quick turnaround."

"A half-year ago in Cedars when I, you know—*she's* who I saw when I died."

Ivan's body locked upon hearing this. "Now, John-O—I thought you were over that stuff."

"Over *what*, Ivan? I have no regrets, but what I did only took me so far. But Susan—she's it. She's gotta be the one."

Ivan was both worried that John was relapsing back into his despondency of the months before, and slightly excited at the idea his friend might be making an emotional connection, something he'd never done before. "What do you know about her, John-O?"

"That's what I've been asking *you*."

"I think her agent's Adam Norwitz. She was with Larry Mortimer until a few years ago. An ugly split. She stalked him. And I don't think she's worked since the grunge era. Say, 1994. A slasher flick? No, wait, it's some new one—*Dynamite Bay*? I'm glad for you, but I've gotta say up front, John-O, she's real C-list. She can't act her way out of a paper bag."

"Ivan, you ought to know not to slag somebody's loved one to his face."

"*Loved* one?"

"Word games."

They heard steps behind them—Nylla, holding a silent baby. "Having our funzies out here on the front steps, are we, boys?"

"Hey, Nylla."

"John, hello. Will you be eating with us in the big house tonight?"

"Nah. Thanks. I'm having Metrecal and celery with Ma down at the house."

"Congratulations on the French numbers over the weekend. Ooh-lah-*lah*."

"We did okay over there?"

"John-O, I tried to tell you back when I picked you up at Gretna Green. Hey Nylla, guess what—John-O's in love! Lovesy-dovesy. Susan Colgate."

"Susan Colgate!" said Nylla. "Oh John, that's so weird. So exciting. I used to love her in that old show of hers, *Meet the Blooms.*"

John's face confirmed the truth.

"Well, I must say," smiled Nylla, "nature works in mysterious ways to get us to propagate the species."

"They met at Ivy today at lunch." Ivan couldn't contain himself.

She's the woman I saw in my out of body experience when I was laid up in Cedars."

The smile muscles on Nylla's face changed like a tide, ebbing from real into phony. "Well then. *Really* now," she trailed off. Ivan, sitting behind John, shot her a worried glance. "Be true to your heart. You two want to come in for a drink?"

"I'm in. You, John-O?"

"Nah. I'm going to go phone Adam Norwitz."

"Adam—" said Nylla. "Say hello for me. He represented me for about six minutes a few years ago."

"Hey. I was talking to his agency today," said Ivan. "His number's still in my cell's memory." He pulled out his cell phone and punched some digits. Two seconds later he said, "Adam

Norwitz, please. John Johnson calling." He handed the phone to John. "Here."

John gave Ivan the hairy eyebrow and took the phone. "Hello, Adam?"

Adam was on: "John Johnson. Good to meet you today. How can I help you? And congrats again on *Mega Force*."

"Yeah, yeah, thanks. Hey, Adam, I need a home number from you. Susan's."

Adam hemmed and hawed as though his morals were in serious conflict.

"Adam, don't give me that discretion routine. I need Susan's phone number."

"I'm not sure if I can . . ."

"It's personal, not business. Call and ask her if it's okay if you want. And I'll owe you a big favor."

"Of course I'll give you her number. But it's not"—he rustled some papers into the phone's receiver—"right here right now. Give me five minutes, okay?"

"Five minutes or no deal."

They hung up. Adam immediately called Susan's line and got her machine, where he left a message: "Susan! Swimming with the big fish now, are we? None other than your strolling companion John Johnson just phoned asking me for your number. He says it's personal. Hmmmmm. Well, just so you know, I'm going to phone back right now and give it to him. A protocol breach, but that's what I'm here for. And phone *me*, why don't you, and let me in on the buzz. I'm on cell all night. Bye."

Adam called back John and gave him Susan's number, which John wrote on the back of one of Ivan's business cards. He hung up. Ivan and Nylla stared at him.

"Yes?" said John.

"Call her," said Nylla.

"What, with you guys here?"

"Yes, with us guys here."

John dialed and got Susan's answering machine. He whispered the words "answering machine" to Ivan and Nylla. And then he left a message: "Susan, it's John—Johnson. I hope you got home okay. Man, was it ever hot today and—oh jeez, I'm stuttering into your machine." He paused to gather his thoughts. "Well, you know what I feel like today? It's like this: the last little while I've been feeling as if—as if I've come back from a long trip away—and I've been continuing on with my life again, but it's only today that I realized something went missing while I was gone. And I think it's you, and I want to see you again so badly I think I'm going blind. So call me." He left his number.

Nylla's eyes were beginning to tear. "Come inside and eat with us," Nylla asked. "Please," she added. The baby woke up and screamed. "I'll ask Doris, too."

And so John went inside to eat with Ivan and Nylla.

Half a year ago, just as John left the city and became a dharma bum, the couple had had a daughter, MacKenzie. She wailed like a crack baby and had a cluster of medical firestorms that had left Ivan and Nylla frazzled, but especially Nylla. Sleepless nights and worries had made her a soccer mom, and Ivan was converting into a soccer dad. Their kitchen was a shambles and all the more pleasant for it. "Watch where you sit," said Nylla. "I think Mac might have had a minor exorcism on that seat."

"Help us choose a name for the next one," said Ivan.

"No!" said John. "Congratulations."

Nylla rolled her eyes. "I feel like somebody's science project."

Ivan said, "I like the name Chloris—what do you think of Chloris—if it's a girl?"

Before John could reply, Nylla asked, "Can Borgnine be a first name if you want it to be one?"

"How about Tesh," suggested John. "It'd work for both."

"*Merveilleux!*" Nylla spoke French.

And so the two parents once again lapsed into banter and John pulled himself away ever so slightly. *This is what Ivan wanted*, thought John. This is a salve for him—his ability to lose himself in a family. And for Nylla, too. The year before, Ivan and Nylla had been like best friends, but now they were absolutely husband and wife. They were content with themselves and with the place their lives had landed. Their train had stopped and this is where they'd hopped off.

John wouldn't dare mention to them the depression he felt when Ivan had told him he was getting married. It was a few years ago, during the emotionally murky period after having two films flop, and their industry currency had been much devalued. To John, two flops meant a time to change and evolve and go forward—but Ivan had chickened out. He'd invented himself as much as he was ever going to. He was going to take the Full Meal Deal and fade away and make medium-budget teen movies that opened big the first weekend and then died of bad word-of-mouth. It was like a slap to John, who had wanted to go on and on, reinventing himself, and had continued to try doing so.

John suspected that his recent crack-up was precipitated by being, if not abandoned by Ivan, then certainly relegated to second place. He felt selfish even thinking about it, and tried to put it out of mind.

But John did want to reinvent himself, still. Even at thirty-seven, after his castastrophic fuckup.

John loved Ivan and Nylla, and he valued the world they'd built for themselves. Yet he knew that fairly soon, there in the kitchen, after Mac was given to the nanny and hauled upstairs, Nylla would gently grill John about Susan Colgate. She'd be careful not to dwell on the negative—his recent past—and then both she and Ivan would try to steer John closer to the road's center.

John wasn't without hesitations in his feelings for Susan. He'd followed his instincts in big ways before, but with his two flop movies and his Kerouac routine, it seemed his instincts now only failed him despite *Mega Force's* current stamina. Yet with Susan he felt only pure emotion. There was nothing strategic about the attraction. It was a rush of feelings that could only be satisfied by establishing further closeness. He wouldn't make money from his feelings. He wouldn't achieve cosmic bliss—he would only be . . . *closer to Susan.*

MacKenzie began to bellow like a Marine World exhibit, and Nylla and Ivan carted her up to her nursery. John picked up *TV Guide* and scanned its pages trying to locate reruns of *Meet the Blooms,* growing frustrated as he was unable to locate any.

Chapter Eight

John's mother, Doris Lodge, had fallen in love with John's father, Piers Wyatt Johnson, a solemn Arizona horse breeder without family or history whom she met at a stable in Virginia, and whom she bumped into again by accident in Manhattan outside the Pierre Hotel, where he'd emerged having just brokered his first five-figure sperm contract. She fell in love with him because she saw this coincidental meeting with him as fateful, but more specifically because of a fairy tale he liked to tell Doris after they'd made love in Doris's one-room apartment on the fifth and top floor of a Chelsea walk-up, an apartment of the sort that had been attracting young Mary Tyler Moores with tams on their heads since the dawn of the skyscraper era. The room, the rental of which had required much finagling on Doris's part, was her first place of her own ("Mummy, *anything* but the Barbizon—this is 1960, we have atom bombs, fergawdsake"). Doris loved the apartment in the way all fresh young metropolitans love the simplicity of orange-crate side tables, and improvised spaghetti dinners eaten by the light of votive candles ("Only a dollar ninety-nine for a box of forty-eight! My Lord, those Catholics have *invented* bargains")—this in an era when spaghetti in non-Italian households had the same subversive allure as stashed military blueprints and smuggled parakeets.

"You see, it's like this," Piers would say, beginning the tale, stretching his milky-white glute muscles on the lumpy mattress of Doris's brass four-poster, her only concession to her froufrou upbringing, "There was this lonely young heiress who was her father's prisoner on their estate out in the country. There was a large brick wall covered in ivy that circled the family's property."

"What was her name?" Doris would ask at that point. It was part of the ritual.

"Marie-Hélène."

"That's so pretty," Doris would say.

"And she was indeed pretty. She was a *catch*."

"It's hard to be a catch," Doris would sigh. Sunlight would stream in through the window, which overlooked a generic brick alleyscape of water tanks and a syringe-poke of the Empire State building above, a bevy of trash cans below, all of which seemed to cry out for wide-eyed sad painted kittens, perched and yowling. Piers's body hairs would catch the sunlight, like light filtered through icicles.

"Absolutely," Piers would add. "Absolutely." Piers's stomach was taut as a snare drum, and he encouraged Doris to tap it with her fingers while he talked. "So anyway, Marie-Hélène spent her days devising schemes to escape, but her family was onto her. They hired extra guards and mortared broken glass onto the top of the brick wall. But then one day she was walking through the many halls of the family's mansion, despairing, when she passed an old oil painting of a forest scene with a hunter, and something about it caught her eye."

"What did she see? Tell me again."

"When Marie-Hélène looked at the young hunter, a strapping lad, she saw him wink at her. And then he spoke to her. He said, 'Marie-Hélène, come in here—come here inside this painting with me—this is your escape route—through this painting.' Marie-Hélène was frightened. She asked the hunter, 'How can I come live in a painting? What will we eat?' This made the hunter laugh, and he said, 'We'll have everything we'll ever need in here. It's not like your world. In paintings, you can go visit other paintings. We'll go visit the feast paintings the Dutch did in the 1700s. We'll go have coffee inside an Edward Hopper diner. Please—come on in. I'm so lonely.'

"Marie-Hélène said she needed to think about it, but the next day she came back to the painting, dressed in hiking clothes, ready for the forest. The hunter asked her, 'Marie-Hélène, will you come into the painting and join me?' and she said, 'Yes, I will.' "

Piers wore Eau de Cédrat, a French citrus concoction that Doris said made him smell like Charles de Gaulle. His already sexy cigarette smoke would mix with his cologne like a spring fog alerting the bulbs beneath the soil to sprout. Piers would say, "The hunter then stuck out his arm and he pulled Marie-Hélène into the painting, into the forest, and slowly the two came together and Marie-Hélène planted a kiss on his lips. She pulled something out of her pockets, and the hunter asked her what it was, but she didn't reply. It was a book of matches and a bottle of her father's lighter fluid. She squirted the fluid out onto the floor of the mansion and lit a match and threw it onto the fluid. The house caught fire and Marie-Hélène said to the hunter, 'Come on, let's go now. Don't look back.' So off they walked, away from the flames, and away from the world where Marie-Hélène could never return."

"The catch fights back!" Doris would say.

Doris and Piers married against her family's wishes in a Manhattan civil ceremony. ("Dor-Dor, he has no family—*none*. Life just doesn't work that way. Johnson—what sort of name is that?") The two traveled the world and then moved to Panama, where Piers had stud farm connections, and Doris became pregnant. One afternoon in her eighth month, Doris was taking an ikebana flower–arranging class in the living room of the wife of a Nestlé executive in Miraflores Locks. Without warning, she fell to the floor in labor pains, screaming like a gorgon, taking with her a zinc bucket full of untrimmed ginger stems. John's birth was so powerful and fast and hot—the air-conditioning had been broken and the room so sweltering—that for decades afterward Doris was unable to tolerate heat or anything that smacked of the tropics, living her life from one air-conditioned space to the next. John was born on the mahogany floor surrounded by tropical flowers and perplexed executive wives. At the time of the birth, Piers was checking out horses in the Canary Islands. His twin-prop plane was lost in a squall, and he vanished.

Her family tsk-tsked and I-told-you-so'd. Her father assigned her to a small family-owned apartment on the Upper East Side, doled out a child-support allowance for young John, plus limited expense accounts at a few grocers and clothiers. Her days of waxy Chianti bottles, Japanese paper lanterns and peacoats were over before they'd even fully begun. She was to become a New York matron. She was to play the part of rich—she was bred to be rich—but she wasn't rich, and this powerless position defined her life. Yet she cherished her lovely memory of Piers in this red roast beef of a baby who wailed like the thrashed clutch of a Chevrolet.

Thirty-seven years later, when John met former child star Susan Colgate, he skipped many pages of the family's story. John was a member of Delaware's Lodge clan—pesticides originally, and then all forms of agrochemicals, plastics and pharmaceuticals, eventually forming a monster that spat out everything from mousetraps to orange juice to nuclear weapons components.

The firm was largely privately owned, and headed by Doris's uncle Raitt, who reigned from the family Tara in rural Delaware.

The family had decided, though not in these exact words, that Doris was a flaky financial drain who had willfully strayed outside the clan's unspoken bounds. She was grudgingly tolerated at annual family events, and she often arrived alone, because young John was a sick child. John was home more than he was at school, frequently in the hospital with infected ears or sinuses or other microbial lapses, which Doris handled with a genial calmness.

"Come along, John, I need to ferry you off to your quack for a checkup."

"Let me finish my breakfast first."

"What is that orangey glop you're drinking there?" She picked up the bottle of drink powder John had begged her to buy the previous week and read the label. " 'Tang'—brilliant. I'll try some with Bombay gin tonight."

"It's for astronauts."

"Really? Then I must have a sip immediately because this afternoon I'll be off to see Raitt at the St. Moritz, and it'll take an extraterrestrial amount of energy to go and pry him away from the charms of Sixth Avenue long enough to discuss raising my allowance just slightly." She sipped it. "Bravo! Now off we go."

John was an imaginative child, but his curiosity was often limited by illness to the confines of the apartment. When Doris was out, John would sneak into her room and go through her treasure box. It contained the shell of a baby turtle she'd eaten for breakfast with Piers in Kyoto in 1961 ("I felt it wriggling down by my voice box, the little dickens"); before-and-after cosmetic surgery photos of saddlebag removal ("Saddlebags are the Lodge family curse, Johnsy. Oh, to be a *boy*!"); the hand-written menu from her wedding dinner catered by an Andalusian chef recommended to her by Gala Dalí—unborn lamb in a mint coulis ("Lambryos, darling, and don't go knocking it until you've tried it, and don't go giving me that Mutual-of-Omaha's-Wild-Kingdom face"). There was one of John's baby shoes (gilded, not bronzed), some seashells and a stack of girlhood horse-jumping ribbons. There was also a photo of Doris water-skiing with Christina Ford, one of Piers on his prized Chesapeake mare, Honeymoon, as well as a faded black-and-white shot, reverently framed and somehow out of synch with the other photos. It was seemingly taken near a stable—Piers was talking with somebody in the background—and showed Doris standing with Marie-Hélène de Rothschild, with Marie-Hélène lighting Doris's cigarette, a wicked grin on Doris's face.

John didn't think it abnormal that his mother spent her days neither learning skills to make her employable nor making thrusts at wisdom. Rather, Doris preferred spending her time pursuing rich men, which she had been raised to do, with the uncritical instinct of terns who migrate from continent to continent each year. John found this fascinating.

"Mom, why do you always go everywhere in a plane?"

"What do you mean, darling?"

"Like today. You went up the Hudson Valley and you could easily have taken a car, but you flew."

Doris preferred flying—even to nearby locales like the Hudson Valley or the Hamptons. "Darling, if there's one thing a man will never admit to a woman, it's that he is unwilling to pay for a plane ticket or charter a craft for the day. A man would sooner eat ketchup soup for a month than to not hire a helicopter to hop to Connecticut with a lady. Easiest just to order the plane and then tell him to pay once you're at the other end." This was not a cynical statement from Doris. She had been taught this on her mother's knee.

Relatives were somewhat kinder to John than they were to

Doris, as families often prefer to skip generations when it comes to conferring affections, and John was a handsome, affable, if quiet, young boy. Spending so much time in bed, he soaked in abnormally large amounts of daytime TV programming—far more than the occasional episode of *Love of Life* or *The Young and the Restless* watched by the typical American teenager. John absorbed everything. TV loaned him a vocabulary and a tinge of sophistication lacking in others his own age. Relatives brought him presents and slipped him envelopes of money. John appeared grateful for these gifts in their presence, and, once they left, promptly gave the cash to Doris. She stashed it away in her mad-money Vuitton valise, up above her collection of Op and Pop outfits that began to infiltrate her sensibility across the decades.

Doris liked arty men. She liked men who lived inside paintings. And these men tended to like Doris at first, when they thought she could buy their way out of paintings, but it usually took about one season before they discerned she wasn't in the Maria Agnelli league and elegantly dumped her. Doris was aware of this cycle, but it failed to harden her in the same way that the serial tribulations of soap opera characters left them similarly undented.

With John, Doris was quite talkative about her family, its source of wealth and its role in the overall scheme of the world. John would squint and try to envision the Lodge Corporation, and he would briefly gather the impression of a massive diseased creature—a sperm whale in which all cells were infected and doomed.

"Darling, all aspects of the Lodge corporation are malignant. Lodge food products are unnutritious and rot quickly. Children raised on Lodge baby formula quickly sicken and die. Lodge electronics fizzle, pop and quickly expire like thrushes hitting the front picture window. Untold thousands of Lodge factory workers routinely become emphysemic by breathing the solvents used in the making of Lodge footwear which, I might add, invariably render their wearers unstylish, lame and beset by fungus infections. Lodge service divisions give sloppy parodies of service at hyperinflated prices needed to pay for Lodge's vast overhead of union bribes, drugs, lynx fur coats and Bahamian holidays for executive wives. Lodge is a goiter on society, draining and taking, pustulant and mute."

John would egg her on: "What kinds of things does Lodge make, Ma?"

"What doesn't Lodge make is the better question, darling. Lodge will make anything. Nothing is sacred: children's cigarettes, Holocaust boxcars, dairy products that are born time-expired, Vatican City parking spots—just call Lodge. Each time somebody in America cries or dies, Lodge nabs its shaved penny from somewhere in the proceedings. Well, darling, that's Lodge."

When he was fourteen, John developed breathing problems, and spent, with minor exceptions, a year in bed while his lungs and bronchial tubes healed. He watched TV, read, chatted with Doris—he had no friends and his numerous cousins were conspicuously kept away from him. Tutors came in and kept him primed with the basics. He wasn't dumb and he wasn't a genius. He liked his world, and he didn't mind its limitations.

John did wonder, though, how he could make up for the lost time in his life. Assuming he recovered, how might he catch up with all the other children who had been out in the everyday world—chasing balls? throwing sticks? shoplifting? John's notions of normal childhood behavior were sketchy. And he worried about Doris, who came close, but didn't "snag herself a may-un." Would she ever be happy? What could he do to bring love into her life? TV had taught him that love was pretty much a cure for all ills.

Doris put a good face on it all. John was the constant in her life, the one thing family could neither take away nor reduce. From her perspective, the more time John spent watching TV in the apartment away from hooligans, third rails and strange men in raincoats, the better.

The year he spent in bed was certainly the longest of his life. When he was older and met other people who had accomplished great things during their stints on earth, he found that invariably, somewhere in their early youth, they had felt the experience of death or incapacity burned into them so deeply that ever afterward they gambled with all their chips, said fuck it, went for broke in the sound knowledge that wasting life is probably the biggest sin of all. John's illness made him value extremeness.

As John was on the mend from his sick year, Uncle Raitt tried to corner the U.S. silver market and bankrupted the family in a scandal that spanned forty-six states, most of Europe and parts of Asia and even, in some complex unprecedented way, Antarctica. Overnight, Doris and John were homeless. A week later Raitt hanged himself from a chandelier in Delaware. Doris felt mainly relief; she no longer had to play the family game.

Hours before the phone was disconnected, Doris made some calls. With her money stash she bought two Amtrak tickets to Los Angeles. A car picked them up at the station and drove them to Beverly Hills, where they were put up in the guesthouse of Angus McClintock, Ivan's father, a film producer who had come close to marrying Doris but didn't quite make the leap. Although there was no ring, they'd remained friendly and intimate through the years, and thus mother and son found refuge, far away from anything smacking of Delaware and lost angry families falling from the sky like a flock of burning birds.

Angus showed them around his guesthouse, a four-bedroom

Spanish Mission lair, and as he handed Doris the keys, something strange happened. It was the end of the day and the sun was low on the hill. John's skin color turned a Kruggerrand gold not available in Manhattan, and the sight of him as a gilded young prince took Doris by surprise. Without thinking she said, "You know, John, I don't think you're going to be sick anymore. It's over now."

"You think so?"

"That's right—all over. You're in the land of gold."

"But it could come back at any moment."

"No. It's all gone now." Doris looked at John and then to Angus, then prayed to the effect of, Lord, stick by me on this one.

They entered their new home.

Chapter Nine

As Susan walked away from her temporary hideout in the Galvins' house—clad in Karen Galvin's wig and sports gear—she was without credit cards, cash, a driver's license or any other link to the national economy. She touched her clean dry face, the face her mother had berated for its blank slate quality: ("Susan, without makeup your face looks like a sheet of typewriter paper. Next week we're getting that eyeliner tattooed, sweetie, and that's *that*"). Susan had once told her friends that being famous was like being Krazy Glued into a Bob Mackie gown, with an Emmy permanently grafted onto her right hand. But without makeup, she looked unconnected to that image. This fuzziness of identity might prove a small blessing in her new life, as it would allow her to roam freely.

Susan's first step was to revisit the crash site, where cranes were lugging the final shards of fuselage onto flatbed trucks. A chess board of police and National Guardsmen shooed away gawkers. Without bodies and popped luggage strewn about, the jet fragments resembled plaza sculptures at the feet of Manhattan bank towers.

Susan ate a chocolate energy bar and felt the warm Indian summer sun on her cheekbones. To her right she saw a burst of colors. She walked closer and found a series of impromptu shrines built of flowers, ribbons, flags, photos and teddy bears, placed by relatives and sympathizers.

All those poor souls, thought Susan, *gone, and yet here I am, as raring to go as if I were backstage in a spaghetti-strapped evening gown waiting to play* Für Elise *for a clump of Ford dealers.* Inside a Ziploc baggie she saw a Sears photo portrait of Mr. and Mrs. Engineer, the Millers, as it turned out. Beside this lay a photo of Kelly the flight attendant who'd told Susan that 802 was her last flight before a holiday in Cancún. Someone had placed a stuffed rabbit wearing sunglasses and a bottle of Tia Maria beside it.

Susan jolted with surprise when she saw a shrine to herself— a color photocopy enlargement of an old magazine photo mounted onto brown cardboard. In the photo she was fifteen, with heavily gelled New Wavey hair, singing Devo's "Whip It" at the Clackamas Mall, Clackamas County, Oregon. In the upper-left corner was her friend Trish, playing a Casio keyboard. Susan looked at her own eyes in the picture, heavily mascaraed, and with an intensity and a naïveté that made her smile. She remembered secretly applying it in the Orange Julius bathroom. She also remembered afterward, the battle royal with her mother, who thought Susan was to be performing a medley of songs from *Grease.* Susan smiled that this funny old picture, of all the Susan Colgate images in the world, would be singled out and stuck in the middle of a damaged Ohio sorghum field as her final tribute.

There was a letter duct-taped to the bottom of the photo. At a glance, it looked to be like the ones she received in sackloads during the peak years of *Meet the Blooms,* letters that had often been postmarked U.S. Federal Penitentiary, Lompoc, or some fellow correctional facility. The letters frequently began with poems that were always sincere but almost invariably dreadful. This letter read:

Susan, my name is Randy James Montarelli and I was born on the same day as you, September 4, 1970. You were kind of a yardstick in my life. There were a lot of people like me, I think, out in the boonies who followed your life's path as if you were a sister, or maybe because you managed to escape a junky life and go on to something better. Regardless, we were always out there cheering for you. Anyway, now you're in heaven and we're still down here and I think I'm too old to find another Susan Colgate, and so life is going to be just that much harder now. I live alone (I'm not the marrying type!) but I have two dogs, Willy and Camper, and an okay job. I guess I never thought you'd go first. Somehow that felt like part of the deal. This is so stupid and all, putting these words on a sheet of paper in Magic Marker letters, when nobody's ever going to read it, anyway. I don't live in Seneca. I live in Erie, that's in Pennsylvania. I drove down here last night (4 ½ hours!) because if I didn't, I couldn't live with myself. I'm sorry your marriage to Chris didn't work out but you were too classy for him, anyway, and I know those party hound types, and they're all flaky in the end. No offense. I always knew you'd get into movies someday, too, and it was fun seeing you in Dynamite Bay just this past month. Well, I could go on here, but my throat feels all tight the way it did driving down here. My friend Casey (she works in the cubicle next to me at the plant) says I make it too easy for people to take advantage of me, but I don't agree. I know sometimes it looks as if I'm getting used, but I really do know what's going on. I'm running out of space here. Say hello to heaven for me, and Jon-Erik Hexum, too. Did you ever meet him? He was on an old nighttime TV soap and . . . well . . . that's <u>another</u> story. Cheers to you, honey.

Your loving and loyal fan always,

Randy
1402 Chattanauqua Street
Erie, Pennsylvania

PS: I found the Wyoming license plate for you at a yard sale the day your plane crashed. I think it was a sign of some sort.

Beneath Susan's photo was the Wyoming plate, a Charlie Brown Pez dispenser with a dozen candy refills, a bottle each of shampoo and conditioner from a Marriott hotel, and a copy of *TV Guide* with the cast of *Meet the Blooms* on the cover. Susan knelt, looked both ways to ensure nobody was watching, took the letter, folded it up, slipped it into her pants pocket, and then put the shampoo and conditioner in her nylon sports bag. She walked away from the crash site, attracting not the slightest hint of suspicion from bystanders, and headed down the four-lane road in the opposite direction from the Galvins'. A bus stopped to discharge passengers and Susan got on, paying for her ticket with four quarters from the sports bag's bottom. She took a transfer and, at the bus route's end, hopped onto another bus which drove her into Toledo. She hopped off at a minimall adjoining the Maumee River, and as her feet touched the ground, she did some arithmetic and figured that if Flight 802 hadn't crashed, at that moment as she stood there in the minimall, she would have been driving to her herbalist after finishing her aerobics class in Santa Monica, then maybe heading home to see what the mail had brought, while checking her answering machine.

Her answering machine. It was probably still connected.

Over by the Blockbuster she saw a phone booth, and once there, she saw that the video store was having a 99-cent Susan Colgate tribute. She dialed her answering system's code numbers, figuring that the odds of anybody analyzing her phone account were minute. A series of bleeps revealed that she had five calls:

• "Susan, this is Dreama. I did your numbers for you and boy, is Thursday going to be a heckuva lucky day for you. As your numerologist, I advise, no, I implore you to rush out and buy as many lottery tickets as possible—and once you win, treat me to a new set of brakes for this heap of mine that keeps breaking down. Dinner at Chin's next Tuesday. Gimme a call."

· "Meese Colllllllgate . . . it's Ryan from West Side Video and you're six days overdue with *The Breakfast Club* and the Hitchcock three-pack. You know how cruel we can be to those who displease us. Oh, and I saw you in *Dynamite Bay* and you were really hot. Shoot. Now I've gone outside the boundaries by saying that to a customer, but still, you *were* really hot. I'm Ryan. Say hi next time you come in."

· A satellite beep followed by the sounds of hanging up.

· Another satellite beep followed by sounds of hanging up.

· Another satellite beep followed by, "Sooz . . ." It was Chris and another beep and his voice sounded highly drunk and highly high. "I . . ." In the background was muffled German and the sounds of a bar or restaurant. "You . . ." Something dropped with a clink on the German end. "I guess it's time for walkies, honey." A man's voice asked Chris who he was speaking with, and he replied, "Max, in Santa Barbara." Chris breathed for a bit and then hung up.

Susan looked out onto the river, caramel and yellow under the dissolving yellow sundown. In the near distance she heard trucks and air brakes. Music blared from cars at the lot's other end—smoking, groping teens. She took her sports bag, hopped over a small pine shrub and walked down over cracked boulders and rusty industrial fossils to the river's edge. She tested the water with her fingers—cold, the temperature of a cheapskate's swimming pool. She then stripped off all her clothes and Karen Galvin's wig—wigs usually made her scalp itchy and sweaty in any role she played—and she gently walked into the Maumee River, her toes touching mud and rock, her inner legs electrified by the chill, her armpits flinching with shock, and then finally an otter's plunge into the brown broth, emerging far out in the middle, her head periscoping the view of Toledo. A short while later she washed her hair with Randy Montarelli's shampoo, then shook it dry. She dressed and rewigged herself.

Susan walked up the bank and over to a commercial strip of fast food, car dealerships and complex traffic lights. It was now almost dark, and she was hungry, and tired of the chocolate energy bars. She strolled the sidewalk-free neighborhood as if seeing her country for the first time—the signs and cars and lights and shop fronts bigger and brighter and more powerful than they needed to be. She caught whiffs of fried chicken and diesel fumes, but having spent her only quarters, she couldn't buy food. She was starving. She walked for hours. She passed eighty Wendy's, a hundred Taco Bells, seven hundred Exxons, and then she came up on her nine hundredth McDonald's, where she decided to use the bathroom.

On the way into the restaurant she noticed a crew chief walking out a side utility door and over to a dumpster where he tossed away a large tray of fully wrapped, unsold, time-expired burgers. Susan saw her chance. She walked to the dumpster and with an agile climb reminiscent of the aerobics class she might well that moment be attending in a parallel universe, she hopped inside and crammed the sports bag with warm, wrapped cheeseburgers. *Loot.* She heard voices approaching. She quickly dropped the bag and contracted herself into a ball beneath the closed right-side door of the dumpster and listened to teenage banter:

". . . gonna go over to Heather's after I lock up."

"She still sore at you?"

"No way, man." The second speaker threw two green waste bags into the bin, which rolled down onto Susan's feet. "I bought her a tattoo, and now she's real nice to me, like . . ."

Whamp!

The left lid crashed down. Susan heard a muffled conversation about women, plus the unmistakable sound of a key locking the door above her.

Chapter Ten

"Think of how gorgeous we're going to be when you wake up."

"Mom, it's *me* doing this, not *you*."

"Susan Colgate, I shucked a helluva lot of bunnies to correct that jaw of yours, and now is not the time to be ungrateful about it. Now hold on to my finger and count back from one hundred."

Susan held on to Marilyn's finger and retro-counted: "A hundred, ninety-nine, ninety-eight, ninety-seven . . ." and closed her eyes. When she opened them, it was to find herself inside a cool, dimly lit gray room. Marilyn was in the corner smoking exactly half a Salem, extinguishing the remains and then lighting another ("Butts are coarse, dear"), all the while avoiding the more intimate questions contained in a magazine quiz about the reader's interior life. She looked up and caught Susan's now open eyes: "Oh sweetie! We look *fabulous*," and then she rushed over to proudly beam at Susan's face, stained from within by lost and dying blood cells—blue, olive and yellow—her broken and reset jaw stitched and swaddled.

Susan touched her face, which felt disconnected to her, like a rubber Halloween mask. She found her nose was set in a splint. "My 'ose! Wha' 'appened?"

"Happy birthday! I had the doctor throw in a new nose at the same time. We're gonna look sensational."

"You let 'em mangle my 'ose?" Her voice felt muffled, as though she were speaking from within a pile of carpets.

"Mangle? Hardly. You now have the nose of JenniLu Wheeler, Mrs. Arkansas America."

"Id's . . . my 'ose." She felt nauseous. Her jaws ached.

"Don't get so exercised, sweetie."

Susan tried to move her body, which seemed to weigh as much as a house. She'd never felt gravity's pull so strongly. Marilyn said, "We have to stay here in the recuperation room for six more hours. How do you feel?"

"Woozy. 'Eavy."

"It's the painkillers. I had them give you a double prescription with two refills. You know how Don the Swan's back can act up." Don, Susan's stepfather had, over the years, evolved into a whisky-sunburnt, perpetually incapacitated repairman.

"Don seems to be able to lift his SeaDoo and his bowling balls from the bed of his pickup 'enever he needs to."

"Susan! We're selling the SeaDoo to move to Wyoming, or are you conveniently choosing to forget this?"

"I don't *want* to go to Wyoming, Mom. It was *your* idea. I'm fifteen. Like I 'ave legal say in the matter."

Marilyn smiled. "Oh! The treachery!"

"Mom, I'm too 'ired to fight. Go get me a mirror." Marilyn paused upon hearing this. Susan said, "I look 'at bad, huh?"

"It's not a matter of good or bad, dear. I speak from experience. You're covered in bandages. You'll look like hell no matter what."

"Mom, just show me the stupid mirror."

Marilyn brought a yellow-handled mirror from the coffee table. Outside in the hallway bandaged figures were being trolleyed by on gurneys. Marilyn held the mirror up for Susan to see her face.

"Ee-yuuu. I 'ook like a used Pampers balled up and stuffed in a trash can."

"Such an imagination, young woman," said Marilyn, whisking away the mirror. "In three weeks it is going to be scientifically impossible for you to take a bad picture. Do you have any idea what that means? I've already lined up a photographer to come up from Mount Hood. An ex-hippie. Ex-hippies make the best photographers. I don't know why. But they do." She lit up a Salem. "Speaking of JenniLu Wheeler, I heard that the night before the Miss Dixie contest, her eyes puffed up from too many cocktails with a handful of senators, and they put leeches under her eyes to suck out the puffiness. I never told you that one, did I?"

"No. You 'idn't."

"She bled like a pig for two days, and she missed the title because of it. Or so the story goes."

"Lovely, Mom." Susan relaxed and sunk into the mattress. A nurse stepped into the room and asked Marilyn to extinguish her cigarette.

"Excuse me, young lady, but are we in Moscow right now?"

"It's rules, Mrs. Colgate."

"Where's your manager?" Marilyn asked.

"This is a hospital, not a McDonald's, Mrs. Colgate. We don't have managers."

"Mom, this is a 'ospital, not the Black Angus. Stub it out."

"No, Susan—no, I won't stub it out. Not until I get an apology from this insultress."

"It's rules, Mrs. Colgate." But the nurse lost her will to push the issue, and walked away.

Marilyn took a deep victorious inhale. "I always win, don't I, Susan?"

"Yes, Mom. You always do. You're the queen of drama."

"And that's a compliment?"

Susan decided the smartest course of action was to shut her eyes and feign sleep. It worked. Marilyn returned to her magazine's personality quiz and smoked her victory cigarette. Susan mentally flipped through a catalog of Marilyn's seamless dramas, such as the time in the changing room she spritzed a tightly aimed spray bottle of canola oil at the swimsuit of Miss Orlando Pre-Teene after a close call in the talent contest. Susan played her Beethoven Für Elise, but Miss Orlando had played a Bach Goldberg variation, which could sway even the most musically naïve listener in her favor. As a result of the canola oil (to which Marilyn was never linked), Miss Orlando was forced to borrow Miss Chattanooga's one-piece and lost the pageant.

Susan won a mink coat and a Waikiki weekend, both of which were exchanged for cash, and used to cover travel expenses and the household bills. The money was nice, but it was by no means the sole reason for pageantry. "Susan, there is no price tag that can be placed on accomplishment and superiority. Even if you were the richest girl on earth, do you think you could simply buy yourself a crown? Winners have an inner glow that cannot even be dreamt of in the soul of a nonwinner."

Marilyn called the pageant business "shucking bunnies," even though the hutches in which she once bred rabbits to raise money for gowns were long a thing of the past—since Susan integrated Barbie into her essence and began winning solidly around age seven in the Young American Lady, West Coast Division.

"Hey, sweetie, looks like rabbit pelting season sure did start today. The bunnies are hopping for their lives tonight!"

When things were good, when both Marilyn and Susan were on the road, stoked to win, their systems charged with the smell of hair products, Susan could imagine no other mother more wonderful or more giving than Marilyn, and no childhood more exotic or desirable. School was a joke. Marilyn regularly phoned in and lied that Susan was sick. In lieu of school, she made Susan read three books a week as well as take lessons in elocution, modern dance, piano, deportment and French. "School is for losers," Marilyn told Susan after spinning another yarn about kidney infections to yet another concerned vice-principal. "Trust me on this one, sweetie—you'll never lose if you learn the tricks I'm teaching you."

And Susan didn't lose. She reassured herself with this thought as her false sleep faded into real dreams.

Chapter Eleven

Half a year after Susan's cosmetic surgery, Marilyn learned in a pageant newsletter that a judge previously unfavorable toward Susan would be on the panel at the upcoming Miss American Achiever pageant over the Memorial Day weekend at the St. Louis Civic Auditorium. Marilyn knew that this judge, Eugene Lindsay, had blackballed Susan after her performance of Für Elise in the talent segment of Country USA pageant at the Lee Greenwood Dinner Theater in Sevierville, Tennessee, the previous fall. After that night's events, from the other side of a freezingly air-conditioned banquette table at the Best Western lounge, Marilyn, drinking a double vodka tonic alone, had heard Lindsay's unmistakable TV-smoothened voice say: "I am so goddammed sick of these wind-up-toy midgets and their goddammed robotic renditions of Beethoven Lite. I hear them play that fucking tune so much that it feels like I'm in a purgatory engineered by whatever asswipe it is who chooses the on-hold music for the Delta Airlines ticket line." Marilyn was taken aback neither by his language, nor the sentiment. But she was deeply surprised to hear such a blatantly truthful expression of the dark thoughts that lurked in the hearts of panel judges. She had wondered herself if Susan's Für Elise was maybe getting a bit thin, and by then had already initiated proceedings to have Susan perform a *Grease* medley.

Eugene Lindsay was to Marilyn an almost unbearably handsome opponent, against whom none of the other pageant moms could be rallied ("Why, sugar," said one pageant mom, torn between propriety and carnality, "I'd let that man hug me *ragged*"). Although Eugene was a weatherman in everyday life, Marilyn knew that when he died, he'd likely land himself the biggest Ford dealership in heaven. Eugene went through life like a Great Dane or a speeding ambulance, exacting the unfettered awe of whomever he passed. He did the nightly weather on an Indiana NBC affiliate, and was hooked into the pageant circuit through his wife, Renata, a mail-order-gown specialist for the generously proportioned, who also sidelined in hairpieces.

The day before the Miss American Achiever pageant, Marilyn insisted she and Susan spend the day visiting Bloomington, Indiana, Eugene Lindsay's home town. "It's research, sweetie. I want to check out Renata's store. It'll be fun."

Soon Susan would decide her mother was out of control, but on this trip she passively flowed along with Marilyn to Bloomington, the two of them surrounded by an asteroid belt of luggage as they strode through Bloomington's Monroe County Airport, Marilyn ensuring that the little clear vinyl windows on the gown bags faced outward: "So that passersby can know they are in the presence of star magic."

There were no cabs at the airport. A buzzing triad of fellow passengers from commuter flights stood on the taxi island pointlessly craning their necks as if, Manhattan-like, a fleet might momentarily appear. Shortly a single cab approached, and Marilyn pounced on its door handle, inflaming the triad. "Hey, lady—there's a line here."

Marilyn swiveled, removed her black sunglasses the size of bread plates, looked at her accuser point-blank and charged ahead.

They checked in to their hotel, then visited Renata's nearby store, which was interesting enough. Susan thought that for somebody dealing in large-size pageant wear, Renata herself had about as much body fat as a can of Tab and three cashew nuts. Marilyn spoke with Renata, and Susan browsed through the far side of the store, which was filled to her pleasant surprise with regular craft-shop art supplies.

Later that evening, up in the hotel room, Marilyn suggested they go for a drive.

"We don't have a car, Mom."

"I rented one while you were in the workout room."

"Where are we going, Mom?"

"You'll see."

"Is this something nasty again, Mom?"

"Susan!"

"Then it is, because you haven't said 'sweetie' once yet, and whenever you fib, you drop the nice stuff."

"Oh sweetie."

"Too late."

Marilyn pursed her lips and looked at her daughter, swaddled in track pants and a gray kangaroo sweater. "Well then. Come along." Marilyn brought two pairs of gardening gloves, a box of trash bags and two flashlights. They drove out into winding residential streets of a repetitive stockbroker Tudor design, the type that, when she was younger, Susan associated with the walrus-mustached plutocrat from the Monopoly board. Now she more realistically associated this sort of neighborhood with car dealers, cute amoral boys, sweater sets, regularly scheduled meals containing the four food groups, Christmas tree lights that didn't blink, the occasional hand on the knee, cheerful pets, driveways without oil stains, women named Barbara and, apparently, weathermen for regional NBC affiliates.

"That Lindsay guy lives here?" Susan asked, looking out at a colonial with a three-car garage, as colorfully lit as an aquarium castle, surrounded by dense evergreens that absorbed noise like sonic tampons.

"*Shhh!*" Marilyn had killed the car's lights the block before. "Just help me out here, sweetie." They sidled over to the cans and Marilyn removed the lid from one. "Beautifully bagged. Like a Christmas gift. Susan—quietly now—help me lift the bag out." The bag made a fruity, resonant fart sound against the can's inner edge as Susan hauled it out, and she laughed.

Five beautifully wrapped bags of trash made their way into the car's trunk and back seat. Marilyn squealed away from the house, with her lights out for the first, almost painful, nervous puffs of breath. "Where now?" Susan asked.

"A Wal-Mart parking lot."

"A Wal-Mart lot? Isn't that kind of public?"

Marilyn turned on the lights. That's precisely why we're going there. We'll look like two lady lunchbucket losers sifting through their own crap, most likely in pursuit of an eleven-cents-off coupon for house-brand bowling balls."

And Marilyn was correct. She parked within ten stalls of the store's main entrance, and not a soul gave a second glance to the mother-daughter team purposefully ripping through deep green plastic umbilical cords and placentas like industrial midwives.

"What are we supposed to be looking for?" Susan asked.

"I'll know when I see it. One bag at a time. Spread the contents evenly on the trunk floor. Good. Now hold open your bag and I'll put things into it, piece by piece." Marilyn hawkeyed the items, which afforded a glass-bottom boat tour of the home and lives of la famille Lindsay. "Bathroom," she said, "bloody Kleenexes, three; Q-tips, two; bunion pads, four, five, six; prescription bottle, contents: Lindsay, Eugene, Stellazine, a hundred milligrams twice daily, no refill."

"What's Stellazine?"

"An antipsychotic. Powerful. Diggety-dawg, this is a *keeper*."
Marilyn's elder sister, a fellow escapee from their yokel origins,
was a schizophrenic who, before jumping off the I-5 bridge in
downtown Portland, had been a pharmaceutical bellwether for
Marilyn. "Let's go on. Disposable razor, one."

Marilyn then found three 8-x-10s of Eugene's face, sand-
wiched together with a layer of Noxzema. "Dammit, why does
he have to be so goddam handsome?"

Susan grabbed one of the photos and her eyes sucked him in.
She felt the way she had when she won a side of beef in her
high school's Christmas raffle. "He is good-looking, isn't he?"

"They always are, honey, they always are."

Susan snuck the photo into her pocket, then shivered.

"You're cold, sweetie."

"No. Yes. Sort of."

"You sound like Miss Montana did in last month's pageant."
Marilyn laughed, and even Susan had to smile. "Only give de-
clarative answers, sweetie."

The next bag must have been from Renata's bathroom, a perfect bin of high-quality cosmetics, items which earned grudging admiration from Marilyn.

Next came several bags of kitchen waste: junk mail, coffee
grounds, mostly unopened upscale deli containers and several
cans of unpopular vegetables—beets and lima beans.

One bag remained: "Come on, Eugene! Give me what I
need." It was evidently office waste: dried-out pens, a typewriter's
correction ribbon, opened bill envelopes from Ameritech,
Chevron, PSI Energy, Indiana Gas and—"What's this?" Marilyn
reached for an askew clump of similar-looking photocopies. She
chose one at random, and began reading it aloud: " 'Ignore this
letter at your peril. One women in Columbus chose to ignore
this and was found dead of carbon monoxide poisoning a week

later . . .' A chain letter." Marilyn skimmed the copy. "Well and good, but why so many of them, Eugene? What the—?" At this point her eyes saucered and her brain flipped inside her head like a circus Chihuahua. "Susan! Look! This weasel's been sending out hundreds of chain letters to dupes around the country—Canada and Mexico, too, and look—he always puts himself at the top of the chain on all the lists."

Susan was young and unfamiliar with chain letters. "Yeah?"

"So even if a fraction of these suckers mail fifty bucks, he still scores big-time."

"Let me see." Susan read the threatening letter more carefully.

Marilyn, meanwhile, yanked out a folder cover: "KLRT-AM Radio, San Jose, California, All Talk, All the Time." Inside the folder were printout lists of names and addresses, each crossed off. There were also folders from other cities—Toronto, Ontario; Bowling Green, Kentucky; and Schenectady, New York. "I get it—these are names and addresses of station listeners who filled out marketing cards."

"Why them?" Susan asked.

"Think about it: if you've nailed down a file of people who enthusiastically identify with whacko call-in radio shows, it's not too much extra work to squeak a fifty out of them. Kid's play. Here, help me put these papers in neat piles. Eugene, I love you for helping dig your own grave."

They stacked and collated their booty. Back in the car Marilyn drove to a dumpster behind a Taco Bell and said, "Chuck the leftover trash in there." Susan took Eugene Lindsay's rebagged garbage and daintily lobbed it over the bin's rusty green rim.

At the hotel, Susan got fed up with Marilyn and her cache of papers. The TV was broken. She lay on the bed and tried to find animal shapes inside the ceiling's cottage cheese stippling. "Mom, are we with a host family or at a hotel tomorrow night?"

"A hotel, sweetie."

"Oh."

"You'd rather we stay with a host family?"

"Yes and no." Yes because she got to peek into other people's lives and houses, invariably more normal than her own, and no because she'd also have to smell the host family, eat their food and have yet another host dad or host brother try to cop a feel or mistakenly enter the bathroom while she was having her shower, and she'd have to put a sunshine smile on everything to boot. Her mind wandered to a group of women who'd picketed the California Young Miss pageant earlier on that year in San Francisco. They'd called the pageant entrants cattle. They accused the mothers of being butchers leading sheep to slaughter. They'd worn meat bikinis. Susan smiled. She tried to imagine beef's feel on her skin, moist and pink, like the skin beneath a scab. "Mom—what did you think of those meat women in San Francisco? The ones with the flank steak bikinis."

Marilyn drooped the papers she was holding. "Angry, empty women, Susan." Marilyn's temples popped veins. "Did you hear me? Lost. Absolutely *lost*. No men in their lives. Hungry. Mean. I feel sorry for them. I pity them."

"They looked like they were having fun, kinda."

Marilyn turned on her with a ferocity that let Susan actually see that human beings have skulls beneath their faces. Marilyn mistook Susan's horror for fear of what she was saying: "No! Don't ever think that—*ever*. Do you hear me?"

"Geez, Mom, I was only joking."

"You'll never give that type of woman any of your time of day."

Marilyn returned to her job of cross-indexing Eugene Lindsay's mail fraud scheme, but her body was obviously now awash in stress chemicals. Susan felt like the young wolf who's just discovered the tender, delicious underbelly of the porcupine.

The next afternoon they checked in to the hotel in St. Louis, whereupon Susan stayed up in the room to read comics while Marilyn confabbed with some other pageant moms, learning that Eugene was staying alone in the same hotel because Renata was stuck in Bloomington coping with demand for the following month's Big 'n' Proud convention in Tampa, Florida. With almost no effort, Marilyn determined Eugene's room number, and shortly after she knocked on his door. He answered, clothed only in argyle socks, striped boxers and an unbuttoned oxford cloth shirt. He was holding a scotch and Marilyn could see he had little hairs bleached gold by the sun on the tops of his fingers. Marilyn knew that Eugene was used to opening doors and letting in exactly whomever he wanted *when* he wanted. He saw Marilyn and said, "What is this—some kind of joke?"

"No joke, Eugene." She barged into his room. She took it by storm.

"What the fuck? Lady—get the fuck out of my room. Now."

"No, Eugene."

"Did the guys at the station set this up? Is this a gag?"

"It's no gag, Eugene, and I don't know any guys from any station." She coquetted her head and sat with her legs crossed on the bed.

Eugene gulped his scotch. "I'm not into mutton, lady. Out."

"Oh, Eugene—you've mistaken my intentions."

"You're a show mom, aren't you? I can always tell you show moms. You're all nuts. You're all freaks." He poured himself a new drink.

"Is drinking a smart thing to be doing?"

"I beg your—fuck it—I'm calling the hotel cops." He moved to the bedside phone.

"I'm not the one on Stellazine, Eugene. I'm not the one who's insane here."

His finger froze on the phone above the zero button. "You know, lady, I ought to—"

"Oh, shut up, you talking hairdo. My name's not Lady, it's Marilyn, which doesn't mean much. What *does* mean something is that my daughter wins tomorrow's title. She's going to play *Für Elise* and it doesn't matter if Miss Iowa cures cancer on stage, or if Miss Idaho gets stigmata, my daughter wins. Period. And *you* will make sure this happens."

"This *is* a joke." Eugene's face relaxed. "The guys at the station *did* set this up."

"No joke."

"You're *good*."

"There's nothing for me to be good *at*, Eugene. This is for real."

Eugene's face clenched and his voice assumed the cool metered speech of TV reason. "This is so totally Gothic, isn't it? You'd kill for your little proxy to win. I bet you and your little Miss . . ."

"Wyoming." The family still had yet to move to that state, but Marilyn had already begun creating technical citizenship by renting a small storage locker on the outskirts of Cheyenne under Susan's name. At the present moment she wanted to unbalance Eugene's thinking. "You're wearing a beef bikini, Eugene."

"Wha—?" He reflexively reached for his privates, which had perhaps escaped containment.

"Read these." From her handbag she removed a bundle of photocopies and slapped them onto the bedspread, and from where he stood, Eugene could tell what they were. "How do we spell 'mail fraud,' Eugene? We spell it F-B-I." Marilyn walked to the door and yanked it open. "You're a big fish in an itty-bitty pond, Hairdo. But it's my pond. Give me what I want and it doesn't go beyond these walls." She stepped outside and looked in. "I could otherwise care less about you. Turning you in would be like spraying sewage onto a burning house. It'd get a job done, but—well, you think it over. Good-bye, Eugene." She shut the door.

Onstage that night, the pageant flowed like soda. Susan made semifinalist, then finalist, played her Für Elise and then stood with the other finalists on the stage directly before the judge's stand. She felt lovely. She had learned to work with the new all-angle beauty her jaw correction and nose job had loaned her. And then, looking through the lights, one face opened up through the optical fog—a face that broke through and became disembodied from all others in the auditorium. It was Eugene—the trash man!—and he was looking at Susan with the same wise, knowing face as his 8-x-10 head shot. Her eyes linked with his, and for the first time in her life she felt sexual. She didn't just put on the pose, she felt naked, proudly naked, and she pulled her shoulders back as if to give more of herself to Eugene. She was being judged, and she knew she was coming out ahead.

Eugene, meanwhile, looked at Susan. He wondered how he could have overlooked this scrumptious little gazelle at a previous competition. Für Elise? Hell, she could play "Chopsticks" with a spatula and he'd vote for her. He pointed at Susan and then back at himself, smiled broadly with film-star teeth, then winked with the force of a blazing iron scorching linen.

Susan heard music and she heard her name. And then a tiara landed on her head and she felt the reassuring cool fluttering sensation of the winner's sash draped from her right shoulder.

Afterward, when the crowds had dispersed, Susan tried to locate Eugene amid the vanishing crowds under the ruse of looking for another show dog, Janelle, from Hawthorne, California.

"Janelle?" asked Marilyn. "You *hate* Janelle."

"I don't hate anybody, Mom."

"Janelle hid your left pump in Spokane two years ago."

"They didn't prove that."

"Winning seems to make you so charitable. Testy, too."

"I'm *not* testy." But she did feel nervous. She was panicking, as her eyes darted about looking for Eugene. Her stomach felt like a kite that was having trouble getting airborne.

"Of *course* not, sweetie. Oh, *look*—there she is over there . . ."

"Where?" Confused, Susan snapped her head in the direction her mother had pointed to. No Eugene there.

"Gotcha."

"Oh Mom."

"Don't worry, sweetie. Whatever's going on, I'm not going to press it tonight. You're a champion."

Chapter Twelve

Susan felt the heat from the cooling cheeseburgers slithering from the trash bag beside her. Having recovered from the explosive clamp of the dumpster's lid, her ears now registered her own slow breathing and the rustle of the bagged trash looming above her like a potential Nerf avalanche. The smell— that was the strongest sensation, sickly sweet—ketchup, buns, fish, beef and potato mingled with their greases and liquids, varnishing the metal beneath her shoes.

There was no light, and in its absence, the shapes she touched burst forth on her fingertips like crippled fireworks. She was hungry, but her repulsion for the dead food overrode her hunger. She tried shrinking herself, like a bird caught inside a house. And then she relaxed. A bit.

She tried to make a seat for herself, batting her hands out into the trash bags and locating a springy one full of paper cups, foam clamshell containers and paper napkins. She sat on the bag in her corner. The smells around her were not diminishing, and her nose refused to acclimatize the way it would around a barnyard's manure. The smell wasn't enough to gag her, but it refused to be ignored.

Her hunger grew worse, but the thought of eating one of the burgers cooling around her made her retch. She was thirsty, and the energy bars in her travel bag tasted like paste and required water to eat. She reached for her bag—her bag! She'd dropped it onto the concrete under the dumpster when the workers came by. She warbled with regret.

Hours passed.

Now she was unbearably hungry. She crumbled, and reached for one of the unsold burgers, its heat gone, recognizable as new only because of its wrapping. She ate it with as much gusto as she might eat Styrofoam packing peanuts.

Her mouth felt like the inside of a catcher's mitt. She ripped open the bag beneath her and rooted through its contents until she came upon a waxed paper cup containing drink remnants. She found a dash of Orange Crush happily diluted with melted ice cubes and downed it in one swig. She rummaged more, culling inert french fries, packets of honey-mustard dipping sauce, prickly drinking straws and smudged napkins. Presto! An almost full medium-sized Diet Coke, metallic and body temperature, flat and wet. She drank it and then tossed the cup to the top of the heap. Then she needed to pee, and her hands fumbled in the trash in search of disposable commodes, two empty milkshake cups.

Using folded cardboard, she built herself an impromptu shanty in the corner. For the shanty's floor she placed a buffer layer of dry garbage to insulate her from the dumpster's bottom, and to one side she built an avalanche shed, so as to be safe if the trash collapsed during the night. For a pillow she used folded cardboard, onto which she placed a bag full of crushed waxed paper cups.

She was surprising herself with her adeptness at navigating inside her new world—in her new life she'd have to start at the bottom—this was her trial by fire. And so it was with a strange pride that she fell asleep, proud she could handle herself no matter what was tossed her way, and her sleep was dreamless.

She was wakened with a stun-gunned jolt of fear by the

industrial crash of steel on steel. Morning—a dump truck come to lift her and her new home away.

She heard the locks above her being unlocked and then almost immediately the dumpster was jolted upward, and her body was compressed by the wall of trash bags that had been against the opposing wall. Her mind raced—a trash compressor—oh God. Within seconds she was upside down and drenched in trickling soda pops which percolated into her sleep nook. Then the bottom fell out of her world and she was briefly weightless while tumbling into a truck bed, pelted with waste, the morning sun blinding her.

The bed was full, and mercifully it had no compressor. Feeling like Bugs Bunny, she poked her head up from her trash and looked over its edge and into the commercial strip she'd walked the night before, haloed in sunlight beaming in low from the eastern horizon. The truck moved onto an interstate with fresh, nonburger winds filling her nostrils and cleansing her hair of ketchup packets and salts and peppers.

It was a long ride, and Susan lay atop the waste and felt the sun on her eyelids.

The truck slowed down, changed gears, stopped, started, made various turns and then rumbled onto the dirt of a sanitary landfill. Trucks around her were beeping as they maneuvered themselves in reverse gear, as did Susan's. Its bed tilted up, up, then up some more, and yet again Susan felt weightless, scrambling up the dumping trash as though she were a monkey walking up a down escalator. She finally came to rest on the crown of a crest of a heap of trash. Sun—warmth—freedom.

She could only see trucks, not people, and she walked down and through the cones of junk, seemingly groomed but utterly filthy.

She came across a scarecrow for seagulls. She stole its mantle, a men's XL down ski jacket with felt pen stains around its hem, and small castanet of sporty ski lift tags chattering on its zipper.

Inside its chest pocket was a pair of bad, cheap aviator glasses of the sort found in dime stores. She put them on. She swept her hair back and left the dump, smiling.

She headed toward Indiana.

Chapter Thirteen

The day John chose for his walkout, he didn't wake up in the morning knowing that would be the day. Rather, he felt a twinge—10:30 A.M. in the Staples parking lot, while closing the door of his Saab under a rainless sky—and realized the time was now. His soul creaked just a bit, like a house shifting off its foundation just ever so. It felt to him like the moment once a year when he smelled the air and knew fall is here; or like the moment when a tamed animal bites its master's hand and reverts to the wild.

He shut the car door, and the annoying sonic blinks from inside stopped. Cindy and Krista had liquidated his chattels and were off once again to pursue their acting careers. He had $18.35 in his wallet, which he placed in the Muscular Dystrophy can by the cashier's till at Staples. He tucked his wallet, containing his driver's license, his credit cards, his various unmemorizable access code numbers, as well as home and studio security card swipes, discreetly inside a littered KFC box, which he dropped in a trash bin.

He was wearing a blue cotton button-down dress shirt, a previously unworn pair of cocoa ("*Never* chocolate," as twin Cindy had informed him) slacks and a pair of shiny black loafers Melody had given him on a distant birthday. He removed his wristwatch and placed it on a bus stop bench. He wore no jewelry.

He remembered his vision of Susan, its clarity and conviction. This reminded him of how he felt when he'd been called up onstage to receive his high school diploma. It had been years since he'd been sick or weak. Beneath his robe he was almost acrobatic with good health as members of the good-looking-girl-clique in the crowd behind him gave him cheeky squeals of reassurance that he was in fact a new person crossing a new line. He had the giddy sensation that came with knowing a part of his life was absolutely over and something assuredly more marvelous lay ahead.

He walked east, and an hour later was soaked in sweat. Food.

It was time to eat and rest. Some blocks ahead was a Burger King, and once inside, it dawned on John that he was moneyless, so he asked for and received a glass of water while he tried to make a dining decision. A quick glance at his reflection in a counterside mirror reminded him that he hadn't shaved that day, and was now entering that small pocket of time in which he would look raffish, and soon after that, unmedicated.

"Can I help you, sir?" asked the manager with an air of understaffedness.

"Not just yet. Thanks." Staying any longer was pointless. In his enthusiasm to run away, he'd skipped over the subject of food, assuming that it would somehow just appear. Walking away from the restaurant's chilled cube of air, he couldn't help but notice the colorful composts of uneaten food that filled its numerous cans, and as he continued his eastward trek, he realized he'd have to quickly invent some sort of nutritious idea.

The sun peaked and quickly fell to the horizon. The thrumming of cars was constant. It grew dark. The neighborhoods he passed through were consistently deteriorating, and soon even the fast food and gas outlets vanished. He was sweaty and thirsty and knew that by now he must be looking rather strange. He wondered how long his $150 haircut would keep him looking like Joe Citizen. His stomach cramped with hunger and dehydration.

A mile farther, at a road junction he spotted a McDonald's. At least there he could shit and wash and devise a food plan. Knowing this, his steps resumed their earlier bounce, and in the McDonald's men's room he sploshed his deranged face with tap water and then entered the main dining area, occupied by a few seniors, three borderline homeless cases and a sullen clump of Asian teens busy flouting California's nonsmoking laws. The counter staff were almost medically, clinically bored, and listened to John's request for water as if he were a dial tone. But he received a glass of water, which bought him time, and then, *eureka!*—the teenagers took off, and in their wake left a Yosemite campground's worth of meal trash. Quickly, under the guise of muttering his moral outrage, he took the food trays and their remnants and stuck them into trash bins, carefully leaving behind the juiciest chunks of burgers, fries and nuggets, which he placed onto a paper place mat, folded up, and carried out of the restaurant like a disco purse.

Outside, he scoured the vicinity looking for a place to eat and chose a small concrete piling behind the restaurant, by some rangy oleander shrubs overlooking the dumpsters and utility hookups encased in wire fencing.

A helicopter flew overhead. He ate his food and then found a place to lie down, behind the oleanders, a spot free of urine, scraping together a pillow of bark chips that made his forearms itch. He smelled something oily. He felt the heartburnt wooziness of having taken the wrong carnival ride.

At midnight the McDonald's lights went off. John watched

two staffers come out back, fill the dumpster with plump white bags, and lock up the caged area. Like a coyote, he caught himself looking for any stray bits of food they might have dropped. Before he fell asleep, he figured the night staff would still be sleeping when the morning employees arrived to open up, and so wouldn't recognize the mumbling transient with a Fred Flintstone five o'clock shadow.

John was a noble fool. His plan to career without plans or schedules across the country was damned from the start. He was romantic and naïve and had made pathetically few plans. He thought some corny idea to shed the trappings of his life would deepen him, regenerate him—make him king of fast-food America and its endless paved web.

Each day John felt dirtier and more repulsive. He stank. He'd tried to wash his underwear in a gas-station sink using granulated pink industrial soap, and he'd put it out across the top of a fence to dry, but it had blown onto a mound of sawdust on the other side.

He learned how to avoid the police. He slept in hedges. He continued wandering east, neighborhood by neighborhood, out into the fringes of Los Angeles County. He came to hate dogs because they recognized him as a roamer and announced it with their barks.

He scraped together aluminum-can money to buy—and he laughed as he did so—bourbon—cheap booze! Nice and sweet, and just as delicious and unsophisticated as the first time he'd tried it in his teens.

In Fontana, a dead steel town sixty miles inland, he fulfilled Ivan's prophecy and stole laundry from a clothesline, a UPS delivery man's uniform which fit him surprisingly well. He scanned the house, and nobody was in. He jimmied the lock on a flimsy aftermarket side door. Inside, he showered, washed his hair, shaved and donned his new uniform. He bundled up his old clothing and wedged it between two plastic stacking chairs on the rear patio as he left.

The UPS uniform was his ticket to respectability. With it, he was able to go almost anywhere in public, regardless of hygiene, with almost no scrutiny. It made him appear casual, industrious, sober, a charmed messenger.

He made no friends, but to his surprise scored with a few women turned on by his UPS togs. He hated himself for having the experiences, not so much for their tawdriness, but because such flings felt as if they were against the rules—which made him suddenly realized he *had* rules, not something he'd expected. He felt moral, a distinctly new sensation. Maybe the road *was* changing him after all.

His first tryst was with a woman—twenty-nine? thirty-two?—tense as an overstretched guitar string. She was reading a copy of *Architectural Digest* in the BP gas-station convenience mart. They locked eyes.

John said, "I'd say the magazine started to go downhill when they shifted their focus from pure architecture to that of Homes of the Stars."

And off they went to her place nearby. She was terrifying in her need, and bayed like a stampeding elk when she saw that John wasn't wearing underwear. That night was his first sleep on a mattress in weeks, but he was promptly booted out in the morning when she left for her job processing spreadsheets at a Dean Witter office.

The following night he scored again, this time with a frowzy-haired plump young mother strolling her eight-month-old past a Pottery Barn. She also lived close by, and offered John a meal afterward—lettuce and a packaged stroganoff casserole, which he ate without talking. The woman and her screaming child struck John as being so alone in the world. It hit him that his own form of loneliness was a luxury, one as chosen and as paid for as three weeks in Kenya's velds or a cherry red Ferrari. Real loneliness wasn't something an assistant scoped out and got a good price on. Real loneliness was smothering and it stank of hopelessness. John began to consider his own situation a frill. The only way he could ennoble it was to plunge further, more deeply and blindly, into his commitment to the life of the road, and garner some kind of empathy for a broader human band of emotions.

The woman asked John to stay the night, but he declined, lest she become slightly attached to him and even lonelier when he left.

In Riverside County he hopped a railway flatcar that carried him to Arizona under a milky night sky. The rhythm was calming and he slept, waking up to pink canyons and coral clouds. There was a fellow Nobody at the other end of the car, hovering over the car's edge to speak in sign language to an invisible friend. John made no effort to talk. It was an unwritten code among Nobodies that they not bother each other, and there were so many of them out there! Once John knew what to look for, he saw them everywhere. In the same way his brain erased telephone poles when viewing scenery, his brain had also blocked out Nobodies.

Nobodies had surrendered their families, their childhoods, their jobs, their lovers, their skills, their possessions, their affections and their hopes. They were still human, but they'd become part animal, too. Two months into his trip, John was pretty much a Nobody, too.

He remembered cruising with Ivan, in the old orange 260-Z, back in the UCLA days of pointless classes, sunshine, large houses filled with rock stars and no furniture, buckets of fried chicken and music that engraved itself onto his brain like script on sterling silver. They were returning from a failed party in the Valley, cresting the Hollywood Hills—Los Angeles lay before them. John had pulled the car to the side of the road and Ivan asked him what was the matter. John was silent. He had suddenly seen a glimpse of something larger than just a landscape.

"John-O, c'mon, what's the deal? You're zoning on me, buddy."

"Ivan, cool down a second. Look at the city."

"Yeah. So?"

"*People* built all of that, Ivan. *People*."

"Well, *duh*."

John tried to explain to Ivan that until then, he'd always unthinkingly assumed that the built world was something that was simply *there*. But now he understood that *people* made and maintained all of the roads as well as the convulsing pipes of sewage that ran beneath every building, as well as all the wires that carried electricity from the center of the planet into the hair dryers and TV sets and X-ray machines of Los Angeles County. And with this news came a further understanding that John himself could build something enormous and do the job just as well as anybody else could. It was a jolt of power.

Ivan *sort of* got the picture. But not totally. John had always looked back on that moment as the one where he became a "big thinker."

But now, on the train at night, John felt as if he'd been leveled, humbled, like somebody gone back to visit the house they'd lived in as a child to find it turned shabby and unremarkable.

Somewhere in Arizona the train stopped and John got off.

Chapter Fourteen

Making hit movies was one of the smaller problems in John's life. Ivan handled the workaday stuff like budgets and wind machines and union haggling. John's role was to walk into a room where nothing really existed except for a few money guys who wanted a bit of glamour, a good dollar return and a few cracks at some industry sweeties. John would conjure up a spell for these Don Duncans, Norm Numbnuts and Darrens-from-Citicorp. He had to cram his aura deep, deep, deep inside their guts, spin it around like a juicer's blade, then withdraw and watch the suits ejaculate dollars. "People, this isn't about cash, this is about the American soul—it's about locating that soul and ripping it out by its root. It's about taking that root and planting it deep into the director's warm beating heart, hot pulsing blood feeding the plant, nourishing it until it flowers and gives us roses and zinnias and orchids and heliotropes and even, fuck, I don't know, *antlers*. And we sit and watch the blooms and we've done our part. It's the only reason we're here. We're dirt. We're crap. We're shit. But we're *good* shit. We're nothing but soil for the director to grow a vision. And we should be *proud* of it." Usually, John would climb right up onto the meeting desk for this portion of the event. People rarely wanted details. They wanted hocus-pocus and John gave it to them. John had good hunches and he acted on them quickly, with almost alien accuracy. He believed that most people had at least a few good ideas each day, but that they rarely used them. John had no brakes. There was no lag time between his idea and its implementation. He was a film commando. Sometimes it frightened him how easily people would follow somebody who conveyed the appearance of direction or will.

Bel Air PI was a reasonably low-budget buddy-cop film in which a has-been rust-belt homicide-detective-turned-PI partnered up with the mayor's daughter, a tawny renegade ("Darling," said Doris after reading the script, "your heroine is a tawny renegade. Whatever *next!*") to establish a PI agency. Their first case was to search for the missing wife of a studio executive who was located in many KFC-sized pieces in an Imperial County lemon orchard. Drugs were involved. Betrayal. A final shoot-out and chase in which Cat and Dog stopped fighting each other to unite against the forces of evil and then Get It On.

The movie relaunched the career of a faded seventies rock star and gave steroids to a film genre then on the wane. Almost immediately *Bel Air PI 2* (*Bel Air* π^2) was in the works, and John had drugs and dollars and pussy hurled into his lap.

Bel Air π^2 became a monster hit, bigger than the original, and was followed by an alien invasion thriller with a soundtrack that number one'd for five weeks, and a terrorists-occupy-Disneyland–style thriller that went ballistic in European and Japanese release but didn't work so well in North America, as copycat directors had glommed onto John's noisy, music-drenched formula. To John moviemaking wasn't formulaic. It was a way for him to create worlds wherein he could roam with infinite power far away from a personal history, free of childhood disease and phantom relatives.

Wherever John went, the volume was up full. Once, John and Ivan drove John's car-of-the-month, a Bentley "the color of Grace Kelly's neck," down to La Quinta for a Polygram executives' weekend retreat. They left the car parked in the desert while they searched for pieces of cactus skeleton Nylla wanted for her flower arranging. Once they'd been in the sun a while, John went to the car and brought back to Ivan's rock perch an armload of items. First was a laminated menu stolen from a Denny's. He rolled it into a funnel, and used it to send item number two, a half bottle of tequila, down his throat. He then reached for the third item, a rifle. He used it to fire five volleys into the car's skin, turning it into a fast, expensive sieve. Ivan yelled, "Studly!" John promptly vomited, and stopped having cars-of-the-month after that, settling on the gunshot Bentley as his distinctive final choice. John had a reputation to keep, and when he entered rooms, success and decadence swarmed about him like juicy gossip.

John's one true friend across the years was Ivan. As an added bonus for Ivan, John came with a mother, Doris—a presence sorely missing in Ivan's life since his father got marriage out of his system just months after Ivan's birth. John and Doris had been living in the guesthouse for two weeks when Ivan was shipped home from an experimental boarding school near Big Sur. He'd been caught sniffing ether from an Orange Crush bottle. The ether had been stolen from the science lab by a student who traded it with Ivan for a set of puffy stereo headphones.

"Why were you sniffing ether?" John asked on their first meeting, in the front hallway of the main house, the floor's stone so smooth and shiny and hard-looking that John thought that anything that dropped on it would shatter—glass, metal, feathers and diamonds. Having never been to California before, he believed he could feel the heat mending his body.

"I was trying to get over something," Ivan said.

"What?"

Ivan looked at this pale, scrawny, unfledged child, more ghost than body. Ivan decided from the start to take John into his confidence. He assumed that such an underdeveloped body could only harbor an overdeveloped mind. "I have this dopey paranoid fear about"—he paused—"the Ice Age."

"The Ice Age?"

"Yeah."

John could hear Doris and Angus sitting in the living room, laughing away.

Ivan went on. "I keep on seeing this picture. These pictures. A wall of ice like the white cliffs at Dover—scraping across Pasadena and then down Wilshire and crushing this house."

"Who told you that? It's a crock of shit. That's not the way it works. First thing that happens is that it snows—but then that snow doesn't melt over the summer. And then the next winter it snows again, and that snow doesn't melt, either. And then it snows maybe a few feet each year, and none of that melts. After a thousand years—a blink in the scheme of things—you've got a slab of ice a mile thick. But you're long gone by then. And if you were smart, you'd have moved to the equator the first year, anyway."

Ivan stood and smiled at John and from then on ceased worrying about the Ice Age. They turned and looked out at the flickering sprinklers in the yard through a small diamond-paned window. "What happened to you?" Ivan asked. "You look like you're dead or something. Like you're on a telethon."

From that point, John's body metamorphosed. He grew tall, almost brawny, but good health arrived too late in his adolescence to entrance him with team sports. He only cared about solo activities in which he could claim pure victory without the ego dilution of teams. John also stopped watching TV, superstitiously equating it with illness.

John and Ivan aligned, making super-8 films as larks, the first of which was titled *Doris's Saturday Night*. It chronicled her cocktailed devolution from Delaware insecticide heiress elegantly tamping shreds of hard-boiled egg onto crustless toast triangles, loving the attention, then shamelessly hamming it up, becoming a haggard *mal vivant* gurgling fragments of sea shanties into the pipes beneath the kitchen sink.

Their second film was more mundane. Angus said they needed to learn about sequencing and editing, so John and Ivan followed Angus through a typical day of work at the studio—capturing his meetings, lunches, drives around the city and a screening at night. It was edited together and shown with goofy subtitles at Angus's fiftieth birthday party under the title *Film Executive Secretly Wearing a Diaper Because It Makes Him Feel Naughty*, and marked their debut into the filmgoing community.

John was a surprisingly confident young man, and a doer, not a thinker. This was an impulse Doris had encouraged him to hone. She didn't want John to be a Lodge in any way, and so fostered in him an enthusiasm for anything that went against the Delaware grain. She encouraged action, creativity and a strong dislike for the past. She had also talked Angus into removing Ivan from the private school system altogether, so both he and John could attend the local high school. Neither flourished, but both were happy enough there, and afterward both young men scraped their way through UCLA, spending the majority of their time making short films and chasing girls. John also experimented with cars. He bought the orange 260-Z from the proceeds of flipping successively more valuable cars, while Ivan drove a mint green Plymouth Scamp he bought from one of Angus's gardeners.

When they were both twenty-four, they founded Equator Pictures, using Ivan's connections and a small loan from Angus. They quickly had their hit with *Bel Air PI*, making them both independently wealthy, independently powerful as well as dependent on each other. John was the unstoppable freight train. Ivan ensured that the vegetables served by craft catering were fresh, and slipped $500 to a crotchety neighbor beside a location shoot who refused to turn off his Weedwacker.

One spring day, somewhere between *Bel Air PI* and *Bel Air PI 2*, John and Ivan were at an ARCO station filling up John's gunshot Bentley. 260-Z, his primary vehicle even though by now he owned the usual industry array of flash-trash cars. John said to Ivan, "I like to pump my own gas into my own car, Ivan. I always go to a self-service pump. Did I ever tell you why?"

"To connect with the man in the street?" Ivan laughed.

"No. Because I like to look at the numbers rev by on the gas pump. I like to pretend each number's a year. I like to watch history begin at Year Zero and clip up and up and up. Dark Ages . . . Renaissance . . . Vermeer . . . 1776 . . . Railways . . . Panama . . . zoom, zoom, zoom . . . the Depression . . . World War II . . . Suburbia . . . JFK . . . Vietnam . . . Disco . . . Mount St. Helens . . . *Dynasty* . . . and then, *WHAM!* We hit the wall. We hit the present."

"So what?"

"This is what: there's this magic little bit of time, just a few numbers past the present year, whatever it is. Whenever I hit these years, then for maybe a fraction of a second, I can, if not *see* the future, *feel* it."

"I'm listening," Ivan said. He was so patient with John.

"It's like I get to be the first one there—in the future. I get to be first. A pioneer."

"That's what you want to be—a pioneer?"

"Yes."

Ivan paused and then, with some consideration, asked, "John-O, have you checked your tire pressure?"

"Nah."

Ivan got out of the car, got a pressure gauge from the attendant, and came back and checked the pressure. "You've got to do the little things, too, John. It all counts, big and small."

Chapter Fifteen

John finished dinner with Ivan and Nylla, then went down to the guesthouse. Doris, having declined dinner with crack baby MacKenzie, was asleep. For the first time since his return from his botched walkout he didn't feel cold dark steel down his spine. He thought back to the women he'd been with briefly during that walkout, then he thought of Susan. Turning the front door knob, it came to him that maybe *he* could sponge away the look of loneliness that he'd seen in Susan's eyes—and John was now pretty sure it was loneliness he'd seen, despite the smiles and the confidences. If he'd learned one thing while he'd been away, it was that loneliness and the open discussion of loneliness is the most taboo subject in the world. Forget sex or politics or religion. Or even failure. *Loneliness* is what clears out a room. Susan could be more to him than his latest box-office ranking. With Susan he might actually help for once, might actually raise something better out of himself than a hot pitch for a pointless film. Something moral and fine inside each of them might sprout and grow.

He phoned and got her answering machine again. He hung up. He felt sixteen.

When Susan didn't respond within an hour, John found his heart racing, his concentration shot. By midnight he was as buggy as he'd ever been on drugs, but without the distractions.

He decided to forward his phone messages to his cell phone, then go rent tapes starring Susan. He wanted to see if the lonely look in her eye had always been there or if it was something new. He also just wanted to see her face. *This is how fans feel about stars*, he thought. *So this is what it's like.* To John, stars were just part of the flow of people through the house, like the maids, the agents and the caterers. But tonight he understood the allure of the tabloids and the fanzines.

He drove Ivan's Chrysler sedan down into West Hollywood. Ivan and Nylla preferred the sedan because of its anonymity. It didn't look like a rental car, and it didn't look, as Doris had said, "ethnic or frightened middle class."

Traffic was tolerable; the night's darkness still felt clean. He found a rental place, West Side Video. On entering he saw it was the kind of shop where the manager asserts personality by laser-printing signs highlighting EVIL MOTHERS, CUTE & DUMB, and arcane subcategories like GORE FESTS and LEMONS, where John was genuinely amused to see his old turkeys, *The Wild Land* and *The Other Side of Hate*.

He realized he had no idea what movies Susan had been in. He asked the clerk, name-tagged RYAN, if he had anything starring Susan Colgate, and the clerk squeaked with pleasure. "Meese Colllllllgate? I should think so. Right this way." He led John to an old magazine rack filled with sun-faded tape boxes. Above the rack was a laser-printed sign reading ST. SUSAN THE DIVINE. The top of the rack was camped up with altarlike candles and sacrificial offerings—Japanese candy bars, prescription bottles, a model Airbus 340 with a missing wing, and a mosaic of head shots of Susan culled from a wide array of print media. Ryan stood patiently, waiting for John's reaction, but John was silent, the inside of his brain firing Roman candles. He felt a sexual need to own the altar.

"She's something, isn't she?" Ryan asked.

"You did this?" John asked, looking at Ryan, a Gap clone—khakis, white T-shirt with flannel shirt on top. A pleasant Brady Bunch face. Like a gag writer at Fox.

"With tender loving care."

"I'll give you a hundred bucks for it, right now."

Ryan was taken aback. "Mr. Johnson—I'm sorry, but I can't pretend I don't know who you are—this is my shrine. It's not like I can just give it away like that."

"Five hundred, but throw in the movies."

"Mr. Johnson. I made it. It's not like a joke or something. Well, maybe a bit of a joke. But I've been saving these clippings for years."

"Nine hundred. Half of what I've got. It's my last money. Everybody knows I'm broke. Even with *Mega Force*—that's in a trust."

"Don't tell me this! Too much information, Mr. Johnson!"

"John."

"Too much information, John." Ryan put his hands on his hips and watched as John scanned the titles on the boxes' spines. The store was empty. They could speak loudly. "John, I'm a stranger to you, but let me ask you something."

"Welcome to detox. Ask away."

"Are you, how shall I say, in *love* with Miss Colgate?"

"What?" John was shocked, not by Ryan's forthrightness, but by the same sort of *ping* he used to get when he discovered whodunit in an Agatha Christie mystery. "Love? I—"

"Go no further. It's okay. I work for the forces of good. And it doesn't surprise me, you know."

"What doesn't? I never said I was in love."

"Psh. You're like the old RKO Radio tower shooting out bolts of Susan."

"You're a ballsy little shit."

"Now, now." Ryan could see John didn't mind. In fact, quite the opposite. "I mean, both of you have done disappearing acts. Her after the plane crash three years ago, and you earlier this year."

John wasn't going to fight it. "Go on. What's your point?"

Ryan rubbed his chin and became professorial. "Well, this would have to be a new thing, wouldn't it? Because if it was even slightly old, you'd already have seen all her old videos by now."

"Bingo, Dr. Einstein."

"When did you meet?"

"Today. At lunch. At the Ivy."

Ryan whistled, then relaxed his posture. "Tell you what, John. Rent all the videos and I'll report them as lost or stolen."

"Yeah?"

"Yeah. And don't waste your last money. I'll throw in the altar, but there's a catch."

"It wouldn't be life on earth if there weren't a catch. "Qu'est-ce-que c'est, Ryan?" John found himself greatly liking this strange young man.

"You have to answer a series of skill-testing questions after reading a script I wrote."

"Fair enough. Deal."

"Good. I'll lock up and we can scan these tapes out of the system and load this stuff into your car."

The two men carried the shrine by its ends over to the counter, where Ryan began to laser-scan the tapes' bar codes. John gave Ryan the address of the guesthouse, as well as his phone number. "Give these out to anybody and you're mulch. And let me ask you something, Ryan—why'd you make a shrine? You're not a stalker, because they don't make shrines—they stalk. What's your deal?"

Ryan looked up from the till, was about to say one thing and then visibly stopped and began to say something else. "Oh, you know, we all need an obsession, and mine's La Colgate: 3184 Prestwick Drive, Benedict Canyon, Wyoming driver's license 3352511, phone unlisted but messages can be left with Adam Norwitz, the IPD Agency."

John stared at Ryan.

"She rents stuff here."

John looked down at the tapes, some episodes of *Meet the Blooms*, *Dynamite Bay* and *Thraice's Faces—On Tour with Steel Mountain*. Crap. "There's another reason you like Susan Colgate. Mind telling me?"

"Fair enough. An LAPD guy told me I was the last person to ever leave a message on her phone line before her plane crashed—a few years ago. I can't explain it. And now here you are tonight. So I'm bonding with her again."

The shrine fit neatly in the car's back seat. The air outside was surprisingly cold and John's skin felt clammy. "Here's the script," said Ryan.

"Yeah, yeah," said John, grabbing it.

"John—listen to me." John stopped—he was unused to being addressed like this but didn't mind. "You're going to read this script and then you're going to get back to me right away. But that's not all."

"It's not, is it?"

"No. You're also going to call me up whenever you need to, and we can talk about Susan."

"Do you have any idea how fucking psycho that sounds, Ryan?"

"Psycho or not, I mean it. Other people aren't going to understand this when it breaks out. And it will. Not from me, but from you, because you're in love so you have a need to blab everything. Other people won't get it."

John laughed. "Okay, Ryan, you win. When my heart gets ready to sing, you can be my Yoko Ono."

"Good luck, Mr. Johnson."

John gave the thumbs-up and drove immediately to 3184 Prestwick, parked across the street and looked at Susan's small blue Cape Cod house surrounded by overgrown ornamental shrubs. A porch light was on, but otherwise it was dark. An hour crept by, and the only activity John noticed was a dog walker and three cars driving by. He gave up, and late in the night he drove back to the guesthouse. The streets were surprisingly empty, and at Highland and Sunset he noticed a fog, but then realized it couldn't be because Los Angeles almost never had fog. His cell phone rang, but the caller hung up. John conceded that something must be on fire.

That night John didn't sleep. He read Ryan's script and drank raspberry juice cut with stinging nettle and mango. He looked at his cordless phone wondering what might be a remotely plausible time to call Susan. Seven-thirty? Too early. Eight? Yes. No. He'd look desperate. Eight-thirty? *Uh, hello, Susan—yes, I know it's kinda early. . . .* Nine? Yes—but how to get there through the ink and murk and smothering slowness of night?

By six o'clock the sky was lightening and a few doves skittered about in the shrubs. He put down Ryan's script, "Tungaska." It was good. A Texas woman inherits a strange metal hoop from her father, which looks like an unjeweled crown or a creweling hoop. She holds it up to the light from a TV set for a better look and suddenly licorice-whip tornadoes descend from the sky, smashing her Galveston subdivision into a landfill of cracked plywood, broken furniture, branches, toys and cars and clothing. Only the room in which she's sitting is spared. It turns out the hoop is a portal that converts human psychic energy into nuclear energy.

John heard a hum up the hill—Ivan's treadmill buzzing to life at its usual six-thirty time slot. Company! He walked up to Ivan, who was also watching the morning news on an ancient 14-inch TV placed on its usual perch on a lawn chair. "John-O."

"Ivan."

"You look like shit. Up all night?" Ivan's treadmill was on 3 out of a possible 10.

"Yeah." This was not uncommon.

"Watch anything good?"

"Actually, no. I read something."

"You *read*?"

"A script, actually."

"My, my. High School Graduates Eat Steak. When was the last time you even touched a script?"

John had to think. "Yeah, yeah. Whenever."

"Something we can use?"

"I think so. It's okay."

"Okay good, or okay crap?"

"Okay good. Okay *great*, actually."

"Spiel forth, pardner."

John started to describe the film.

"What happens after the Galveston blowup?" Ivan was hooked.

"We go back in time—to the famous Tungaska 'meteor explosion' of 1909."

"Isn't that the one where half the trees in Siberia got knocked down?"

"That's it—except it turns out it wasn't a meteorite explosion. It was this hoop thing."

"Not aliens, I hope. The market's supersaturated with alien shit." Ivan timed some sort of pulse or throbbing in his body with his stopwatch.

"Not aliens. The hoop is from Switzerland. From Bern, Switzerland. It's from 1905, and it was made by a voluptuous Russian Jew down the hall from Einstein's apartment. That was the year he discovered the Theory of Relativity."

"Voluptuous? What kind of word is that? Where are we, John-O—1962?"

"Okay okay. But she's hot."

"She's *hot*? Are we in 1988 now?"

"God, Ivan. She's hot in a cold kind of way. Her parents died and she had to go back to Siberia from Bern. But when she's there, there's the accident—the Tungaska explosion."

"What kind of psychic energy creates an explosion that levels half of Siberia?"

"The woman's first orgasm accidentally funneled through an amplifier ring within the hoop."

"*Jawohl.*"

"Anyhow, she's at the center of the explosion, so she's safe. That's part of the deal. Imagine the special effects on this one, Ivan. Anyhow, by now the bad guys know all about this hoop."

"Who are the bad guys?"

"A Swiss banking consortium just before WWII. The guys who were about to rake gold fillings out of the death camps."

"Go on."

"These banking guys want it. All of the governments want it, but she keeps both herself and her hoop hidden until 1939 and the war. She's sent to a death camp and the Nazis get the hoop. Then the Americans steal it from the Germans, and the Americans use it to nuke Japan. And after that the hoop moves to Nevada, where they suck in the gambling energy and the desperation energy from Las Vegas to do their nuclear tests. But then the woman's son, a ballistics scientist working there at the Nevada test site, makes these connections and realizes what the hoop is really about—and also that it belongs to him.

"So he manages to swipe it—that's when the nuclear testing

stops—in the eighties—and he smuggles himself and the hoop down to Galveston. But he has a stroke. His daughter, played by the same actress, puts the hoop into a luggage closet. It's when she's cleaning out the closet that she has the accident with the hoop up against the TV set. The tornado alerts the bad guys, and so there's this chase and it ends with a hurricane of blood. Fish turn inside out. Roses bloom at midnight. It's Revelations. At the end the woman takes the hoop to Hawaii and throws it into one of the live volcanoes on Oahu. Whaddya think?"

Ivan was measuring his breath as his treadmill kicked into a hill simulation. "Sounds to me like there's lots of debris flying around in it."

"Debris? What? Yeah—I guess so."

"I was meeting with these nerds at ILM and SGI up in San Francisco before I went to Scotland. Their computers can do perfect flying debris and litter now. They're looking for a show-case for their new techniques and this sounds like just the thing. Story needs some work, though. Who's the writer?"

"One of these young turks—Ryan Something. He's boiling hot right now."

"I haven't heard his name. Is there an auction on it?"

"We have the option to make a preemptive bid."

"How much you think?"

"Five hundred."

"Make it three. You feel good about this?"

"First script in years to give my brain a hard-on."

"It's the first script you've *read* in years."

A bell rang, announcing somebody at the front gate. Ivan switched off the treadmill. "Come on, John-O, let's see who's here." They walked around the patio, which was dripping with flowers and lush branches. Out front a police car was at the gate, one officer standing beside the car manning the intercom, another in the passenger seat. Ivan buzzed them in with a remote. The four of them formed a congress on the front steps.

"Officers?" Ivan said.

"Hello, Mr. McClintock," the tall one said. "And you, too, Mr. Johnson. Do you have a moment, Mr. McClintock?"

"Call me Ivan. Of course. What's this regarding?"

"Doing a check. Do you own a white Chrysler sedan, license number 2LM 3496T?"

"Yes."

"Were you driving the car last night around two A.M. in Benedict Canyon?"

"That was me," John said.

"Could you tell us where you were last night, Mr. Johnson?"

"Easy. I was getting tapes at West—West—West Side Video on Santa Monica."

"What tapes?"

"About ten of them. Susan Colgate stuff—*Meet the Blooms*, and some cheesy B flick."

The policeman shared a flickering meaningful glance. "What time would that have been, Mr. Johnson?"

"The guy was just closing the shop. Around one A.M., I guess."

"What then?"

"Then I—went and parked in front of Susan Colgate's house. For about an hour."

"Why was that, Mr. Johnson?"

"Is something wrong? What's going on here?" John was getting edgy.

"It's a routine check, sir. Why were you parked outside her house?"

"John-O," said Ivan. "Just talk, okay? We're not cutting a distribution deal here."

"She didn't answer my phone message. Susan Colgate. I thought she might be coming home late."

"You live here, Mr. Johnson?" asked the shorter officer.

"In the house down there. With my mother." The police looked down at the guesthouse, almost unchanged since the day John first saw it. "I lost my old Bel-Air tree-fort last year. You probably read about that in *People*."

"You didn't lose it, John," said Ivan, "you gave it *away*."

"To the IRS. That's not me giving. That's *them* taking."

"Is that the Chrysler down there?" asked the tall cop.

"That's it," John said, his stomach turning to slime as he remembered the shrine still in the back seat. "There's a—oh fuck. You'll see."

The four walked down the hill, the police clicking into almost paramilitary action as they discovered the shrine in the back. One called HQ requesting something technical immediately. The other blocked John from the car.

"Am I under arrest? Do you have a warrant?" John asked.

"No. And we don't have to go through that if you agree."

"John, it's my property," said Ivan. "Go right ahead, guys." He looked in the back seat. The white towel around his neck dropped onto the gravel driveway and he didn't pick it up. "John-O, there's a goddam Susan Colgate parade float in the back seat of the car—you *made* this?"

"Did you make the shrine in the back seat?" the cop asked.

"No. I bought it from the kid at West Side Video. I think it's one of those campy queer things."

At this point Doris came out of the house, cloaked in shawls, her bunned gray hair a porcupine of flyaway hairs. "Oh Christ—it's my mother."

"Morning, darlings. Oh my—the fuzz."

"The *fuzz*?" said John.

"I'm merely trying to be contemporary, darling. Officers—has there been a crime?"

There was mild confusion. A police photographer and forensics expert went over to the car. Ivan went back up to his treadmill and John phoned Adam Norwitz. "What the fuck is going on, Adam?"

"Susan's gone AWOL. She had a six A.M. makeup call for a Showtime Channel kiddy movie and she didn't show up. So the producer phones and screams at me, and I go racing from my gym straight to her house and the doors are all open. There's nobody there, but her car's still out front. The coffeepot was still on, but the coffee was like tar, like it'd been on for twenty-four hours. So I called the cops. You tell *me* what's going on. I nearly had to donate my left nut to science to get her that stupid part on Showtime, and she fucks it up."

"Compassion, Adam."

"Yeah, right. Is she doing a project with you? Is she jumping into a bigger pond now—no more time for the little fish?"

"How can you make this woman's disappearance about you, Adam?"

"Spare me the melodrama."

"Did you call the hospitals or anything?"

"That's the cops' job."

Adam knew nothing. The police knew next to nothing. John refused to panic. Susan could be out on a tequila jag or maybe she was whipping one of those creepy Brit directors with birch fronds. *She's not that type,* he thought. He sucked in a breath, then phoned Ryan to buy the script.

Chapter Sixteen

Their first flop was a love story: *The Other Side of Hate*. Nothing about it came easily. To begin with, Angus, in the final depressing stretch of prostate cancer, told him the title was wrong. "John, 'hate' is a downer word, and it doesn't matter if you make *Citizen Kane*, a title like *The Other Side of Hate* is box office poison from the word go."

Doris had other concerns. "A love story? *You*, darling? Just keep making things that go bang and you'll be hunky-dory."

"You don't think I can do a love story?"

"That's not it, darling. Love stories need to be made by . . ."

"Yes?"

"Oh, I *have* put my foot in it, haven't I?"

"Love stories need to be made by . . . ?"

"They need to be made by somebody who's actually been in love, darling, and I think I'd better have something very bubbly very quickly." Over the years Doris's life had devolved into a pleasant timeless succession of sunny days, clay modeling, bursts of watercolor enthusiasm, gossip with a small clique of "card fiends," and a well-worn path between her front door and the Liquor Barn a few miles away. John saw her twice a week and she remained a close confidante.

"I've been in love before."

"With whom?"

"With . . ."

"Really, darling, it's okay, and doubtless you'll one day find some lucky young starlet who'll sweep you right off your feet. And until then, keep blowing things up in Technicolor."

"Technicolor? I think I hear Bing Crosby ringing the doorbell."

But John wondered why he hadn't fallen in love. He'd been in lust and in like countless times, but not something that made him feel like a part of something bigger. The energy from his filmmaking—as well as filmmaking's rewards, the delirium of excess—it all conspired to mask this one simple hole in his life.

It seemed to John that people in love stopped having the personality they had before love arrived. They morphed into generic "in-love units." John saw both love and long-term relationships as booby traps that would not only strip him of his identity but would take out the will to continue moving on.

But then again, to find somebody who'd be his partner on the ride—someone to push him further. That's what he'd held out for. And as the years went on, the holding out got sadder and more solitary. He began to hang out with people younger than he as older friends drifted away. But even then he sensed the younger crew were contemptuous—*That fucked-up old wank who can't even get himself a girlfriend. He lives in a house like a nuclear breeder facility. Sure, he has hits, but he always takes his mom to the premieres.*

Ivan was less doubtful than Doris about the fate of *The Other Side of Hate*, but during the production cycle he was sidetracked by an onslaught of collapsing real estate deals in Riverside County, and wasn't able to assign himself fully to his usual pre-production grind of rewrites, casting changes, and cleaning up

John's well-intended messes. The director and the lead actress discovered they were sleeping with the same script girl and subsequently refused to listen to each other. The male lead tested positive for HIV two weeks before shooting and arrived on the set with a new and medicated personality greatly at odds with the cavalier froth demanded by the thirteenth and final script rewrite. The grimness continued through the dailies, through the storm that bulldozed a third of the Big Bear location set and through John's initiation into the world of crystal meth on the eleventh day of shooting.

After a profoundly dismal test screening in Woodland Hills, Melody said to John, "John, I know you meant well by this film, but if you want to do the right thing, go out and buy a can of glue and stick it onto the back of the negative and sell the whole thing as packing tape."

"Mel!"

"Johnny, don't be a retard. It's crap. Burn it."

"But it's tender—lovely . . ."

"Please. Don't even put it on video. Don't even dub it into Urdu. Burn it."

Angus died shortly thereafter and Doris came unglued. They hadn't been lovers for decades, but he'd been her good friend. She lapsed into a cloudy fugue. Ivan inherited the estate and Doris stayed in the house.

The Other Side of Hate was released after John ignored what proved to be sound advice from Melody. The film was violently thrashed by media organs with the glee of vultures who have long awaited the giant's first fall. It died on opening weekend, taking in just under 300K, close to the amount John spent on under-the-counter pharmaceuticals in any given year. There were the inevitable industry backlash rumors that the golden days of Equator Films were over. Some viewed the film as a burp, others a death cry. John and Ivan were unable to rustle up even the faintest, most vaguely kind word from a 200-watt radio station in the middle of Iowa. ("Slightly amusing!" KDXM, La Grange, Iowa.) Nothing was salvageable.

All eyes were on the next film, *The Wild Land*, a historical saga set in early-twentieth-century Wyoming. The script was adapted from a best-selling novel by a two-time Academy Award–winning screenwriter. The cast was six of filmdom's most in-demand stars, all of whom got along famously with the Palme d'Or director. It came in on budget, with a sweeping musical score, and when it came out in theatrical release, it . . . flat-lined. It garnered none of the venom and acid of *The Other Side of Hate*. The film simply *vanished*, a response more deeply wounding than any of *Hate*'s hatchets and chain saws.

After *The Wild Land*, John and Ivan had a dozen films in development. Time passed. Studios mutated and merged and vanished and some were born. Japan entered the arena. Tastes changed. New audiences evolved. The men had lost their footing.

John completed construction of his high-tech fuck-hut, which had been ongoing for five years. He tried to clean up his substance act, and lost entire years at a time in the effort, the very name Johnson becoming industry shorthand for slipping and lapsing and falling. He lost interest in making movies. His world narrowed and his circle shrank. John began to feel like some old mirrors he'd seen in Europe, at the once-grand old palaces, the glass that had slowly, fleck by fleck, over the years shed the flecks of silver that had made them originally reflective.

"Oscar season again," sighed Ivan. "Is it March already?" They were in the back seat of a car, being driven to Century City for a morning legal meeting. Ivan was immaculately dressed and his skin had the shine of eight hours of drugless sleep. John's face looked like a floor at the end of a cocktail party.

"What are we up for this year?" asked John.

"Don't be facetious, John."

John was doing lines of coke from a small oval of safety glass he stored in his attaché case. He noticed Ivan give him a glower. "So what is your point, Ivan? I've got to stay awake. You know lawyers hit me like animal tranquilizers." Ivan waited.

A flatbed loaded with jumbo gold statuettes was headed off to the venue—a tourist's dream photo. The truck paused beside them at a light. John caught Ivan eyeing the statues. "No, no, no, Ivan. I can see that 'I wish we had an Oscar' gleam in your eyes. Well, forget it. Oscars are for freaks."

"You can't honestly believe that, John."

"*Oohhhhh*, look at *me*—I've got a little statue for being this year's token Brit, or this year's on-screen hooker with a disability. *Oohhhhh*, look at *me*—in twenty-four hours nobody's going to remember my name. *Oohhhhh*, the studio can put lots of little Oscar™'s all over ads for my movie—not simply *Oscars* but Oscars with the little trademark ™'s up on top: *Oscar*™'s." He chopped up a crystal. "Oops—excuse me, I forgot to put the ™ at the end of it. Off to Alcatraz we go."

"*John* . . ." Ivan adapted his baby-sitting voice. "Go easy on that stuff. The guys we're meeting are ball-breakers."

"*Oscars* . . ." John began to mumble, not a good sign. Ivan began to brace himself for a crash-and-burn morning, and downgraded his expectations for the upcoming meeting accordingly. Ivan, like John, had been seduced by the rewards and extremes of filmmaking, but unlike John, he wanted a traditional life now. In his mind he was "officially disgusted" with his life up to that point. He was "officially through with carousing" and was now ready to begin "officially looking to settle down." And it was at this point that he saw Nylla, at the foot of an office tower, tears trickling down her cheeks, swaddled in a printed silk scarf that fluttered over her right shoulder. Running up her neck and into her cheek was a mottled scar left by a massive jellyfish sting from off the Australian coast two years previously. Its trace had nipped her acting career in the bud. Her new agent, Adam Norwitz, had seen her jellyfish scar a month before and had finally succeeded, just minutes prior to her appearance on the sidewalk, in breaking her spirit. He convinced her that the scar would keep her out of work, "unless you want to do soft porn, in which case a scar like yours could be a definite asset."

Ivan stared at her silk dress, patterned with gardenias, fluttering in a warm wind, and he felt sorry for her. Meanwhile, behind him, John's sinuses and lungs clapped and glorted. Ivan watched Nylla chew her gum. She removed it from her mouth, and instead of flicking it onto the hot concrete, took a small paper from her purse, and placed the gum inside the paper, and tucked the result in her purse. It was the cleanest thing he'd ever seen anybody do.

"Look, she's crying," said Ivan, entranced, as though witnessing the world's smallest rainstorm. He got out of the car.

"Ivan," John said, "isn't the meeting in the next tower over?" He heard Ivan ask Nylla if she was okay, and then say to her, "Can I help you out here? I'm Ivan. I'm on my way to a meeting, but I saw you here and . . ."

She said, "Oh God, I must look like an idiot."

"No you don't. Not at all. What's your name?"

"I'm Nylla."

"That's a nice name."

"It's spelled N-Y-L-L-A. My father came to the States from Europe after the war. He wanted to name me after New York

State because the States had been so good to him. My mother wanted me named after her mother, Bjalla. And there's the result."

"I'm Ivan."

And they were married six months later.

Chapter Seventeen

Eugene Lindsay, Ford dealer of the gods, was alone in bed making a list in a small notepad:

No. 63: You can get almost any food you want at any time of the year.

No. 64: Women do everything men do and it's not that big a deal.

No. 65: Anybody on the planet can have a crystal-clear conversation with anybody else on the planet pretty well any time they want to.

No. 66: You can comfortably and easily wake up in Sydney, Australia, and go to bed in New York.

No. 67: The universe is a trillion billion million times larger than you ever dreamed it would be.

No. 68: You pretty well never see or smell shit.

He was writing a list of things which would astound somebody living a hundred years before him. He was trying to persuade himself that he was living in a miraculous world in a miraculous time. Having taken early retirement from his job as a local TV weatherman, he'd subsequently retreated for a decade inside his mock-Tudor house in Bloomington, Indiana. He made art from household trash and watched TV. He jotted the occasional thought in his notebooks, such as the evening's list. And in his basement he used a Xerox 5380 console copier and a CD-ROM–based computer to execute far more elaborate mail scams than he had ever dreamed of in the eighties.

His wife, Renata, had years ago moved to New Mexico, where she paid the bills burning herbs for neurotic urban refugees. She abandoned decades of starvation dieting, and had grown as big as a pile of empties on the back stoop. She wore no makeup and made a point of letting people know it. When she divorced Eugene, she had asked for nothing, which confused and frightened him more than a nasty divorce fight would have done.

No. 69: We went to the moon and to Mars a few times, and there's really nothing there except rocks, so we quit dreaming about them.

No. 70: Thousands of diseases are quickly and easily cured with a few pills.

No. 71: Astoundingly detailed descriptions of sex acts appear on the front page of *The New York Times*, and nobody is ruffled by it.

No. 72: By pushing a single button, it's possible to kill 5 million people in just one second.

Eugene looked at number 72. Something was wrong—what? He figured it out: buttons didn't exist a hundred years ago. Or did they? What did people do back then—did they pull chains? Turn cranks? What did they have that they could turn on? Nothing. Electric lights? Eugene didn't think so. Not back then. He made a correction:

No. 72: By pushing a single lever, it's possible to kill five million people in just one second.

He looked at his clock—deepest night—3:58 A.M. He dropped his pen and marveled at his body, lying on the bed, still well proportioned and lean, still dumbly beautiful and betraying no evidence of inner weariness.

His bedsheets felt dry but moist, like the time he lay down on a putting green in North Carolina. Surrounding him was that month's art project—thousands of the past decade's emptied single-portion plastic tublets of no-fat yogurt, their insides washed squeaky clean, stuffed inside each other, forming long wavy filaments that reached to the ceiling like sea anemones. The finished piece was to go inside Renata's old gift-wrapping room, a concept she'd stolen from Candy Spelling, Aaron Spelling's wife—a whole room devoted to wrapping the nonstop stream of trinkets and doodads from her old gown business.

Eugene had to take his weekly bag of trash out to the curb. He looked at his clock—3:59 A.M. now. He procrastinated and added to his list:

No. 73: Bad moods have been eliminated.

No. 74: You almost never see horses.

No. 75: You can store pretty well all books ever published inside a box no larger than a coffin.

No. 76: We made the planet's weather a little bit warmer.

Trash time. Since the episode with the crazy pageant mother back in Saint Louis, giving anything away to the trashman was cause for personal alarm. Trash night had never been the same since. To make his current bag of garbage seem fuller and hence more normal, he fluffed up its contents and carried the full bag, weighing no more than a cat, down to the front door. Eugene paused and tightened his robe, which bore the embroidered logo of the Milwaukee Radisson Plaza Hotel from which it was stolen during a meteorological conference. He darted out to the curb, lobbed the bag onto the concrete, then ran back to the door.

On the way back to his room he beamed with a creator's joy at his three pillars made of Brawny paper towel shipping boxes, a trio that filled the front hallway from floor to ceiling. Take that, Andy Warhol.

Cozily back in bed, Eugene heard an unmistakable thump from downstairs. He knew the noise couldn't be a tumbling mound of his art—he stacked his goods in stable piles, the way he'd seen them stacked in museums. Perhaps a raccoon had snuck in during his brief trash haul. Eugene reached for his gun in the bedside drawer and released the safety. Seated on the floor between the wall and his bed, he plotted his strategy.

Then came another bump from below. Confident and collected, he slipped through the Brawny towel box totems. Sliding on his buttocks, he lowered himself into the foyer, lit only by the candle power of a half moon in the clear sky. He crouched behind some of the totems and scanned the living room. Somebody or something was rooting behind a 1:4-scale Saber fighter jet made of Bumble Bee tuna and SpaghettiOs tins.

Eugene swept across the foyer like a cartoon detective. Stealthily he maneuvered to the base of the statue, its wheels resting atop a plinth built of stabilized Kraft Catalina salad-dressing boxes. He was calm. He stood up and, with kickboxing speed, lunged over to the other side of the base shouting "Freeze!," and pointed the handgun onto what appeared to be a drifter—a wino—who yipped like a squeak toy, and cowered against the boxes. Eugene flipped on the light switch, shocking the room and flaring his retinas. "Well fuck *me*," he said. "If it isn't Miss Wyoming."

"Put down the gun, Ken Doll."

"Lordy! Miss Congeniality."

"Yeah, like I always keep a speech about world peace prepared."

"Hey—" The adrenaline was wearing off. He grew confused. "You're supposed to be—"

"Dead?" she laughed. "Well, technically *yes*."

Eugene paused and crossed his arms while studying Susan, now hoisting herself up. "Boo," she said. "I'm not a ghost. I'm real. I promise. Nice place you have here."

Perplexed, Eugene asked how she got in.

"I scampered in while you were on the curb. I was sleeping outside your front door."

"You were sleeping outside my front door?"

"No. I was waiting in the soundproof booth to answer a skill-testing question." Eugene was still digesting the scene before him and was silent. Susan wanted a reaction and added, "Gonad."

He lit a cigarette and relaxed just a smidge. "I can see you're a feisty one. Ten out of ten for deportment."

"Oh, let it rest. I came here on purpose. What do you think."

"You came *here*? Why *here*? And as I said, you're *dead*. I saw the crash on TV a hundred times."

Susan stood up and removed the scarecrow's down jacket. "You've been doing weather for how many years now, Eugene—how many times are you ever right?"

"I was a good weatherman."

"*Was*? I guess your station saw the inside of your house and decided to can you." Susan was both pleased and surprised that she and Eugene so quickly fell into patter. More to the point, the sense of powerful first-crushiness initiated with "the wink" back in St. Louis was in no way diminished by the physical sight of an aged Eugene. He'd aged in the crinkly, weather-beaten manner of action heroes, sheepherders and five-star generals. His eyes remained as gemlike and clear as she'd remembered. He was also a kook and already kind of fun.

"Susan, what could you possibly have come to me here for? I've never even *met* you."

"Where's Renata?"

"Renata's not here anymore."

A good sign. Susan's insides thrummed. "You two split?"

"Years ago. You didn't answer my question. Why did you come *here* of all places? You've gotta know dozens of people within hours of the crash site." He threw up his arms. "Shit. Look at me, trying to be logical with somebody who's supposed to be a *ghost*, fer Chrissake."

Susan wondered herself why she had come there. All she'd known along the way was that she was in the Midwest and that Eugene's house seemed like the only safe place between the two coasts. She *had* no plan prepared for what came next. As this dawned on her, the lack of immediate response goaded Eugene.

"So let me get this straight—you thought Renata and I would give you a blanket, some Valiums and a phone line to 911? Your crash was a *week* ago, Miss Wyoming. Something's not right here. If you wanted blankets and cocoa, the time limit on *that* expired five days ago."

Meanwhile, all Susan knew was that since her initial crush on Eugene she'd spent her life trying to find him in some form or another, mostly through Larry, and maybe now she wanted to see what the real goods were like. "Maybe I'm not sure myself why I'm here."

"Oh, this is nuts!" He let out a breath. "Are you okay? After the crash? No broken bones? No bruises?"

"I'm fine."

"You're going to tell me what happened?"

"Of course. Not now. Later."

"You hungry?"

"Thirsty."

"Come on. I'll get you some water."

Susan brushed herself off and looked at Eugene's sculptures. "All this stuff made of trash. But it's so clean. How do you keep it all so clean?"

"It's my art. It's what I do. Come on. Kitchen's this way. How'd you get here from Ohio?"

The house was warm and dry. "It's pretty easy to get anywhere you want to in this country. All you have to do is find a truck stop, find some trucker who's flying on ampheta-mines, hop in the cab, drive a while, and then start foaming about religion—that way they dump you off at the next truck stop and you don't even have to put out."

"I remember seeing you on that stage, you know."

"You *do*?" Susan was thrilled.

"Hell, yes. The night you won, you would have even if your mother hadn't done her little blackmail routine."

Susan didn't want to dwell on Marilyn. "I'm thirsty, Eugene."

Eugene gave her some water. The kitchen ceiling's lights wore milk carton shades, beacons of missing children, and cast a yellow light on the sink. She checked the expiry date on one of them. "April 4, 1991. That's when you started to become Picasso?"

"Sunshine, you're crazy as a fucking loon. And your voice. Your manner. You probably don't even know it, but you've become your mother. I only met her for maybe five minutes, but baby, you're *her*."

Susan closed her eyes. She had a small puff of recognition. "Oh God—you know what, Eugene? You're right. I actually do feel like her right now, the way she moves. Funny—this has never happened to me before. It took me a plane crash to bring out my inner Marilyn. All it took *her* was fifteen years being the youngest daughter in a hillbilly shack full of alcoholics." She put down her glass. "Now where am I going to go sleep?" They could hear a garbage truck outside, bleeping and throbbing.

Eugene was curious but exhausted. They inched back into the dining room. "My brain feels like Spam. Are you sure you're okay?"

"Yeah."

Eugene became officious. "How'd you manage to survive that crash?"

Susan took a sip. She was beginning to feel level. The sense of having taken flight was gone. "You know, I've been thinking about that for seven days solid. I drew ticket number 58-A and won. I don't think there's anything more cosmic to it than that. There just isn't. I wish I could say there was, Eugene."

"But where were you this past week?"

Susan yawned and smiled. "Save it for the morning. I've been up thirty-six hours."

Eugene was too tired to probe further. "There's still a guest-room with furniture in it. Probably a bit dusty, but it ought to be fine." Eugene led her there. Susan, meanwhile, was inwardly glowing: Eugene was single, retired and, like her, didn't have too much interest in the outer world. Once in the room, she lay her aviator glasses down on the bedside table and sat on the bed.

"You know, if it hadn't been for Mom pulling that stunt with you, then I never would have stolen your 8-x-10 and fallen in love with you."

"Love!" Eugene seemed amused but then yawned. He said to Susan, "I phone in my grocery order tomorrow afternoon. Think of what you want to eat over the next week."

"Why not go out and just buy them?"

"I don't like leaving the house."

Susan hadn't heard such good news in years. It was all she could do to contain her sense of sleeping on Christmas Eve. "Good night, Eugene. Thanks."

"Night, sunshine."

Eugene sighed and walked down the hall. He loudly thumped the top of a totem. "And the winner is . . ." he said, "Miss *Wyoming*. What a fucking *ride*."

At noon the next day Susan awoke to the sound of an electrical rhythmic thunking sound coming from the basement. *Eugene's house.* She rolled over and faintly purred.

A minivan drove by outside. The rumbling beneath her, precise and gentle, continued. She found an old housecoat on the guestroom door peg and walked down to a paneled oak door beneath the main staircase. Blazing green-white chinks of light escaped from around the door's edge, as though the door were shielding her from invading aliens. She opened it and discovered the basement. Eugene was dressed in slacks, socks and a polo shirt, orchestrating the Xerox 5380 console copier's collation of hundreds of mail-outs. There were shelves of blank paper, file folders and CD-ROM's containing thousands of U.S. and Canadian names and addresses Susan would soon learn were culled by a demographics research firm in Mechanicsville, Virginia, accompanied by information on incomes and spending patterns.

Eugene glanced up at Susan on the stairs. "Good morning, sunshine. Dressed for casual Friday, I see."

On the walls surrounding Eugene's work area were dozens of wood and velvet plaques of clouds and sun and snow and temperatures ranging from −30 up to 120. She walked down the steps and picked up a velvet sun. "Whoo-ee! I'm all sunny today." She noted Eugene's flash of disapproval and placed the sun back in its correct orbit.

"Thank you," said Eugene, who continued with his clerical chores. Susan came up close to get a better peek at his documents, backing into Eugene.

He turned around. "Can you work a copier?"

"Back on the set of Meet the Blooms, whenever the writers got pissy and superior, I used to bring script production to a halt. You know how I did it? I wrote OUT OF ORDER on a sheet of scrap paper and taped it onto the copier's lid. All these people with IQs higher than Palm Springs temperatures, and not once did they consider challenging my paper signs." She picked up a wooden plaque numbered 110°. "Did you ever use this one much?"

"Near the end. A few times. Once the weather got wrecked."

"I guess you'd know." She sat down on a stacking chair and watched Eugene. "When the show was canceled, Glenn, the head writer, loaded a commissary drinking straw with Nutra-Sweet. Back on the set, he opened the copier's top and blew the NutraSweet into the machine, onto the drum. Killed the machine dead. They had to throw it out. It's like the worst thing on earth for copiers."

"This house is a Nuclear Weapons Free Zone. We'll be having none of your white-collar sabotage during your stay here." But he couldn't hold back a smile.

The copier created a relaxing rhythm. Susan's eyes glazed and her thoughts wandered. "Did your TV station can you because you were nuts?"

Eugene, sorting papers, spoke: "Nah. They didn't can me. I was injured on the job. I took early retirement."

"You were injured doing the nightly weather?"

"As it happened, yes. You want to know what happened? I was crushed by a Coke machine."

"On the job?"

"In the studio, so it was insured and unionized up the ying-yang. They installed a talking Coke machine which weighed, like, a ton more than a normal mute Coke machine. So this ugly little twerp with hockey hair shakes the machine back and forth, getting a rhythm going, until a can or two pops out, and the thing toppled down on top of him and it crushed him like a piñata. I happened to be passing by and my right foot got smashed. Look . . ."

Eugene removed his sock, and Susan bent down to look at Eugene's right foot, which, with its scars and stitches, resembled a map of Indiana divided into small, countylike chunks. "Ouch City, Arizona," said Susan.

"You said it, baby. The kid was a goner, and I didn't walk for maybe seven months afterward. In the meantime they brought in a new guy with a fresher, perkier smile than me, who also focus-grouped like a royal wedding. I didn't have it in me to flog my butt around to the other stations. Too old. And if you're old in the weather biz, you either turn into a wacky eunuch real quick, or take a hike. So I hiked."

"Let me see your foot more closely." She sat down. "Put it in my lap."

Eugene turned off the copier, and silence, like solidified Lucite, filled the air. He sat on a chair opposite Susan and hoisted his leg up and dropped it into Susan's lap.

Susan said, "Mom trained me *never* to say a word or a sentence without imagining that a pageant judge is out there secretly listening in. So my whole life I've been followed by this invisible flotilla of soap opera actresses, Chevy dealers, costume designers and TV weathermen who scan my every word. It's a habit I can't shake. It's like those people whose parents made them chew food twenty times before swallowing, and so the rest of their life becomes a hell of twenties." She looked Eugene in the eyes: "Does it hurt when I do *that*?" The atmosphere for Susan took on the it's-not-really-happening aura of life's better sex.

"No. Some of it I can't feel at all. And some of it feels like regular touching and . . ."

Susan looked him in the eye and applied more pressure but was also more thoughtful, kneading both the bottom leathery pads and tender spots between the toes.

"I saw you that night—at the pageant. You winked. Your wink almost bruised me," Susan confessed. Her hands locked onto his ankles. She stared him down: "I've been through a lot this week. I need a shower, Eugene."

He led her up out of the basement. They reached the bathroom. Susan turned on the water, clean and hot, and in an instant they were naked and wet and all over each other like scrapping dogs. Susan felt her skin shouting with relief, as though it had been long smothered, and her insides felt like she was riding in a fast elevator. They slammed into each other, releasing unknown volumes of anger and lust and loneliness until finally the water went cold and they left the tub. Eugene opened a cupboard which contained, to Susan's surprise, fresh towels.

A few minutes later, Susan was looking into Renata's old closet for something to wear. "I'm going to borrow one of these Bob Mackie gowns here. I see she left her stuff behind." There were hundreds of dresses and outfits hanging from a dry cleaner's mechanized conveyor belt. The outfits did a dainty little jig as Susan turned the system on and off. "Boy, if Mom could see this."

"Christ, turn that thing off. The noise is like the theme song to a show I don't watch anymore."

"She can't have been that bad."

"You used to be married, too."

"Still am, technically. We never divorced."

"Rock star guy. Rough stuff, I imagine."

"Chris? Rough, yes, but stuff, no. He's gay as a goose. I married him so he could get a green card and so I could remain close to his Catholic and very married manager Larry Mortimer." She stopped playing with the clothing rack.

Eugene was dialing on the cordless, ordering groceries. "Oh God."

"What?"

"You're real," he said.

"As opposed to . . . ?"

He lay back on the bed and stared at the ceiling fan. "I've got a good thing going here. My time is all my own. I don't have to deal with . . ."

"With what?"

"With *people*," Eugene spat out.

Susan looked at him. "I agree. You *do* have a good deal going here."

Now they were both looking at the ceiling and holding hands. Eugene asked her, "What did the focus groups say about you?"

"What do you mean?"

"You know. The focus groups. The ones they brought in to pick you apart so the network could figure out what makes you *you*."

Susan was intrigued. "Why?"

"I'll tell you what they said about me. Then you tell me what they said about you."

"Okay, deal."

"Women said, 'What's with his hair? Is it real? Is that his real color?' They said, 'Ooh, me so horny, me want humpy astronaut.' They said, 'I'd go metric for you, baby.' Guys weren't as descriptive. They just called me nothing, but once they saw my face, they knew the sports segment was over and could switch off the set." He lit a cigarette then lay back and chuckled. "TV. Ugh."

Susan spooned into him. The sheets felt like cool pastry marble.

She said, "Near the end they knew they had enough episodes to syndicate, so they stopped focus-grouping. But at the start I got stuff like 'I can see the zits underneath her makeup. Can't you guys find her a putty knife? That's one helluva thick paper bag she's trying to act her way out of. Her tits are like fried eggs gone all runny.' That kind of stuff." Their eyes caught and they both laughed.

"I've gotta phone in this grocery order." Eugene punched a phone number into the cordless, and the touch-tone beeps reminded Susan of a song she used to like back in the eighties.

Chapter Eighteen

Susan had performed in shopping strips many times, and her afternoon stint at the Clackamas County Mall was by no means unusual. In fact, as opposed to pageant judges, she found the overwhelmingly geriatric mall crowds emotionally invisible, and performing before them neither chancy nor stressful, her only stings arising from the occasional heckling teen or a stray leering pensioner. Once in Olympia, Washington, mall security had removed an old lech who'd been wanking listlessly down by the left speaker bank, like a zoo gorilla resigned to a sterile caged fate. Susan thought it was funny, but hadn't quite understood what it was he'd actually been *doing*. She'd told both her mother and the mall cops she thought he'd been "shaking a donut," which made the cops snort and Marilyn screech. When the cops briefly left the office, Susan had said, "Mom, please don't go filing another lawsuit. Not over this. Just let it go."

"Young lady, who knows what harm that man did to you."

"What harm?"

"It'll be years before you even know, sweetie."

"Mom—no lawsuit. I'm sick of your suing people all the time. It's my birthday. Make it my present, okay?"

Marilyn's face froze but then immediately thawed. "I'll just keep on shucking bunnies to help pay the rent. I suppose *some*body has to work in this world."

At the Clackamas Mall it had been arranged for Susan to perform a *Grease* medley, her routine that somehow dovetailed with the mall's Campaign for Drug-Free Kids. Susan's friend Trish had just turned sixteen, and drove Susan up to the mall from McMinnville. Marilyn was to follow shortly, after stopping to meet with a seamstress in Beaverton to go over Susan's autumn look.

Susan and Trish parked, hooked up with their mall contact, and then crammed themselves into the Orange Julius bathroom where Susan's poodle skirt remained untouched within its paper Nordstrom's bag. From a gym bag, she and Trish removed black jumpsuits and thin red leather ties. Both combed their hair into spikes and applied gel and heavy mascara, then headed backstage. Susan's name was called, and the two climbed up onto the carpeted plywood risers. They walked like robotic mimes, Trish to her Casio keyboard, Susan to center stage. To the bored and distracted mall audience they might just as well have been dressed as Valkyries or elm trees, but Susan felt for the first time a surge of power.

Trish hit the opening notes, at which point Susan lifted a riding crop she'd borrowed from one of Don's army buddies. She began to crack the whip in time with the rhythmic nonsense of "Whip It," a by-then-stale new wave anthem. For the first time, Susan didn't feel like a circus seal onstage. Trish kept the synthesizer loud, and Susan could feel all other times she'd been onstage drop away—those years she'd been trussed and gussied up, barking for fish in front of Marilyn and every pageant judge on earth, joylessly enacting her moves like a stewardess demonstrating the use of an oxygen mask.

But now—the faces—Susan was seeing genuine reactions: mouths dropped wide open, mothers whisking away children— and at the back, the cool kids who normally mooned her and pelted her with Jelly Tots, watching without malice.

Suddenly the speaker squawked and moaned, and Susan turned around to see Marilyn ripping color-coded jacks from the backs of the Marshall amps while a mall technician lamely protested the ravaging. Heads in the audience shifted as if they were a field of wheat, in the direction where Susan now turned, glaring like a raven.

"What the hell are you doing, Mom?"

Marilyn plucked out more jacks, and her face muscles tensed like a dishrag in the process of being squeezed.

Susan cracked the riding crop at Marilyn, where it burned Marilyn's hands, a crimson plastic index fingernail jumping away like a cricket. "Mom, stop it! Stop!"

Marilyn grabbed the crop's end and yanked it away from Susan. She looked to be rabid and scrambled up over the 2-x-6 trusses and onto the stage. Susan turned to her audience. She was raging. "Ladies and gentlemen, let's have a big hand for"— she paused as Marilyn raised herself awkwardly, like a horse from thick mud—"my overenthusiastic mother."

The audience smelled blood and clapped with gusto as Marilyn cuffed Susan on the neck. Three hooligans over by the Sock Shoppe shouted meows, at which point Susan went momentarily deaf from Marilyn's blow. Time stopped for her. She was lifted up and out of herself, and she felt aware for the first time that her mother didn't own her the way she owned the Corvair or the fridge. In fact, Susan realized Marilyn had no more ownership of her than she did of the Space Needle or Mount Hood. Marilyn's connection was sentimental if Susan chose it to be that way, or business, which made some sense, but no longer was Marilyn able to treat Susan like a slammed car door every time she lost control.

Marilyn looked in Susan's eyes, realized she'd blown it and would never regain her advantage. This sent her into a larger swivet, but its ferocity now didn't faze Susan. She now knew the deal.

Marilyn lunged at her daughter, enraged, but Susan looked back at her and with a gentle smile said, "Sorry, Mom, you're thirty seconds too late. You're not going to get me—not this time."

Marilyn's arms went around Susan's chest, half as if to strangle her, half for support. The clapping stopped and Trish ran over. "Mrs. Colgate, *please*."

"You backstabbing little whore," she shouted at Trish.

"Mom!"

"She doesn't mean it," Trish said, trying to wedge Marilyn and Susan apart. "We've got to get her off the stage."

Mall security arrived. Susan and Trish stood locked in place as two beefy men used all their might to keep Marilyn away from Susan.

"Come with us, ma'am."

"No."

Susan said pragmatically, "Guys, let's get her into an office or something. She's jagging on diet pills. She needs a cool dark place."

"*Traitor*," Marilyn hissed.

Susan grabbed her mother's handbag. She and Trish followed Marilyn into an office, where Susan made her mother swallow some downers. She phoned Don to tell him they'd be late. Trish left at Susan's asking, and Susan drove her mother home to McMinnville. Dinner was take-out Chinese, and they all went to bed early.

The next day was sunny and unseasonably hot for April, and Susan sat on the back lawn, suntanning her face between the two inner faces of a Bee Gees double album covered in aluminum foil. Marilyn beetled about between the car and the yard, planting multiple flats of petunias, daisies and white alyssum. This struck Susan as odd, but not unusual. The previous year, Don's workers' comp kicked in and the family had upgraded from a trailer to a house, albeit a small, weed-cloaked and rain-rotted house. But living in a genuine house seemed to satisfy Marilyn, who didn't give much thought to interior design, exclaiming only how thrilled she was not to have to disguise axles with rhododendron shrubs.

Susan continued sunning herself, and in midafternoon she came in for iced tea and found Marilyn holding Don's hunting knife, a big honker from one of Karlsruhe's most sadistic factories. She was using it to carve notches into the wood of the door frame between the kitchen and the TV room—dozens of slits at various intervals ranging from thigh height up to her shoulders.

Susan said nothing.

Marilyn took a Bic pen and a pencil and began writing names and dates beside the slits "Brian 12/16/78, Caitlin 5/3/79, Allison 7/14/80," and so forth.

Don came in from the front hallway, his hands black with SeaDoo crankcase oil. "Mare," he said, "whatthefuck are you doing to the door frame?"

"Raising the price of the house, honey."

Don and Susan exchanged looks.

"Don't think I can't see the two of you exchanging concerned looks." Before her the mythical young Brian had broken the five-foot mark.

Don reached for his hunting knife, saying, "Gimme that."

But Marilyn flinched away, then swiveled around like a Shark versus a Jet. "Like fuck I will." Susan and Don were stunned. "We're leaving this little sugar shack, kids, but before we do, I have to raise its value." She continued carving slits. "Studies have shown that the price of any home can be raised by a consistent ten percent or more by simply planting about a hundred dollars' worth of annual flowers." Allison reached four feet eight. "Flowers make a home feel lived in. Loved. So do growth charts. Growth charts indicate happiness, pride, devotion and stick-to-itiveness. Adds 5K to the asking price."

"And where might we be moving?" asked Don.

"Wyoming, you cretin. Cheyenne, Wyoming."

"Oh, Mom—not *that* again."

"Yes, *that*, again. Houses are cheaper there. We'll have a guest bedroom and three bathrooms. And *you*, sweetie, can represent an entire *state* in the nationals. Only a handful of people live there. The competition's nil. *Fifty-one gorgeous contestants and only one will win. Who will replace Susan Colgate as the next Miss USA?*"

"We're not moving nowhere," Don said.

"We're not moving *anywhere*, honey, and yes we *are*. This house is in my name, so off we go."

"She's loony today," Don said to Susan. "Leave her be."

Susan went back to her tanning, and assumed the mania would pass. Later on, up in her room, she heard the normal clinks and clatters of dinner preparation below. Marilyn called Susan and Don to the table, and the tone of the night seemed altogether normal. Too normal. At that point, their ears roared and the house shook like a car driving over a speed bump. Susan's water glass tipped over and a framed photo fell from a wall. The three stood up—all was silent save for a faint hiss coming from the kitchen.

They walked through the newly scratched door frame to see a manhole-sized gape through the ceiling, and another one directly beneath it in the floor between the stove and the fridge. Don looked down: "Jesus H. Christ—it's a meteorite."

Susan and Marilyn peered down at the blue-brown boulder that lay on the cracked concrete beside the deep freeze containing

Don's venison from the previous fall. Don raced down the stairs, looked at the boulder and then looked up, speechless. The two women ran down to join him.

"It's a miracle," said Marilyn. "We've been spared. It's a sign from the Lord above that we are on the correct path, an omen to fill us with respect." She fell to her knees and prayed as she had once before when visiting her kin back in the mountains. Susan looked more closely at the boulder. "Hey—it's melting, or something."

"Holy shit," said Don, "it's shit."

It was a frozen ball of shit, accidentally discharged from the hull of an Philippine Airlines flight from Chicago to Manila, which paid for the new house in Cheyenne. Don called it "the shitsicle." The airline settled swiftly and quietly. Within six weeks they were living in Cheyenne.

Chapter Nineteen

The police finished scrutinizing the Susan Colgate shrine in the car's back seat and left the property. John spent the remainder of the day spacing out in front of the shrine and phoning Susan's answering machine, hanging up on the beep each time. He tried sleeping but instead had choppy naps, like pieced-together cutting room floor scraps punctuated with frequent eye openings and anxious pangs. In the late afternoon he gave up, took a shower, drank an algae shake, had a quick chat with Nylla, who was just returning from her exercise class, then drove the car down to West Side Video. Ryan was with a customer.

Do you know the name of the movie, sir?" Ryan was asking the customer.

"Oh, you know—*that movie.* I think it came in a blue box."

"Do you know who stars in it?"

"That guy. You know?"

"I'm not sure. Is it a comedy or a drama or—?"

"It's really good."

"Okay—any idea who directed it?"

"That famous guy."

"Right."

John moved in. "Hey, buddy—go take a pill, and when your brain clicks in, send us a memo."

The customer was chuffed. "Excuse *me*. I'm trying to choose a movie, Mr. Whoever You Are. Do you have a problem with that?"

John looked the customer in the eye: "You *care* what I think?"

"Well, um, *no*."

"Then why are you asking me? Scram. People who know what they want have to get on with their lives here."

The customer skulked away, visibly distressed.

"Oh *thank* you, John," said Ryan. "You've no *idea* how long I've been wanting to say something like that."

"The sad residue of too many days lost in meetings with professional time-wasters."

"If you *ever* decided to make a film titled *You Know—That Movie*, it'd be the most popular rental of all time."

John scanned the store, then said, "Ryan—get off work and come on. We've got business to do."

"Not now—it's the dinnertime rush, I have to phone in the overdues, and tonight is the 'Women Who Love Far Too Much' Special."

"Ivan and I want to buy your script."

Ten minutes later, in separate cars, they drove to the St. James Club bar. John arrived first, and ordered two scotches. Ryan arrived, breathless. "Before we discuss anything, John, I have to tell you that the police were in this afternoon and they were *totally* all over me about (a) my having built the Susan Colgate shrine, and (b) giving it to you. It was like I was strapped to an anthill and slathered in marmalade."

"She's gone missing. She didn't show up for some Showtime Channel movie she was doing. The cops harassed me, too. But I had to explain to them what I was doing sitting parked outside her house for an hour in the middle of the night with a Susan Colgate shrine in the back seat."

"Oh God—you're a freak!" Ryan laughed.

John didn't laugh.

"Aren't people supposed to be gone for at least forty-eight hours before they become a missing person?"

"I don't know." John put his head in his hands. "Drink."

Ryan drank.

"Nylla—that's Ivan's wife—before I came down here tonight, we were chatting about this and that, and she told me that after the crash Susan was gone for a whole year before she came back. I didn't know it was for that long! I didn't. And it turns out nobody has any idea where she went. Not even the cops."

"But you knew she was in a crash . . ."

"I was in and out of Betty Ford so much in '96 I don't even know who was president, you little smartass."

Ryan was slightly unsure of his footing with this powerful movie producer intent on buying his script, and didn't push the matter, but John went on. "This is to say that if Susan Colgate, who's like the patron saint of missing persons, goes missing, even for one day, then Missing Persons ought to get right on the case, right?"

Ryan asked, "When you two met, she knew who you were? How much did you guys talk? How did you leave it? What was she wearing?"

"We went walking. Must have been three miles. It was damn hot out, too. She didn't break a sweat once. It was like in high school, like we were off to get milkshakes with Jughead and Veronica." Some cashews appeared on the table. "Ryan, do you know that before I made my decision to put myself out of commission I'd been really sick?"

"No."

"I was. I technically kicked the bucket over at Cedars—that's what the doctors said. And you know what I saw when I flat-lined?"

"What?"

"Susan."

"What can I say to that?"

"You tell me."

"John—come to the light!"

"Alright, so it was a *Meet the Blooms* rerun that was on the hospital TV a few minutes before I bottomed, but it took me months before I figured that out. But it was still *her*. You know what I mean? And I'd just gotten used to the idea that seeing her face and voice was meaningless, and then *today* happens—and now I don't think it's so meaningless anymore."

A waiter came by. Ryan's drink was empty. He ordered another. "A Singapore sling, please." He didn't know what to say to John.

"A Singapore *sling*?" said John. "Where are we? In a Bob Hope movie? I feel like I'm having drinks with my mother."

"It's a jaunty ironic retro beverage."

"You little twerp. I pioneered irony and retro back when you were shitting your Huggies." John looked at the waiter: "A rusty nail, please."

Ryan was fidgeting. John said, "Well, I suppose you probably want to discuss your script. We'll buy it. Don't get an aneurysm or anything." Ryan looked relieved but nervous. John said, "You don't have an agent, Ryan, do you?"

Ryan's face was flushed. "Nope."

"Good for you. You just saved yourself forty-five grand."

Ryan's flush drained away. His face stopped.

"Oh, this is good," said John. "I can see the little cartoon cogs and wheels in your head trying to do the arithmetic to figure out the offer. I'll put you out of your misery. Three hundred grand."

"You're messing with me."

"You have a shitty poker face, Ryan."

Ryan's drink arrived, but he pushed it away. "I want to remember this clearly."

"You've got a stronger constitution than I ever had." He held his glass up. "A toast." They clinked glasses, sipped and then John said, "Ivan doesn't trust something unless it's way overpriced. If I told him I'd gotten 'Tungaska' for five grand, it would have ended right there. I pulled the number 300 out of the air. I could have made it more."

Ryan sat, immobilized.

"Hey, c'mon, Ryan," John said. "Sing—dance—do a little jig or something. Make me feel like an aging benevolent fart."

"No. John. You don't understand. You've just changed my life as if you'd given me wings or blinded my eyes. I feel dizzy."

"Believe me, this isn't the way it usually happens. Normally, Ivan and I would be trying to engineer some way of fucking you ragged on the deal. But I'm feeling mentorish. I'll hook you up with a lawyer. Sign the paper and you're set."

A cocktail of money, shared secrets and ironic beverages made Ryan bold. "John—what was the deal with last year? I know about as much as anybody does who reads the tabloids. What happened? What was it you were wanting to do back then?"

John looked at Ryan kindly but sternly. "Not now. Not tonight. Tonight is about success."

They soon split up, but some hours later, after zooming through Susan's tapes, John phoned to ask Ryan if he could take him up on his corny offer to indulge his feelings for Susan. It was past one in the morning, and Ryan was polishing "Tungaska" and didn't want an interruption, but John persevered. And then Ryan revealed he had to go out on an errand and would be busy.

"Okay, Ryan, you can just tell me your offer to riff about Susan was a courtesy, like telling some loser actor to come play squash sometime to get rid of him."

"John, I've got to go help my girlfriend with something."

"Girlfriend?"

"What's that tone in your voice?"

"Me? Nothing. All I said was 'Girlfriend?' "

"You think I'm gay."

"Did I say that?"

"It was in your voice."

"Well, you are, aren't you?"

"No."

"I don't believe you."

"God, let me make a phone call. Hang up, eat a Scooby Snack and I'll call you in five minutes."

John hung up. Three minutes later the phone rang. "Vanessa says you can come help us."

"Help with *what*?"

"You'll see." He gave John Vanessa's address in Santa Monica. They agreed to meet in one hour, but John was early.

Vanessa opened the screen door, calm and bookish in horn-rimmed glasses and a wool sweater set imported from some other part of the century. John thought Vanessa looked like one of the murdered Clutter daughters of Kansas. She asked him to sit on a side chair. "Would you like something to drink, maybe?"

"Uh—a Coke."

"Sure."

She went into the kitchen. John heard the fridge open and close, along with other friendly kitchen sounds. Vanessa looked smart in a way John knew she was helpless to conceal. She had the laser-scanning eyes of the highest-paid personal assistants, the ones who single-handedly made Neanderthal teensploitation film producers seem classy and hip by scripting the brief, urbane speeches they gave while donating comically large checks to well-researched and cutting-edge charities.

Vanessa was quite obviously some freak of nature marooned on the shores of the bell curve's right-most limits. "What do you do for a living, Vanessa?" John asked, stretching out his neck as if it would help lob his words around a bend in the wall.

"I work at the Rand Corporation."

This didn't surprise John. "No shit. Doing what?"

"Think-tanking."

"You sit around in beanbag chairs all day and think up military invasion strategies and ways to suppress the development of electric cars?"

She pretended not to have heard that and came in and handed him his Coke. He took a sip and paused. "Hey—this is really delicious!" The sweetness delighted him, and he chugged down half the glass. "Wow. I'd forgotten how good a simple Coke could be."

"It's not the Coke, it's me. I added sugar to it. Two teaspoons."

John hacked. "You added sugar to Coke? That's revolting."

"Don't be stupid." She sat down on an IKEA couch–sofa bed then in the couch mode. "Everybody bitched and moaned when Coca-Cola went and changed their formula in the eighties. If you want 1950s–style Coke, add some bloody sugar to it. Besides, John, you seemed to like it."

They sipped in silence for a minute, and then Vanessa said to John, "Ryan says you think he's gay."

"Well?" Obviously she didn't.

"He's my boyfriend, John." She took a sip of her drink. "Mine's a Diet Coke, but I mixed sugar in with it. It has a really perverse taste." John stared her down. "I love Ryan, and he loves me."

"I love my friend Ivan, but I don't date him."

"Oh, shut up. Eros. Agape. Sex. Friendship. All of that. I'm not dense."

"You mean there's some eros in there?"

Vanessa's eyes glinted, but she said nothing. "Well, it's not like Tarzan and Jane, but it's real. He's genuine about *me*."

John bit an ice cube. "You're obviously the Nurse Crandall type. You know, Nurse Crandall lets down her hair and Dr. Hunnicutt says, 'Nurse Crandall, good God but you're gorgeous. I had no idea.' "

"That would be me." She looked out the window. "Ryan's car's here. We didn't have this chat, okay?"

Ryan walked in and the trio was off to Long Beach. Ryan leaned in between the driver's seat and the front passenger seat and said to John, "If you want to talk about Susan with Vanessa, go right ahead. She's totally cool."

"Thank God," said John, embarrassed.

"Susan Colgate was an idol for me, John," said Vanessa. "You know, the role she used to play on TV—the smart daughter finding meanings and patterns in this nutty world. It's like my own family."

John said, "I know what you mean. I have this feeling like she's got my keys. You know, like she knows my combination even though I can't get it right."

"That's what Vanessa does for a living," Ryan said. "At Rand. She finds meanings and patterns. Combinations."

"What's your specialty?" asked John.

"Like Ryan said, I'm a finder."

"A finder?"

"Just what it sounds like. Ever since I was a kid, if something got lost, people came to me to find it for them. I'm able to *locate* things. I ask questions. I look at data. I make connections. And then I find what's lost."

"Bullshit."

"My my, a naysayer—how quaint." Vanessa took on the charged aura of an ATM about to feed forth large quantities of cash.

"Give him an example," said Ryan.

"Fair enough. Let's talk about *you*, John Lodge Johnson, born November 5, 1962, Miraflores Locks, Panama Canal Zone. You have one undescended testicle and you smoked Kent cigarettes heavily between the years 1983 and 1996. You've been questioned but never charged in a dozen assorted narcotics investigations since 1988. You're right-handed, but you use your left hand for throwing baseballs and masturbating. As of two years ago, you owed the IRS just over 11.3 million dollars, which was repaid eight months ago after a complete liquidation of your assets, as well as a cleansing of your bank accounts, two of which, in Davos, Switzerland, you didn't think the IRS knew about, but they did, and you're lucky you revealed their existence or they would taken a fork and dug out your undescended testicle and eaten it for lunch. You blood type is O, and your IQ is 128. You've been prescribed over thirty different psychoactive pharmaceuticals in the past decade, invariably obtained with overlapping prescriptions throughout Los Angeles, Ventura and San Bernardino counties. You're heterosexual but have done three-ways with guys a few times, only at the request of the present female. Months ago, before your much publicized vanishing, you attempted to transfer all of your copyrights and future royalties to the Ronald McDonald House, but thanks to your friend Ivan, the courts rejected the transfer and instead set up a trust, which will soon be convening to evaluate your mental fitness, restoring to you a whack of dough you had seriously thought was gone forever. I'd send Ivan a fruit basket, John Lodge Johnson."

John was mute.

"Isn't she great?" said Ryan.

"You want more?" Vanessa said. "Almost ninety-five percent of your phone calls go to either New York or California. Your monthly consumption of phone sex averaged ninety-five hundred dollars across the years dating from 1991 up to your vanishing. If you've made a sex call since, I have yet to know about it. Your single most frequently dialed number is that of celebrity madam Melody Lanier of Beverly Hills, who, I bet you didn't know, has recurring bouts of malaria and who also lost her left baby toe in a Vespa crash in Darwin, Australia, in 1984. Nobody avoids the scrutiny of I, Vanessa Humboldt. There. *Ta-da!*"

"Melody is not my madam. And *you're* a monster."

"Don't be so thick. It's all out there. You just have to know where to look."

"She's good, eh?" said Ryan. "She could find you an abortionist in Vatican City."

"If it makes you feel any better, I'm not creative. I leave that to my boy genius here." She patted Ryan's knee.

Quickly the car off-ramped, and Vanessa pulled into the front of a sterile blue mirrored-glass cube, a large laboratory building surrounded by a dense putting-green lawn. "We're here," she announced. "This is the office where a certain weasel named Gary Voors cheated me out of a few grand in freelance research commissions."

"She got hosed," said Ryan.

"Fifteen grand. But I did some research on him and this company and it's doubtful I'll ever get my dough. My mistake. I should have checked their financial patterns beforehand. Come on, now—out of the car."

Standing in the parking lot, Ryan asked Vanessa which window was by the staff lunchroom. She pointed out one nearby.

She then went to the trunk of the car and removed a 4-gallon red plastic gas can. John skittishly approached Vanessa, who said, "Put out your hand." John balked. "Oh, be a *man* about this, John." He held out his hand and she poured a fine, granular substance onto it.

Vanessa said, "These tiny, almost invisible little bowling balls are clover seeds. And now we are going to use them to have fun with spelling."

She began pouring the seeds out in a large flowing script, onto the putting green grass. John understood that she was writing something. "What are you writing?"

"She's writing out the words 'Gary's banging Tina,' " said Ryan.

"Who's Tina?"

"The CEO's wife. They leave a sloppy trail behind them, too. And I wouldn't have dragged Tina into this except that she's the one who made sure that Gary got the credit for my ideas."

"Clover seeds quickly penetrate the turf," said Ryan. "And once they seed, their roots are like tentacles—the shoots show up a deep, dark green in about ten days."

"Just a few days before Gary returns from Bermuda. What a coincidence," said Vanessa. She finished her large, graceful lasso-ing of letters.

"The only way to get rid of the words is to remove the turf," said Ryan. "Smart, eh?"

"Done." She headed back to the car.

"That's it?"

"Chop-chop. Let's get a move on."

A minute later they were on the freeway again. Vanessa was still driving. John was getting the jitters. He was having dark thoughts about what could have happened to Susan. Though his movies were violent and their characters often sick, John had never thought of them as being *real*. For the first time in his life he began visualizing the violence of his films entering his life and it made him feel queasy, and now he knew a bit of what the people who sent him letters chiding him for gore might be feeling.

Ryan said, "Vanessa and I are going to help you find Susan."

"Leave it to the cops," said Vanessa, "and she'll be luncheon meat before anybody finds her. Let me put out a dragnet tonight. Come over to my place tomorrow afternoon at five. I'll give you the results and throw in dinner." She paused. "Are you okay, John?"

"Why?"

"You look like you've seen a ghost."

"I'm fine. Vanessa," he said, "I have a question for you."

"Uh-huh?"

"Why are you helping me? I mean, you don't know me— you don't—"

"Oh, stop right there. My angle is Ryan. You helped him, and so I'm helping you."

"And?" asked John.

"And that's all. Please, why don't you tell me the real reason you're so obsessed with finding Susan Colgate, huh? For all I know, she could be wearing a Girl Guide costume and decomposing underneath your front porch—and maybe all of this search stuff we're doing is a ruse designed to deflect attention away from you."

John was dismissive: "Not the case."

"Okay then, why look for Susan Colgate, John?"

"It's because . . ."

"Yes?"

John squeezed and squeezed his brain with his fingers like a hard-to-open bottle of olives. "It's because she knows that people were meant to change. She knows it's inevitable. And she seems to recognize I'm at a point in my life where I can't transform anymore. I sound like a country-western song. Sorry."

"Well, to me it looks like you're stalking her. It could seem kind of creepy to her."

"I'm not stalking her, Vanessa. I'm trying to find her. Nobody's taking this disappearance seriously, except us."

"Hey, what's in this for Susan?" Ryan asked. "Assuming we rescue her from being tied up on top of the railway tracks."

John glared at him.

"Sorry."

But Ryan's question got John to thinking. What *did* he bring to Susan's table? Was he just another fucked-up Hollywood guy for her to take care of? No, because—because what? John reached down deep into the hole of his mind, trying to grasp onto a nugget of reason. He thought of the desperately lonely woman reading the *Architectural Digest*, and he thought of the woman he'd met outside the Pottery Barn who'd fed him dinner, the secret nation of Eleanor Rigbys who existed just under the threshold of perception. That this secret nation existed was new to him. That he might help fix it was even newer. "We have a lot in common," he blurted out.

"Huh?" Both Ryan and Vanessa had each gone on to new thoughts.

"Haven't you noticed that the couples who stick together the longest in life are the ones who shared some intense, freaky experience together? Jobs—school—a circle of friends?"

"Yeah?"

"Well, Susan and I did that, too."

"But you have no idea where Susan went after the crash, John. I mean, you're talking about disappearance, right?"

"Ryan, that's what we learned about each other during our walk—that we both went to the same place. At the moment I don't know her specifics, but that'll happen once I find her."

They fell silent. Vanessa was frozen at the wheel, as if driving through a snowstorm. They were in one of thousands of cars on a ten-lane freeway jammed with cars, even in the darkest part of the night, rivers of cars headed God knows where. Nobody spoke.

John slept all of the next day. That night, over a simple pasta primavera, Vanessa emptied out her net for John and Ryan to see her bounty. "Susan Amelia Colgate was born on March 4, 1970, in Corvallis, Oregon. Her mother, Marilyn, was married to a Duran Deschennes, but never actually got divorced."

"She's a polyandrist," said Ryan.

"A *what?*" asked John.

"It's the opposite of bigamy. When a woman has two or more husbands at once."

"This Duran Deschennes guy got killed in 1983 and the mother married Donald Alexander Colgate in 1977, so for seven years she was a polyandrist. But my hunch is that Don Colgate has no idea he was hubby number two. I bet we three, along with Marilyn herself, are the only people in on her secret."

Vanessa continued. "Susan grew up in McMinnville, Oregon—in a trailer, at that. She was a frequent entrant, finalist and winner in literally hundreds of beauty pageants during her youth. Her biggest win was the 1985 Miss USA Teen pageant in Denver, but she surrendered her crown there onstage, to LuAnn Ramsay, now wife of Arizona's governor, I might add."

"This stuff I already know," said John. "Internet. Library. Magazines. Tell me something new."

"In 1997 she was presumed dead in the Seneca plane crash, but she wasn't, and to this day nobody knows where she spent almost exactly one calendar year. Even I couldn't find anything there."

"Such modesty."

"Well, I did find *something*."

"*What?*" John pounced.

"It may be nothing, but when I was patterning her phone data—"

"What phone data?"

"Oh, grow up. The era of privacy is over. As I was saying, I was patterning her phone data and found an anomaly. Her most-dialed phone number is to a guy named Randy Hexum. He lives out in the Valley. So I did a scan on him, and it turns out he's from Erie, Pennsylvania. His real name's Randy Montarelli and he lived thirty miles away from the police station where Susan turned herself in and claimed amnesia."

"And?"

"They both arrived back in L.A. at the same time a year ago, and he went to work for Chris Thraice. Randy Montarelli-slash-Hexum also has almost no data attached to him since leaving Erie. It's damn hard to have a dead data file, but he's done it. It's bloody suspicious."

"He's in the Valley?"

"Yup."

John was up in a second, carrying the emptied plates into the kitchen, screwing the cap back on the Coke. He put it in the fridge. "Let's go."

Chapter Twenty

When John was young, back in New York, in the third grade on one of his few nonsick days, a math teacher named Mr. Bird, who also filled the roles of gym teacher and guidance counselor, took the entire shivering class out onto the playing field. He pointed out white chalk marks which outlined a large square. Onto each of these marks he made students stand in place, and once everybody was in their assigned location, he used a megaphone he'd brought to shout out the following words: "Class, look at the area in front of your eyes. This is called an acre. For the rest of your lives you're going to be hearing people talk about acres. Five acres. Three thousand acres. An acre and a half. Well, this is an acre. Look at it hard. Burn it into your memory because this is the one time in your life you're going to see a perfect, one-hundred-percent-pure acre."

John remembered that acre, cold and wet and trampled. Its size did truly stay in his mind, and as he crisscrossed the country on foot, he saw nothing but acres, on all horizons, all of them one hundred percent pure, one hundred percent empty and most of them ownerless. He was truly a Nobody now, the land was his. He felt like a king during his few good moments, but these decreased as he nose-dived deeper into the American landscape. The sex had ended. Most forms of communication had quieted. Women vanished from his life and he missed them with the dull hunger of homesickness. He caught only glimpses of them, sleek, well fed, possessing clear goals and usually behind a car window in the process of rolling it up. John knew that he'd become the cautionary story their mothers had warned them about. He longed for female company and the ability of women to forgive, to care about hurts, and their readiness to laugh and be amused. His mother, Melody, Nylla and even the Florida twins, whose names he'd forgotten.

Nearly all of the Nobodies he saw were men. Women, he thought, had so many more ways to connect themselves to the world—children, families, friends.

John was an expert at looking in people's eyes and knowing when they wanted something from him. Nobody gave him that look anymore. But he wasn't astute about looking in people's eyes and recognizing when they wanted to give him something. Sometimes he'd see a woman watching him as he walked from a Denny's rest room back to the counter, or in a grocery store, tending to squawking kids and errant grocery carts. What were they offering? A meal and a dose of love to get him to the next way station? Women became to him portals back into a better place he'd always seemed to have overlooked.

Five drunk farm kids in a pickup rolled him one evening at sunset because he was there and they felt like doing it. His UPS uniform was Rorschached with blood puddles and he had to throw it into a gas-station litter bin. He spent his accumulated recycling money, fifteen dollars, on a discounted yellow T-shirt that read MY OTHER SHIRT IS A PORSCHE and a Corona beer wind-breaker that came free with a six-pack, which he drank, metabolized and pissed away in the space of one thunderstorm.

One night in Winslow, Arizona, he met a friendly-enough guy, Kevin. They'd both been checking out the pickings around an Exxon station's groceteria. It was around sunset. One or two stars had risen in the sky. John had just found a pack of time-expired hot dogs when Kevin said, "I've got a place not far from here. We can go eat there." Kevin seemed friendly enough and John missed simple conversation. Truth be told, he hadn't had a profound thought in weeks.

Home was underneath a sun-rusted bridge that crossed a dry gully, decorated with high school graduation graffiti, so-and-so-was-here felt-pennings, sun-rotted condoms and a mattress so verminous that John consciously swept his way around it, as if he might catch athletically hopping crabs.

"Here. Get a fire going." He helped John light a twig fire beneath an inverted Chevelle hubcap filled with the lame trickle of water dripping down the gully's bottom-most rift. The water came to a boil and John put his time-expired hot dogs into it and the two watched them cook and said nothing. John figured so much for conversation.

They ate the hot dogs, shared only the most cursory of stories—mostly about planned trips, whether the other was headed east or west, or what the weather might do; neither offered up his past—and then the sky was dark. Kevin went to sleep on the mattress. John found a sandy nook high up in a corner underneath the bridge where it joined the road. He'd learned that there was little, if anything, for a Nobody to do past sundown. He fell asleep to the sound of the occasional vehicle passing overhead.

Somewhere in the night he felt a jolt of pain inside his dream, and he woke up to find Kevin walloping him with a broken-off metal rear flap from a shopping cart. Kevin was spewing out random invective: "Take my hot dogs away from me, will you? Steal a man's food right from under his nose, you're no better than Detroit automakers . . ."

Blood dripping from a gash in his cheekbone, John ran away, down the road, into flat landscape, nothing on either side, finally far enough away to feel safe. He scuttled off the road, into a patch of desert, found a rut, crept into it, heard small animals scurry away, and then once more slept.

The next day in Flagstaff he ate a discarded hamburger for lunch. The meat tasted strange, but he ignored it. Four hours later he was walking down a gravel road in what he thought was the direction of a meteorite crater he'd read about as a sick kid in Manhattan, when his gut collapsed as if he'd been judo-chopped, and he keeled over, into a dry ditch alongside the road. He began to shit and vomit as though all the cells in his body were screaming to empty themselves of toxins. In the haze of illness he removed his pants, knowing he had to keep them clean, and clumped his still clean clothes in a heap above him. He lay on the gritty soil and his body exploded. He could see the mountains and the mesas on the horizons, and billions of acres. John tried to imagine a bunch of children—all the kids in Arizona—standing around the edge of this landscape so savage and broken and freshly ripped from the kiln, and imagined as he clutched his stomach that children might one day play on this desert, this blank space; but he knew they never would, the land would always outsmart them, always be just one notch more cruel.

He asked the stars to give him some kind of word, but the stars gave nothing. Then he recalled being in the hospital a few months before—had it been so recently as December?—the night of his flu and the vision. He remembered seeing Susan Colgate on TV—before he conked out completely—and he suddenly realized that his vision of Susan's face was a rerun that had been playing on his bedside TV, and it meant nothing. His time on the road was a sham as well. His exercise in going solo was a cosmic joke. He was inside a hellish one-panel New Yorker cartoon captioned, *"Her face was just some TV actress your neurons glommed onto."* And here he was, near death again, except this time he just didn't care.

He fell unconscious, and when he woke up, he didn't know how much later, he saw the Milky Way and some shooting stars, and knew that the worst had passed, but his body felt like a chunk of salt licorice, as if all its moisture was gone. Then he heard an idling engine and a woman's voice. The woman was carrying a flashlight and she told him he was going to be okay, he could come with her. He forgot he was naked and crawled up the crumbling ditch. A man's voice said, "One wrong move, asshole, and I'll blow you into hamburger."

The woman said, "Eric, put that thing down and pass me the bag of groceries. Jeanie, get the blanket from behind my seat." Jeanie, a teenage girl, was videotaping John. "My name is Beth," the woman said. "Here . . ." She placed an Arapaho blanket around his shoulders and then opened a cardboard carton of orange juice. "Here, drink this up. You're dehydrated."

John guzzled the juice and collapsed on his knees. His teeth chattered. Beth retrieved his bundled clothing. He saw the man in a truck. "Eric, goddammit, help this guy out. Get out here." Eric put down the gun and reluctantly helped Beth lift John onto the truck bed. She spoke to John over the bed's rim. "What's your name, hon?"

He said, "John."

"John, you lie down and we'll have you home in a few minutes, okay?"

John said, "Okay," then lay back and watched the blinking red light of Jeanie's camcorder taping him. Then he tilted his head back and looked at the stars, and he began to cry because it had all been a waste and because the voice of Susan was only a sound buried under a laugh track he'd heard by accident in a stale white room.

Chapter Twenty-one

Even the most anal of the 4 A.M. bread-baking monks would be unable to compete with Eugene Lindsay's compulsion for getting his postal fraud mail-outs into the local postbox before morning pickup. Susan was drafted into this work pronto, and even when she was half a year pregnant, Eugene still had her lugging box loads of heavy documents and paper up and down the basement stairs. Susan could have cared less. For the first time in her life she felt as if there were no tightly coiled springs waiting to lurch out from beneath her skin. She felt as if she were on holiday. Added bonus: wild sex, up until the baby got too big.

"Yooj, I feel like a Cambodian peasant or something, freighting these—what *are* they?"—she looked down at the envelopes in the box she was holding—"mail-outs to the Greater Tampa, Florida, postal region. I could drop Junior into the rice paddy and be back on threshing duty the next afternoon."

Eugene attended his Xerox 5380 console copier like a surgeon with a patient, bathed in strobes of Frankenstein green light. "Hey, sunshine, God bless Florida. All those seniors with nothing but free time and too many radio stations. They hand in their mailing addresses like they were spare change. Now let's get them up to the front door. Mush!"

When winter came, the air in the house became drier, but the daily schedule went on unchanged. In December, when Susan had realized she was pregnant, Eugene forbid her to go near the microwave oven or to drink alcohol.

Spring and summer came and went. She liked her job. She opened the daily mail, which Eugene picked up at a post-office box a few streets over. Inside the envelopes came crumpled money, sent in by superstitious radio enthusiasts whose names Eugene purchased from an old college pal who'd become a tele-marketing whiz—*suckers*! Most often it consisted of two twenties and a ten, but sometimes Susan collected wads of ones and fives in dirty little clumps, likely scrounged from under the front seat of a teenager's car. What did these people want? What kind of cosmic roulette wheel did they hope to spin by responding to Eugene's fraudulent thrusts?

Susan's stomach felt as if it contained a great big ski boot that rolled around inside her. The Seneca plane crash seemed like a lifetime ago, her precrash life, a miraculous story of out-rageous behavior relayed to her the morning after a drink-ing binge blackout. The only real reminders she had of her former days were the passing glimpses of herself on TV—reruns of old shows—as well as the image of Marilyn, now dressed like a Fifth Avenue stick insect, hair chignoned regard-less of time of day or season, scrapping it out in court with the airline.

The crux of Marilyn's case was that Susan's physical remains were never found despite indisputable evidence she was on the flight (a GTE Airfone call and the testimony of four ground staffers) and that, unlike other family members of crash victims, Marilyn was alone in not having so much as a fingernail with which to memorialize her daughter.

Susan saw Marilyn royally milking the situation for all it was worth. With public sympathy on her side she was likely to win her case. Eugene would egg Susan on. "You're going to just sit and let her rake in millions on this and do nothing?" But the topic was one that made Susan turn remote, and so he stopped forcing it. To Susan, the sight of her mother on camera was too distant, too unreal to enter into.

Life in Indiana went on. Eugene ventured out to do his mailings and make minor shopping runs. Susan occasionally went along, but she was much happier cosseted away with her lifelong sexual paragon, helping with the family business. It wasn't even until her third month there that she realized she hadn't once had the urge to make a phone call.

In early September, Susan was heavily pregnant and began to grow bored and cranky. "Hormones, Eugene. I get them hot and spicy like my mother." She told him she wanted to take the car out for a spin.

Eugene, testy after disassembling an overtaxed air conditioner in the basement, unsure if he might be able to reassemble it afterward, had no interest in joining her. A heat wave had made the basement the only cool area in the house. The floor was covered in wires and screws, one of which Susan stepped on, sharpening her own mood until it broke.

"I want to drive to the Drug Mart and get some alcohol to cool my boobs. And it'll be fun to do some makeup, slap on a wig."

"What if you—"

"Go into labor?"

"Well, *yeah*."

"I'll bring the cell phone."

"Let me gas up the car then."

"Gas up the car?"

He went around the corner from where he was rewiring the

air conditioner and opened up some sliding doors to reveal several 55-gallon drums Susan hadn't seen before They'd been loaded through what appeared to be locked hatches in the ceiling above.

"What the hell are these, Eugene?"

"Gas. I panicked during the Gulf War. I stocked up."

"Are you nuts? Keeping these in the basement?"

"Cool yer jets, sister. It's nearly all gone. You should have been here in 1991. It was like a refinery down here."

"This stuff's been down here the whole time?"

"I only drive maybe three miles a month. So, yeah."

"That's not the point, Eugene."

"Go get your wig. The weather's making us both nutty. I'll gas the car."

Susan went upstairs to disguise herself. That day she was Lee Grant in the movie *Shampoo*, complete with frosted wedge-cut wig, and a beige pantsuit of Renata's modified to fit her smaller yet pregnant body. She also chose one of Renata's many purses, filled it with a small pile of clutter, makeup and baubles—her "pursey stuff"—and looked at herself in the mirror—sporty! Feeling a tiny bit better, she went into the carport, and called down to Eugene. "I'm going, Yooj."

"Can you pick me up some gum?"

"Gum?"

"Cinnamon Dentyne."

"Yes, my lord."

"Ouch!"

"What's that?"

"This goddamm wire just sparked in my hand."

"Careful now. See you in a half hour."

She got in the car, still slightly annoyed. The sun was almost down, but none of the day's heat had dissipated. And soon the alcohol would be an extra cooling treat. She parked at the strip mall and bought a few things at the drugstore. Her mind wandered. She thought about how soon it'd be before she'd be going there regularly for Pampers and breast pads. On impulse she bought a bottle of bourbon at the Liquor Barn next door, and then got back in the car. Sirens were flaring down the street and she heard a boom a few blocks away.

She turned the corner onto her block to see the lower portion of the house completely ablaze, flames shooting out the windows like water raging down a river. More fire engines arrived, as if from the sky, just as Susan saw the top half of the house collapse into the bottom half.

It was the plane crash repeated—the flames, the havoc, the unreality. She closed the car door tightly and walked toward the pyre. A fireman warned her to stay away, but she ignored him, stumbled over a fire hose and heard the firemen yelling at one another:

- "Fastest fire I've ever seen. Zero to sixty in two seconds."
- "Almost like it was planned this way."
- "Anyone in there?"
- "Won't know until tomorrow. Assuming there's anything left."
- "Family? Christ."
- "No. It's that old weather guy—Evan something. From back in the eighties."
- "Before my time."
- "Real coot. Lived alone. Collected trash, the neighbor said."

The front facade of the house tumbled into the barbecue pit that was once home. All eyes were on the fire, none on Susan, who felt trapped and damned in some sort of sick cosmic loop as she turned around and ran back to the car.

She started the car. Already the show was ending outside— not much remained to burn. She pulled away, wanting to find a highway, any highway, crying furiously, hitting her face, bruising it in anger. She found the freeway and raced onto it. She drove with the high beams on because she knew she was now in some rarefied darkness.

Susan remembered a New Year's Eve she'd once had, back in the eighties. She'd been in Larry's Jaguar and the two of them had gotten lost on the way to a party at Joan Collins's house. They'd already gotten a late start, and then the car needed gas. They'd taken the wrong freeway exit, and the net result was that at the stroke of midnight they were on the Hollywood Freeway, one car among hundreds—millions—around the world, driving through the night, through all the great changes, through those moments when one era turns into another.

Her eyes became cosmetic blots. She couldn't see and she pulled into a gas station and washed her face in the rest room. She fumbled in her purse and cried when she found a small photo of Eugene among the other things. And then she found the folded-up letter she'd rescued from the shrine to her back at the Flight 802 crash in Seneca—Randy Montarelli of 1402 Chattanauqua Street, Erie, Pennsylvania. She went into the convenience store, full of rush-hour shoppers, stole a map and got back into the car and drove, north and then east, from Bloomington to Indianapolis to Akron to Cleveland.

Around midnight she drove into Erie, Pennsylvania, where she pulled out the map and rattled through its flaps until she found what she wanted. Then, in what turned out to be a dozen or so contractions later, she banged on the front door of Randy Montarelli's town house. He opened it wearing a cucumber facial mask, with a TV blaring in the background playing a pre-taped episode of *Matlock*. The odor of popcorn filled the air like hot salty syrup. Red-eyed, Susan ripped off her wig. Her hair was sticky, her brain racing. She crossed Randy's threshold and dropped herself onto the couch where she produced, before the TV program was over, a perfect baby boy.

Randy's afghan dogs, Camper and Willy, were whimpering in the spare bedroom. Randy held the baby in his arms while Susan yelled at him to cut the umbilical cord, which he did.

Chapter Twenty-two

"You *hag*, stop trying to change me. God*dammit*, I can't ever remember a single moment in my life when you weren't trying to twist me into something other than who I am."

"Are you *through* yet, sweetie?"

They were in Denver for the Miss USA Teen competition. Mother and daughter were conducting their conversation through clenched teeth, mouths smiling. They were breakfasting in the Alpine Room of the Denver Marriott. It was seven-fifteen Thursday morning, at an orientation meeting and "Prayer Wake-Up with Turkey Sausage—Turkey, the Low-Fat Pork Substitute."

Such pre-event meals were standard pageant procedure, and at them, gown lockers and keys were assigned. Susan also filled out sign-up sheets to set up a time slot for a video photo-op tour of the city of Denver, the footage to be edited into a big-screen montage and shown during the Sunday night awards ceremonies.

Meal time changes were announced, and lunch that day was to be shared with a local den of Rotarians. "So we can hook ourselves up with a fuck-buddy," Susan laughed.

"Susan!" Marilyn slapped her daughter, who smiled, because as with most slappings, it's the struck who wins the match.

"Classy, Mom. Real swankeroo! I don't think anybody in the room missed it. There goes my Miss Congeniality trophy."

"Only losers win Miss Congeniality, Susan. Aim higher."

Since the move to Cheyenne a few months before, just after her cosmetic surgery, Susan had grown positively mutinous. She had no friends in that surprisingly flat and dusty Wyoming city, and her high school days were finally over after having received a C− average from an exasperated McMinnville school, blissful to have Marilyn out of its hair. Susan lived her days as might the favored member of a harem, painting her toenails, foraging for snack foods and absorbing anything possible from the local library up the street, eager to broaden her world's scope and to learn of possible ways out of pageant hell: Thalidomide, the Shaker religion, witch dunking, the Yukon Territory and Ingrid Bergman.

On the drive to Denver from Cheyenne, Susan did some math in her head. She realized that counting all of her wins over the past decade, little if any money was ever fed back into improving the Colgate family's quality of life. All the loot, she figured, was cycled right back into gowns, surgery, facials, voice and singing lessons. Susan had, until that math exercise on the drive down to Denver, thought of herself as the family breadwinner, the plucky little minx who kept her family away from the destructive intrusion of social workers and the rock-bottom fate of shilling burgers at Wendy's. She now understood that in continuing the pageant circuit, she was only fueling the fire of her own pageant hell.

The Miss USA Teen pageant was a national contest, but not one that Marilyn would concede was A-list like Miss America, Miss Teen America—or even Mrs. America. The winner of the Miss USA Teen pageant would receive a Toyota Tercel hatchback, a faux lynx fur evening coat, $2,000 toward college tuition, and $3,500 cash, along with a gown endorsement contract.

Susan had easily clinched the Miss Wyoming Teen title, and

Marilyn acted like a crow raiding another bird's nest as Susan twinkled her way through a competition that was hokey, amateur and pushover. It was essentially four car-stereo speakers, a borrowed room at the community center (the sound of basketballs from the next room punctuated the event like a random metronome) and a feedlot of tinseled yokels who knew nothing about ramp walking, cosmetics, accessorizing, stage demeanor or the correct manner of answering skill-testing questions. The question asked of Susan had been: "If you could change one thing about America, what would it be?" Marilyn knew that the easy and obvious answer would be peace and harmony, but Susan's answer, delivered in tones Marilyn found suspiciously heartfelt, was, "You know what I'd change?" A pause. "I'd like to make us all stop squabbling for just one day. I'd have citizens sit down and talk about what it means to live in this country— all of us sitting down at the world's biggest dinner table, agreeing to agree, all of us trying to find things that bring us together instead of the things that keep us apart."

Storms of applause.

Title clinched.

Marilyn found that Susan had been difficult of late, alternately insolent, silent, crabby and apathetic. The Miss Wyoming title, rather than making Susan buoyant, merely threw her into some sort of moody teenage dungeon, and afterward each time Marilyn and Susan needed to talk about pageant business, Susan would merely roll her eyes, moo, and return to one of what was an ever growing pile of books with disturbingly uncheerful titles like *Our Bodies, Our Selves* and *Mastering Your Life*. The drive to Denver had been particularly taxing, owing to both Susan's sulkiness and to an Interstate pileup outside of Colorado Springs that left one trucker dead, six cars munched and a confetti of broiler chickens and Nike sneakers strewn across the median.

The remainder of the drive was somber, and nearing the hotel, Susan seemed to have reached a decision of some sort, and cheered up once more, the way she'd been back before—back before *when?*

Marilyn watched Susan flow through that evening's pageant with a previously unseen ease. She walked like a Milanese model and held her head up high like a true Wyoming cowgirl. She was good, and Marilyn knew it and, like most show moms, kept one eye glued to her offspring, the other on the evening's quintet of semi-loser judges: the local modeling school doyenne, a drive-time FM radio jock, a disco-era Olympic gymnast, a walking hard-on from the local baseball team, his leg in a cast, and "Steffan," a humorless local designer with a midlife-crisis ponytail. Marilyn looked at the faces of the judges, the speed and confidence with which they jotted their numerical ratings onto the score sheets, and knew Susan was a shoo-in as a finalist. Backstage during the final costume change, Marilyn couldn't help but preen: "Sweetie, you're just *killing* them out there."

Susan removed her key from where she and many other contestants stored theirs—duct-taped to her belly just above the pubic hair so as to preclude vandalizing of gowns and accessories in the locker areas. She and Marilyn prepared the final gown. "You'll never guess *why* I'm doing so well tonight," Susan said.

"Whatever it is, just keep on doing it."

"You sure about that?"

"Win, sweetie, win. It's all there is." Marilyn zipped Susan up and checked her hair. "Turn around—lint check."

Susan turned and the overhead lights blinked: time to get back onstage. "What's tonight's secret then, sweetie?" Marilyn asked. "Let me in."

Susan stood in the wings with the four other finalists, Miss Arizona, Miss Maine, Miss Georgia and Miss West Virginia. The stage lights glowed like the sun through a grove of leafy trees. "The reason is," she said, just before the emcee called out "Miss Wyoming," "that I no longer give a rat's ass."

Marilyn's heart chilled. Susan went onstage. With dread, Marilyn returned to her table, where a broad assortment of now drunk show moms and show dads were clapping with near Communist precision and zest. Trish, living in Denver that summer, was along for the evening's ride. She occupied a $45 seat to Marilyn's right. She asked Marilyn if she was okay.

"Just fine, hon. Just fine."

The emcee introduced the skill-testing-question portion of the evening's events, and asked the five finalists to enter the "Booths of Silence," which were actually a series of plywood stalls painted robin's-egg blue, fronted with a sheet of clear Plexiglas. Inside, Whitney Houston music blared to the exclusion of all other noises—just the sort of yesteryear propping that Marilyn thought kept this particular pageant entirely B-list.

Susan was fourth out of her stall, having watched Miss Maine, Miss Georgia, and Miss Arizona come onstage before her. She left her booth, hearing the click of Plexiglas on plywood. She sashayed up to the green electrical tape strip that was her floor marker. She saw that the emcee was as handsome as Eugene Lindsay—*Why is there never a woman emceeing these things? Why is it always some variation of a Qantas pilot crossed with a Pentecostal evangelist?* His teeth, lips, Adam's apple and chin worked in symphony, and Susan heard: "Susan Colgate: A UFO lands in your back yard and a little green man pops out of it and says to you, 'Hello, Earthling—please tell me about your country.' What do you tell this little green man?"

Susan thought about this question. Why would an alien even know about the concept of countries? Were countries a universal concept? Did they have countries on Betelgeuse or on Mars? She thought about what a ridiculous spot she was now in. How many times had she been in just such an artificial situation where she was put on trial with fatuous, clownlike questions like something out of the Salem witch trials? Susan looked into the emcee's eyes and she could tell he was hosting the evening's event because he needed the money. Gambling debts? An addiction to sexual novelties or to Franklin Mint collectible ceramic thimbles? What was with his hair? Was that a trace of a scar on his left eye? Oh *God*, there still remained this idiotic question to be answered. The audience was so quiet. The lighting was so bright!

Aliens . . . She thought of cartoon aliens endorsing presweetened breakfast cereals. Pictures of Mexicans flashed through her head. She recalled the moods she had when she was on the road, driving to pageants—the hotel rooms and freeways and taxis and forests and grocery stores and all of the people she'd ever seen across the country, churning, scrambling and going—going forth—into some unknown.

She replied, "I'd tell that little green man that we're a busy country, Ken." Marilyn safety-pinned the names of the emcees onto gowns before storing them in backstage lockers. "I'd tell him that we like getting things done here in the USA, and that we're always on the lookout for newer, better ways of doing them. And *then*, Ken"—Susan decided to speak to the emcee as a person and not a robot— "and then I'd ask the little green man if he'd take me for a ride in his UFO, and I'd say, 'Take me to Detroit! Because there's tons of people there who'd like to learn from this little UFO ship of yours—because you know what? These UFOs look like a dandy new way of doing things faster and better. That's the American way.' Then, I guess, the two of us would lift off and cross this big country of ours. You might even call it a date. That's what I'd say, Ken. That's what I'd do."

Her smile was clean, her eyes direct, and the crowd loved her.

Miss West Virginia was next. She was going to tell the little green man that the USA was a free country and that if he had a problem with that, he could leave, then and there. This was a negative reply and only garnered weak clapping, and sure enough, Miss West Virginia came in as fourth runner-up. Miss Maine was third, Miss Georgia was second runner-up and then, "In the event that Miss USA Teen is unable to fulfill her duties the first runner-up will assume those responsibilities. The first runner-up is Karissa Palewski, Miss Arizona, making Susan Colgate, the new, Miss USA Teen!"

A flash of kisses, flashbulbs and roses. A sash. A scepter. The previous Miss USA Teen, Miss Dawnelle Hunter, formerly Miss Florida USA Teen, emerged from the wings with a platinum tiara which she nested and pinned onto Susan's hair. From all sides came clapping, and a gentle tickle in the small of the back from Ken propelled Susan up to the front where she was to make the briefest of acceptance speeches.

Marilyn was at their table, electrified. The runners-up, or, as Marilyn would say, "the losers," formed a sparkling multi-colored backdrop behind Susan.

The floor calmed.

All was silent.

Susan wondered how to be truthful without giving offense. She said, "Thanks all of you. Thanks so much. As we know, this is an important pageant, and winning means a great deal to me." She paused here, looking for words. "And I think one of the traits we value most in any Miss USA Teen is honesty. So it's only fair I be honest with you now." She looked at Marilyn, and waited an extra few seconds for full impact. "The truth is that I've got my nose in the books these days—I got a C− average in high school and I know I can do better than that—I'm even thinking of applying for college. I simply won't have the time to fulfill my duties as Miss USA Teen. To properly give justice to the role is a full-time job and requires a girl who can give it a thousand-percent dedication." Susan was winging it now. "It's only from winning that I can see how sacred the role of Miss USA Teen is. And so, in the spirit of truth and pageantry, with a clear head and a happy heart I pass the crown on to Karissa Palewski, Miss Arizona Teen and now, Miss USA Teen. Karissa?" She turned around and beckoned Karissa who, so recently awash in loser's hormones, failed to immediately register her bounty. "Please come forward so I can pass along my crown to you." The sound technicians sloppily cued up Vivaldi's *Four Seasons*.

Marilyn's tortured "No!" was drowned out in the applause as emcee Ken shrugged and escorted Karissa to Susan for a transfer of the tiara, sash, scepter and roses. Mission accomplished. Susan hopped efficiently off the stage and said to Marilyn, "Sorry, Mom, but this is a jailbreak. I'm no longer your prisoner." She left the banquet room while a confused Trish, justifiably wary of Marilyn's wrath, darted after her.

A week passed in which Susan holed up at the home of Trish's aunt.

Marilyn and Don were back in Cheyenne, where Don was making pay phone calls to Susan, as he didn't want any telltale evidence of communiqués with Denver on the monthly phone bill. "I've gotta tell you, Sue, your mom's pissed as a jar of hornets on this one."

Susan could easily imagine Don fumbling with a roll of quarters in a booth beside a shoe store. She said, "You know, Don— what *else* is new? I mean, you're married to her, I'm born to her. Neither of us has any illusions, and I just can't take her anymore. I'm out of high school now. Do you really want me hanging around the house for weeks on end with nothing to do but bask in Mom's loving glow?" There was silence on Don's end, and a cash register kachinged in the background. "I thought so.

For the time being I'm here with Trish and it's a harmless enough life. I've got a job flipping dough at Pizza Slut. It's a start."

"Well, Sue, that sounds good to me." Don possessed no initiative but considered any trace of it in others a good sign. "What else is new down there? I used to have a brother in Denver. He's in Germany now, Patches Barracks, outside of Stuttgart."

Susan said, "I hang out with Trish by the pool at the Y. She's into numerology now. She's changing her name to Dreama." Susan could sense every fiber of Don's body instantly spasm with boredom. "Not much else, I guess."

"A guy called. From Los Angeles. An agent. Named Mortimer. Larry Mortimer. He says you should give him a call. He read about your chucking the pageant in the paper." Susan took down the number and then she and Don exchanged polite good-byes, both happy to leave the business of what to do to calm Marilyn to some other call, another day.

A few hours later, Susan and Trish, armed with fake IDs and Trish's aunt's Honda Civic, whooped it up in keggery bars and hot spots, releasing sugary bursts of energy with the fervor and desperation of the young. The partying went on for two weeks, after which Trish's aunt Barb suggested the two girls accompany her on a road trip to Los Angeles in her car. They could share in the driving duties.

And so they left, and yet again Susan saw and participated in the country's landscape—hostile, cold and magnificent, dull and glowing. They pulled into Los Angeles around sunset, arriving in Rancho Palos Verdes on the coast just as a full moon pulled up over the Pacific. They were just in time for a dinner of sloppy joes at Barb's friend's house, and they watched the lights of Avalon over on Catalina sparkling in the distance. Dinner was almost ready and adults and teenagers scurried about. Susan found a quiet den and dialed Larry Mortimer's number. She connected to a personal assistant and then a few breaths later, Larry was on the line. "Susan Colgate? You're one brave woman to go and quit that pageant the way you did."

Susan was flattered to be called a woman. "It wasn't quitting, Larry. It was—well—there was no way around it. You go and do a hundred pageants and then write me a postcard. We'll compare notes."

"Such spark. You could really harness that—make it work for you."

"I'm happy enough just having my mother off my back."

"Have you ever acted before?"

"Have you ever been in a pageant with cramps before? Or the flu?"

"Touché. How old are you?"

"I'm out of high school, if that's what you mean."

"No—I meant—"

"With a beret and a kilt I look fourteen. With makeup, cruel lighting and two beers in me, I can pull off thirty. Easy."

"What's the most ridiculous pageant you ever did?"

"I was Miss Nuclear Energy three years ago. I had this little atom-shaped electric crown over my head. It was pretty, actually. But the pageant was dumb. It was organized by men, not women, and the only other thing they'd ever organized was a Thanksgiving turkey raffle. The whole thing was so—corny. Instead of sashes we had name tags."

"We should meet. We should get together."

Susan's stomach made a dip, like cresting a roller coaster's first and biggest hill. She was excited. She hadn't expected this. "Why's that?"

Barb passed by the door to tell Susan the sloppy joes were ready.

"You could really go places," Larry said.

"Like where?"

"Movies. TV."

"Be still my heart."

"Come into town. Tomorrow."

"We're going to Disneyland tomorrow."

"The day after then."

Susan had the sensation that this was just another emcee calling her up onto some stage where she would be judged again. After a few weeks of freedom from pageantry, she felt old strings being tugged and that spooked her. Trish, now answering only to "Dreama," called Susan to the table. "Dinner time, Larry. I ought to go."

"What's for dinner?"

"Sloppy joes."

"I love sloppy joes."

"It gives me cellulite."

"Cellulite? You're a child!"

"I'm seventeen."

"Ooh. I'll back off now."

They were quiet.

Larry asked her, "Meet me?"

"What do you look like?" Susan asked.

"If I were in a movie, I'd be a sailor like back in the old days, with a sunburn and a duffel bag, and I'd be on shore leave wearing a cable knit sweater."

Two days later Susan, Dreama and Barb met Larry for lunch at an outdoor café where the linen, china and flowers were white and the service was so good they didn't even realize they were being served. Larry was late, and when Susan saw him rush toward the table, her heart did a cartwheel. Larry was older, curly-haired, gruff and in a glorious twist of fate, a clone of Eugene Lindsay, the winking judge.

Susan fell into a reverie. She hoped that Larry's breath would smell like scotch. She realized that Larry was to be her devirginizer, and a wash of sexual energy and nervousness bordering on static cling came over her. She caught his eye as he approached, and sealing his fate with Susan, he winked.

"I'm late," he said.

"You're just in time," she said. Their eyes locked and they held each others' hand a pulse too long. "Larry, this is my friend Dreama and her aunt Barb." They shook hands, and Barb sized Larry up in a manner that was blatantly financial, embarrassing and amusing.

Lunch was a blur. Afterward, Susan left with Larry, ostensibly to test for a new TV show. Once inside his Jaguar, Aunt Barb and Dreama out of sight, Larry told Susan that the test was actually for the next day. He then looked up at the sky innocently. Susan wasn't fazed. She told Larry this was pretty much what she'd figured. *Oh God*, she thought to herself, *I'm a jaded harpy and I'm only seventeen. Mom did this to me. She's gone and turned me into . . . her.*

Larry asked, "So where do you think we might go now?"

Years later, with hindsight, Susan would find it appalling that Barb had left her so readily in the hands of an L.A. predator.

Later that night, after Susan and Larry had exhausted themselves in Larry's bed, they would briefly chuckle over the clunky roving eye Aunt Barb had focused on Larry, then phone Barb and say, "Barb? Larry Mortimer here. We're late like crazy. We didn't even get a chance to audition. The tests were slowed down by a union walkout. It'll have to be tomorrow. We'll be back at your hotel in an hour. Here. Susan wants to speak with you." He passed the phone over the sheets to Susan.

"Barb? Wasn't lunch today a *dream*?"

The next day at the actual audition, Susan clarified in her own mind one of the larger lessons of her life so far, the one which states that the less you want something, the more likely you are to get it. As she uttered her very first line, "Dad, I think there's something not quite right with Mom," the character of Katie Bloom, two years younger than her, melted onto Susan Colgate's soul, and as of 1987, the public and Susan herself would spend decades trying to separate the two. Katie Bloom was the youngest of four children, a distant fourth at that. Her three on-screen siblings were played by a trio of better-known TV actors who couldn't seem to make the bridge into film, and they chafed madly at any suggestion that their Bloom work was "only TV." Off-screen, the three were patronizing and aloof to Susan. On-screen they looked to their younger free-spirit sister Susan to give them a naive clarity into their problems, and as the years went on, their problems became almost endless.

When Susan emerged as the keystone star of the series, it was in the face of outright mutiny by her costars. At the beginning she thought their coldness was the angst of tormented actors. Then she realized it was essentially fucked-up bitterness, which was much easier to handle. Far more difficult to handle was the issue of Marilyn's continued involvement in her life. The procedure, for insurance reasons, demanded that Susan live with a family member near the studio. The glimmer of TV fame quickly outshone the gloom of pageants lost. Marilyn and Don rented the upper floor of a terrifyingly blank faux-hacienda heap in deepest Encino. Susan did the easier thing and lived in Larry's pied-à-terre in Westwood. Thus, Marilyn's presence was minimized to that of a bookkeeping technicality.

Larry was like all of the pageant judges in the world rolled into one burly, considerate, suntanned package. He knew how the stoplights along Sunset Boulevard were synched and shifted his Porsche's gears accordingly. He had a writer fired who called Susan an empty Pez dispenser to her face. He made sure she ate only excellent food and kept her Kelton Street apartment fully stocked with fresh pasta, ripe papayas and bottled water, all of which was overseen by a thrice-weekly maid. He lulled Susan to sleep singing "Goodnight, Irene," and then, after he nipped home to sleep with his wife, Jenna, he arrived at work the next day and saw to it that Susan received plenty of prime TV and film offers.

When she thought about her new situation at all, it was with the blameless ingratitude of the very young. Her life's trajectory was fated, inevitable. Why be a wind-up doll for a dozen years if not to become a TV star? Why not alter one's body? Bodies were meant to photograph well. Mothers? They were meant to be Tasmanian devils—all the better reason to keep them penned up in Encino.

Every night she took two white pills to help her sleep. In the morning she took two orange pills to keep from feeling hungry. She loved the fact that life could be so easily controlled as that. Inasmuch as she had a say in the matter, she was going to keep the rest of her life as equally push-button and seamless. In the mornings when she woke up, she couldn't remember her dreams.

Chapter Twenty-three

John, Vanessa and Ryan were driving from Vanessa's house to Randy Montarelli's out in the valley. The three were crammed into the front bench seat, Vanessa in the middle. John was sweaty and pulled a pack of cigarettes out from the car door's side pocket and lit one.

"You smoke?" Vanessa asked. She made a serious, unscrutinizable face.

"As of now, I've started again. I'm worried about Susan. I can't unstress."

Once in the Valley, John pulled the Chrysler into an ARCO station for gas and gum. He went to pay at the till, and on returning to the car found Ryan and Vanessa in the front seat giggling like minks.

"Christ, you two."

"We're young and in love, John Johnson," Vanessa teased.

"People like you were never young, Vanessa. People like you are born seventy-two, like soft pink surgeon generals."

Driving along in the accordion-squeezed traffic of Ventura Boulevard, John said, "So, are you two wacky kids gonna get married or something?"

"Absolutely," said Ryan. "We've even got our honeymoon planned."

John considered this young couple he was driving with across the city. They were like rollicking puppies one moment, and Captain Kirk and Spock from *Star Trek* the next. Both seemed bent on discovering new universes. John thought that they were, in a way, the opposite of Ivan and Nylla, who he was convinced had married in order to compact the universe into something smaller, more manageable.

"Where are you two clowns going to honeymoon then, Library of Congress?"

"Chuckles ahoy, John," Ryan replied. "We're actually going to Prince Edward Island."

"Huh? Where's that—England?" John was driving at an annoyingly slow speed in order to torment a tailgater.

"No," said Vanessa. "It's in Canada. Back east—just north of Nova Scotia. It has a population of, like, three."

"We're going to dig potatoes."

John put his hand to his forehead. "Dare I even ask . . . ?"

"There's this thing they have there," said Ryan, "called the tobacco mosaic virus. It's this harmless little virus that's lolling about dormant inside the Prince Edward Island potato ecology, not doing much of anything."

"Except," said Vanessa, "it's highly contagious, and if it comes in contact with tobacco plants, it turns them, basically, into sludge. So what we're going to do is rent a van and fill it up with infected potatoes and then drive down to Virginia and Kentucky and lob them into tobacco fields."

"We're going to put Big Tobacco out of business," said Ryan.

"Romantic," said John, "but it does appeal to my Lodge pesticide genes."

"Vanessa's dad died of emphysema."

"Don't make me sound like a Dickensian waif, Ryan, but yes, Dad did hork his lungs out."

"Vanessa likes to fuck things up with the information she finds," said Ryan with a note of pride.

"You know what, Ryan? I have an easy time believing that. I'm also going to light up another cigarette. Sorry, Vanessa, but I'm flipping out here."

Ryan shouted, "Hey—that's Randy Montarelli's street over there," and John pulled into a leafy suburban avenue. The tail-gater whizzed off in a huff. Randy's wood-shingled house was pale blue and tall cypress tree sentinels were lit with colored floodlights.

"Well," said Ryan as they parked across the street and peeked at the house. "We're here."

"We are," said John. It was a quiet moment, like being on holiday, after flying the whole day and navigating through cabs and crowds, arriving in the hotel room, shutting the room and taking a breath. What came next was unknown, and John realized he hadn't given this moment much thought. He was stage-struck.

"I just saw somebody move inside a window," said Ryan.

"We have to go down there," said John.

"Ryan . . ." said Vanessa. "Maybe we should wait here. Maybe John should be alone for this."

"No. Come, you guys—I need you."

Like clueless trick-or-treaters, they headed to the front door. From inside the house they heard a TV blaring, feet pounding an uncarpeted floor and a door shutting. John rang the bell before he had a chance to change his mind. All interior sound stopped. Vanessa rang it again three times quickly. A minute passed and still nothing. Ryan tried the doorknob to see if it was open. It was.

"Shut the fucking door, Ryan," said John.

"Just checking."

"Hellooooo . . . ?" Vanessa called into the crack in the door.

"Oh jeez," said John.

"You are such a chickenshit, John." Vanessa cooed into the house, "Hello—we're from Unesco."

Ryan turned to Vanessa: *"Unesco?"*

"It was the first thing that popped into my head."

"Right," said John, "like you're Audrey Hepburn and ready to hand over a clod of Swiss dirt if they donate five bucks."

From down the hallway came the sound of somebody tripping over a small heap of suitcases. A man appeared, pale as linguine, in a black bodysuit, a cell phone dangling from his right hand.

"Well, well, it's the Mod Squad. I'm Randy. You're John Johnson, aren't you? What are *you* doing *here?*"

"Perhaps we could come in?" John asked.

"No. I—*can't.* I mean, I know you're famous and rich, but I don't know you personally. And I don't know these two here at all."

"I'm Ryan."

"I'm Vanessa."

"I'm sorry, but I still can't do it."

"That's okay," said John. "We're looking for Susan Colgate."

Randy didn't flinch. "And why would you be talking to me about this?"

"You are Randy Montarelli?"

"I was."

"And you are Randy 'Hexum,' then, too?"

"Yes, but what is your point? It's a free country. I can change my name. So you guys know stuff about my past. I'm not scared or anything."

"We're not here to scare you," John said.

"Okay, but why are you assuming I've got something to do

with Susan Colgate? Do you have any idea how random it is to have you three show up on my doorstep like this? Asking about some washed-up soap actress? I can already feel my spirit entering therapy as a result of this visit."

"So you're saying you don't know her," said John.

"I didn't say that."

"Do you know her?"

"We've met."

"And?"

"I used to work for Chris Thraice a few years ago when I came to L.A. As far as I know, he and Susan are still friends, but I don't think they ever talked much." Randy added, "Hey, kids, I have an idea. I won't tell the cops that you were here if you don't tell them you were here, either."

"Deal," said John.

Randy's face changed like still water brushed by a breeze. "Wait . . ." He looked at John with a degree of calculation. "Maybe there is something you need to know—something you should have." John, Ryan and Vanessa exchanged Hardy Boy glances. "Hold on," he said, and headed down the hall, knocked a piece of luggage out of his way and entered a room. A minute later he returned with a sealed manila envelope and offered it to John. "I hope you're feeling better," he said to John.

"What was wrong with me?" John was taken back.

"Well," said Randy, "I recently heard that you were suffering from Jeep's syndrome."

"Oh jeez," said John, "that's one of those bloody Internet rumors. Who starts those things?"

"What's Jeep's syndrome?" asked Ryan.

Vanessa said, "It's when an ingrown hair follicle above the anus becomes infected, causing a massive buildup of waste fluids, requiring a surgical excision and drainage. The most famous sufferer was English pop star Roddy Llewellyn, who once dated Princess Margaret."

"Did we *really* need to know that?" John asked.

"Ryan *did* ask. And besides, I've heard the rumor, too. That's why I looked it up."

Randy handed John the envelope. "You should find this interesting." He closed the door.

A minute later they were back in the car. John was agitated, mad at himself for not having better strategized the encounter. "Shit, that guy's balling town somewhere and he's our only clue. He could have *Susan* in those suitcases for all I know. Ryan, open the envelope. What's in it?"

"It's a script: 'Scratch 'n' Win,' by Randy Hexum."

"Shit—a script." He slammed the steering wheel.

Vanessa said, "I have another clue," but at that exact moment Ryan locked bumpers with a car identical to John's own—same color, same year—and their car was hobbled onto the other like animals in heat. "Oh *wow*," mumbled a surf brat loitering on the corner with a friend, "two gay Chryslers fucking."

Chapter Twenty-four

One night back in 1986, Susan came within an eyelash of being introduced to John Johnson at a party Larry Mortimer had thrown. Larry was eager to showcase Susan and to network her with as many people as possible. Meet the Blooms was riding high, and of the eighties crop of "It Girls," Susan was the one most coveted by the networks.

For some reason there was a giraffe at the party. Susan heard somebody ask why, and someone else replied it was to help plug a disastrously overbudget chimp comedy that had tanked that weekend on 1,420 screens across North America. Susan was standing with people from Johnny Carson's production company. It was then that she noticed John speaking with that toilet-mouthed lady from Disney—Alice?—something about an Oxford don and a punt—and Susan deemed John date-worthy, and that he would be even more so once he had a few years to . . . ripen. She was going to ask Larry for an introduction when a woman on her right said, "Hello, Susan Colgate."

Susan turned to the speaker who was, according to the framed photos on Larry's desk, Larry's wife, Jenna Mortimer, lovely, with hair like spun black glass, baby-doll features, dressed in a black chiffon evening dress that featured the linebacker shoulder pads of the era. This look, combined with a flash of teeth, created an aggressive posture.

"Hello—Jenna—Mrs. Mortimer. Hello."

"It's a pleasure to finally meet you, Susan."

"Oh—nice for me, too. How did we ever get this far without being introduced? Shouldn't Larry have done this, like, an hour ago at the very least?"

"Cuckoo, isn't it?" said Jenna. "Larry can be so forgetful. Such a business this is."

"Larry's always talking about you."

"I'm sure he is." She motioned toward a buffet table. "Have you had something to eat?" She was making it clear that she was the hostess. Susan was overeager to sound like an appreciative guest and she blurted out a dumb lie: "Yes, I had some cheese."

"But I'm not serving any cheese."

Susan was flustered.

"Is your mother here?" asked Jenna, knowing full well that Susan lived on Larry's Kelton Street property. The truth was that at that exact moment Marilyn was scouring the streets of Encino hoping to find Don's car, hoping to find Don inside a bar with a slut, knowing there was a far greater likelihood of simply finding Don with a bottle, which was somehow worse.

"No. It's a lovely party. Really beautifully done." Susan felt mature using the words "beautifully done." It was the way she thought rich people spoke.

Jenna looked around. "It is, isn't it?"

"And the giraffe!"

"The *giraffe* just ate the neighbor's prize Empress Keiko persimmon tree. There'll be hell to pay tomorrow." She looked at Susan appraisingly. "Clear shoes and nude hose—trying to lengthen our legs tonight?"

"An old show dog trick. Miss USA Teen, 1985."

"Miss Nevada, 1971."

"No!" Susan smiled. "What a racket, huh?" She found herself beginning to like Jenna.

"Oh yes. The *crap* I spouted during those pageants," Jenna said.

"I always thought the good thing about being Miss Wyoming was that I'd get to go last when they called out the states. You know, the letter *W*—and that I'd get to see the other girls' ramp-walking errors, and learn from them."

"Did you ever win Miss Congeniality?" asked Jenna.

"Me? Never. I should have won Miss Why Am I Here?"

"I *always* got Miss Congeniality."

"Did you?" Susan was curious.

"Those nuns. Catholic school. They nabbed me when I was young."

"I didn't go to religious school. We're hillbillies in our family."

"The thing about Catholic school is that they manage to make you put a smile on absolutely anything."

"Yeah?"

"*Everything.*"

Susan now understood where Jenna was working the conversation.

Larry saw the two women talking and bolted their way. "Jenna! Susan! I've been waiting for the special moment to introduce you."

"No doubt you have," said Jenna.

"Larry," said Susan. "I didn't know that Jenna used to be a show dog, too.

Jenna said, "It was actually me who put Larry onto you. I read about you throwing your crown back in their faces. I wanted to send you a box of roses and a trophy. I figured it'd take a personality like a freight train to pull off a coup like that."

"You ought to meet my mother, the locomotive."

Larry wanted to get the two women apart. "Susan," he said, "I want you to meet this producer named Colin. He's from England, but he's still useful to us over here. Jenna, can I steal usan away from you?"

"I have a choice?"

Larry flashed teeth and escorted Susan toward the patio doors. Susan called back, "Bye, Jenna—nice to meet you."

Larry moved her around a corner and said, "Christ."

Susan said, "Larry, I can't see you anymore." Her body began to feel as though it were rising upward like a helium balloon. A string had been cut.

He wiped his forehead with a paper doily from a table of mineral waters. "We'll talk about this tomorrow."

"Yeah, we will."

Larry stood still and appraised Susan's face. "You're young. It'll pass."

"But I don't want it to pass."

"It's called getting older. I'll send you the coverage on it."

"Ryan O'Neal's here," Susan said to change the conversation.

"I'll introduce you."

And so the evening went on. Susan drank German mineral water—Sprudel-something, with a name like a pastry—and swished the water about inside her mouth, almost burning her tongue with bubbles—it tasted geological. She watched Larry squirm and lie to the people around him who were squirming and lying right back.

"Susan, this is Cher."

"Hello."

"Susan, this is Valerie Bertinelli."

"Nice to meet you."

"Susan, this is Jack Klugman."

"Great. Hi."

"Susan, this is Christopher Atkins."

"Hey."

"Susan, this is Lee Radziwill."

"Hi."

The party felt like it went on all night, when, like most film industry functions, it actually ended around nine. She couldn't have known that the party was to be her high-water mark within the entertainment world's social structure.

The morning after the giraffe party, a car from the production company picked Susan up at 6:30 A.M. She sat in the back seat, memorizing her lines for the day. She performed her role. She stood for publicity photos with her TV parents and siblings. She had a fight with Larry and dead-bolted him out of the Kelton Street apartment. Days passed. Her strength passed. She let Larry in. She disgusted herself. She'd built no other substantial friendships during her TV blitzkrieg. It was either back to Larry or careen into outer space, and she couldn't face that. Any discussion of Jenna or divorce led to a brick wall which Susan acknowledged with the ever more edgy tag line, "Excuse me, Larry. Pope on line three."

Susan was never a particularly good actor, but at the start of the TV series, she did have a naturalness that stood out and looked good against her actor-since-birth costars. But the naturalness began to wear thin and she became increasingly self-conscious about her body, her face, the words that came out of her mouth and the overall effect she had on people. The scrutiny was a thousand times more intense than any pageant. Her encounter with Jenna at the giraffe party opened some inner sluice of her conscience, and her acting became abysmal almost overnight. She told Dreama: "It's like the part of my brain that used to allow me to do an okay acting job got all warped. It's merging with the part of my brain that makes up lies. I can just *feel* it. I get a simple line like, 'Mom, I'm going to volleyball practice,' and it sounds forced, like it's filled with all this innuendo. My retakes per episode are up like crazy. The network thinks I have a drug problem. The cast thinks fame is wrecking my head. And the thing is, Larry knows it's all because of Jenna and keeping our big lie going, and it's kind of turning him off. And that's freaking me out and making it even worse."

Susan guested on *Love Boat*. She did a walk-on part in a James Bond movie. She was on the cover of *Seventeen* magazine. She had her wisdom teeth removed and discovered the Land of Painkillers. She mended the fence somewhat with Marilyn. Dreama also moved to Los Angeles and into Susan's apartment. Sex with Larry cooled considerably and, as Larry predicted, she grew older.

Chapter Twenty-five

John sat beside his rescuer, Beth, in a security office adjacent to the private jet facility at Flagstaff's airport. Outside the wired-glass windows, in the warm gray air, hydro and aviation towers blinked rubies and diamonds. John was wearing clothes Beth had assembled from her husband's castoffs. His pale aqua shirt was crisply ironed and his skin was brown as if he were baking on the inside, like a bird just removed from the oven. His hair had been hacked off a few weeks before with a hunting knife in a Las Cruces, New Mexico, Shell station rest room. His eyes were clear and wide like a child's. Beth said to him, "I'm sorry about Jeanie and that tape. She's a wild one. I've never known what to do with her."

"It doesn't matter." said John.

Beth bought two weak coffees from a grumbling vending machine. "Here," she said, "take one."

"Oh—no thanks."

"Go on."

John held on to his coffee with the same unsureness he'd felt when holding a baby for the first time, Ivan and Nylla's daughter, MacKenzie. A fuel truck drove by in a mirage of octane. Beth said, "Your friends really have their own private jet, then?"

John nodded.

"Jeanie never would have done it if she hadn't found out about that jet."

"It doesn't matter. Really. It doesn't."

Beth's daughter, Jeanie, had sold the tape of John's naked climb from the ditch and the hour that followed to a local network affiliate. It would be a lead story on a nationally broadcast tabloid show the next night.

"What makes me mad," said Beth, "is that she's going to use the money to pay for her boyfriend's car, not even her own. Dammit, she doesn't have to do that. Royce has a good job already."

"Young people."

"You said it."

A shrillness called out from the black air, and John, staring at the floor, placed it as quickly as a dog recognizes the firing pattern of the cylinders in his master's engine. It was Ivan and the G3. John heard it land and then taxi. He heard the heavy metal staff doors opening, footsteps and voices: Ivan, Nylla, Doris and Melody.

"John-O?"

John stood up and tried to raise his head, but his eyes were too heavy. "John-O?" Ivan crouched down and looked up at John. "We're here, John-O." But John couldn't speak or look up. The coffee dropped from his hand and the cheap plastic cup rattled on the floor. Nylla, Doris and Melody kissed him on the cheek and John could smell their perfumes, so kind and decent that he choked.

Ivan looked over at Beth, who was holding John's laundered clothes inside a paper grocery bag. "Are you . . . ?"

"Yes, I'm Beth."

Ivan handed John over to Melody and Nylla. "Thank you for your . . ."

"It was nothing. But your friend here, he's in a bad way."

Ivan handed Beth an envelope from which she pulled out a stack of hundreds. "Jeremy from my office got your address and numbers?"

"He did."

There was nothing left to do but go out onto the tarmac and into the plane and head west. Beth said good-bye and hugged John, whose arms flailed out from him as if made from straw. The two younger women escorted John on each side up the stair ramp, and Ivan followed behind, a glen plaid jacket draped over his left arm. Soon they were up in the warm night sky, but John had yet to make eye contact with his old friends.

"Johnny," said Melody, "can you hear me okay?"

John nodded.

"You're not on drugs are you, John?" asked Doris.

John shook his head.

Melody said, "Do you want a drink? Ivan, where's that whisky? Pour him a shot." She held a crystal glass up to John's lips, but the taste triggered a convulsion. He felt as if his chest were being crushed by ten strong men.

"John," said Nylla, crouching down beside him, "breathe. Breathe deeply."

"What's going on?" asked Ivan.

"John," Nylla continued, "please listen to me. You're having a panic attack. You're panicking because you're safe now. Your body's been waiting all this time until it felt safe enough to let go. And you're safe now. You're with your friends. Breathe."

John's stomach felt as if it had been given a swift boot. Melody sat on the floor and held him from behind as he rocked. "Johnny? Where've you been? Johnny?"

John said nothing. He'd wanted those rocks and highways and clouds and winds and strip malls to scrape him clean. He'd wanted them to remove the spell of having to be John Johnson. He'd hoped that under a Panavision sky he'd wake up to find the deeper, quieter person who dreamed John Johnson into existence in the first place. But there was nothing any of them in the plane could say or do. They were just a few pieces of light themselves, up there in the night sky, and if they flew twenty miles straight up, they'd be in outer space. It was a quick flight and soon they were back at the airport in Santa Monica, and they drove into town.

John's old house and its James Bond contents had been sold to pay off the IRS. With his royalties caught in a legal snag, he was cashless. As though traveling back in time, John returned to his old bedroom in the guesthouse. Doris was now a living, breathing mille-feuille of ethnic caftans and clattering beads. During his first few weeks home he tried to give the impression that all was fine with him, like a defeated nation embracing the culture of its conqueror. Each day he wore a suit and tie from a selection Melody bought for him. He went without drugs. To see him on the street one would think he was swell, but inside he felt congealed and infected. He felt as if he were soiling whatever he touched, leaving a black stain that not even a fire could remove. He felt as if people could see him as the fraud he knew he was. His skin was sunburned, his hair had grayed, and sunlight now hurt his milk blue eyes, which he was unable to look at in the mirror, as if it could only bring bad news.

He tried finding shaded cafeterias in the drabber parts of Los Angeles, where there was no possibility of encountering old acquaintances. He occasionally spotted geriatric scriptwriters from the DesiLu and Screen Gems era beached like walruses in banquette seats eating Cobb salads, but he never made contact. John would sit and read the daily papers, but they held the same sterile appeal of grossly outdated magazines in a dental office reception area. He wanted to go home, but once he got there, he felt like a bigger misfit than he did out in the city. He tried but couldn't think of any single thing that might make him feel better.

A few months passed, and nothing within him seemed to change. Then without at first being aware of it, he one day realized he was taking a measure of comfort in following a rigid schedule. He quickly developed a notion that he might just be able to squeak through if he could keep his days fastidiously identical. He told this to Ivan, who then lured John back to the production offices with the absurd promise that his days would be "utterly unsurprising." Both Ivan and Nylla were at wits' end as to how they might reintegrate John back into L.A. *Mega Force* finished while John was away, was scheduled for release, and there was no doubt that it was going to hit big. Test screenings in Glendale and Oxnard evoked memories of the old days of *Bel Air PI*—yet to John it was nothing, not a flash of interest.

Among industry people John was considered a mutant. Consensus had been reached that he really *had* been out crossing the country on some sort of doomed search. This made him seem charmed in an interesting but don't-get-too-close way. In a deeply superstitious environment, John was bad and good luck at the same time. If people wanted to do business, they went to Ivan. If they wanted a bit of gossip to pass along at the dinner table, they popped their heads into John's office.

Around Doris, John felt like a burden. She'd come to enjoy her privacy and unaccountability over the years. While she was patient with John, he couldn't help but feel like an anchor roped around her waist—and yet the thought of being alone in a place of his own was inconceivable. Ultimately, beneath Doris's *Darling!*-rich exterior John also sensed a veiled hostility—and he couldn't quite identify its root.

Until one night, just after John had returned home from the offices of Equator Pictures—six fifty-five, in time for the news on TV—Doris came through the door in a filthy mood. Her car had been broken into during her lunch with a friend at Kate Mantilini, and her favorite dress, just back from the cleaners, was stolen, along with a sentimental cameo brooch she kept in the dashboard's beverage caddie. She cut her fingers removing the pile of shattered glass strewn about the driver's seat, and she'd driven to Bullock's to meet another friend. There she realized, after waiting in a long lineup, that her credit cards and ID had also been swiped. She worried she was getting Alzheimer's because she hadn't noticed sooner. She had a fit, and during an angry drive to the police station, ran a red light, receiving both a ticket and a scolding from a traffic cop. She was mutinous.

"Oh God, do I need a drink," she blurted as she scrambled for the liquor cabinet. "Want one?" John said no. "You don't have to be such a priss about not having a drink, John."

"I'm—not—drinking—these—days," he said in precisely metered tones.

"Aren't you a saint."

Out the side of his vision, John watched Doris pour a Cinzano, gulp it down, pour another, this time with a lemon zest, gulp it down, and then in a more relaxed state, pour a third. He wondered what was going on with her, but he didn't want to miss the news.

Doris was looking across the room at John, his posture self-consciously erect, sitting on a stool watching reports from some war-torn ex-Soviet province. It was like he was six and sick again, trying to be a good little boy. The emotions she'd been feeling about her crappy day did a 180, and without warning, her heart flew back to the New York of decades ago when John was the child who didn't want to be sick or a burden.

The shutters were drawn, but late afternoon sun treacled in through the chinks. Doris had the sensation that the hot yellow air would feel like warm gelatin against her body were she to venture outside. She sighed, and suddenly she didn't want to drink anymore. She felt chilly and old. She wanted to slap John. She wanted to hold him, and she wanted to chide him for his recklessness and to tell him how much she wished that she'd been out there with him, out in the flats and washes and foothills and gorges, begging God, or Nature or even the sun to erase the burden of memories, and the feeling of having lived a life that felt far too long, even at the beginning. She called to him, "John . . ."

He looked around. "Yeah, Ma?"

"John . . ." She tried to find words. John pushed the MUTE button. "John, when you were away—out on your jaunt a few months ago, did you . . ."

"Did I what, Ma?"

"Did you find . . ." Again, she stopped there.

"What, Ma? Ask me."

Doris wouldn't continue.

"What is it, Mom?" John was now alarmed.

And then it just flooded right out of her, in a rush: "Didn't you find even one goddam thing out there during the stint away? Anything? Anything you could tell me and make me feel like there was at least one little reason, however subtle, that would repay me for having been sick with fear all those nights you were gone?"

Doris saw John open his eyes wide, religiously. She immediately felt queasy for having been so vulgar, and apologized, though John said there was no need for it. But John knew his mother was mad at him because he was still seemingly unchanged at thirty-seven, because he was still alone and because she'd pretty much surrendered hope that he would ever acclimate, marry and procreate like the sons of women in her reading group.

"It's my back," said Doris, thumping the base of her spine as though it were a misbehaving appliance. "It hurts like stink and I have the one Beverly Hills doctor who doesn't like to overprescribe for his patients."

"It's still that bad?"

"As ever."

"I thought you were trying a new—"

"It's not working."

"Can't you go to another doctor? Get more pills?"

"I could. But I won't. Not now. I'd feel so—I don't know, slutty, openly hunting for drugs like that. And Dr. Christensen knows my life story. I'm in no mood to start from scratch with someone new."

"So you'd rather be in pain?"

"For the time being? Yes."

Her temper was brushed over. When the CNN news ended, John had an idea. He went into his room and looked through his old address book. All these numbers and names and not a friend in the lot. John wondered why it is people lose the ability to make friends somewhere around the time they buy their first expensive piece of furniture. It wasn't a fixed law, but it seemed to be an accurate-enough gauge.

He flipped through pages of numbers and memories and meetings and sexual encounters and deals and washed cars and flights booked Alitalia and Virgin, and tennis games catered—a small stadium's worth of people who would find John Johnson whatever he needed.

He removed his working clothes and shed them into a pile in the corner. He was sick of being Mr. Corporate Office Guy. He rooted about his cupboard and found some old clothes Doris hadn't thrown out—old mismatched shirts and pants used for painting the kitchen drawers and for yard work. Every day was now going to be casual Friday for John.

He returned to his old address book. In it he located the name of Jerr-Bear, a child actor of the *Partridge Family* era who as a grown-up had gone terribly skank, dressed in the homeless version of Milan's latest offerings, with matted hair that smelled like a barn. John tried to remember Jerr-Bear's full name and couldn't, yet he fully remembered Jerr-Bear's portrayal of the loyal son on a long-vanished cop show.

Jerr-Bear may have gone skank, but the goods he carried were the finest. John looked in his bedside table and found eighteen hundred dollars remaining from a five-grand float Ivan gave him for the month. It was all in twenties and looked sleazy sitting in a heap the way it did. He dialed Jerr-Bear, and against the odds, Jerr-Bear answered.

"Jerr-Bear, it's John Johnson."

"The happy wanderer!"

"Yeah, that's me." John heard chewing sounds. "Are you at dinner now? Do you want me to call back?" The thought of Jerr-Bear at a nonrestaurant dinner table seemed almost impossible for John to visualize.

"Yeah, it's dinner, but big deal. What are you, a telemarketer? How can I help you, John?"

"Call me back."

"Right."

Jerr-Bear maintained a complex system of cloned cell phones so as to avoid tapping by authorities. A minute later John's line rang. Even then, the two spoke in veils.

"Jerr, what do you give someone who's in a lot of pain?"

"Pain's a biggie, John. Life hurts. Specifically—?"

"Back pain."

"Ooh—most people need heavy artillery for that one."

"You have any artillery?"

"I do."

They arranged for lunch the next day at the Ivy.

Chapter Twenty-six

After the scuff with the other Chrysler, Vanessa took the wheel of the car and John sat in the back seat spinning theories about Randy and semipacked luggage.

"Drugs. It *has* to be drugs."

"No, John," said Vanessa. "There's nothing in Susan's banking or Visa card patterns that indicates a consistent drain of drug-caliber discretionary cash."

"You got her banking info?"

"I gave her Susan's Visa number," said Ryan. "It was in the video shop's computer. I mean, once somebody's got your Visa number, they can pretty well clone you."

"Not really," said Vanessa. "In order to clone you they'd also need your phone number."

"Why do I bother even trying to generate ideas?" asked John. "You two are the most drag-and-click people I've ever met. You're wearing the pants here, Vanessa. Why don't you tell me what we ought to be doing next?"

"Okay, I will. We are currently en route to the North Holly-wood home of one Dreama Ng."

"She's a numerologist," said Ryan.

"Is she going to give us potatoes, as well?"

"Oh, grow up," said Vanessa. "Susan's been giving Dreama Ng twenty-five hundred bucks a month for a few years now."

"I told you, it was drugs."

"Your naïveté yet again sickens me," said Vanessa, adding, "You, who spent maybe 1.7 to 2 million dollars on both drugs and drub rehab programs over the past six years."

"Oof. That much?" asked John.

"Probably more. I wasn't able to access one stream of data out of Geneva." Vanessa continued steering the car with a pinky around a sharp curve. "You know as well as anybody, John, that drug consumption only escalates. It docs not remain stable month in, month out over several years. I also ran a check on Ms. Ng's finances, and, lo and behold, who do you think she signs over her check to each month?"

"Drum roll . . ." said Ryan.

"Randy Hexum."

"Well, I'll be fucked," said John.

"A bit less color, if you please," said Vanessa. "Anyway, we're almost there. I already phoned ahead and made an appointment to get our numbers read."

"What else have you done that I don't know about?"

"When you two were out unlocking the bumpers a few minutes ago, I phoned my brother Mark, and he is now parked across the street from Randy Montarelli's house, and you're paying him twenty-five dollars an hour plus meals so that he can maybe get an inkling where that luggage is headed."

"Where were you when I was making The Other Side of Hate?" asked John. "If you'd been running things, it could have been a hit."

"No, John. It was unsavable."

Vanessa and Ryan plunged invisible peacock feathers down their throats. John went quiet. They spun onto and then off the Hollywood Freeway, and parked outside Dreama's apartment building. John had a déjà vu, but then realized it was actually a flashback to the beginning of his film career. The smell of

Dreama's elevator was identical to the hallways of his first apartment in a building off Sweetzer, a blend of cat piss, cigarettes, incense and other people's cooking. Vanessa asked John, "What do we do once we're in there, John?"

John shrugged. "We'll know when we get there. I hope. Look for clues."

"Hi." Dreama answered the door. "Come on in. You're Vanessa?"

"I am. This is Ryan and this is John."

"The apartment's a mess." The most obvious aspect of Dreama's apartment was luggage on the kitchen table, evidently in the final stages of packing.

"I'm sorry," said Vanessa. "Are we interrupting you? Are you heading somewhere?"

"Yes, but to be honest, I need the money. I hope that doesn't sound crass. I don't want you to feel exploited." She moved a stack of dreamcatchers off a stool.

"Where are you going?" asked Ryan, feigning nonchalance.

A lying flash passed across Dreama's eyes. "To Hawaii. To a seminar on square roots."

"Hmmm."

"Well, let's get started. Who first?"

"Me," said Vanessa. "Vanessa Louise Humboldt, that's one N, two S's, with Louise spelled the normal way, and Humboldt spelled with a d, as in Humboldt County."

"Okay . . ." Dreama sat down and reached for a box of sparkly pencils and a light-powered calculator bearing a $1.99 price tag.

"Do you always let people in here?" asked John. "Strangers? Right into your home?"

"You're friends of Susan. That's good enough for me."

"Yes, John," Vanessa cut in, "Susan's been wanting us to do this for years." Vanessa turned to Dreama: "Just ignore him. Susan says your accuracy is chilling."

"I guessed the Seneca plane crash the day before it happened."

"That's amazing," said Ryan, who suppressed an itch to tell Dreama that his message on Susan's answering machine had been the last before the accident.

"I got the message to her too late," Dreama said, "but she made it anyway. Her prime number that day was so high she could have been struck by a Scud missile and walked away with no more than a nice new set of bangs."

"Prime number?" asked Vanessa.

"That's how I work. With prime numbers—they're the ones that can only be divided by either one or themselves. Like 23, 47, 61 and so on. There's a prime number for all people and events." Dreama's fingers twiddled the calculator's buttons. Her pencils produced spidery loopy letters and numbers so faint they were like strands of thin hair fallen onto the page.

"What's mine? asked Vanessa.

"Give me a second here." She fiddled a bit more. "One hundred seventy-nine."

"That's good?"

"That's excellent. You have strong instincts, you'll never lack money and, as I understand the psychic makeup of 179s, you'll probably go through your life with a man as your slave."

"Why a man?"

"All 179s are het." To emphasize this, she said, "It's a fact, but not one you should let dominate your choices."

"I'll remember that."

John was standing in a corner, pretending to read the spines on Dreama's CD rack, a blend of folk and earth sounds, as he tried to think up a probing question. He spun around, a touch overtheatrically, with his face caught in a patch of light coming off a paper lantern. "Your last name is Ng. That's a strange name—Asian—you don't look Asian. Is there a Mr. Ng?"

Dreama was nonplussed. " 'Ng' is the Cantonese word for the number five. I chose it for that reason, and also because it doesn't have any vowels. And there is no Mr. Ng anywhere. I'm a lesbian." She paused. "Does it bother you . . . ?"

"John."

"Does it bother you, John, to have a strong fertile woman shed her father's name and assume one on her own?"

"Uh . . ."

"What's your full name, John?"

"John Lodge Johnson."

Dreama began doing John's number, then dropped her pen and stared. John asked what was wrong, and Dreama told him she'd made a mistake. She redid his numbers and said, "Well, I'll be . . ." Dreama looked up at him with fresh eyes now, as if he'd been revealed as the murderer at the end of the final reel. "I have to ask you a question, and you have to give me a straight answer. Are you lying to me?"

"What?"

"Are you here under false pretenses?"

"What are you . . . ?" John was adrenalized.

"Let me see your driver's license."

He pulled out his driver's license, just one month old, and handed it to Dreama. She looked at it, handed it back to him and said, "Sorry. I had to see if that was your real name—if this was a hoax of some sort. You're a 1,037, John Lodge Johnson. Do you know what that means?"

"No. You tell me."

"You're a four-digit prime number. Most numerologists go their entire lives without encountering a four-digit prime."

Dreama grilled John, asked what he did for a living and took a distinctly arch manner with him. Ryan then asked to have his number done. It was 11.

"Eleven?"

"Sounds like you're set for a career in the dynamic and fast-growing world of fast food, Ryan," said Vanessa.

"Eleven?" Ryan was crestfallen.

"Eleven is a perfectly good number," Dreama assured him.

"I hear 11s are really loyal," said John.

John paid Dreama, who gave them a sheet describing their prime number's characteristics. Dreama became fidgety and scuttled the three out of her apartment.

Back in the car, John said, "Well, that was a fucking waste of time."

Vanessa's phone bleeped and she answered it. "It's my brother," she told the other two. She finished the call and pressed END. "Randy is in a minivan headed this way."

"Do you have your GPT?" asked Ryan.

"What's that?" asked John.

"My global positioning transmitter. It's the everyday equivalent of the black box they use behind the cockpit in jetliners. I keep it sewed into the hem of my purse." She yanked a small black rectangle from her bag, smaller than a TV remote control. "A satellite can track me down at any place on earth plus or minus a freckle."

"You're giving it to me?"

"For a 1,037 you can be awfully dim. When young Randall's Ford Aerostar van pulls up in"—she looked at her wristwatch—"under two minutes, you are going to have to stick this onto the car without being seen. And as we seem to be fresh out of duct tape, what exactly will be your brainy plan to attach it to the vehicle, John?"

John shut his eyes to concentrate. "A man, a plan, a canal—I was born in Panama, you know."

"Oh, shut up."

"Juicy Fruit." He wrenched open the glove compartment and from it threw packs of unopened gum to Ryan and Vanessa, taking several for himself.

Randy's van swung into a spot directly in front of Dreama's building and across from their car. The three watched Randy walk to the building's main door, buzz and head to the elevator.

John gently opened the side passenger door and crawled behind the car. He roadrunnered across the street and fastened the GPT to the inside of the rear bumper with a cooling glob of his gum. The dogs, sensing John beneath them, grew frenzied, scratching at the windows and barking. Just then the apartment's door opened, and Randy and Dreama came out with her luggage. Both looked worried. There was nowhere for John to hide except underneath the van, where he quickly rolled, listening to the doors above him open and shut. Randy shouted at the dogs to sit. Finally, John heard the engine ignite and watched the van drive away, leaving him facing the sky where he saw the lights of jets preparing to land at LAX sweep in from the distance.

Chapter Twenty-seven

In Erie, Pennsylvania, three weeks after Susan's arrival at Randy Montarelli's house, she floated down the stairs, her nightgown trailing. "Christ, Randy, my nipples feel like hand grenades. What are you doing up at"—Susan looked at the clock on the top right-hand corner of Randy's Mac—"four twenty-seven A.M.?" Upstairs, Baby Eugene, three weeks old, screamed for milk.

"Oh, you know, no rest for the wicked."

"Are we out of pineapple juice again?"

"We are."

"Right. Do we have any Goldfish crackers left?"

"Cupboard above the toaster."

"Good." Susan foraged about. "What lies are you cooking up tonight?"

"You just gave me a good idea. Here, let me try it out." Randy read aloud the words he'd just typed into an Internet chat room:

> That's not what I heard from my friend who does the
> makeup on the Friends set. *He* told me that Jennifer
> Aniston delayed taping for three days because she had
> nipple fatigue.

"Know what it reminds me of?" Susan asked, running her finger around the rim of a peanut butter jar. "Last month, when you started the rumor that Keanu Reeves has 'reverse flesh eating disease.' "

"That *was* a classic, wasn't it?"

"It's like your brain doesn't know what image to conjure up." Susan tasted the peanut butter and found it delicious.

"That's the coolest kind of rumor," said Randy. "Like the one I did about Helen Hunt—having the operation to remove the remains of a vestigial beaver tail from the base of her spine."

"Yet another classic." Susan cradled a box of Ritzes and some apples in her arms. She kissed Randy's forehead, sprinkled crumbs onto his keyboard, then gallumphed upstairs.

Randy was a rumormonger. Before the 1990s he thought of himself as a gossip, but more tellingly he considered himself a zero, some sort of alien love child abandoned on an Erie, Pennsylvania, tract house doorstep where he grew up clumsy and socially inept. Randy was 30 percent over the national recommended body weight for his height, and possessed a sensibility so totally not of Erie that he was unable to be even the class clown or a bumbling mascot to the cruel and good-looking girls. The only friends he ever attempted to make were the brassy, cynical girls with whom he dissected *Mademoiselle* and who seemed to have affairs only with married men girls who bolted from Erie the moment they graduated high school.

Checking out of Erie was an act Randy hadn't been able to do himself. It was a case of the devil he knew versus the devil he didn't. As a teenager, he had first seen the devil he *didn't* want to know in a 1982 TV news documentary. The devil was on-screen for perhaps fifteen seconds, but that's all it took.

The devil still burned in his mind fifteen years later, in the form of a diseased gay clone, emaciated and mustached, wasting away as he guarded the gates of hell. He made bony come-hither disco dance hip sways, and his skin was pitted with prune-tinted Kaposi's sarcoma lesions. His eyes had become white jelly from a cytomegalovirus infection.

In Randy's mind, somewhere around 1985, the image of the sick man acquired chaps and a cowboy hat. Around 1988, each time Randy thought of the sick man, the man began to wink back at Randy with dead white eyes. If the cowboy signified adulthood, then Randy wanted nothing to do with it. If that was the image that stood for sex, then Randy was going to be a monk. And so he hadn't left Erie, which, whatever else it didn't have going for it, was also seemingly lacking in people with AIDS.

But then over the years he began to see the devil everywhere he went. On a trip one night in 1988 he kissed a trucker at a stop outside of Altoona. He shut down emotionally and spent the next five years waiting to die. When he didn't, he decided he was going to live, but his was to be a life without love or affection save for that which came from his two spindly café-au-lait Afghan hounds, Camper and Willy. He'd bought them as puppies from the trunk of a 1984 LeBaron parked outside a Liz Claiborne factory outlet. Its driver was a hippie girl who said the puppies would be drowned that afternoon unless they found homes, because God had summoned her to Long Island where she was to cornrow the hair of teenagers as well as monitor the sunrise.

As he aged and lost his hair and wrinkled, Randy figured he deserved no love or affection because he hadn't been brave or suffered or fought a good fight across the years. The newer, younger, more beautiful children arrived, and with annoying ease inherited the rubble of the sexual revolution, plus the freedom and the easy knowledge of love, death, sex and risk. Randy extracted his revenge on the world for poisoning both his coming-of-age and his youth, through the creation of lies and rumors. Locked inside his Erie town house at night, numbed by his day job doing payroll for a roofing company, he fed thousands of deceptions into a Dell PC which multiplied them like viruses, out into the world of electrons. Most of his rumors died, but some became self-fulfilling prophecies. Who could have known that young ingenue truly *was* so ripe to become a compulsive handwasher?

And then one September night Susan Colgate fell into his life. He was watching *Matlock*, had a refreshing cucumber facial scrub on his face, and was drinking weak Ovaltine, when there was a thump on his front door. He braced himself—midnight jolts on the door, even in Randy's relatively safe neighborhood, were not a good sign. He looked through a small pane of a bay window and saw a pregnant woman, whom he didn't recognize, slumped on his doorstep.

He raced to the door and opened it. The woman was evidently in great pain, and Randy carried her into the living room and lay her down on his two-week-old Ethan Allen colonial couch. He started to dial 911, but the woman screamed, "No!" and yanked the cord from the wall before he could even dial the third digit. She lowered her voice. "Please. Randy Montarelli. Help me. You were the only person I could think of to come to. I saved your letter."

Randy wondered what she could mean by a letter. She briefly calmed down, and Randy realized that this was Susan Colgate.

"You're not dead!"

Susan burst into tears.

"Oh good Lord, you're alive!" Randy ran over to hold her tightly and he whispered, "Oh, Susan—Susan—please—you're safe here. Everything's going to be fine. Just fine."

"I'm scared, Randy. I'm so *scared*." she grimaced, then yelped like a coyote. "Shit, the contractions are close. I'm landing any moment now."

A Boy Scout pragmatism seized him. "I'll get things ready. What do you need right away?"

"Water. I'm thirsty."

"Right." Randy raced into the kitchen, his thoughts scrambled like popcorn. Nothing in his life had prepared him for an event like this. He filled a plastic jug with tap water and relayed it to the living room with a plastic cup. He ran into the guestroom and grabbed a pile of down comforters and told Camper and Willy to stop whining. Random thoughts went through his brain. Susan was supposed to have been long dead. He clearly remembered his pilgrimage to Seneca, one of his few forays outside the Erie region. He then remembered reading in a magazine that Prince Charles wished he hadn't witnessed Prince Harry's birth. He'd wondered what it was Charles had seen, and now he'd soon find out and the idea made him woozy. Was that bourbon he smelled on her breath?

He raced again into the living room; the TV was on. He turned it off. He laid the blankets on the floor but Susan's bag of waters had already burst. He ignored the stains on his couch and rug. Susan reached over sideways into her purse and pulled out Randy's letter. "Here . . ." she said. "You wrote this to me. It was the nicest thing I ever had anybody say about me. Come here, Randy. Hold me a second."

Randy hugged Susan tightly. She held him away from her and looked deeply into his eyes: "We're going to get through this okay, Randy. We've been having babies for a trillion years. This isn't something new. Let's just breathe and play it cool. Here . . ." Susan straightened out some blankets. "We're going to do just fine."

"Does it hurt?" Randy asked. "I've got some Vicodins left over from my root canal."

"I'll take them."

Randy ran into the bathroom and fetched them and some towels. Back in the living room Susan was screaming, "This is it, Randy!"

The next twenty minutes were wordless. They became a grunting, shouting push-me–pull-you animal team, and a baby boy finally emerged in a squalling pink lump. Susan held him up to her chest and Randy severed the umbilical cord. All three of them cried, and by sunrise, they were asleep in the wreckage of the living room.

That morning Randy phoned in and quit his job. He had become privy to some, but not all, of the details of Susan Colgate's precrash and postcrash life. By the afternoon he had the living room pieces hauled away. He ordered a vanload of groceries and baby furniture. He emptied his bank accounts. He stripped Susan's car of Indiana plates and replaced them with fakes he bought from a junkyard. He had momentum. The action made him thrive. He didn't feel like Randy Montarelli anymore. He felt like . . . Well, he wasn't sure yet who or what he felt like. That would come. But within the week he'd thrown away many of his clothes and knickknacks and photos and things that to him reeked of the old Randy—sweaters he wore out of duty to the relatives who joylessly gifted him with them every year; drugstore colognes purchased not because he liked their scent but so as not to inflame redneck strangers with overly exotic aromas; his high school ring, which he kept because it seemed the only piece of jewelry he'd ever have earned the right to wear. He also began legal proceedings to change his surname to Hexum, something he'd always wanted to do but had never found the will to act on.

Randy had been offered this one doozy of a chance to rewrite himself, and he wasn't going to blow it. He'd kill for Susan and little Eugene if need be, and he hoped that in the near future Susan might go into further details on what she hinted was a plan for leaving Erie. In the meantime, Susan spent much of the first month either crying or locked in silence. Randy didn't push her. And the thought of Randy phoning somebody to announce this Bethlehemical miracle was out of the question. This was something for him alone: no mocking relatives or evil coworkers and chatterboxes from his model railway club allowed.

"Randy," Susan said, "why bother reading those infant care books? Any kid of mine is going to be tough as nails. His genes are made of solid titanium."

"We want the baby to be a god, Susan. We want him to *glow.* He has to be raised with care."

Whether to alert the authorities to the birth was not an issue. In Susan's mind, Eugene Junior wasn't to enter the public realm. He was to be unknown to the world and protected from its stares and probes and jabs. "Especially," said Susan, whenever Randy broached the subject, "from my *mother.*"

The more Randy had Susan and Eugene Junior to himself, the happier he was. He was a born provider, and now he had been blessed with souls for whom to care.

Late one night in her fourth week in Erie, the trio was watching TV—an old episode of *Meet the Blooms*. Eugene was clamped onto Susan's left breast. The TV's volume was low. On the screen was an episode in which Mitch, the eldest child, develops a cocaine habit for exactly one episode. Susan watched the TV as if it were an aquarium, garnering neither highs nor lows—just a constant dull hum.

A log in the fireplace burst aglow with new vigor. "Do you ever miss Chris?" Randy asked.

"Chris? I barely ever think of him, the old poofter."

Randy's eyes goggled. "Poofter? You mean—no *shagging*?"

"Good Lord, no. I mean, I like Chris now, but at the beginning we were about as close to each other as you'd be, say, to some FedEx guy dropping an envelope off at Reception. Well, that's behind us now, isn't it? Far, far away." She drained her glass.

"But those pictures," said Randy, "and all those stories that were in the tabloids week in, week out—'Chris and Sexy Sue's Hawaiian Love Romp'—big burly Chris with the scratch marks on his back. I *saw* them."

"Those scratch marks? His masseur, Dominic. I was over in Honolulu getting blepharoplasty on my eyes."

"Your tattoo—it said, CHRIS ALWAYS." Randy's disillusionment was growing more vocal. "But then I guess I didn't see it when Eugene was being born."

"No, you didn't. I had it done for a *Paris Match* photo shoot. It was laser-removed in 1996." Susan stood up, shook her head as though her hair were wet, then positioned her body to meet Randy's full on. "Randy, look at me, okay? It's all lies, Randy. All of it. Not just me. Chris. Them. *Whoever. Everybody.* Everything you read. It's all just crap and lies and distortions. All of it. Lies. That's what makes the lies you spread so funny, Randy. They're *honest lies.*"

The baby snored. A tape that had been spinning in the VCR without playing hit the end of the reel and made a *thunk*. Susan tried to change her tone. "Having said that, Randy, tell me, what's the big lie of the day?"

Randy chuckled. "Whitney Houston."

"Oh *dear*."

"It's true."

"About her left foot."

"What *about* her left foot?" Susan played along.

"You haven't heard?"
"Break it to me."
"It's pretty weird."
"Just *tell* me!"
"Cloven hoof."
"Oh *Randy*."

Chapter Twenty-eight

After shooting her Japanese TV commercial in Guam ("Hey team—let's Pocari!"), Susan arrived back in Los Angeles fresh with the knowledge that the network had decided not to renew *Meet the Blooms*. Larry was in Europe, and he spent hours on the phone with Susan, reassuring her that her promising career had barely yet begun.

She threw a duty-free bag filled with folded Japanese paper cranes into a cupboard. She waited three weeks to unpack her luggage from the trip. She took long baths and spoke only to Larry until she visited her First Interstate branch and learned that her long-term savings account, into which she'd been regularly depositing good sums for years, was empty.

Her lawyer was in an AIDS rehab hospice and unable to help her, and her accountant had recently left town in the wake of savings and loan scandals, so Larry hired new and expensive lawyers and accountants. They did a forensic audit of Susan's life, and after months of document wrangling, playing peeka-boo with receptionists and marathon phone tag, Susan learned that Marilyn had, quite legally, soaked up and then dissipated Susan's earnings—Marilyn who had been little more than a duty visit once a month up in Encino.

"One of my numerology clients was a child star," said

Dreama, then living on her own in North Hollywood. "He got fleeced, too. The government has the what—the Coogan Law now, don't they? I thought the system was rigged so that parents couldn't swindle the kids' loot anymore."

Susan, heavily sedated, called Dreama frequently during this period. She murmured, "Dreama, Dreama, Dreama—all you have to do is come home late from a shoot wired with about three hundred Dexatrims, sign one or two documents buried within a pile of documents, and you've signed it all away."

"You two must have talked . . ."

"Battled."

"What does she say? I mean . . ."

"She says I owed it to her. She says I'd have been nothing without her. And you know what she told me when it became clear that she'd swiped everything I had? She said to me, 'That's the price you pay for being a piece of Tinseltown trash.'"

Dreama, not a shrieker, shrieked. "Tinseltown?"

Larry continued paying the rent on Kelton Street, but he told Susan his accountant would only let him do it for one more year or until Susan had her own income again, if that came sooner. Jobs were hard to come by. Casting agents knew she wasn't a skilled actress and didn't think her marquee value canceled out her bad acting. Lessons did nothing to improve her skills, and the fact she was even taking lessons made her a subject of snide whispers in class. Larry seemed to be giving her far less attention, too, not because of her unbankability but because he knew that Jenna was the root of the problem.

By the end of the Blooms run, Susan overheard Kenny the director say that if Susan ever got a role even as a tree in the background of a high school production of Bye Bye Birdie, it would be as an act of pity. The taping of the final two-hour episode was a bad dream to which Susan returned over and over.

"Susan, dear, you've just learned your father has prostate cancer. Your face looks like you're trying to choose between regular or extracrispy chicken. Let's do a little wakey-wakey because we're close to union overtime, okay?"

The cameras rolled: "Dad, why didn't you tell me before? Why all the others but not me?"

"Cut! Susan, you're not asking him 'Where is the *TV Guide?*' You're asking him why he didn't share with you the most important secret of his life."

The cameras rolled: "Dad, why didn't you tell me before? Why all the others but not me?"

"Cut!"

Susan stopped again.

"Susan, less *TV Guide* and more cancer."

"Kenny, can I use some fake tears or something? This is a hard line."

"No, you may not use fake tears, and no, this is not a hard line. Roger? Give me my cell phone." A bored P.A. handed him a phone. "Susan, here's a phone—would you like me to give you a number and you can simply phone this line in? Or would you like to do it for the camera, for which you're being paid?"

"Don't be such a prick, Kenny."

The cameras rolled: "Dad, why didn't you tell me before? Why all the others but not me?"

"Cut! Roger? Please bring Miss American Robot here some fake tears."

Soon Susan began going to parties each night, not because she was a party hound but because her celebrity status entitled her to as many free drugs as she wanted, as long as she tolerated being fawned over or mocked by the substance suppliers.

· *I can't believe Susan Colgate's here at this party.*
· *Basically, for a gram she'll go anywhere in L.A. County. For an ounce she'll be the pony that takes you there.*

As time went on, she learned not to stand outside the kitchens, where the acoustics were better and where she was more likely to hear the worst about herself. She had far too much free time on her hands, and with it she began to obsess about Larry. One early evening when Susan was feeling particularly alone and the phone hadn't rung all day, she decided she was sick of being iced out of his life, and went to his house. Larry had mentioned that Jenna would be away that night at her mother's birthday in Carson City. Susan knew that if she tried to use the intercom at the gate, or open the front door, she'd be frostily ignored. She cut through the next-door neighbor's yard, once home to a prized Empress Keiko persimmon tree, and approached the house from the back patio.

She was shortcutting through the yard when suddenly the place flared up like Stalag 17. Five Dobermans with saliva meringues drooling down their fangs formed a pentagram around her, and what seemed like a dozen Iranian guys with Marlboro Man mustaches circled the dogs, handguns drawn. She saw Larry amble out onto his veranda next door wearing his postcoital silk robe, the one he'd stolen from the New Otani back when he'd been negotiating the Japanese TV commercial deal. A naked little fawn named Amber Van Witten from the TV series Home Life scampered out after him, eating a peach.

Larry yelled to the Iranians, "Hakim, it's okay—she's one of mine," and the Iranians, gaping at Amber, called off the dogs who, happy as lambs, bounded toward Susan to smell the urine puddle at her feet.

Larry beckoned Susan into the house. She followed him into his den, where he made Susan sit on a towel he placed on the fireplace's flagstones, making her burn with humiliation.

"Susan, it's over."

She started to say, "But Larry," but her pants chafed, the urine had gone cold, and Amber poked her head in through the walnut wood doors. ("Oh, hi Susan.") Susan stopped speaking.

Larry said that he still wanted to be friends—and then Susan really *did* realize it was over. Larry said he had an idea, and that he could use Susan's help if she was willing to go along with it. He'd begun managing a new band out of England called Steel Mountain—"head-banger stuff for mall rats." There had been a screw-up at the Department of Immigration and Naturalization, and the band's lead singer, Chris Thraice, needed a green card or an H-1 visa. If Susan agreed to marry him in order to get him into the country, she could earn 10K a month, live at Chris's house—no more Kelton Street—and have access to the social scene as something *other* than unbankable former child star Susan Colgate. So she asked him what the catch was, and he said that there wasn't a catch, that Chris was a closeted gay, so she wouldn't even have to deal with sex.

A week later she married Chris in Las Vegas—cover of *People* in a black, almost athletic, Betsy Johnson dress. She'd never had so much coverage of anything like this in her career. Music was indeed a whole new level.

She toured 140 concerts per year: all-access laminates; catered vegetarian meals; football arenas and stadiums. Everywhere they went little trolls out on the fringes pandered to their most varied substance needs. It was fast and furious but full of dead spots and time holes in Hyatt suites and Americruiser buses and airport business lounges. Susan felt like she was in a comfortable, well-stocked limo being driven very slowly by a drunk chauffeur.

Larry was around full-time, but he was business only now; fun was over, or rather, fun had moved on. Sex was easier for Chris to find than for Susan. If Susan had liked stringy-haired bassists with severe drug problems and colon breath, she would have been in luck—but she didn't. The only thing that kept her around was access to free drugs, but a few well-placed questions to the people out on the scene's fringes allowed her to set up her own supply in Los Angeles, and she camped out at Chris's Space Needle house in Los Angeles.

"I'd introduce you to my lesbian friends," said Dreama, "but I don't think you'd find what you're looking for. And how can you continue to let yourself be in such a phallocentric and exploitative situation?"

Susan ignored Dreama's PC dronings. "Chris tells me I should just phone up hustlers and bill them to the company. What a hypocrite he is. He found out I was seeing other guys—or at least trying to—and he turned into the Killer Bunny from Monty Python because I was putting his green card in jeopardy. If he were to walk into the room right now, we'd probably rip each other up."

"There ought to be some way for you to meet somebody."

"The only way anybody meets anybody in L.A., Dreama, is through work, which I don't have."

Just under three years into their marriage, Chris had an album tank. In the magical way of the music industry, Steel Mountain was, out of the blue, *over*. The record company withdrew support, money shrank and Chris had to start playing smaller arenas and cities, and he accrued the bitterness that accompanies thwarted ambition. Susan saw his snide side. Chris had his lawyer pay Susan her monthly 10K in the form of two hundred checks for $50, and then the checks started coming less frequently and there wasn't much she could do about it. One morning Susan went out to her car—a pretty little Saab convertible—and Chris had replaced it with an anonymous budget white sedan which Susan called the Pontiac Light-Days. "It's like driving a tampon, Dreama."

A year later Susan had a new agent, Adam, who took Susan on

as a mercy client. He owed Larry fourteen months' rent on office space his B-list agency rented from Larry's holding company. He phoned and told Susan she had a big break, that a young director with a development deal at Universal wanted her to play the deranged ex-girlfriend in a high-budget action movie he was making. "Susan, this kid is young and he is *hot*."

"What's he done?"

"A Pepsi commercial."

There was silence from Susan's end of the line. Finally she asked him, "What's it called?"

"*Dynamite Bay.*"

"Why do they want *me*?"

"Because you're an icon and you're—"

"Stop right there, Adam. Why *me*?"

"You undervalue yourself, Susan. The public *worships* you."

"*Adam?*"

"He approached each of the cast members of the old *Facts of Life* show before you, and none of them wanted to do it. So he chose you instead."

"Oh. So I'm now retro?"

"If being retro and hot is a crime, you're in jail, Susan. In jail with John Travolta, Patty Hearst, Chet Baker and Rick Schroeder."

Susan made the movie, and enjoyed herself well enough, but afterward was again unoccupied, which was worse than before, because she'd tasted work again. Chris was off-tour, and in the house much of the time. He and Susan fought all day, both reeling with disbelief that they were bonded to each other. Susan eventually moved into Dreama's place, where incense burned incessantly, and where Dreama's numerology clients barged into the bathroom to ask Susan if a 59 should date a 443. Between her pitifully small savings and her monthly income, she had just enough to rent a tiny Cape Cod house on Prestwick.

As *Dynamite Bay*'s 1996 release neared, Susan began doing

press. She was in New York doing an interview with Regis and Kathy Lee. It was familiar, and this time she loved it. Chris finally got his green card and the two agreed to divorce after the movie had run its cycle. The movie fared reasonably well, but led to no new offers. At the hotel in New York, before leaving for JFK, Susan spoke with Dreama, who reminded her about an upcoming dinner at the house of a mutual friend named Chin. Dreama was going to bring Susan a new set of numbers to help her make future decisions.

Susan felt rudderless. The harmless nonsense of Dreama's numbers made as little sense to her as anything else. On the way to the airport, Susan asked the car driver to pull over at a deli just before the Midtown Tunnel, where she popped out and bought some trail mix, bottled water and a Newsweek. She had mentally entered the world of air travel, and put her brain into neutral, not expecting to have to use it again until Los Angeles.

Chapter Twenty-nine

Vanessa dissected her first brain one hour before she learned the correct technique for making a moist, fluffy omelet. It was in the tenth grade at Calvin Coolidge High School, Franklin Lakes, Bergen County, New Jersey. She was in biology class, where students were divided into groups of four, each assigned a pig. They were told to stockpile their observations, and then afterward the class would discuss brains. Vanessa had been given her own brain. In the Bergen County School system, Vanessa was always being given a brain to herself. It wasn't so much that she was a round peg in a square hole—it was more that she was a ticking brown-wrapped parcel in an airport waiting lounge. *Treat Vanessa Humboldt differently.*

Vanessa dissected her pig's brain quickly, with a forensic speed and grace that chilled her teacher, Mr. Lanark. Next came home ec, in which Mrs. Juliard demonstrated for the class the proper way to whip eggs, pour them into a buttered nonstick pan (medium-low heat) and use a Teflon spatula to gently lift up the edges of the nascent omelet to allow the runny egg on top to trickle underneath and cook. Once done, the eggy disk was folded over onto itself and presto, "a neat-to-eat breakfast-time treat."

The students followed Mrs. Juliard's technique. Near the end of Vanessa's omelet creation cycle, as she folded the egg over onto itself, her life was cut in two. Vanessa stood in home ec, undoing the fold, and then folding it again over onto itself in different ways. The other students finished their omelets, ate them or disposed of them, according to their level of eating disorder, and prepared to leave, but Vanessa stood rapt. Her classmates were students who'd known Vanessa since day care, who'd seen her reject Barbies, hair scrunchies, Duran Duran and sundry girlhood manias of the era, opting instead for Commodore 64's, Game Boys and the construction of geodesic domes from bamboo satay skewers. They giggled at her.

"Vanessa, honey—you're not angry or anything, are you?" asked Mrs. Juliard, who, like most of Vanessa's teachers since kindergarten, trod on eggshells around her. They feared an undetermined future torture that would subtly but irrevocably be dealt them should they in any way displease this brilliant Martian girl.

As for Vanessa, she looked upon high school as a numbing, slow-motion prison, to be endured only because her depressingly perky and unimaginative parents refused to make any effort to either enroll her in gifted-student programs or permit her to skip grades, which they worried, ironically, might cripple her socially. Her parents viewed high school as a place of fun and sparkling vigor, where Snapple was drunk by popular crackfree children who deeply loved and supported the Coolidge Gators football team. They viewed Vanessa'a intelligence as an act of willful disobedience against a school that wanted only for its students to have clear skin, pliant demeanors, and no overly inner-city desire for elaborately constructed sports sneakers.

But all of this was different now, because of her omelet.

"Vanessa? Are you okay, honey?"

Vanessa looked at Mrs. Juliard. "Yes. Thank you. Yes." She looked at her dirty utensils. "I'll wash up now."

She skipped her next class and waited until noon, sitting on a radiator near the cafeteria. She knew nobody would ask Vanessa Humboldt if anything was wrong for fear that the response could only complicate their lives.

The noon bell rang. She waited five minutes, then walked through the staff area into the faculty room, where teachers were lighting up cigarettes and removing lunch from Tupperware containers and the microwave oven. The vice principal, Mr. Scagliari said, "Vanessa—this room is off limits to—" but he was cut short.

"Can it, Mr. Scagliari."

Voices simmered down and then stopped. A student in the faculty room was still, in late 1980s New Jersey, a rarity.

Vanessa was straightforward with them, as though she were informing them about a transmission that needed fluid changing, or the proper method for planting peas. She said that she was leaving school that afternoon, and that she was probably as happy to be gone as they would be to have her out of there. She stated what the staff had known all along, that she could ace any graduation test they could throw her way, including SATs and LSATs. She also said she would be contacting the American Civil Liberties Union, the local TV and print media, and that she would locate a hungry, glory-starved lawyer to do her dealings. She had $35,000 in savings stashed away from waitressing and playing the horses and could easily support such a gesture.

The staff masked their surprise with pleasant faces. She sounded so reasonable.

Vanessa went on to say that contacting her parents wouldn't gain them much ground, as they were more concerned about her prom dress than her future ambitions. In her own head she was already at Princeton and Calvin Coolidge High School was only a bad dream after a strong curry.

She walked out the front doors and over to the parking lot,

where she got into the battered Honda Civic she'd paid for herself and put her plan into operation. Within a month she was out of the Bergen County school system, and accepted at Princeton for the next fall in a joint mathematics–computer science program. But as she drove home that afternoon, Vanessa thought of eggs and she thought of brains. She wondered how it was that maybe twenty thousand years ago human beings didn't exist—and yet suddenly, around the globe, there appeared anatomically modern people capable of speech, language, agriculture, bureaucracy, armies, animal husbandry and increasingly arcane technologies dependent on refined metals, precise tools of measurement and elaborate theoretical principles.

It all had to do with the brain—which upon dissection struck Vanessa as a large flat gooey sheet of omelet elaborately folded over onto itself into the gray clumpen hemisphere. Vanessa had decided that twenty thousand years ago the human brain decided to fold itself over one more time, and it was that single extra fold that empowered brains to create the modern world. So simple. So elegant. And it also helped to explain why Vanessa was such a freakazoid, so cosmically beyond the others in her school. Vanessa realized that her brain had made the next fold—that she, in some definite and origamilike way, represented the next evolutionary step of Homo sapiens—Homo transcendens—and that her goal in life was to seek out fellow Homo transcendens and with them form colonies that would bring Earth into a new golden age.

At Princeton she encountered fellow advanced humanoids and she no longer felt so alone. But she was disappointed to discover that such petty failings as jealousy, political infighting, fragile egos and social ineptitude were just as prominent among her new colleagues as they were among the old. Phil from the Superstrings Theory group was a pig. Jerome the structural linguist was a pedantic bore who lied about meeting Noam Chomsky. Teddy the quark king was a misogynist. Vanessa correctly surmised that her life needed balance, and one polar afternoon, when ducking into an arts building for a dash of heat, she attended a surprisingly enlightening lecture on the Abstract Expressionist paint dribblers. From this lecture she decided that balance in her life would come from the arts, and that fellow Homo *transcendens* must surely await her in that arena.

She sought out any artistic gesture that proposed human evolution beyond Homo *suburbia*. She attended *The Rocky Horror Picture Show* at midnight screenings for two years running, dressed as Susan Sarandon, which left her with a lifelong yen for midwestern twin-set outfits. She read sci-fi. She tried joining Mensa but was turned off by the bunch of balding men who wanted to discuss nudism, and women who refused to stop punning or laughing at their own spoonerisms.

Half a year before graduation, a dozen companies battled to employ Vanessa, but she chose the Rand Corporation because they were in Santa Monica, California, close to Hollywood and what could only be a surplus of advanced geniuses. She was not above movies—they were the one genuinely novel art form of the twentieth century.

Her work in California was pleasure, and at night she went out into the coffee bars of Los Angeles, meeting dozens of young men with goatees and multiple unfinished screenplays. Some were smart and some were cute, and some were quick to charm, but it was Ryan, three years later, whom she deigned to be the first other member of the new species. She found him by accident late one night, at West Side Video after an evening of hmming and uh-huhing her way through another round of goatees-with-screenplays. She was returning a copy of an obscure but technically interesting early eighties documentary,

Koyaanisqatsi, and muttered, more to herself than to anybody nearby, that the film's repetitive minimalist soundtrack didn't induce the alpha-state high she'd read about.

"Oh, then you'll have to listen to it again, but you have to watch it at a proper theater, and it will work, you know. You'll reach alpha every time."

"You did?"

"Well, yes. That's one of my favorite films."

Vanessa spoke with pleasure. "I liked it, too, but . . ."

"Oh, you know—you have to see it on a big screen. You really *do*. Maybe I'm being too forthright here, but let me ask you this—would you come with me tomorrow night? There's a nine-thirty showing of *Koyaanisqatsi* at the NuArt. If you came here at eight, we could eat something vegetarian beforehand. You are vegetarian, aren't you? I mean, your skin. . . ."

There was a weighted pause in which emotion and options blossomed before them like time-lapse flowers.

And they were off. They went to *Koyaanisqatsi* the next night. They went to more movies. Vegetarians, they refused to eat any food that might have tried to resist capture. Ryan was a screenwriter and woodworker, and he was the only Hollywood writer Vanessa had yet encountered who didn't feel as if the world owed him both a Taj Mahal and a large clear rotating lottery ball stuffed with fluttering residual checks. "Tungaska" was genius. Vanessa twinged with the urgency felt throughout the ages by all women who have struggled to put their loved ones through med school or its equivalent. Vanessa was determined to be the one who discovered him, who pollinated his talents and supported him during his rise.

Then one night she snuck into the video store and found Ryan entwining his signature into that of her own. She felt sure it must be love. She had a few doubts about him—his Susan

Colgate worship, his Caesar hairdo and his underwear, which looked not merely freshly laundered but freshly removed from the box. But no one whom she found tolerable had ever enjoyed her company before.

"Vanny look—it's a Class 3 electrical substation with" (gasp) "a WPA bas-relief on the doors. Pull over!" They were on the way to a Hal Hartley re-release Ryan insisted they not miss. Ryan let Vanessa drive. Their children would be magnificent.

Chapter Thirty

The morning after John, Vanessa and Ryan had their numbers read by Dreama, John sat on a towel outside the guesthouse and bombarded Vanessa and Ryan with phone calls. It was an effort to spur progress in the hunt for Susan. On John's fourth call to Vanessa's office, her patience was taxed.

"John, I could get fired if the company learned I was using their system to track down two nut cases across south central Wyoming."

"So they're still in Wyoming?"

"Three hundred miles west of Cheyenne, passing through . . . at this moment . . . Table Rock, Wyoming."

John then phoned Ryan and grilled him about Susan's history in Wyoming.

"Susan's mother returned to Wyoming after Susan left TV. But Susan's originally from Oregon."

"So her mother may be in Wyoming, then?"

"She was a few years ago, back when Susan recovered from her amnesia."

"*Amnesia—pffft.*" John sounded disgusted. "Amnesia's bullshit, Ryan. It's only a movie device."

"Either way, nobody knows where she went for that year. For that matter, where did *you* go when *you* dropped out of sight, John? You've still never told me."

"I went nowhere."

"Brush me, Daddy-O. Jack Kerouac, *man*!"

"No—Ryan—you know where I went? I really went *nowhere*. I ate out of dumpsters. I slept under bridges. I traipsed around the Southwest and got gum disease and my skin turned into pig leather and I didn't learn a goddam thing."

John hung up. He mulled the morning's information over and became convinced the key to the mystery of Susan's whereabouts lay in finding Marilyn. He phoned Vanessa and ran this idea past her.

"John, the LAPD tried locating Susan's mother and they couldn't find her. And besides, Susan and her mother hate each other. I've had two solid years of Sue Colgate trivia drizzled onto my brain. I've had to drive Ryan to the twenty-four-hour Pay-Less at two-thirty A.M. to buy two-sided mounting tape for his shrine. I've been forced to watch *Meet the Blooms* re-runs on tape instead of going to chick flicks since around the death of grunge. Sure, I know all that stuff I pulled out of data bases. But I know the tabloid stuff, too, and Sue Colgate *hates* her mother."

A neighbor's leaf blower turned off and John marveled at how quickly the world became silent. He walked back inside the house with the cordless phone. "Vanessa, *please*. Wherever the mother is, we'll find Susan. You know it, don't you, Vanessa?" Vanessa didn't answer. "I *know* you know it, Vanessa. You're the professional finder, not me." He sat down on a couch and watched sun break through woven slots in the curtain, like a cheap hotel in Reno back in the seventies. An unwashed dish in John's sink settled with a clank. John took a breath.

"You're smart, Vanessa. You're pretty. You could easily pass as a human being if you wanted to. It gives you a kick to fool the others. But I'm worried about Susan Colgate, and I'm worried about her in a way I haven't been worried about anything before. You may not be worried, but I know you care. I know you do."

Vanessa was quiet a moment and then said, "Okay."

John sighed and looked at the ridges in his fingernails as he continued. "Susan. Shit—she's been around the goddam block so many goddam times that it makes me cry. And yet there she is, still this glorious creature."

The sun went behind a eucalyptus tree and John's room became cool and gray. He could hear the leaves rustle behind him and through the phone line he could hear occasional office noises from Vanessa's end.

"I need you to help me, Vanessa. You're my agent of mercy. My oracle. You may be a space alien, but you're a *good* space alien. Superman was a space alien, too. And this afternoon—this is the chance fate's throwing your way to replace that uranium heart of yours with blood."

Someone called Vanessa from across the office. She called back, "In a second, Mel." John could hear her breathe. Vanessa said, "Her name's Marilyn, right?"

"Yes."

John went outside and lay back and basked in the sun. This was his first real solar exposure since the day he was sick in Flagstaff.

Ryan phoned him. "John, how'd you get Vanessa to agree to do an MSP?"

"A *what?*"

"I have to call Vanessa. I'll call you right back." Both men speed-dialed Vanessa, but Ryan got to her first. John's body began to throb with curiosity, with an urge to know that felt like an urge for sex. He walked back inside the guesthouse, picked at a piece of cold pizza in the fridge and tossed some Chinese food flyers into the trash.

The phone rang. Vanessa said, "So I see that Number 11 has gone and blabbed about the MSP."

"Not really," said John. "But you know what? Here's my guess. You and your egghead palsy-walsies have some scary new gizmo that can locate a lost hamster from outer space. Am I correct?"

"You're a smart one. Meet me for lunch at the Ivy by the Sea. I don't want to leave Santa Monica. Use your big macho clout and get a table for three."

John was there early, then Vanessa arrived. They were surrounded by chattering dishes, tinkling glasses, car noises and seagulls screeching outside. Both were slightly twitchy with their own worries. Vanessa was speaking her thoughts aloud. "I'm going to lose my job if I get caught. What am I saying? I will get caught. It's only a matter of how many minutes before they catch me."

"Caught doing *what*, Vanessa?"

"You'll find out soon enough." She made a tetrahedron of cutlery, using the tines of her forks to join a spoon and a knife. John knew she wanted to ask him something, and he was right. "John . . ."

"Yes, Vanessa?"

"Do you think I'm—"she took a big gulp of breath—"cold?"

"What? Oh Jesus, Vanessa, please don't go taking me too seriously. It's not a good idea."

"Don't flatter yourself, John. But I mean it. Do you think that I'm capable of —."

"Of what?"

Vanessa blushed. "This is so embarrassing. Okay, I'll say it: of being *loved*." Vanessa looked as if she'd suddenly discovered she was naked in public.

"Yeah, of course you are, Vanessa. But—"

"But *what?*" Vanessa's voice expressed weakness for the first time John had noticed.

"You're lovable, Vanessa." John tried to think of how to phrase what he said next. "But you've gotta rip your chest open and expose your heart to the open air, let it get sunburned, and that's bloody scary." He bit an ice cube. "Even still, most people seem to do it automatically. But you and I—it makes us balk."

"And . . . ?"

"Shit. Like I'm the person to speak? Thirty-seven and single. But I did make *The Other Side of Hate*, and you know why it bombed?"

"Why?"

"Because I thought I could fake it. It was so humiliating when it tanked. People think I don't care, but I do. Those reviews were just—*ouch*."

"But now?"

"I guess the thing about exposing your heart is that people may not even notice it. Like a flop movie. Or they'll borrow your heart and they'll forget to return it to you."

The air between the two of them was thick and warm like in a tent. Neither knew what to say next. Ryan came in out of breath. "Try finding a taxi in L.A. My car battery's dead." He made does-he-know? eyebrows at Vanessa. She shook her head. John had the desperate look of somebody who's about to quit a job they've held for twenty years.

Vanessa explained to him what an MSP was—a complex computer program, the opposite of a SpellCheck—a Mis-SpellCheck. The premise of the MSP is that all people consistently misspell the same words over and over, no matter how good a typist a person might be. Misspelling patterns are idiosyncratic—unique like fingerprints, and the MSP also takes into account punctuation patterns, rhythms and speeds.

"You could log on as Suzanne Pleshette or Daffy Duck, but the MSP will identify you after about two hundred fifty words. It's so finely tweaked, it can tell you whether you're having your period or if your fingernails need trimming."

John asked why the cops hadn't run an MSP already. Vanessa said: "This is hush-hush stuff, John. They only do it if they think you might be linked to a missing plutonium brick or to trace you if they think you're violating your position in the witness protection program. It's not a standard security check, let alone for a starlet missing a few days. It also sucks up so much memory that all the in-office computers develop Alzheimer's while it's in use."

John slapped a $100 bill on the table. "Come on," he said. "We're going to Vanessa's office."

John and Ryan were in the car following Vanessa. John phoned Ivan to see if he'd fly them in his jet stowed not far away at Santa Monica Airport. John could feel Ivan's sigh on the other end. "To go *where*, John-O?"

"Wyoming, probably—I'm only guessing. For Susan."

Ivan hesitated. If nothing else, the Susan Colgate fixation had brought John back from the dead after Flagstaff. "There's the European marketing meeting for *Mega Force* this afternoon. You said you'd be here." Ivan was silent a moment, then spoke. "Okay, John-O."

"Great. We'll be on the tarmac in a half hour."

It was a brainless sunny day, and the high noon sun flattened out the world. The trees looked like plastic and the pedestrians like mannequins. Patches of shade formed deep holes. As arranged, Vanessa parked her car in her company's lot while John and Ryan parked across the street. "It's Security City in there," said Ryan. "They don't just take your picture when you drive in there. They take your dental X-ray."

"Do you have any idea what Vanny's doing right now, Ryan? She's going to get fired for using this MSP thing."

Ryan said, "You call her Vanny?"

John waved his hand in a well-of-course-I-do manner. Ryan then asked John, "Well, we knew she might get fired. Is she doing it for me, or is she doing it for you?"

John laughed a single blast of air.

Ryan fiddled with the rearview mirror outside the passenger door. "You know, John, when you grow up these days, you're told you're going to have four or five different careers during your lifetime. But what they don't tell you is that you're also going to be four or five different people along the way. In five years I won't be me anymore. I'll be some new Ryan. Probably wiser and more corrupt, and I'll probably wear black, fly Business Class only, and use words like 'cassoulet' or 'sublime.' You tell me. You're already there. You've already been a few people so far.

"But for now—for now me and Vanessa—Vanny, really do love each other and maybe we'll have kids, and maybe we'll open a seafood restaurant. I don't know. But I have to do it now—act quickly, I mean—because the current version of me is ebbing away. We're all ebbing away. All of us. I'm already looking backward. I'm already looking back at that Ryan that's saying these words."

They sat and stared at the low-slung corporate-plex. The tension of waiting for Vanessa was becoming too much. They didn't talk. They tried the radio, but it came in choppy so they turned it off. A bus stopped beside them and John and Ryan watched the passengers inside it, all of them focused forward and inward. The bus pulled away and they saw Vanessa burst out of the company's front door carrying a cardboard bankers' box. Her stride was off as she speed-walked to her parked car. She pulled away onto the main road, up beside John's car. She rolled down her window and said, "C'mon, let's go to the airport." Her eyes were red and wet.

"Are you okay?"

"Just go. I'll meet you there." She sped away.

By the time they reached Vanessa at the Santa Monica Airport's parking lot, she'd composed herself. "Shall we go to Cheyenne, then?" she asked.

"Honey?" said Ryan.

"It's okay," Vanessa said. "I didn't like it there anyway."

"I never even got to see your cubicle."

Vanessa opened up the bankers' box and Ryan looked inside. There was a Mr. Potato Head, a framed four-picture photo booth strip of her and Ryan, a map of Canada's Maritime region, and several plump, juicy cacti.

Ivan was at the airport. John slapped him on the shoulder and introduced him to Ryan and Vanessa. Ten minutes later they were up in the air.

"I found her," Vanessa said.

"Where?" said John.

"She's working for a defense contractor. In the paralegal pool. Radar equipment. Guess what name she's using."

"Leather Tuscadero."

"Ha-ha." She looked out the window below at the warehouse grids of City of Industry. "Fawn Heatherington."

"That's so corny," Ryan said. "It's like something right out of *The Young and the Restless.*"

"Ivan," said John, "make sure we have a car waiting for us on the tarmac at the other end. And make sure there's a map inside it. We'll be there in a few hours."

Vanessa said, "There's something else strange I found out."

"What?" asked John.

"Judging from various spikes in her typing speeds and frequencies compared against her other data—she used to do data inputting for the Trojan nuclear plant up on the Columbia River back in the late eighties—particularly as regards her use of SHIFT key and the numbers one to five, I'm going to make an educated guess here."

"What would that be?"

"Marilyn's going through menopause."

John looked at Vanessa and then turned to Ivan. "Ivan, Vanessa now works for us."

"Good," said Ivan. "What will Vanessa be doing for us?"

"Running our world." John felt a bit better for having conspired to make Vanessa lose her job. He was smoking furiously now.

"I thought you quit last year," said Ivan.

"I smoke when I'm worried. You know that."

Ivan noticed that John made no connection between his current posture in the jet, alert and driven, versus the crumpled heap he'd been on the floor months previously.

They landed in Cheyenne. An airport worker directed them to their car. Ivan asked Vanessa to be navigator. "No time to start your new job like the present." She sat in the front, and Ivan leaned over and whispered to Ryan, "The secret to success? Delegate, delegate, delegate—assuming you've hired somebody competent to begin with."

Ryan felt like a thirteen-year-old being given advice by a cigar-chomping uncle.

They drove through the city. It was a cold hot day on the cusp of a harsh autumn. The air felt thin and they managed to hit every red light as they wended through this essentially prairie town that was more Nebraska than Nebraska, certainly not the alpine fantasia conjured up by the name Wyoming, or from John's prior experience in the deepest Rockies filming *The Wild Land*.

"Over there," said Vanessa, "the blue sign. Calumet Systems—purchased just last week by Honeywell."

They encountered yet another low-slung corporate glass block surrounded by a parking lot full of anonymous-looking sedans and a wire fence topped with razor wire. A security Checkpoint Charlie precluded their entering the lot. Vanessa made John pull the car into the Amoco station across the street. John said, "Ivan, did you bring the binoculars like I asked?"

John looked, but didn't know what to expect to see—Marilyn making coffee in the cafeteria? Filing a letter? Readjusting her Peter Pan collar?"

"Can I see those, John?"

He handed Ryan the binoculars and Ryan scoured Calumet's lot. John turned on the radio and settled on a Spanish dance station, which Vanessa turned off. "This is no time for the Cheeka-Chocka."

Ryan said, "I can see her car."

"Bullshit," said John.

"No. I do. It's a maroon BMW. I remember it was in the news footage when Susan went home to her mother's."

John said, "Paralegals for prairie defense contractors don't drive BMWs."

Ryan continued staring at the car through the binoculars. "John, you forget the settlement Marilyn made and then lost with the airline after the Seneca crash. She's clinging to her last remaining item of wealth like a lifeboat."

"It was a claret-colored BMW," said Vanessa, adding, "So

what's the deal, John? I mean, we find Marilyn and then what? We trail her all day and all night? To what end?"

"She'll lead us to Susan."

"How do you know that? My professional finding instincts are baffled."

"We don't know where Susan went that year—nobody does. But Marilyn vanished, too, and now suddenly we find she's Fawn von Soap-Opera working here in Cheyenne at a defense plant. I mean, two people in a family vanish? That's no coincidence. Defense contracting? Spying? Espionage? Who knows. But there's a link. A strong one."

"Oh my," said Ryan. "I don't quite believe this myself, but La Marilyn has left the building. She's walking toward her car. Jeez, what a mess she is."

"Let me see," said Vanessa. "Work isn't over until five. Why's she leaving early? Shit—Ryan's right. It is her—with a $6.99 hairdo and a pantsuit ordered from the back of a 1972 copy of USSR This Week. I thought she was supposed to be stylish or something." She kissed Ryan. "Agent 11, you are good."

John started the engine to follow Marilyn, who was pulling out of Checkpoint Charlie. They turned onto the main strip, just then plumping up with the beginnings of rush-hour traffic. They skulked three cars behind her for many miles, past a thousand KFCs, past four hundred Gaps, two hundred Subways and through dozens of intersections over-loaded with a surfeit of quality-of-life refugees from the country's other larger cities, with nary a cowboy hat or a crapped-out Ranchero wagon to be seen in any direction. They drove out of Cheyenne's main bulk, and into its fringes, where the franchises weren't so new and the older fast-food outlets were now into their second incarnations as bulk pet-food marts, storage facilities and shooting ranges. Marilyn pulled the car into the lot of the Lariat Motel. She got out of the car and ran into room number 14.

"Well, kids," said John, "guess where we're spending the night."

Chapter Thirty-one

Erie was having a bad winter that year and Randy's heating was on the blink. Randy, wearing several layers of sweaters, was channel surfing around dinnertime, chili vapors drifting in from the kitchen, when he found CNN announcing that Marilyn had settled her airline lawsuit for *ka-ching*-point-four million dollars. He whistled, slapped his thighs and yodeled, "*Soozan-oozan-oo-AY-oo*." She came in from the laundry room, where she had been changing Eugene Junior's diaper, and watched the coverage stone-faced: Marilyn, her arm around her lawyer's shoulder, was emerging like a catwalk model from a Manhattan courthouse.

"She's got gum in her mouth, the old crone," Susan said. "You can tell because of the slight lump behind her left ear. She doesn't think people can tell, but I can. She thinks gum chewing develops your smile muscles."

Marilyn spoke into a copse of network mikes. She said that justice had prevailed, but dammit, she'd happily forfeit every penny of her settlement for the chance to speak to Susan again for even one minute.

"Oh, Randy, this is *so* Oscar clip."

Randy's eyes darted between the screen and Susan's face. The trial had cast a spell on the house in the three months since

Susan had arrived. She pretended not to care, but she did. Even on the days she claimed not to have read the paper, she was invariably up-to-the-minute on the trial's progress, and never lost a chance to assassinate her mother's character. More importantly to Randy, Susan had let it be known over the past months that once Marilyn finalized her suit, she, Randy and the baby would move out to California and put into action "Operation Brady," which Randy hoped would be the next phase of his life.

"Look, Randy, she's still wearing those cheesy Ungaro knock-off outfits, and she's even got those fake Fendi sunglasses she bought at the Laramie swap meet." She smiled at Randy. "Well, there, pardner, looks like we're a packin' up and headin' west."

Their plan was not complex. Randy, Eugene Junior, and the dogs were to drive to Los Angeles. Once there, Randy would rent a Brady Bunch house in which he and Dreama would raise the baby in a deftly twisted version of nuclear familyhood. Susan would have to live close by until what could only be an enormous amount of fuss died down. Susan wanted to minimize any public glare Eugene Junior might have to endure. But most of all, Susan wanted to keep Marilyn away from the child. "That greedy old battle-ax's claws are never going to touch Eugene. *Ooohh*, that's going to torture her—more than anything— no access to Eugene. Finally I'll have a bit of youth I can take away from her."

Randy said, "Sooner or later the kid's going to need a Social Security number, Susan. I mean, technically, in the eyes of the U.S. government, Junior doesn't even exist."

"Randy, Eugene Junior is going to be a Stone Age baby. There's going to be no paper trail on him at all—not until things quiet down. It's going to be a tabloid shark frenzy. We can do paperwork then."

They worked quickly. On the day of her reemergence into

the world, she drove down to Pittsburgh with Randy and Eugene Junior, and waved them off in an unparalleled spasm of blubbering. A chapter of her life was over as neatly as if followed by a blank page in a book. Then, wearing an anonymous, untraceable Gap outfit—unpleated khakis with a navy polo-neck shirt—she sauntered into a suburban Pittsburgh police station. She'd styled her hair in the manner she was famous for in *Meet the Blooms*, the lanky girl's ponytail, and despite the years, she looked deceptively young, and not too different from the way she once looked on the cover of *TV Guide*. She walked up to the front window and could tell right away that the female duty officer had recognized her—instant familiarity was a sensation Susan remembered from the heightened portion of her career. The officer at the counter, name-tagged BRYAR, was speechless as her brain reconciled what she was seeing with what she thought she knew.

"Hello, Officer Bryar," Susan said thoughtfully, as though she were about to offer a sample of low-fat cheese ropes at the end of a Safeway aisle. "My name is Susan Colgate. I—"she paused for effect—"I'm kind of confused here, and maybe you can help me out."

Officer Bryar nodded.

"We're in—I mean, right now we're in, let me get this straight, Pennsylvania. Right?"

"Pittsburgh."

"And today's date—I read it on the *USA Today* in the box outside. It's—what—September 1997?"

Officer Bryar confirmed this.

Susan looked around her and saw a generic police station like one on the studio lot: flag; presidential portrait; bulletproof windows and video cams. She made a point of looking directly and forlornly into all of the cameras, knowing that the police department might well earn enough to finance a new fleet of patrol cars from selling the footage she was generating for them. She turned back to Officer Bryar: "Well, then. Last thing I remember I was heading to JFK Airport in New York to catch a plane to the Coast and now it's— Forget it."

A media zoo ensued, and Susan was grateful to be housed in a cell in an unused portion of the civic jail. Her life of privacy with only Eugene, and then Randy and Eugene Junior was over. Her holiday from the variety pack of Susan Colgate identities for which she was known had come to an end.

A deputy brought Susan a small tub of blueberry yogurt and a KFC lunch pack of chicken and fries. Susan said thanks, and the deputy said, "I thought you were really good in *Meet the Blooms*. You were the best on that show."

"Thank you."

"I rented *Dynamite Bay* just three weeks ago with my girl-friend, and we watched the whole thing without even fast-forwarding and we returned our backup video unwatched. She's not gonna believe I actually met you here."

Susan ate a fry. "What was your backup video?"

"*America's Worst Car Crashes*. Reality TV."

The deputy walked away and Susan ate a clump of fries and then spoke to herself. *Well, Eugene, am I going to screw my life up all over again, now? You think I've learned anything over this past year?* She nibbled on a thigh, salty and greasy. She realized she was hungry and ate her lunch.

Susan's public story, planned long in advance by her and Randy, was that she remembered not a thing between arriving at JFK Airport and reading the *USA Today* in the box outside the po-lice building. She would tell people that the photo of Marilyn on the front page was perhaps the trigger. The police interviewed Susan for hours, and it yielded them nothing.

Susan let it be known that she chose not to speak with the press as she sat safely within the cool, echoey stillness of the jail cell. For the time being, they could snack on the security camera images she'd provided. She also declined to speak with Marilyn. She was in no hurry because, as her story line went, she didn't feel she'd been missing. She felt no pangs of homesickness. The airline offered to fly her to Cheyenne that night. She accepted. The flight arrived past midnight, and at her request, she was to reunite with Marilyn the next morning. She said she was tired and confused and needed to sort things out in her head.

She was put up at the local Days Inn, and she slept soundly. She woke up at six-thirty the next morning, showered, and put on a Donna Karan ensemble provided by the airline. She was driven in a minivan through Cheyenne, the city that hadn't really been her home. It had been an extraordinarily hot and dry summer, and the leaves on the trees looked exhausted and the roads were dusty. Already her bowels felt like lead and she missed Eugene Junior and Randy. In a dull, aching and car-sick way, she missed Eugene Senior, too. He would have loved and applauded the performance-art side of the act Susan had planned for the morning.

The vehicle approached an expensive-enough-looking Spanish-style house with a maroon BMW and a Mercedes in the drive-way. So this was the House on the Hill up to which Marilyn had leveraged herself. Trailers with satellite feeds circled the yard. Neck-craning neighbors stood behind yellow police tapes and the cameras rolled as Susan slowly walked up the front path-way to the house, toward the double doors inlayed with a sandblasted glass kingfisher holding a minnow in its beak. The doors opened and Marilyn emerged, eyes flooded with tears, and she stumbled toward Susan, who hugged her mother the way she used to hug first runners-up during the pageant days. If the pageants had trained her for nothing else, it was for this moment: *Susan! Mom!*

It was mechanical. A pushover. The cameras needed this. The world wanted it. But what neither the cameras nor the world got to hear was Susan whispering into Marilyn's ear, jeweled with a gold nautilus shell earring, "Guess what, Mom? You really *are* going to have to give back every single penny you were set to receive from the airline. So that makes us even now, okay?"

"Susan!"

Don came out the doors and approached Susan, giving her a hug, with Marilyn barnacled between them. "Good to see you, Sue. We haven't had a single quiet moment since we got the news yesterday." Susan laughed at this, then smiled at Marilyn, who was crying out of what Susan was now convinced was a real sense of loss.

The press camera lenses whirred and zoomed and the apertures clicked and chattered among themselves. Susan, Don and the tearful Marilyn stood on the front steps of Marilyn's house. Susan said to the cameras, "Sorry guys. We need to go inside for a spot of privacy. See you in a short while."

Good old Sue! Always kind to the press.

Marilyn, Susan and Don stepped in the house, and almost immediately Don fled to the cupboard above the telephone and pulled out a magnum of molasses-colored Navy rum. "It's woo-woo time," he said, pouring four fingers worth of the liquor into a highball glass, which he topped off with cartoned chocolate milk. "'I call it a Shitsicle in honor of that wad of crap that got us here to Wyoming. I live on 'em. You want one, Sue?"

"No thanks, Don."

"You sure? Aw, c'mon. We need to celebrate."

"No. It's too early," said Susan.

"Have it *your* way then," said Don, a nasty new spark to his voice. He glugged down a sizable portion of his drink.

Marilyn was mute. She stood by the kitchen table, her arms

folded over her chest. Susan looked around the kitchen, bright and clean and dense with appliances, and by the telephone she saw an array of envelopes and letterheads from CBS, CNN, KTLA and assorted cable and network outlets. "It's been a busy year here, I can see," Susan said.

Marilyn opened her mouth, about to speak, and stopped. The three were as far away from each other as it was possible to be inside the kitchen.

"You're wondering where I've been," said Susan, "aren't you?"

"It's a reasonable question."

Susan picked up a Fox TV letterhead with a note on it:

Dear ~~Mrs. Colgate~~ Marilyn,
Please find enclosed a check for $5,000.00, and thanks again for
providing yet another compelling and inspiring story segment for our
viewers.

Yours, Don Feschuk
VP Story Development

"Maybe you ought to be talking to Don Feschuk instead of me, Mom."

"Don't be willfully cruel. It's not becoming."

"Today's festivities must have caused a bidding war. Who won, Mom?"

"CBS," said Don.

"Let me hazard a guess," Susan said, not releasing her eyes from Marilyn's face. "An exclusive interview, scheduled for pretty soon, I'd imagine, so as to be ripe for tonight's East Coast prime-time slot."

"I didn't want pandemonium here," Marilyn said. "It was a way of simplifying things."

"Heck, no—we wouldn't want pandemonium here, would we. Mom."

"Stop saying Mom like that."

Susan tried to remember the last time she'd seen Marilyn in the flesh. It was at Erik Osmond's accounting office in Culver City. Marilyn had called Susan a "bitsy little slut," and Susan had called her a thief, and then Marilyn threw an ashtray as Susan was leaving the room. The ashtray had shattered and Erik shouted, "That was a gift from Gregory Peck!" Susan had shut the door and that had been it.

Marilyn lit a cigarette. "You could have called."

"Are you dense, Mom? I don't even know where the hell I was."

"I don't believe it."

"Then don't." Susan found the Fendi glasses. "But aren't *you* the one faking it."

Marilyn came over and snatched them away from Susan. "Not *these* days, *daughter*."

"This is the most ornery homecoming I've ever seen," Don said.

"Don," said Susan, "Look at it from my point of view, okay? As far as my brain is concerned, there *was* no last year. Suddenly I'm standing on a street in the middle of Pennsylvania, and then I'm whisked home to see Mummy here who, as far as I'm concerned, is the same thief who swiped not only the sum of my TV earnings, but who also made me shake my moneymaker onstage in front of an unending parade of Chevy dealers and small-time hairstylists for all of my childhood. I had no desire to speak to her a year ago, and I have no desire to speak with her now."

Don was somehow cast in the role of debating coach and nodded fuzzily.

"Do you honestly think," said Marilyn, "that I walked around that crash site—and don't try telling me you don't remember it, because I know you do—amnesia my ass—and saw those body parts and shoes and wristwatches and dinner trays piled up and charbroiled like so much pepper steak on the grill at Benihana's—that I could walk through all of that and wish my own girl dead? That I would say to myself, *Hey Marilyn, your ship's finally come in but hey, too bad about the kid?*" Marilyn walked over to the sink where Don put the rum and the chocolate milk, and she poured herself a drink and took a slug. The rest of the drink soon vanished. "I wouldn't wish that crash on anybody, not even my worst enemy. But I don't even *have* a worst enemy because I don't even have any friends. What do I have? Really? I have Don and I have you, and I don't really even have you. Yes, I almost made a shitload of money from your disappearance, where*ver* you went to, but let me say here for the record, *you* disappeared. You vanished. It was torture, never having a true ending. All the money I made over the past year is mine. I didn't earn it, and maybe I didn't even *deserve* it, but I'm not ashamed of it."

Outside on the street, through the kitchen window's sheers, Susan saw a network van, and some guy beside it switching on a rumbling generator. "I wonder what those people out on the street think we're doing in here right now," she said.

"Oh, hugging, or some sort of crap like that," said Marilyn.

Susan thought of Eugene and Eugene Junior. A small wave of possible forgiveness lapped over her. "Mom, have you ever once, even for a fleeting moment, felt sorry for stealing my life the way you did?"

"Stealing your life?" Marilyn plunked her glass down on the counter. "Give me a break. I made you what you *are*."

"What I am?" A small pin of hope pricked Susan's skin. Maybe she'd right now find out what it was she'd become. "You've got my full attention, Mom. *Please*, go ahead and tell me what I am."

"You're my daughter and you're tough as nails."

This useless reply dashed Susan's brief hope. "What a sack of crap."

"If it weren't for me you'd be driving a minivan full of brats to a soccer game in small-town Oregon."

"That sounds bloody marvelous. I might have wanted that."

"Bullcrap you would have. You were made for bigger stuff. Look at you now. And look outside the window. You're getting more coverage now than an embassy bombing."

"Is that all you care about? Coverage? What if I *did* have a bunch of kids, Mom. What if I *did* have a whole goddam Chevy Lumina vanload of squalling brats, and all of them looked just like you."

Marilyn paused a fraction before saying, *"Kids?"*

"And what if I never let you see them. Ever. What if I told them you were dead and they'd never know their grandma?"

"You wouldn't do that."

"Wouldn't I?"

Don cut in, "Guys, maybe we should take a break—"

"Shut up, Donald," said Marilyn. "Go ahead, Susan. Tell me more. What would you do to hurt me?"

Susan, suddenly aware of how well Marilyn could read her, pulled back. "All I'm saying is that I'm not over it, Mom. The money. The lawyers. Those scenes we had. The *everything.* You know that, right?"

Marilyn's index finger clickety-clicked the rim of her empty glass. "Fair enough."

"You own the house?" Susan asked.

"The bank."

"You're going to have to sell it now. And all those chichi outfits I can just imagine you pigging out on and buying in New York."

"Yeah, we probably will. Make you happy?"

"It does. I lived on bulk yogurt and three-day-old vegetables for years after the show ended. Larry didn't foot the bills. He dumped me pretty quick. I don't know what would have happened if the Chris gig hadn't come up. Everybody was laughing at me behind my back, and it was you who put me through all that."

Marilyn looked at her coldly. "Been practicing that one a long time, dear?"

Susan decided to cut it off there. "I'm going to leave," Susan said. "The airline's going to fly me to Los Angeles."

Susan paused and looked at Don with a question that came to her just then. "Did you ever meet Chris?"

"He's an asshole."

Susan laughed. "Yeah, well, you're pretty well right on that score. But there's nobody can trash a hotel room as well as he can."

Susan blew Don a kiss and then paused in front of Marilyn. She shrugged, turned around and left. It hadn't been the triumphant touché fest she'd hoped for, but not much in life ever was.

Three hours later she was back in Los Angeles; four hours later she was in Chris's house, alone; Chris was in South America. The house on Prestwick had been emptied after the crash, her things sold or given away.

In just a year, the city Susan had known was gone. Larry Mortimer had quit managing Steel Mountain weeks after Susan's crash. He'd divorced Jenna and was living with Amber in Pasadena, producing CD-ROM games for preteens. She called and left a message that she was back, and he drove over to visit her, cutting through the gaggle of press people on the street.

"Sue? Sue! It's me, Larry—open up."

"Larry . . ." Susan opened the door and was stilled as always by Larry's resemblance to Eugene. But this time she'd known

Eugene the man, and Larry was a pale match for Eugene's quirky, arty crustiness. Larry was . . . just another Hollywood manager unit. Susan found herself trying to mask the flood of emotion she was feeling for Eugene. Larry mistook this for Susan's pleasure at seeing him and came toward her in a slightly seductive manner. Susan in turn gave him the most sisterly of hugs. He asked how she was feeling and they exchanged small talk.

"How's Amber?"

"Pregnant. The show dropped her because they didn't want to fit it into the script."

"Well, congratulations. You finally left Jenna, huh?"

"Oh, you know."

"No, I don't know. Forget it. How's the band? Chris?"

"The band," replied Larry, "is in physical, moral, creative and financial chaos. But then I've moved away from rock-and-roll management. Too many aneurysms every day." Susan and Larry had migrated to the kitchen, where Larry poked around the fridge for something to eat. Neither was hungry, but it was a ritual they'd developed years before to squelch awkward moments. They talked some more about the comings and goings of various old acquaintances.

"I checked, but there's no hope in hell of you getting any, how shall we say, 'back wages,' from the Steel Mountain Corporation. There's nothing there to pay you with. And by the way, you'll have to do a photo-op with Chris and sign some divorce papers. I can make it a one-stop deal. He's back from Caracas on Monday."

"Adam Norwitz is supposed to be managing my life these days."

"Adam's become a bigger fish since you were here. Two pilots he was connected with got picked up."

"Life's so rich, isn't it, Larry?"

"Snippy, snippy." Larry found a can of house-brand cola. He looked at it, paused, and asked Susan, "Can this stuff go bad?"

Susan shrugged and said, "Go nuts. Live dangerously."

Larry opened it, poured two glasses, they toasted her return and he soon left. An hour later Dreama came over. She was deeply lonely, without a focus and was only too eager to enter the new family fold. She was given instructions to meet Randy and Eugene Junior at the airport. Randy by then had officially changed his name from Montarelli to Hexum. He and the baby moved in with Dreama that night, and would hunt for a Brady Bunch house the next day. It was all Susan could do not to abandon all her plans, run to Dreama's and inhale Eugene Junior's sweet baby smell.

Public interest in Susan's reappearance, at first blazing, died down to near nothing. Susan did nothing to encourage publicity, and at first Adam saw this as a clever device to jack up her price for an exclusive interview. But Susan rested firm, and Adam had a hard time forgiving her for blowing the chance to sell at the peak of public interest.

Susan was able to rent her old Cape Cod house from the Steel Mountain Corporation, who'd bought it after the plane crash. It was eight minutes from Eugene Junior. She landed Randy a job in a music PR office as an assistant. He used this money to rent the agreed-upon house in the Valley. The Cape Cod house existed almost purely as an elaborate ruse to deflect any possible public awareness away from Eugene Junior. Susan was still trying to think of the lowest-profile manner possible of "taking Eugene public," but finding a solution was proving difficult, as any solution meant a media deluge.

Susan slept in her Cape Cod house at night. Otherwise it was useful only as a shell for her answering machine. It received calls, almost all from Adam Norwitz, to inform Susan of offers for the rights to tell-all cable network dramatizations of her life. These were offers she had to refuse because she publicly stood by her amnesia story, and technically she had no real story to tell. The only other calls were psychiatrists from around the world specializing in memory retrieval who had obtained her number on the sly. ("I know it's bad form to sneak in the back door like this, but I think I can help you out, Susan Colgate.")

"Christ, Randy, these losers think that ambushing me on my private line somehow predisposes me to like them. Whatta buncha lepers."

Randy agreed. His job had given him a small measure of media savvy. His office handled what press remained for Steel Mountain, and he brought back reports that the band's five members had succumbed to road fatigue, catastrophic drug use, hepatitis C, assault-and-battery lawsuits, and musical irrelevance.

"My days are only a little bit starfucky. Mostly they're spent photocopying legal documents and fetching arcane health-food products from halfway across town. Starfucky's more fun."

Susan was cutting melon wedges into zigzag shapes for a barbecue at the Brady house. "Steel Mountain's really over now, isn't it?"

"I don't want to be disloyal—they pay the bills," said Randy, "but how much more energy is it worth to make five grizzled Liverpudlians with teeth like melting sugar crystals look like sexual and moral outlaws for kids maybe two decades younger than themselves? It's obscene past a point."

"How's Chris doing?" Susan asked. She and Chris rarely spoke.

"My boss claims he has a few brain cells left."

"He was the brains of the group."

"But . . ."

"But what?"

"I don't know if it's the drugs or the album sales or the closet but . . ."

"What? Is he hitting on you?"

"No. Susan, I'm just an assistant, not like an agent or someone. But I hear his memory's like cheesecloth."

"Coke."

"He can afford it?"

Five weeks later Chris was jailed in Nagoya, having been caught with a picket fence of coke lines beneath his nostrils during a police raid of an after-hours club. Three grams of coke were found in his jacket pocket and the Japanese correctional system threw the key to his cell down the well. Randy caught the news on CNN on a Thursday morning shortly after his return. Within days what remained of Steel Mountain's infrastructure was dismantled, and its legal bills were staggering. Susan had until the month's end to vacate the Cape Cod decoy house. Randy lost his job and his back pay and took on another PR gig at half of his previous salary. The baby was sick a few times, and Susan squeaked him through the pay-as-you-go medical system by disguising Dreama as a Canadian tourist flashing a wad of bills that were actually the remains of Randy's savings. Dreama kicked in her numerology money, but it only went so far. There were taxes. Rent. Groceries. Phone. Dog food for Camper and Willy.

In the midst of this, Randy enrolled in a screenwriting night school course. He came to realize that his life's 'narrative arc' was, like that of most everybody else in the world, cruelly and pitilessly dictated by the most mundane of financial straps and, in Randy's particular case, a troglodyte goon from a collection agency who showed up at his offices during a sales meeting, demanding either payment or return of the TV set.

And so the money ran out. Everybody was doing what they could, but Susan decided it was her turn to bring home the bacon. She arranged a lunch meeting with Adam Norwitz at the Ivy. She was going to sell her privacy.

Chapter Thirty-two

Marilyn meandered through the Seneca crash site and remembered a movie she'd seen years before, one where the wife of a Hollywood movie executive is hacked to bits and left strewn about a lemon grove. But Seneca—this was no movie, this was the odor of burning plastics, her shin scraped from bumping into a sheared aluminum panel. This was the crackle of walkie-talkies, the wail of competing sirens. She saw a drink service trolley, little liquor bottles and all, flattened like a cardboard. She saw a Nike gym bag run over by a fire truck. She saw prescription bottles, juice cartons and exploded cans of ginger ale pressed into the Ohio soil like seeds, watered with aviation fuel and germinated by fire.

She'd been at O'Hare in Chicago, and was heading back to Cheyenne after helping organize a regional pageant in Winnetka. Inside one of the air terminal's snack bars, she'd seen crash footage with Susan's old promo shot inset in the upper left corner. Within a blink she had checked the departure screens, purchased an electronic ticket and boarded a flight to Columbus, where she rented a car. She was at the crash scene within three hours. Once there, Marilyn learned that there are no rules for crash sites. They occupy huge amounts of space in the strangest locations. Most local disaster crews are overwhelmed by the workload and are sickened by the things they see. There had been a yellow plastic tape hastily strung up around much of the site to keep away the gawkers, and Marilyn knew that the easiest way to get inside the tape without hassle was to give the impression of already having been there. To this end she smeared her face, blouse and jacket with rich Ohio soil and nimbly stepped inside, into the space where chaotic orders were barked through megaphones, past blue vinyl tarps fluttering over stacked bodies and inside the supermarket meat trucks used to refrigerate body fragments for later DNA examination.

There were any number of photographers on the scene, and one photo of Marilyn in particular, with her lost face and soiled wardrobe, made the cover of several national publications ("One Mother's Loss"). Marilyn bought four dozen copies of each issue.

In Marilyn's mind, Susan was either completely intact or completely incinerated. Any point between these two extremes was intolerable, for Susan was a beauty, a result of Marilyn's own good looks and teaching. Marilyn's own pursuit of beauty had raised her out of the Ozarks of the Pacific, out of the family's Oregonian mountain shit shack, with its seven children, two of whom were alcoholic by the time Marilyn began generating memories. Hers was a beautiful looking family, but one with a hellish ugly core, no morals, too many guns, no God to fear, reared in isolation, mostly illiterate and sticking their dicks wherever the opposition was overcome. She abandoned the shit shack at sixteen, pregnant by one of two brothers, and miscarried in a Dairy Queen bathroom after a fourteen-hour walk into McMinnville. Using one of three dollar bills she'd stolen from her father's rifle bag, she bought a banana split and marveled at the free red plastic spoon that came with it. The other two dollars she used to buy foundation at the Rexall to cover up her tear-blotched complexion. She hitchhiked out of town and got a ride with Duran, a half-Cajun drainage pipe salesman. Almost immediately he asked her to marry him, and she accepted because she had nothing else going for her, and besides, Duran was a gentleman who didn't wake her up in the middle of the night, heavy, wet and pounding. In fact, except for the first few times that produced Susan, Duran didn't touch her much, and that was just fine. Duran's love was more like worship, and he insisted Marilyn do all she could with what she had, yet he was also a pragmatist and insisted she learn a non-beauty skill. To this end he oversaw Marilyn's two-part education of daytime courses at the Miss Eva Lorraine Institute of Cosmetology (since 1962), and night school courses in typing and office procedures, which Marilyn soaked up like a cotton ball.

Susan was born, but Duran insisted Marilyn continue with her studies, which ultimately raised her to paralegal status. "Marilyn, please stop talking and study the woman on TV."

"I'm tired of watching her."

"That is not an issue. Just keep watching." Duran was convinced that the most useful accent a woman could use was the concise nasal telegraph of the network news goddesses, and made Marilyn watch and mimic their style.

"Durrie, why are you making me learn all of this stuff?"

"Because, Marilyn, you know I'm not going to be here forever, and please don't talk like such a heek."

"What do you *mean* you're not going to be around? And by the way, it's hick, not heek, and please don't call me a hick."

"I need to know you'll be able to make it on your own. The world is hard. You need skills."

"And when am I going to be alone?"

"When you're twenty-one."

"And then what, Durrie?"

What Duran did was leave, just as he said he would, and Marilyn accepted it without rancor and thought she had gotten good value for her time with him. As Marilyn had cultivated no friends, and had pretty well jettisoned her family, she didn't mention him again to anybody else.

But when the screen door slammed, Marilyn sensed an absence in her life as blunt and frightening as a freshly cut tree stump. And it was at this point that her enthusiasm for Susan's entry into the world of pageants was born.

Miss Eva Lorraine's primary cosmetological message was that the traits humans perceive as beautiful are those that bespeak of fertility. "Big titties mean milk, girls, no secret about that. Shiny hair means healthy follicles, and our eggs, girls, come from follicles just as surely as does our hair and fingernails. And so that's why we keep a buffin' and a primpin'."

Marilyn found the message eminently scientific, and thereafter as a rule she let the pursuit of babies govern all of her future beauty decisions—push-up bras, rouge in the décolletage, cellophane rinses on her hair and, as time wore on, silicone injections to plump up some facial sagging. But the injections didn't come until long after Don Colgate entered her life, a hefty logger from Hood River. He was blown away by a looker who worked at a genuine legal office, with a daughter like a china figurine on his granny's mantelpiece.

After they got married, he insisted she quit working, and so she did. Marilyn saw this as decidedly old-fashioned thinking, but it also implied that Don wouldn't go leaving her like Duran.

It was with her conquest of Don Colgate that Marilyn obtained the final proof she needed that fertility and the proven ability to bear beautiful babies were integral to her allure and her sense of being. But then there was the issue of Don and his fertility. His sperm were dead or lazy or stupid or overheated, and he and Marilyn didn't conceive. As his sterility became more evident, so did his drinking and the number of pageants in which young Susan was entered increased. The bunny hutches behind the trailer increased, too, and it was a trailer, never a house, because Don just didn't seem to get promoted at the lumberyard.

Marilyn found that she could funnel her native intelligence into the world of pageants, an intelligence she was convinced she had passed on to Susan. Other pageant girls whined and screeched and pulled princess routines, but Susan sat like a hawk on one of the Interstate light posts, scanning for roadkill, watching and learning from the others. She tended to win, and after a point released Marilyn from the need to shuck bunnies.

Don said that some of the makeup and attire Marilyn made Susan wear was cheap and slutty. She told Don that she'd once read that girls in China have babies at the age of nine, "so if girls can have babies that early, there's nothing wrong with high-lighting that capacity."

"It's bad morals is what it is, Marilyn."

"Don, cool your jets. Get off the pulpit."

"Marilyn, nine-year-old girls do not wear tittie-bar stilettos."

"Don't be so coarse. They're *evening* shoes."

"I thought hill folk were supposed to be so wise, like the Waltons."

The issue of morals usually quieted Marilyn, if only briefly. Knowing about morals was in no way the same thing as actually having them. She'd been raised in a hog pen and was lacking in ethics. Some nights she genuinely did worry about the sins of the parent being handed down to the child—her own feral up-bringing overriding Susan's angelic manner. But she wouldn't speak these thoughts aloud. Instead, for example, she told Don that morals were whatever got the job done at the time. "Like those Polynesians who eat Spam."

"The whats who eat *what?*"

"Spam. That's what Mr. Jordan, my old boss, told me. He'd read that in supermarkets down in the South Pacific they have whole aisles that are devoted to nothing but Spam. The Americans tried to figure out why these island people liked Spam so much, and it turns out that nothing else approximates the taste of cooked human flesh like the salty porky taste of Spam."

Don's mouth hung open.

"We think of those jolly little Island people down there in their jolly little hula skirts and being oh so moral. But to them, cannibalism is perfectly moral, so it seems to me, Don Colgate, that morals are a pretty flexible little concept, so don't go getting preachy on me."

But it was Marilyn whose mouth was agape while walking through the sprays of cooked human flesh at Seneca. She was asked her name by a person inside one of the many biohazard protection suits swarming the site. She replied, "Susan Colgate is my daughter. I'm her mother. Have you seen her?" Marilyn's shoes' heels had broken. She was wearing a pair of pink women's running shoes she'd found intertwined with a stereo headset a few minutes back when she'd scraped her shin.

At sunset a Gannett reporter named Sheila drove Marilyn to the local Holiday Inn and gave Marilyn her bed. Sheila filed her stories and bounced between her laptop PC, her cell phone and the TV. Marilyn called Don. He arrived the next morning. Both spent the day at the local ice rink, temporarily converted into a morgue. Skating music serenaded family members of crash victims who appraised what remains were "readable." There were rows upon rows of limbs and torsos and shards, all covered in black vinyl tarps, arranged like 4-H projects atop plywood sheets that straddled sawhorses. Five days went by and still they found no trace of Susan. Marilyn donated blood samples for DNA testing, to help analyze those bodies too far gone for visual or dental identification. They returned to Cheyenne, their spirits fogged like wet car windows, their emotions on hold. Sheila called each day to see if an ID had been made, but no. This in itself became a story, and the local coroner, in conjunction with the airline and the civil aviation authorities, were at a total loss as to where Susan's remains might have ended up. There hadn't been enough heat for vaporization to occur, and all eye-lashes and fingernail clippings within a half-mile radius had been DNA-cataloged. It was at this point that Sheila hooked up Marilyn with a prominent claims litigator, Julie Poyntz, who spent the next year winning her claim, arguing about the pro-found stress for family members arising from the airline's losing the body of a passenger, a body that might very well be in the deep freeze of some psychotic fan.

"You just don't lose a body, Mrs. Colgate—Marilyn." It was early on in their lawyer-client relationship. "And I don't want to dwell on the possibilities of what might have become of her re-mains, but ..."

"What if she's alive?" asked Marilyn.

Julie tsk-tsked. "You were there, Marilyn. Everybody on that flight was dead and/or severely mutilated."

Marilyn squeaked.

"I'm sorry, Marilyn, but you can't be squeamish. Not now. We're going to win this. They know it. We know it. It's only a matter of how much and how soon. It's no compensation for losing Susan—who, I might add, was a role model for me from Meet the Blooms—but at least the money is something."

Money was flowing into Marilyn's life from many directions at that point, and each new development, or each new recently discovered baby photo of Susan was carefully brokered with all facets of print and electronic media. She bought two new cars, a Mercedes sedan for Don, and a BMW the color of homemade cherry wine for herself. She also took out a mortgage on a Spanish mission–style house and indulged herself with clothing and jewelry, her prize being a pair of genuine Fendi wraparound sunglasses which, not five minutes after buying, she wore as she snapped arms off the fakes she'd bought years ago at a Laramie swap meet. Marilyn spent like a drunk in a casino gift shop. There was no overall scheme to her buying—she simply thrilled with the burst of power each time a piece of loot that once belonged to somebody else suddenly belonged to her.

Yet for all this, Don and Marilyn didn't speak much about Susan, mostly because long before the crash, back in 1990 after her TV show was canceled, Susan had eliminated them from her life with a finality that approached death. Marilyn truly saw no reason why Susan should be as angry about the money as she was. Hadn't Marilyn done half the work?

They'd read of Susan's marriage to Chris in the Arts & Lifestyle section of the local weekend paper. They met Chris only once, at a midnight vigil for Susan that Marilyn had staged in a Cheyenne town square (exclusive continental European photo rights to *Paris Match*, UK rights to *Hello!* magazine, U.S. and Canadian rights to the *Star*, film and TV rights reserved, as live footage was to be inserted into a possible A&E special about Susan to begin production the following year). Marilyn and Chris hugged for the cameras, lit candles, and bowed their heads for the cameras. All the while, Chris's young fans chanted from across the square. Afterward, Chris left and didn't speak with Marilyn again. ("Guess what, Don—I think Sir Frederick Rock Star is an asshole.")

Then came Julie's phone call one morning: "Marilyn, come

to New York. It's over." When Marilyn found out the amount, she whooped with pleasure, then immediately apologized to Julie for whooping in her ear. She tried to find Don, and did, passed out in the back corner of his favorite seedy sports bar. So that afternoon she left for Manhattan without him. The next day, with Julie, she walked down the courthouse steps and spoke with the press. That afternoon she spent $28,000 while shopping on upper Madison Avenue.

The next day Marilyn went home to Cheyenne, and the day after that she got the call from a sparkle-voiced airline PR woman about Susan's return to the living. She hung up the phone and reached for half a Shitsicle Don had left beside the phone book. Susan would be home the next morning.

Chapter Thirty-three

Back in Cheyenne's outskirts, Marilyn lurked inside her motel room with the drapes closed, the TV blaring. Vanessa and Ryan were standing behind the rental car keeping sentinel on her, while Ivan and John headed to the lobby.

Ivan called Cheyenne's airport about the jet's overnight parking and then rented rooms for the group in case they had to watch Marilyn into the evening. John was looking out the window covered in grit and credit card stickers, also scoping the door to Marilyn's room. The group reconvened at the car, where Ryan said, "I'm starved. We didn't eat lunch."

"Me, too," said Ivan. "I'm going to go make a burger run. There's an A&W a quarter mile back on the road."

"Well, you can't use the car," said John.

"What?" said Vanessa. "As if Marilyn's going to vamoose right now or something? We're all sugar crashing. It's a worthwhile risk to get ourselves properly nutrished. Get me a large fries—make sure they use vegetable oil, no lard—and an iced tea."

John was too hungry to fight and he gave Ivan his order. As he left in the rental car, Vanessa walked up to the door of number 14, and knocked loudly. Even from a distance, the sound of blaring cartoons and commercials tumbled from the room, the windows rattling as if they possessed stereo woofers.

Vanessa's unexpected charge shattered John and Ryan's complacency, and they dive-bombed behind Marilyn's BMW.

"Hellooo . . ." said Vanessa, and she knocked again, louder this time. "Hellooo—Mrs. Heatherington? Fawn Heatherington?" Vanessa rapped the windowpane and then a slit in the curtains, which were yellowed, nicotine-soaked and threadbare, fluttered open. The room's door opened a crack. "Yes?" Bugs Bunny shrieked from within.

"I'm Mona. My uncle runs this place. Did you leave a twenty-dollar bill lying on the counter by mistake?" She held up the bill.

The door opened a notch wider. "Why yes, I did—how thoughtful of you."

"Think nothing of it, Mrs. Heatherington. Wyoming hospitality."

Marilyn plinked the bill from Vanessa's fingertips and mumbled the words "Wellthankyouverymuchgoodbye," to Vanessa, but Vanessa stuck her foot in the door so it couldn't close. "Excuse me?" said Marilyn in a forced huff.

"Sorry to disturb you even more, Mrs. Heatherington, but—"

"Fawn. Call me Fawn."

"Sorry to disturb you even more, then, Fawn, it's just that . . ." Vanessa's eyes saw the aged curtains. "It's just that for the past year I've been trying to get my uncle to buy new curtains for the units. See how ratty these are?"

"Well, I suppose, yes."

"Exactly. If you could just mention this when you check out, it would sure help me build a stronger case. He's kinda cheap."

"Absolutely," said Marilyn.

The door shut and Vanessa strode over to her room, number 7. She was followed by John and Ryan, who scrambled out from behind the BMW, then beneath Marilyn's window. They came into the room and Vanessa said, "She's not alone."

"How can you tell?" asked John.

"I heard someone rattling about in the bathroom. Even through the cartoon noise."

"Did you see anything else in there? Clothing? Books? Magazines?"

"No. It looks like an unoccupied room."

Ryan asked if the room was the same configuration as the one they were in, and Vanessa suspected it was. "Then come back here with me," Ryan said. "Let's see if there's some kind of escape route we should watch for." They walked back to the bathroom and inspected the window beside the sink.

"I don't know if that window is crawl-out-of-able," said John.

"I think it is," said Ryan. "Watch me." He hoisted himself up, his stomach resting on the dusty and blackened aluminum slide rail.

"Ryan," said Vanessa. "Get down from there."

"No. I just want to see if—" He was cut short by the sound of Marilyn's BMW charging out of the parking lot and left, westward, onto the highway.

"Shit," said John. He kicked a hole in the door of number 7.

"Don't be so melodramatic," said Vanessa. "Ivan'll be back soon enough. Let's sit tight."

"I bet she saw us behind her car," said Ryan.

They waited outside for Ivan, and John was visibly falling apart. Vanessa asked him if he was going to be okay, and he wasn't sure if he would be. The sun was still above the foothills off to the west, but only just. Wind whistled by, and John recalled the wind, back when he'd been lost. He remembered how it never leaves the air.

Ryan tried to atone for his having distracted the trio away from Marilyn's exodus. He went up to the door of 14 and tried turning the knob. It did and the door opened. He inspected the room but found no clues.

"Gosh, Sheriff Perkins," said Vanessa, "those darn crooks left a book of matches from the Stork Club. Look—there's even a phone number written on the inside: Klondike 5-blah-blah-blah-blah."

"A bit more support, a bit less sarcasm, Vanny."

Ivan pulled in and the trio rushed into the car like puppies. "That way," said John. "She has a two-minute lead."

The car skidded out in a lazy spray of gravel. They flew west down the Interstate, back toward Utah and California, amid the truckloads of lettuce and hay bales and lumber that John thought seemed to never leave the roads, as if they existed in some sort of perpetual caffeinated loop.

An Exxon station lay ahead like a beacon. Ryan scoped it out with the binoculars. "She's there," he said. "Parked over by the tire pump."

"Thank Christ," said John. "Ivan, pull in, but not too far, because she might see us and bolt."

Ivan veered into the station, then empty.

"Is she in the office buying gum or something?" asked John.

"If you're like me," said Ryan, "whenever you're being pursued, your first impulse is to stop the chase and stock up on gum."

"She's probably in the bathroom," said Vanessa. "I'll go look." She got out of the car and walked to the ladies' room entrance by the side. She knocked on the door and Marilyn's voice called out, "Yeah?" Vanessa faked a southern accent and said, "No hurry then, ma'am," then gave the thumbs up to the men in the car, and walked back.

John got out and stood at the back of the car, absentmindedly eating a cheeseburger. "If we keep following her, we could be on the road for hours," he said. "She could be driving anywhere."

A black minivan drove by. Susan was at the wheel. She saw John and wrenched the van to a halt. Camper and Willy avalanched into the dashboard. She and John locked eyes, smiled. She recovered her wits.

"Shit, Susan," Randy yelled, a drink spilled in his lap. "What the hell are you—?"

Susan plunged the minivan into reverse gear and made a crazy donut, then looped around and pulled up beside John's car.

"Your mother is in there," John said, pointing to the rest-room. "I found her for you. You were looking for her, weren't you?"

Susan climbed out of the van, lifted her arms up to her mouth, and started to rock back and forth slightly, like a stick in the wind. She said, "Oh, John . . ." but her voice vanished, and instinctively Randy and Dreama, now out of the van, stepped back in surprise, as though Susan were a highway smash-up during rush hour. She took geisha steps toward the rest room door.

Vanessa quickly pulled back from the door, allowing Susan to approach alone. The others in the group formed a semicircle around her. A truck zoomed by on the freeway. The sun was halfway behind a mountaintop and their shadows were black ribbons. The dogs romped and yelped in the grass scrub behind the station. Susan knocked on the door. Marilyn shouted out, "Jesus Christ, I'm hurrying, I'm hurrying. I'm changing a diaper in here, okay?"

"Mom?"

Everybody felt the silence from within the locked bathroom. The last glint of sun went behind a hill and their shadows vanished and the air became that much cooler.

The station's attendant rounded the corner to check out the crowd. Randy asked him, "Do you have an extra key to the ladies' room?"

"No sir, just the one."

From inside the door came a child's crying. Instantly, Susan bolted toward the door and tried smashing it with her shoulder, unsuccessfully. She slammed into it again, then Marilyn opened the lock and Eugene Junior raced out. "He's okay," said Marilyn, then Susan grabbed him and swept him over to a small wall beside the propane filling tanks where she held him close to her chest. Marilyn sat down on the toilet in haggard defeat.

"Mom," said Susan, "it's okay."

Marilyn didn't come out of the bathroom. Her body deflated and she took a breath. The group's eyes peered into the small, harshly lit room.

Chapter Thirty-four

Susan slammed the door of the house in Cheyenne, and almost immediately Marilyn felt as if she were on fire. But the fire didn't go away. It burned within her, underground, flaring up hourly across the following months, and when she burned, she lost her head and said hateful, vengeful things, which finally drove Don away. She beetled about inside her clean, white petrified house with nobody to talk to and nobody to phone. She felt like her head was filled with larvae. Her doctor said it was "the change," and Marilyn said, "Dammit, why can't you just call it menopause?" The doctor said, "We look at things differently these days. This isn't an end. It's a beginni—" Marilyn said, "Why don't you just shut the fuck up and prescribe me a suitcase full of pills and make this blasted fire go away."

The fire didn't go away, and pills were useless in snuffing it out. She cried and then she felt elated, but mostly she was bewildered and burning. And then the bills came due and all of the money was gone. She'd been proud, and didn't want to give Susan the satisfaction of seeing her mother cash in on paid interviews, so she did no press after Susan had left for California. Yet at the same time she hoped that Susan would see her mother's refusal to pocket some money and then maybe, just maybe, Susan would forgive her. And if Susan forgave her, then maybe she'd one day allow Marilyn access to the brood of children she'd seemed suspiciously intent on mentioning.

In the end, Marilyn's pride and hope had left her vulnerably broke. She phoned the networks, but it was too late, the Susan Colgate story stale. Marilyn offered no new angle.

Marilyn pawned what she could, yard-saled some more, and then rented a cheap apartment. She developed a phobia about touching her lower stomach. She was afraid of her fallopian tubes and her uterus, sure they'd dried out like apricots or chanterelle mushrooms, and she didn't think she could cope at all were she to feel their lumpiness within her.

Fertility. Babies. Desirability. Love. These words were so fully joined together in her head, like pipes and wires and beams in a building. And now, suddenly she was barren. A houseplant.

As if on cue, parts of her face started to migrate and shift. Silicone injections from a decade ago became like rogue continents within her skin, and Marilyn ran out of supermarkets and convenience stores in the Cheyenne area because she had shrieked at the clerks in the stores for focusing even a blink too long on the inert sensationless bulges beneath her left eye, her right cheek or the bridge of her nose.

She lost her energy. She became unable to drag herself out of bed in the morning. And then the landlord's henchmen gave her a month to leave her apartment. So she threw what she could into the BMW (which she refused to surrender) and sold what remained to a guy from a local auction house. She went out onto the road, like so many people had done before her, discharged from a world that no longer gave a damn if she burned or mummified or vanished or was sucked up into the sky by a spaceship.

And then one day, somewhere in Colorado, it all stopped. Her head cleared, and it was as if the months of hell had been merely a fevered patch. Though she had lost her husband, her house, almost all of her possessions, she felt—*free*.

She took a room by the week over by the Cheyenne air force base, where weekly rentals were common. She changed her name to Fawn because she saw a fawn behind her rental unit one morning, and Heatherington because that was the fake I.D. name they gave her in the back room of Don's old sports bar haunt as she exchanged her Piaget wristwatch for a new identity.

Good old Duran had been spot on about Marilyn's needing a skill not tethered to beauty to help her through her life. She resumed including him in her prayers, when she prayed, which wasn't too often. He'd been dead for maybe fifteen years. In 1983 she'd read that he'd whacked his car into the side of a dairy van. She said, *"Hey Durrie, at least I sound like a lady on TV announcing the news. Sleep tight, honey."*

Marilyn's clerical and organizational skills, acquired so many years back, landed her a job at a company called Calumet Systems, which, as far as she could tell, built UFOs for the government. Nobody there recognized "Fawn" as Marilyn, despite her recently televised reunion. She'd morphed into somebody utterly new. She was now a cropped brunette with pitted skin who bought her Dacron frocks off the rack that in a previous life she wouldn't have deigned to use to wipe crud off the snow tires in the garage. She was cool and serene and proud to help her government manufacture UFOs at Calumet.

This went on for a year. She assembled bits and pieces of daily necessities from thrift shops, and she went out once a month to see a movie with two of the girls from Calumet, who ribbed her about her BMW, which she said her brother gave to her. She watched TV. She was happy because she figured she could live this unassuming life until she died and she wouldn't ever again have to put so damnable much energy into being a complicated person with tangled relationships that only seemed to wear her out in the end.

She typed like a woodpecker, even with long fingernails. She was so good at it that a man from a company outside Calumet was brought in to witness her skills for himself, to identify her "metrics." He praised Marilyn for her low error rate and he noted her biggest weakness, her frequent inability to capitalize sentences that began with the letter T. The man had smiled at her just before he left, and it was then that Marilyn intuited that he knew she might not be Fawn Heatherington. He'd asked her if she'd ever worked anywhere else before, and she'd said she hadn't. This had to seem like a bald-faced lie, but it actually wasn't. Her job with Mr. Jordan, the Spam Man, had been in another era altogether, and her only other typing-based work was time spent in a satellite office of the Trojan nuclear plant, raising money for Susan's gowns.

That same night the fire in her body came back again, and it was worse than before, possibly because its reemergence seemed like such a sick joke and she'd worked so hard to erase Marilyn Colgate, the Burning Woman. The loneliness that she thought she had so effectively thwarted began to rip apart her insides. She phoned in sick to Calumet. She screamed and wept in her car, and drove to California with a plan to beg for Susan's forgiveness, though she knew this was only dreaming.

She drove past the Cape Cod house on Prestwick and parked in front of a house down the street. It was garbage night. Nobody saw her. She picked up Susan's small zinc garbage can and threw it into her car's back seat. She drove to a Pay-Less lot past the Beverly Center and dissected the contents of the can: two nonfat yogurt tubs, an unread paper, three Q-Tips and a phone bill with thirty-eight long-distance calls to the same number in the San Fernando Valley, plus a receipt for a jungle gym delivered to a Valley address. Bingo.

She went to a pay phone and dialed the Valley number, and a man's voice answered, "Hello?"

Marilyn said she was from the company that had delivered the jungle gym and wanted to see if they were satisfied customers.

"Eugene *adores* it—*lives* on it, practically. And it really does help pull together the whole back yard."

"That's good, then," Marilyn said. "Would Eugene be needing anything else for the back yard?"

"Oh you relentless sales folks. Not now, but he's getting a real thing going for airplanes, so don't be surprised if we order the Junior Sopwith Camel in a half year or so."

"We'll look forward to it."

The call ended. Marilyn went into the Pay-Less and bought a foam 747 made in Taiwan. She drove out to Randy's house, parked down the street and slept there overnight. In the morning she carried the plane around to the edge of the house and there saw the most beautiful child she'd ever laid eyes on—a child of almost celestial beauty. He looked so much the way Susan had as a child, and like someone *else*—a face she couldn't quite place. Suddenly she knew something about where Susan had spent her year of amnesia.

Marilyn wanted desperately to hug this child. She held up the 747 and made it loop up and down with her arm until Eugene Junior noticed her. He skipped delightedly her way. Two minutes later, with Marilyn in tears, they drove away from the jungle gym in her BMW.

Randy had been folding laundry in the living room, and though it had been less than five minutes since he'd last checked on the child, his radar blipped. Something was wrong. He looked in the back yard and his spine froze. Then he saw the car pull out of the driveway. He phoned Susan, just back from her walk with John Johnson. Before he could speak, she burst out, "Randy! I just got a ride home from the cops—and I met this guy—"

Randy interrupted and told her what had happened.

Chapter Thirty-five

The police dropped Susan off at home. She made a pot of coffee and phoned an old TV contact, Ruiz, now at the Directors' Guild. She had asked for John Johnson's home number, but Ruiz was hesitant. Susan reminded him that she was the one who arranged for his sister's nose job in '92, and so he gave her the number. The pen Susan was using had dried out. She was repeating John's number over and over, searching for something to write with, when the phone rang. It was Randy with news of the kidnapping.

After she hung up, she stood amid her cheerful anonymous kitchen and her skin no longer felt the room's air-conditioned chill. Her ears roared with so much blood that she went deaf. The sink and the potted fern in front of her seemed unconnected, like a convenience store's surveillance camera image. Only her sense of taste seemed to still work, albeit the wrong way, as tingling coppery bolts shot forward from her tonsils. She'd been waiting for a moment like this since she severed connections with her mother in the Culver City legal office amid the shards of Gregory Peck's ashtray. She'd always felt that nobody ever gets off an emotional hook as easily as she had.

The agitated chemical soup in her bloodstream thinned slightly. Her senses returned to her and she ran to the hallway, grabbed her purse and fished through it quickly: keys, wallet, ID, cell phone, photos and mints—that's all she'd need. She dashed out the door and into her car parked in the driveway, leaving the house unlocked and the coffeemaker still brewing. The sun had set and rush hour was almost over, but the Hollywood Freeway was packed five cars abreast, as tightly as a movie audience, all flowing at sixty-two miles an hour. She phoned Randy, and both of them screamed into their receivers, Randy demanding to call the police, Susan ordering him not to. They entered a cell hole and the line cut out. Susan called back, but her budget cell phone's drained battery began beeping. She told Randy she'd call again once she had recharged it in the cigarette lighter, which would take about three hours, by which time she would be near the California–Nevada border.

"Randy, it's not your fault. She'd have gotten into Fort Knox if she'd wanted to."

"But Susan, why are you—"

Vzzzt zzzst . . .

"She'll be back in Wyoming, Randy. She wants this on her turf. It's how she—"

Dzzzzzt . . . vvvvdt . . .

The phone died, and Susan was alone with her thoughts in the car, driving east, seeing only a few stars and a few jet lights in the sky.

She was furious with her mother, but she was also furious with herself for having been so vengeful and stupid in Cheyenne. She'd been so full of pride, twisting the financial knife, and most stupidly of all, mentioning grandchildren. Stupid, stupid, stupid. Something in her voice and eyes had given Marilyn the clue. Dammit. She slapped the steering wheel and felt nauseous with worry. She turned on the radio, but it made her head buzz to hear the outrageous opinions and meaningless chitchat that drenched the sky. She turned it off.

She looked at the road signs. She was nearing Nevada. Randy said Marilyn had a one-hour lead, and Susan knew her mother was a speed demon, so she was likely a fair distance down the Interstate.

Susan looked back over the past year for other clues as to why this craziness was happening. The biggest hint was that after Susan's return to Los Angeles from Erie, not once had she seen Marilyn in the news—either on TV or in print, aside from the endlessly replayed hugging scene on the front steps of Marilyn's house. Susan knew Marilyn's media embargo was her way of communicating by not communicating—of letting Susan know she was up for a challenge. Susan mentally tried to imagine the amount of money Marilyn lost by being silent and had a grudging admiration for her strength. Why couldn't her mother use her strength to clip newspaper articles and knit baby booties like everybody else's mother?

She looked back over the day. She sighed and tried to hook her arm over the back seat to snag a bottle of orange juice in the back. The car swerved, another car honked and she pulled over to the shoulder and breathed deeply.

She'd met John Johnson only that afternoon, what seemed like forever ago. It was the first real connection she'd made in so long. He was as colorful as guys got, with a cordiality and freshness she doubted he was even aware he possessed. And he'd seen her face in a vision! It was so sweet. Normally she'd have thought this was just a manufactured come-on line, but with him it wasn't. And Susan was moved that she could represent an image of . . . *cleanliness* to somebody else, somebody with whom she seemed to share such a unique set of experiences. And with John she'd also had that sexy charge-right-into-conversation feeling. And what fun it would be again to have a man's razor and shaving cream in the medicine cabinet.

The next time John would hear of her it'd be in some tawdry, cheesy tabloid slugfest she'd always dreaded, with Eugene Junior used as a pawn. Randy was right. She ought to have brought the child into society more quickly. What were the rules on these things? If she told about Eugene, would she be tried as some sort of arsonist? If she had DNA tests done, proving the child was definitely hers, would people suspect Eugene Junior was the child of rape? The scenarios spun out of control in her head. Could she be deemed unfit to parent? Could the child be taken away from her?

Randy. The phone was charged. She called; he was in the Valley house bathroom vomiting with fear, guilt and worry beside Dreama on the cordless phone. They wanted to come meet Susan, but Susan said, no, to stay there in case Marilyn called the house. Dreama was doing what she could to calm Randy.

Susan drove through the night. By dawn her eyes were bloodshot and stung in the sunlight. Somewhere in central Utah she bought apple juice and a ham sandwich at a gas station. She ate, realized she was going to collapse if she continued right away, and took a tranquilizer from her purse, garnering a fitful spate of sleep in the parking lot. The cell phone jolted her awake. It was Dreama and Randy calling for news.

She sped off again. Her map told her there were 1,200 miles between Los Angeles and Cheyenne. She spent hours dividing miles-per-hour into 1,200. It always seemed to come out to around a fifteen-hour haul. When she factored in the nap, she calculated she'd arrive in Cheyenne around 7 A.M. local time. In Utah her engine died. She lost more than half a day there. She arrived in Cheyenne at sunup, ragged and starving. She showed up at Marilyn's old house, rang the doorbell, ready for war, and the new tenants answered, a pleasant young couple, the Elliots, getting ready for work.

"Your mother moved out a year ago," said Mrs. Elliot, Loreena. "We get people knocking here maybe once a week still, looking for either her or you. We certainly never thought we'd see . . . *you* here." Loreena didn't mean any disrespect. Susan could only imagine how bad it looked, arriving in the morning not even knowing where her mother lived.

They offered Susan breakfast, and she ate in the kitchen, which was eerily the same as it had been the morning of the reunion. Loreena offered a bath, but Susan declined, far too frazzled to lather and rinse her hair. Loreena offered her a clean outfit, which Susan did accept. While changing in the upstairs bathroom, she could hear a muffled conversation downstairs. Susan was paranoid about the police being brought into the matter. When she returned to the kitchen, she confessed that she and her mother had stopped speaking, but now she needed to connect with her. The husband, Norm, said the situation reminded him of his sister and his mother, and Loreena nodded.

Susan and Loreena combed the phone books for all possible variations of Marilyn's surnames, maiden names, middle names and pet names, but their work yielded nothing. Susan then methodically scoured every street in the city—it was just small enough to do so—looking for a maroon BMW. After the sun had set, she conceded defeat.

She phoned Randy, who was clomping about the Valley house packing things up, anticipating Susan's request for him to drive to Wyoming with Dreama.

Susan assembled a degree of composure and thanked the Elliots, then spent the next twenty-odd hours in her car driving around Cheyenne. She phoned Randy's cell and told him she'd drive to Laramie, to the west, and meet them there.

When they showed up, Susan collapsed into their arms in tears. She ditched her car in a gas station, and they drove in Randy's minivan back to Cheyenne. Randy and Dreama tried to calmly assess the situation and tried to decide what to do next.

What confused Susan amid this was news of John Johnson's

appearance at both Randy's house and then at Dreama's. This stopped her thinking dead, as if she'd been slapped.

"He's not a creep," Susan said. "He just . . . isn't."

"I never said he was, Susan," Dreama said. "But he is a four-digit prime."

"Not numerology. Not now, Dreama." Randy was cranky from the drive.

"He was looking for me?" Susan said. "He doesn't even know about Eugene Junior." Susan mulled this over: John was looking for her. Once again her mind hit a wall. But now she had what felt like a new battery placed inside of her. Someone was looking for her—someone she herself had tried to locate. She looked out the window at the prairies. Suddenly they didn't feel quite so large and terrifying. Suddenly they didn't seem like a place in which she could be hopelessly lost.

On the outskirts of Cheyenne, Susan took her turn at the steering wheel of the minivan.

Chapter Thirty-six

Susan was holding Eugene Junior on the concrete ledge beside the propane tank. Her body felt deboned with relief, but the child showed no signs of anything other than simple pleasure.

Randy had gone to calm the Exxon duty manager's nerves, worried that this sudden burst of people might constitute a situation of some sort. Ivan's cell phone rang; he answered it, began speaking Japanese, and withdrew inside the rental car. Dreama hovered by Susan, while John, Ryan and Vanessa crept up to the opened rest room door and stared in at the harshly lit, unkempt sprawl that was Marilyn, slouched on the toilet lid. Her eyes were wide and red.

"Marilyn?" John said into the echoey tiled room. Marilyn didn't respond. "Are you okay?"

The back of Marilyn's head rested against the wall. She turned toward John at the door.

"Can I get you anything—Tylenol? Food? A blanket?"

"No," Marilyn said. "It's okay. There's nothing I want. Really. Truly. Nothing." She looked at John and saw a resemblance to Susan's child, which was, in a way, a resemblance to Eugene Lindsay. "You're the father?"

"No, ma'am."

"He's a beautiful child," she said.

"Sure is."

"Susan was more beautiful, though. She was. She was like a Franklin Mint souvenir figurine. People would *gasp*." Marilyn then glared at Vanessa. "*You*. How'd *you* catch me? I knew the jig was up when you talked about the curtains. You don't look like the curtains type."

Vanessa gaped, unable for once to come up with a reply. Marilyn cut her thinking short. "To hell with it. I don't *want* to know. It'd probably scare the shit out of me anyway. I knew I shouldn't have stopped at Calumet for my bonus check." She lit a cigarette. John thought she looked like a drag queen. "So what's the deal—are you guys cops or something?"

"No. We're friends of Susan," John said.

Randy had just come back and told everyone that no police or state troopers would be forthcoming.

"I ought to be in jail," said Marilyn. She turned her head to look at the graffiti-free wall.

"There's not going to be any charges, Marilyn," John said.

The Interstate traffic punctuated the sky with its dull Doppler-shifted roars. John remembered back to less than a week before—when he was the schedule-obsessed robot watching the CNN six o'clock news—and he remembered Doris's yelling at him to cough up the goods on his solo road trip. John put his arms out to Marilyn.

Marilyn was disdainful. "Give me one good reason I should even come near you."

John thought a second and remembered Vanessa's telling him about Marilyn's polyandry. What was his name? He remembered and blurted out, "Duran Deschennes would have wanted you to be close to Susan."

Marilyn let out a thimbleful of air, and her face lost all harshness, briefly becoming young, and John could see the beauty she had obviously once been. She tottered over to him, as though walking on a wobbling dock. They went outside, where she and John sat down beside a transformer box and some scrub pines. "You know, I've been broke before, Marilyn," he said. Marilyn nodded. "And I've been jobless before, too." She nodded again. "But mostly I've had nobody to join for dinner at six-thirty every night," he said. "That was the worst of it for me—sunset—six-thirty P.M. and nobody for dinner."

Susan, Randy and Dreama were by the van, their breathing harsh and quivering. Ivan was still in the car speaking Japanese. Ryan and Vanessa were discreetly turned away from John and Marilyn, but still trying to take in each word, and John shooed them off like children past their bedtime.

"Ryan, would you get Marilyn a cup of coffee. Vanessa, can you grab my coat from the car."

As they went off, Ryan whispered to Vanessa, "Oscar clip," and Vanessa giggled. A minute later they were back. "Drink some coffee," said Ryan. "It'll be good for you." He handed Marilyn a paper cup filled with hot coffee.

John walked over to Susan, who was holding her child upside down by the ankles. A cold breeze shot by and he buttoned up his jacket.

Susan looked up and smiled and said, "Seems like a hundred years ago since our little walk together, eh?"

"A thousand."

Randy and Dreama, fifth wheels, made quick hellos, and walked away with the two dogs.

"So how'd you do it? Find my mother, I mean. I've been here in Wyoming going crazy for days now. I haven't slept in, like, forty-eight hours. How'd you even know I was looking for her?"

"I didn't. I was looking for you." He sat down beside Susan. "I had some luck and I followed a hunch or two. And the *Hawaii*

Five-0 crime lab pitched in." He pointed to Ryan and Vanessa. "Don't ever cross those two. They're so smart, even their shit has brains."

Susan brought Eugene Junior right side up and hugged him while smiling at John. "Never a dull moment when Mom's around, that's for sure. Hey, know what? I know your home phone number."

"Really now?"

She told him.

"Aren't *you* the sphinx." John turned toward the child, who was fumbling with pebbles to his far left. "How old is . . . ?"

"Eugene."

"Eugene?"

"He was two last week."

"You gonna go talk to your mother?"

"I suppose I have to." Susan grabbed him by the arm. "You want me, you better see this, too."

The two walked over to Marilyn, who had the lost look of a seabird covered in oil. Susan was going to speak, made a false start and stopped. It turned out for once, Susan didn't have to say anything. Marilyn whispered, "I'm sorry about those pageants."

Susan made a noise, emptying her lungs of air and stress. She said, "Mom, look. If I *ever* hear you so much as a hint that my kid needs a haircut or has to go to the gym to develop brawny shoulders or even that he needs a dab of Clearasil, then I'm going to stop inviting you over for Christmas, okay?"

Marilyn sighed.

Susan and John went over to the minivan and sat down beside it, Eugene on Susan's lap. Susan said, "I got your number from a friend at the Director's Guild. I was about to call you when the shit hit the fan known as my mother." She gave a lusty yawn. John picked up a piece of cardboard and played peekaboo with Eugene.

"I can't act," Susan said.

John snorted. "Oh God, where did *that* come from?"

Susan smiled. "Well, I don't want you getting it in your head you can save me from myself by starring me in one of your movies. I'm a crap actress. I really am."

"You can take lessons and—"

"*Stop.* I don't *want* to be an actress. I never *did.* It just happened. I want my life to change, but not in that direction."

"So you still want to change, then?" John tried to ask this casually.

"Well, yeah. Don't you?"

"How about I'll stop if *you* stop."

"You think you can?"

John thought this over. The wind seemed to get stronger, blowing down from the Rockies onto the Plains. "Look at us," said John, "two clowns who went over Niagara Falls in a barrel."

Susan put her hands in her face and said, "Oh God, my mother is back in my life."

Ivan had finished his phone call and sidled over. He reached John and Susan just as their hands touched. "*Mega Force* blew them to bits in Nagasaki, John-O."

"Ivan, this is Susan. Susan, Ivan."

John's and Susan's hands were carelessly touching. "John-O, I tell you what—why don't I pile everybody into the rental car and take them back to Los Angeles?"

Susan's eyes were as wide and as open as the cobalt sky above.

"Okay," John said.

Susan got behind the wheel of the minivan and John jumped

in and rode shotgun with Eugene Junior on his lap. Susan started the van and drove off.

Looking back, John saw the mystified crowd, with Ivan preparing a plot synopsis for their next six hours.

Susan, exhausted or not, was a confident driver. The three sped across the dark flat continent, nobody in the minivan knowing where they might be heading, just that they were heading away from where they had been before.

Eugene Junior fell asleep in John's lap. John turned his head and looked out the window. Outside, there was a barbed-wire fence, a road sign saying OMAHA 480, and John also saw what he thought were the eyes of an animal.

He looked at Susan's reflection in the black window glass. John remembered once yelling at a cameraman on a film, whom he was convinced was color-blind. During a break John went off to props and brought back with him a piece of shiny black plastic. He gave it to the cameraman, and the cameraman asked him, "What's this for?" and John said, "It's something the Impressionist painters used to do. Whenever they were unsure of the true color of something, they'd look at its reflection in a piece of black glass. They thought that the only way they could ever see the true nature of something was to reflect it onto something dark."

Police lights erupted behind them, but the police were after another car, not theirs. Susan looked over at John and arched her eyebrows in conspiracy. John watched the pale black road, and he remembered a single moment during his time away in the wilderness. He wished he had told Doris about it—a single moment in Needles, California, months and months ago, facing west in the late afternoon. There had been a heavy rainstorm over just a small, localized patch of the desert, and from the patch beside it, a dust storm blew in. The sun caught the dust and the moisture in a way John had never seen before, and even though he knew it was backward, it seemed to him the sun was radiating black sunbeams down onto the Earth, onto Interstate 40 and the silver river of endless pioneers that flowed from one part of the continent to the other. John felt that he and everybody in the New World was a part of a mixed curse and blessing from God, that they were a race of strangers, perpetually casting themselves into new fires, yearning to burn, yearning to rise from the charcoal, always newer and more wonderful, always thirsty, always starving, always believing that whatever came to them next would mercifully erase the creatures they'd already become as they crawled along the plastic radiant way.

Douglas Coupland

Microserfs

'About as Zeitgeisty as it gets.' *GQ*

At computer giant Microsoft, Dan, Susan, Abe, Todd and Bug are struggling to get a life in a high-speed high-tec environment. The job may be super cool, the pay may be astronomical, but they're heading nowhere, and however hard they work, however many shares they earn, they're never going to be as rich as Bill. And besides, with all the hours they're putting in, their best relationships are on e-mail. Something's got to give . . .

'A funny and stridently topical novel. Coupland continues to register the buzz of his generation.'

JAY MCINERNEY, *New York Times*

'The kooky aphoristic ripeness of Coupland's writing almost succeeds in making us forget the hollowness of these live-to-work lives. In the first 50 pages, there are more one-liners than in a decade of Woody Allen films.'

ROBIN HUNT, *Guardian*

'Coupland is the crowned king of North American pop culture.' *NME*

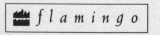

Douglas Coupland

Girlfriend in a Coma

'I was amazed by it. The dialogue is some of the most brilliant
I've ever read in a novel. It's a great wake-up call to young
Americans everywhere.'   MARK LAWSON

'At the start of Douglas Coupland's new novel, 17-year-old
Karen loses her virginity to boyfriend Richard on a ski slope
in Vancouver. An hour later she collapses at a party and falls
into a vegetative coma . . . Fortunately, Coupland's concern
isn't a teen-sex-is-death homily, but the need to live life to the
full. *Girlfriend* is a richly associative novel, ranging from
the dysfunctional teendom of *Twin Peaks* to the chilly meta-
physics of *The Sweet Hereafter, en route* to winding up as a
post-apocalyptic version of *It's a Wonderful Life*. This media
literacy is one of the conspicuous pleasures of Coupland's
fiction . . . Coupland's "end of the world" is a brilliantly
constructed setpiece, and very scary: you'd have to be cold as
ice not be truly engaged and stirred.'   *Independent*

'A millennial novel of a very subtle and interesting kind . . .
it's visually brilliant, full of extraordinary imagery, fresh like
new paint. I was absolutely knocked over by it.'
                                        TOM PAULIN, *Late Review*

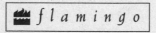